THE WANDERING MAGE

BOOK TWO OF CONVERGENCE

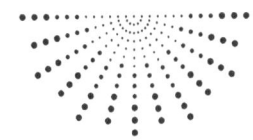

MELISSA MCSHANE

Night Harbor Publishing

AUTHOR'S NOTE

A glossary and pronunciation guide appear at the end of this book.

PART I
BOOK SEVEN, CONTINUED

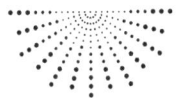

CHAPTER ONE

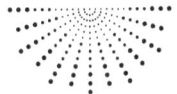

Probably 17 Coloine

I feel so much better now I'm not half-naked, even though my left palm still stings where the skin is missing. There are a few patches where more than just the surface tissue is gone, but those are small enough I'm not worried about infection. Fortunate, given that I didn't have any way to bandage it until now.

It's funny how I've gotten used to using the walk-through-walls pouvra, when it used to terrify me. I mean, I'm never going to love the feeling of my bones and organs sliding through stone or wood, but I sort of take it for granted now, and not just because it seems to have saved two worlds. But while I was rummaging through that woman's dresser looking for something to wear, I realized I'd gone through her bedroom wall without thinking twice about it. Maybe it was just that I was anxious about wandering around in nothing but my breast band, but I think after what I went through in the convergence kathana, it's a pouvra I feel more or less comfortable with.

I still don't really know what happened. I mean, it's clear the worlds aren't destroyed, but since this is a Balaenic village in the far southwest, judging by the stars, it's possible Castavir was destroyed and I was somehow transported back to my own world, which was spared. But I can't bear the thought of Cederic, of all my friends, being dead.

So I'm going to assume the worlds came back together success-fully, the damage was minimal, and Cederic is still, for the moment, in Colosse. What's worrisome is that it's going to take me a couple of weeks to walk there from where I am right now, and who knows where he'll be by then?

Time for a list, so I can calm down and stop panicking about whether I'll ever find my husband:

1. I am, as I wrote, somewhere in southwestern Balaen. Probably.

2. This is where Viravon is, in Castaviran geography.

2a. Who knows what the consequences of 1 and 2 might be?

3. I have no money, but I think I can sell Audryn's hair clips (sorry, Audryn) and get enough to speed my trip along.

4. I still have these books, though this one is filling up fast. It's the one Cederic gave me, so it's doubly precious.

It took me two days to reach this town, which fortunately for me lies on a well-traveled road running north and south through the forest. I don't want to think about what might have happened if I'd been well and truly cast out in the middle of nowhere, because it's been a long time since I've had to live off the land, and this time of year it's hard to find ripe fruit that hasn't either been harvested or eaten by birds. As it is, I was starving by the time I reached this place.

I scouted around the outskirts, very carefully, until I found a house whose owners were out. Then I did the walk-through-walls pouvra and helped myself to some food and a shirt that's a little too big for me, but better than nothing. They had some clean rags I used to bandage my hand after I washed it really well. I waited until night-fall to do all that, since I've learned it's bad to rely too much on the concealment pouvra. Although this isn't a big town, closer to a village really, there were still a lot of eyes that might be able to see past the pouvra's compulsion to look elsewhere. So I'm going to sleep in the woods again, more comfortably this time, and go into town openly tomorrow to find someone who'll pay me for these clips (sorry again, Audryn).

It's late in the season, but I might be able to find a ride at least some of the way toward my goal. But I'm not counting on it. I doubt a town this size has anything worth hauling two weeks' east to the Myrnala River and the handful of settlements along its banks. Handful of *Balaenic* settlements, I should say. I wonder what people thought when Colosse appeared out of nowhere? Not that I know that's what happened.

I'll see what I can learn from these villagers tomorrow. They might not know anything's changed, because this place doesn't look as if the convergence touched it at all. There's certainly no activity of the kind you'd expect after a disaster, no broken buildings, nothing out of the ordinary. It's just a typical village like you find all over the borders of Balaen, out on the frontier: houses of wooden beams with plaster between them and thatched, peaked roofs, mostly single story except for a couple of buildings near the center of town, like the inn —oh, that's good news, I hadn't thought about it, but if they have a building for hosting travelers, they're likely not as suspicious and xenophobic as some of the places I've been to.

This one's also more cheerful than most because so many of the houses have brightly painted doors and shutters, and I saw flowers growing around the ones on the edge of town where I did my scouting. So I feel fairly positive about my chances of learning something valuable. And who knows? Maybe I'll find someone heading north who's willing to give me a ride.

19 Coloine

Well, that was interesting.

It's—honestly, I don't know where to begin, so much has happened in the last two days. Except that's stupid, of course I should begin at the beginning, when I walked into the village yesterday morning.

I'd debated whether to enter early, when there would be fewer people around to be suspicious of the stranger, versus mid-morning, when business would be in full swing and I'd have more options for selling the hair clips and therefore might get a better price. I decided on mid-morning, because the village was big enough I figured they'd be accustomed to visitors and I wouldn't attract as much attention.

Hahahaha.

I attracted *all sorts* of attention when I came strolling down the main street—unfriendly, fearful attention. The sort of attention where you can tell people are nerving themselves to accost you. By the time I realized how universal this attention was, I was a good way into town and had to decide what I should do, other than pretend I wasn't aware of the whispering.

No one had actually attacked me, so I casually veered over to inspect some apples in a bin outside a store, making the owner take a few steps back over the threshold and shut the door in my face, then sauntered back the way I'd come.

Or tried to. I'd only gone a few paces when I saw people moving in on both sides of me, trying to act casual, but they were so tense I started to feel afraid. It's true I can turn the walk-through-walls pouvra on other people now, but only one at a time, and with physical contact. Besides, after what happened at my nearly-disastrous "wedding" to Aselfos, I'm more than ever convinced that trying to walk through a person could be seriously fatal. And there were a lot of people moving in on me, maybe fifteen or twenty, some of them much bigger than me.

I stopped walking and surveyed the crowd, looking for a place I could summon fire that might get me out of this. The group of men encircling me stopped about ten feet away, close enough that I had to keep myself from panicking. Other villagers were coming up behind them, watching to see what might happen, making me feel more panicky because they represented one more obstacle I had to get through.

So I held my hands away from my body, spread wide to show I wasn't holding anything, and I said, "I don't want any trouble," which is clichéd, but getting eloquent in a situation like that is the sort of thing that gets people dead.

Then the strangest thing happened, and even now, knowing why they reacted that way, it still strikes me as odd. The crowd backed away, the way you do when you're surprised, this sound like wind rushing over ripe corn rose up as every one of them took in a startled breath, and then they grabbed me.

I fought and shrieked and kicked, and I know I hurt at least a few of them, but there were too many for me to escape—so many that they could carry me away rather than dragging me. *Now* I can be grateful for not being dragged, but at the time I was terrified. I kept shouting at them to put me down, but that only made them move faster. In no time they'd wrestled me into a shed, where three of them held me still while others searched my pockets and took the hair clips and the books. That's when I lashed out with fire because the thought of losing those books terrified me more than the thought of what they might do to me.

This made them all start shouting, and one of them hit me hard in the side of my head, which made me lose control of the fire so it went out. I don't remember much after that, but when I finally regained my senses, I was alone in the shed, my hands and feet were tied, and my things were gone.

I lay there for a while, trying to become calm and figure out what to do. My first instinct was to burn my way out of there and run, but that would mean leaving the books behind, and that wasn't going to happen. On the other hand, they now knew I could do magic, so it was possible they were planning my death, and staying in the shed might be a bad idea.

On a third hand, though, they hadn't killed me outright, which meant...what? That they weren't sure what to do with me? True, there aren't any actual laws requiring mages to be put to death, but the fear of them is so widespread, particularly in small towns like these, that no one in authority so much as blinks if somebody executes vigilante justice on someone proven to be a mage. Assuming anyone in authority ever finds out. So it was strange they'd locked me up instead.

I decided to untie myself, at least, because the floor of the shed was mucky and smelled bad, and lying on it was disgusting. Manipulating the ropes with the mind-moving pouvra wasn't too hard, though it did take time because the ropes were thin and the knots were tight. Then I got up and explored my cage.

It was about ten feet square, with a roof of wooden shingles about six feet high, no windows, just an old door hanging on leather hinges. I could see three ways of escaping that didn't even require magic. They were probably as panicked as I was, to resort to confining me here. I sat down, thought better of it, and stood to lean against the back wall. I stared at the door and made a list. I don't remember exactly what it included, but this is my best guess:

1. I can either leave now, or wait for them to come for me.

2. If I leave now, I get away clean, but I leave my things behind, which is unacceptable.

3. If I wait for them to come for me, I might not be able to escape again.

4. If I leave now, I can search the village for my things...which could take forever, and I can only stay concealed for so long.

5. If I wait, I might be able to find out why they attacked me and why they didn't just kill me when they saw I could do magic.

Much as I wanted to run away, I decided I would have to take a chance on staying. It was reckless and dangerous, but I think I've said before that I hate not knowing things, and in ten years of traveling through tiny, hostile villages, I've never once been attacked simply for walking into town. It was strange, and it bore investigating. So I stood there and waited.

It was boring. I went over plans for escaping, plotted a journey to the Myrnala, wondered why the kathana hadn't returned me to Colosse and if Cederic was going out of his mind with worry yet, thought about pouvrin and whether I could create one based on a kathana or at least part of one. There are so many things I'd like to do with magic, now I know how th'an and pouvrin are related—the enhanced hearing pouvra, for one, and the memory one so I don't have to feel bad about making up bits of the conversations I record because I don't remember everything exactly.

I also practiced the binding pouvra, the one I'd learned just before the convergence that was based on th'an from Vorantor's original kathana to bring the worlds together. I still have no idea how to make it do anything, but it's the first pouvra I've ever created, and knowing that made me feel confident even though everything else around me was uncertain.

It must have been two or three very boring hours before the door opened, slowly, and someone stuck a pitchfork through the narrow gap, pointed at where I would have been if I'd still been tied up. I waited.

Gradually the head of the pitchfork was followed by the man holding it, who was followed by two other men. All three of them were looking down, squinting the way you do when you go from a bright room into a dark one, so I cleared my throat and then had to swallow a laugh because the pitchfork swung up fast, and the three men all tried to move in different directions at once. Then it was less funny because the one man thrust the pitchfork at me, abruptly, and I had to step to one side because I didn't want to reveal the walk-through-walls pouvra by letting it pass through me. "I'm not going to hurt you," I said, raising my hands again.

In hindsight, their reaction was funny—they looked as if they'd just heard a dog comment on the weather. At the time, it was baffling. The man with the pitchfork said, "How do you speak our language?"

That confused me so much all I could say was, "What?"

"It's a trick," one of the other men said. He had very short brown hair, as if he'd had his head shaved and it was only just growing back. "She only knows a few words."

"What else can you say, outsider?" the pitchfork man said.

I looked the three of them over. They didn't look like farmers—the pitchfork man was definitely not familiar with his "weapon." But they also didn't look like aldermen or councilors or whatever it was this town had for government. People like that have an air about them that marks them as different. I looked past the trio and saw a crowd gathered behind them, but no sign of anyone holding a position of responsibility. So I said, "I want to talk to your mayor."

The pitchfork came a little closer to my nose. "That sounds like memorizing to me," said the third man, who was shorter and skinnier than the other two and had a nasally whine to his voice.

"I was born in Thalessa," I said, "I've spoken this language all my life, and I don't know why you're so afraid of me, but I—" I was about to say *I haven't done anything you should fear* and then I remembered the fire, so I shut my mouth.

"She's a sorcerer," the brown-haired man said. "We should kill her before she does like the last one did."

"You're from Thalessa?" pitchfork man said, ignoring his friend. "I was there once."

"I haven't been back in ten years, but yes," I said. Actually, I was born in Venetry, and when my Dad lost his rank and his surname when I was two, we moved to Thalessa, but this man didn't need to know my tragic history.

"She looks like *them*," the short man said. "It's a trick."

"And even if it isn't, she's still a sorcerer," the brown-haired man said.

Pitchfork man chewed his lip in thought. Then he said, "Yakon, go get Riona. She'll have to make the decision. You—" He jabbed the pitchfork at me. "You may be Balaenic, or you may not, but either way you've got magic and I'm not letting you out where you can use it on folks."

I nodded and kept my hands high. The short man ducked away into the crowd, which parted for him but otherwise stayed put. I guess this was more entertainment than they saw around here all year.

"So, how long ago were you in Thalessa?" I said, though I didn't think I'd get a response. Sure enough, he grunted and wouldn't meet my eyes. So I stood there and ran through more escape plans—conceal myself, step backward through the wall of the shed...which still left me without my books. I'd just have to see where things went.

Eventually the crowd parted in reverse, and the short man came through, bringing with him a woman who looked to be nearly two feet taller than he was. I don't think that's an exaggeration. She was maybe ten years older than I am, with short brown hair, and she had a dusting of flour over the neck of her dress, just where an apron wouldn't have protected her. She moved with an air of authority that told me whatever else she might be, she was used to being in charge. I wondered why she hadn't been at the front of this attack, but she said, "I thought I told you I'd deal with her once the rest of the council members got here," which answered some of my questions.

Pitchfork man had the decency to look embarrassed. "Thought she might try to magic her way out," he muttered.

"I told you if she wasn't going to burn down the shed, she wasn't going anywhere," Riona said. "Sorcerers got only one magic in them."

That was interesting, and I rated my chances of getting out of this alive much higher at that point, because they wouldn't be expecting me to have any other tricks at my disposal. But then pitchfork man said, "Outsiders might have any number of magics. Who knows what they can do?"

"I'm not an outsider," I said. At this point I had the beginnings of an idea of what was going on here, but I decided to make sure before jumping to conclusions. "I'm from Thalessa. I'm guessing you don't see many people in this part of Balaen who look like me."

Not that I look all that strange. Even though I wasn't born in Thalessa, Mam's family came from the northeast, so my skin is darker than the villagers', and my hair is dark blond instead of the brown most of them seemed to have. But I doubt most of those people have been more than thirty miles from their village in their whole lives, so any difference probably looked exotic to them. And if a Viravonian town had "appeared" somewhere nearby, full of blond-haired people who didn't speak Balaenic, it would definitely have these people worried.

"She looks like the outsiders!" Yakon insisted.

"Where did you see these outsiders?" I said. "Did they come into town, or did you meet them outside? Maybe someone went to their village?" I probably shouldn't have said all of that, but it suddenly occurred to me a Viravonian town might have a mage who could contact Colosse, and I was so eager to reach Cederic I forgot to be cautious. And sure enough, this put everyone on edge. The pitchfork came back up, and Riona didn't do anything to stop it. In fact, she looked as if she wanted to take hold of it herself.

"You must be an outsider, to know so much," she said.

At that point I could see no graceful way out of the situation. Placating them was useless. I'd already decided I wasn't going to run. So I took the approach I'd taken with the God-Empress—I can't believe it was only two weeks ago; it feels like forever—and went with brazen audacity.

I stepped to one side, took hold of the pitchfork just where the metal met the wooden handle, and set it on fire. The man holding it shouted and yanked his hand away. Riona tried to step back, and I threw the pitchfork down and grabbed her by the collar. I pulled her close, praying I hadn't burned my uninjured hand in that foolhardy move.

"I am *not* an outsider," I snarled at her, "but you ought to be asking yourself, if I know so much about them, whether I might be persuaded to turn that knowledge to your advantage."

"You're a sorcerer," Riona said. I was impressed she wasn't afraid of me, but not impressed enough to let her go.

"I'm a mage," I said, "and I know why these outsiders are here."

She thought about it for a moment, then said, "Let me go, and we'll talk."

It wasn't that easy. She had to convince the crowd to stand down. Then there was some discussion about a number of people who were supposed to be there but weren't—the missing councilors, I gathered. *Then* she took me to her—I thought it was her home, but it was a bakery, and instead of living quarters above it was a big room with a lot of comfortable chairs that turned out to be where the town council met. There are four councilors besides Riona, and they all just call her Chief, so I'm not sure if she's the mayor, or first among equals, or something else. The important thing

Actually, the important thing is I'm falling asleep here. I hate getting behind in my record, but I'll have to finish it tomorrow. I hope Jeddan is being treated well, wherever he ended up in this place. I half expect to find him gone in the morning, even though he was pretty adamant about staying close to me. At least his first exposure to Castavirans is more pleasant than mine was, though unfortunately we don't have Terrael and his Cap of Death to confer instant fluency on him. But all that can wait for morning.

CHAPTER TWO

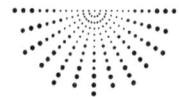

20 Coloine, early

I can't believe it only took a handful of weeks for me to grow so accustomed to my big soft bed with all the pillows that this ordinary mattress feels thin and lumpy. I didn't sleep well, and when I did sleep I dreamed of being in this enormous house with a million doors, looking for Cederic, and every new room I entered had ten new doors leading out of it. I miss him so much. I wish these Viravonians—but I want to bring this record up to date.

So I met with the council—it occurs to me now I have no idea what that village is named. Nor do I care. They seemed so reasonable, but it turned out they were just like every other isolationist hamlet on the borders of Balaen. But I'm getting ahead of myself.

The first thing I did was demand the return of my things. They refused, trying to establish their authority over me, so I sat and refused to speak until Riona, exasperated, said, "It doesn't matter, does it?" and called for a messenger to bring me the books and the clips. I half expected them to pretend the clips had disappeared, since they are valuable—Audryn's people must be wealthy for her to go around wearing that kind of jewelry so casually—but no, they brought everything back. I don't know if anyone read the books,

though I think not, or our conversation would have gone very differently. I was just happy they were undamaged.

The council meeting was far too long—it seemed everyone had to
have their say, and their say was usually a repetition of what someone
else had already said, so I'll sum up:

Three days before, they'd experienced the same effects we had in
Colosse—the pulling sensations, the confusion, and there had been
some actual tremors, but (of course) they'd passed by late afternoon,
and there were no lasting effects other than some furniture and boxes
being knocked down. So it was a curiosity, but nothing anyone
worried about.

The next day, some people came into town, people with hair like
mine, armed with strange swords, looking suspicious. (No detail on
what "suspicious" looks like, but I'm guessing the Viravonians were
being as cautious as anyone would be in investigating a village that
appeared out of nowhere, from their perspective, and that probably
looked furtive.) The council didn't know how the first interaction
began, but it was immediately clear the strangers didn't speak
Balaenic.

It was, on the other hand, unclear (and here I have to commend
the council for not just blaming the outsiders) how the altercation
began, or why, but swords were drawn, people were injured, and one
of the Viravonians used magic to help them escape. This made the
villagers terrified and angry and, as a result, disinclined to give any
stranger the benefit of the doubt. If I'd approached the village from
the other direction, I'd have seen the fortifications they threw up to
defend against the outsiders returning. They'd sent out a group of
men with some military experience to follow the Viravonians, and of
course they all came running back when they discovered a village
where one hadn't been before. That was two days before I showed up.

The whole time this discussion was going on, I was working out
how much to tell them. Explaining about the convergence was probably a bad idea, given that they had no concept of magic except as
something scary bad people use to hurt good people. But I couldn't
think how else to explain about a Viravonian town appearing two

miles down the road from them. And I also couldn't think of a good lie that would help them understand the truth. So in the end I went with the truth, though I had to gloss over the details of how magic works to accommodate their lack of understanding on that front.

When I was done, they all sat there, as I'd expected. Then one of them (I don't remember their names except for Riona, and even she didn't give me her surname or placename, so I couldn't call her by *any* name) said, "I would say you're lying, but no lie is that elaborate."

I could think of several more elaborate lies I've told over the years, but I kept my mouth shut. Another one said, "So what should we do now?"

I didn't realize at first that question was directed at me. Then I said, "That's not my responsibility. You people govern this city. You need to decide."

Riona said, "Will they have many...you said, mages?"

"I don't know," I said, "but probably more than just the one. Maybe not many more. I got the impression most mages go to the big cities for work. But magic isn't feared in Castavir, so it's certainly possible they'd have several."

"And you will fight on our side?" said one of the councilors, a round-cheeked woman with silver hair.

That startled me. "I don't know that it has to come to a fight," I said, "and I have to leave in any case."

"We have no way to communicate with them," the woman said, "and they've already shown themselves to be aggressive. If you don't fight with us, we will be overrun. Where's your loyalty?"

"If you're thinking like that, then you have a bigger problem than neighbors you can't communicate with," I said. "This is how the world is now. It's not Balaen versus Castavir, or shouldn't be." But I already knew how this was going to end. I couldn't guarantee the Viravonians wouldn't be hostile; they're in rebellion against an empire that has been trying to crush them for over a century. True God alone knew how they'd feel about the new world the convergence had thrust them into.

"You're right, it isn't your fight," Riona said, standing up to show the meeting was over. Since I am occasionally stupid, her giving in just then didn't rouse my suspicions. "Thanks for explaining it all. We're sorry for the misunderstanding. Can we do anything to help you on your way?"

Well, *that* had me suspicious, but it was getting late and I was tired from having slept on the ground for several nights in a row, so I just said, "I was hoping to sell these clips so I could buy food for my journey."

"Oh, don't worry about it," Riona said, and called for another messenger. While she was giving the girl her instructions, I talked a bit to the other councilors about the weather, and was there a larger city nearby where I might find transportation, and so forth. I wanted to ask them why they didn't want me dead because of my magic, but decided not to remind them about it in case it was all an oversight and they might try to execute me if they remembered.

The girl came back after about twenty minutes with a knapsack full of food, and I thanked Riona and the councilors and followed them down the stairs and out of the bakery—where I was seized by about a dozen hands that threw me down and wrapped rope around my body, tying my arms to my sides. I kicked, and shouted, and summoned fire, but they were ready for that and flung me from one pair of hands to another as they carried me off down the street, breaking my concentration.

They took me down a few steps and along a short stone corridor to a room even smaller than the shed, also windowless, made of rough brick, with a heavy wooden door that was black as if it had been burned long ago. Then they cut the rope off, but before I could break away they slapped manacles on my wrists and pulled the chains they were attached to taut so I was spread-eagled against the wall, which was damp and gritty and clung to my hair.

I shouted at them some more, and Riona came forward and said, "There's nothing to burn in here. We'll give you some time to change your mind, but you're not leaving this place until you agree to fight for us." Then she and the others left the room, and I was alone in the darkness.

I was so angry all I could do at first was shout and swear and yank on the chains, which only made my wrists hurt. Then I did the see-in-dark pouvra and looked around. They'd actually left the bag of food with me! And I still had my books and the hair clips in my pockets! I started to laugh, then stopped when it occurred to me someone might be listening. I slid my wrists through the manacles—this was hard because I kept accidentally turning them insubstantial with me —and rubbed them where the edges had cut into flesh, then I gathered up the pack of food and had something to eat before slinging it over my shoulder. If I had to leave in a hurry, I didn't want to waste time fumbling around.

I hadn't seen anything more of this cell than the door and the hallway that led to it, so I was reluctant to try to exit by any of the other walls, in case it was further underground than I thought—I've already experienced being trapped inside a large solid object and I don't need to repeat it. So I decided to wait a couple of hours until dark, for extra security, then I was going to leave the village and... well, I didn't exactly hope the Viravonians overran them, but I was angry enough I didn't much care if their stupidity hurt them.

Only I didn't get that far. About an hour after I'd been thrown into the cell, while I was trying to decide where to go next, I felt a horribly familiar sensation in my left arm—the queasy, slippery feeling of flesh sliding through immaterial flesh. I squeaked and threw myself in the other direction, coming up hard against the wall and scraping my cheek against the rough brick. I got quickly to my feet and tried to make my breathing slow as I looked around for whatever had passed through me.

It was a man, taller than I am, broad in the neck and shoulders. The see-in-dark pouvra told me he had short dark hair and was wearing the same kind of clothing the villagers did. That, and he couldn't see in the dark the way I could; he was fumbling around with his hands outstretched, searching for something. "Who are you?" I said, which wasn't a very good question, but it was better than all the other ones that occurred to me.

He stopped moving and felt behind him for the wall. "I'm here to get you out," he said. "I'm a sorcerer. Like you."

"Oh," I said. It seemed ungrateful to tell him I could get myself out. So I said, "You can walk through things?"

"Yes, and see inside things, but I don't think that's useful right now," he said. He sounded proud, and I remembered what they'd said about mages having only one trick. And *then* I realized what he'd said.

I grabbed his hand and said, "Can you teach me?" I didn't care that we were both crammed into this tiny, damp, horrible cell; all I could think was that I'd finally met someone like me, and he knew a pouvra I didn't!

"No, but I can make you immaterial long enough to get out of here," he said. I realized he'd misunderstood me just as he closed his hand tightly over mine and said, "You have to hold your breath." Then I felt the familiar sensation of my bones and muscles slipping between the wall. It was a good thing I'd reflexively taken a breath, because the stranger dragged me through the back wall of the cell without waiting for my assent. I was annoyed, a little, but—well, he still hasn't taught me the see-inside pouvra, so I've decided not to call him on his impertinence.

It wasn't quite full dark outside, and the moon was overcast by high, thin clouds. We'd come out into an alley behind a row of buildings, all of them wooden except the cell. I tried to yank my hand away from my rescuer's, but he held on and said, "You have to follow me exactly or we'll be seen."

"I'm not going anywhere until you tell me your praenoma," I said. I realize how rude it was to demand that gift of him, but he was asking me to trust him with his life, and that's an intimate enough relationship to justify it.

"Jeddan," he said, as casual as you please, so he must have felt the same way. "Now follow me."

"No," I said. "I have a better way."

He turned to look at me, and even in the dimness I could see his mouth open to argue with me, so I worked the concealment pouvra on both of us and enjoyed how his expression went from annoyed to confused to awestruck before the pouvra forced me to look away. "It's not invisibility, but it will keep people from looking at us," I said, "and we have to go on holding hands or I can't conceal you."

I've known Jeddan for a few days now, and it's true he has some habits that irritate me, but he's quick to grasp the essentials of a situation and he doesn't waste time exclaiming about how wonderful or impossible something is. He took us through the back streets of the village, not that there were many of them, and into the forest that lies to the east without raising any alarms. Once we were safely inside the trees, I released the pouvra and we both stood there rubbing the feeling back into our fingers. "Thanks," I said, again deciding not to tell him I could have escaped on my own.

"They were going to kill you," Jeddan said. "I couldn't let that happen."

"They weren't going to kill me, they wanted me to help defend the village," I said.

He shook his head. "That was the council. There were a lot of villagers who wanted you dead. They're afraid of any magic, and yours...I didn't even know fire was possible."

"Oh," I said. "Then I really am grateful." I probably would have escaped on my own before the villagers were a threat, but if not, I couldn't have fought them all off.

"Like I said, you're a fellow sorcerer," Jeddan said. "I knew there had to be others, but I've never met any."

"We're called mages, and neither have I," I said.

"I've never heard that word," he said.

"It's in most of the oldest books, and I like it better than 'sorcerer.' Can you teach me your see-inside pouvra?" I said.

"I don't know. Is...pouvra...what you call magics? Can you teach me yours?" he said.

"We'll have to see," I said, and then I remembered my actual goal. "But I don't have time to find out. I have to be on the road again."

"I'm coming with you," he said.

That threw me. "No, you're not," I said, which sounded stupid then and still sounds stupid when I write it now.

Jeddan was just a big dark shape against the trees, but I could tell he'd squared his shoulders like he was expecting a fight. "I've been studying magics—pouvra—for four years," he said. "I was caught in a mudslide, thought I was dead, then I was sliding through it—*between* it—and I knew I'd done something I couldn't bear to give up. Magic is everything to me, and I'm not going to lose the chance to learn more of it. And I know you want to learn what I know, too. So I'll stay behind, if that's what you want, because I'm not going to force my company on anyone. But I think you want me with you."

It was true. I did. "You're right," I said. "We need each other. And there's so much more to magic than you realize." I looked around, remembered Jeddan couldn't see in the dark, and reached for his hand, which is really big and strong. I keep forgetting to ask what he does for a living. "We're going to find a place to sleep, and then in the morning we're going to pay a visit to some people who may or may not be friendly. And they don't speak our language. So you'll just have to trust me, okay?"

"All right," he said, but he sounded dubious. He's been patient since then, even letting the Viravonians take him to his own room rather than stay with me—I'm sorry, but even though I'm excited about meeting someone else like me, I draw the line at letting strange men share my bedchamber.

Anyway, we slept under some trees that had already begun to shed their leaves, so with the dampness it wasn't a very comfortable sleep. I probably shouldn't bitch about the mattress I slept on last night, since it was far better than a pile of wet leaves on the hard ground.

In the morning, before we went anywhere, we shared some of the food and I told Jeddan my praenoma—return courtesy for courtesy and all that—and all about the convergence. Everything, not just the event and what came of it—all about th'an and kathanas and Castaviran magic, and what I knew about pouvrin, and that I was trying to find my husband and that's why I was going north, or would be going north eventually.

Jeddan listened in silence, only interrupting me with questions once or twice, until I explained about my pouvrin, and then he got the kind of look you get when you find out your grandmother's paste brooch is a twenty-carat diamond.

"Show me," was all he said, and I demonstrated everything except the see-in-dark pouvra, which has no discernable effect and would only make me blind in the daytime, anyway. Then he sat there staring at me, or past me, or something, until I said, "Are you all right?"

"I thought I was doing well with two," he said, but in a joking way.

"It took me ten years to master all those," I said. "But who knows what we might accomplish if we work together? It has to be easier than reading those old books."

"I didn't read any old books," he said, and now it was my turn to look stunned. "Seeing inside things...it's a variation on being able to slip between them. I didn't know it was impossible to learn a pouvra that way. I didn't even know they were called pouvrin."

"If you hadn't already told me you were coming along, I might have kidnapped you," I said, and he laughed, probably because there's no pouvra in the world that would let me overpower someone his size.

Anyway. That took a few hours, and then we circled around the village and headed off south down the road toward the Viravonian town. We decided it would be best for us to approach it in the opposite direction to the one facing Jeddan's village, in case they were also expecting foreign invaders. It took us about an hour and a half, between walking the couple of miles to the town and then staying out of sight while we made our way around to the southern side. Then we walked up the road and through its gates.

We got a friendlier reception than I had at the Balaenic village, even if I did have Jeddan in tow; people hailed us and wanted to know if we'd had any trouble on the way from Kinis, which I gathered is the next Viravonian village south of Erael (once again I'm spelling their words my way, and I—damn it, I was about to write "I plan to get Terrael to teach me to read Castaviran as soon as possible." That reminded me I have no idea where he is, where any of them are, and learning to read is so far down the list of things I have to do it might as well not even be on there. And now I'm trying not to cry. It's been a long day, and I've learned too many discouraging things, and I'm being stupid) anyway, Erael is the name of this village, and not one of them imagined I wasn't Castaviran.

Of course I didn't correct them, just said "I have news for the person in charge" and hoped they wouldn't think it was too strange that I didn't say "the mayor" or whatever it is their local government is. And they didn't, because they led Jeddan and me to a large house and ushered us inside.

It's obvious at even a casual glance this is not a Balaenic village; everything's made of planed wood painted white, though most of the buildings look like they could use another coat, and the roofs are a funny pinkish-grey slate I've never seen before. I doubt they came from very far away, because that would be too expensive for the people who live here. I wonder if the quarry they came from survived the convergence. I wonder if the desert around the Darssan is plains now. I wonder if the Darssan is even still there. More things I don't have time to investigate.

We waited for a few minutes, and then this old man with a short gray beard and long white hair came into the room. "Travelers," he said, "my name is Wilfron Kasselen, and I am the elder of this village. Please, sit down. Do you have news from the south? Are there more strange appearances? And what of the pagan invader's troops?"

That was a lot for me to take in all at once, so I decided not to answer any of it. "Elder Kasselen," I said, hoping that was the correct form of address, "my name is Thalessi Scales, and despite how I look, I'm not Viravonian. I'm one of the...you know the village that appeared north of here? I am one of their people. I mean, of their country, not that I come from that village. If that makes sense."

That stunned him, and he looked like he was about to shout, so I overrode him and said, "Ask me how it is I speak your language."

He closed his mouth. Then he said, "I don't understand any of this."

"I'll try to explain," I said, and even though my explanation to Kasselen was longer than the one I'd given the council in Jeddan's village, it was much easier because he at least knew about the shadow world, even if he didn't know the details of the convergence. I didn't tell him about the pouvrin, since that would have taken forever to explain, or how the final kathana worked, but it was still a very long story. The longer I spoke, the more intense his expression grew, until I reached the end of my story and said, "Could I have some water, please?"

He got up without saying anything and went to the door, where he called to someone, and then returned to his seat bearing a tray with a pitcher of water and three glasses. "So their world has joined ours?" he said, after a long silence in which we all drank some water and stared at each other. I wondered what Jeddan thought—he must have been bored, listening to me babble in a language he couldn't understand. He really is very patient.

"It's more accurate to say both worlds have returned to their original state," I said. "We're both invaders, in a sense."

Kasselen didn't like that, but he didn't challenge me. "Then what are we to do?" he said.

That was the second time someone had tried to put the burden of decisions on me. "You'll have to work that out for yourselves," I said. "I'm not the leader of this village. But you will have to find a way to come to terms with the Balaenic villages around here. And that might be difficult, because they're afraid of magic."

"A great challenge," he said. "But what of the pagan invader's troops? What has happened to them?"

"The God-Empress's soldiers?" I said.

"We do not call her that," Kasselen said, looking grim. "She usurps the place of God and wants to see us subjugated to her rule."

"I know," I said, "but what I don't know is how she was going about it down here. I'd heard only that she had most of an army in Viravon, trying to maintain control."

"Yes," Kasselen said. "So what has happened to them in the convergence?"

I shrugged. "Nothing, I imagine," I said. "Though they might have lost contact with Colosse during the coup." He gave me a startled look, and I realized I hadn't said anything about Aselfos's uprising against the God-Empress, so I told that story. He looked happier when I was finished.

"They receive their orders from Colosse," he said, "and with luck they will be in confusion, and we will have an opportunity to strike at them." He stood up, so Jeddan and I did too. "We will give you a place to sleep, and food," he said, "before you start your journey north.

I realized I was hungry enough it must have been dinnertime, so we joined Kasselen for a meal, and it wasn't until it was over that I remembered the most important reason I'd had for coming here, and asked if they had a way to contact the mages in Colosse. They

I've just realized it's almost three o'clock in the morning, and my eyes are burning, so I'll have to sum this up even though my conversation with Lineta was really interesting. Interesting, and depressing, and a little frightening—anyway. The conversation went all over the place, so I've rearranged the details so it makes more sense. I kept dragging it off course by asking questions, but in the end, this is what I learned:

Something strange happened in Erael in the days since the convergence. It has five mages—two who live here, and three who were on their way to something relating to the Viravonian resistance Lineta didn't want me to pry into, so I didn't. And the day after the convergence, suddenly only Lineta was still capable of working magic.

Coincidentally, or maybe not coincidentally, she has the same green-gray eyes I do, and Jeddan has. Cederic once told me those eyes indicate a predisposition to do magic, but it can't be a coincidence that those four other mages, who don't have those eyes, all lost their magic at the same time.

I remember somebody, probably Terrael, said the worlds coming back together would restore the original requirements for magic;

suppose the green-gray eyes are one of those requirements? Or that they indicate the innate ability to work magic Cederic's research implied was part of the original world? It sounds silly, but based on

Oh no. Terrael's eyes are blue. So are Sovrin's. Oh, please let me be wrong about this. If Terrael...I can't even imagine it. I'm not going to think about it anymore. It's a stupid idea and it has to be wrong.

The important thing is that the loss of their mages has thrown this village into more turmoil than the convergence did, and they've (she's) been trying to contact Colosse ever since that horrible discovery, to no effect. Lineta says the Firtha thanest, whatever that is, is not only not responding, but acting as if it isn't there anymore, and she doesn't have any friends in the capital she might be able to contact.

I must have looked awful when she gave me the news, because she said a lot of comforting things I tried to be grateful for, because she was trying to help. But I can't stop remembering how the palace was coming down on our heads, there at the end, and Aselfos's troops were fighting the God-Empress's soldiers all around us, and the God-Empress is who knows where—it's impossible she's dead, she's too evil to die without taking a hundred innocent people with her. I can't stop imagining everyone I love is dead, or thinks I'm dead, I'm not sure which is worse, but either way I just want to curl up somewhere and cry.

I hate feeling that way. I hate feeling helpless and weak, because I'm not weak. I've had a lifetime of fighting every challenge the world has thrown at me. They aren't dead. I *will* find them. Cederic's the Kilios, damn it, and there's no way the Kilios is just going to disappear. So even if he's not in Colosse when I get there, someone will know where he went, and I'll chase after him as long as I have to.

There. I feel better now. I think I can sleep a few hours, and face breakfast, and then I can start planning a route to Colosse. And Jeddan and I can work on teaching each other pouvrin.

CHAPTER THREE

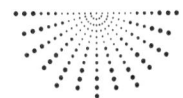

20 Coloine, very late

It's taken me nearly an hour to convince myself to write the events of the day. So much has happened that I'd rather forget, because I feel so guilty about it all. It was so easy to tell myself the Viravonians have a right to defend themselves in the ways they've learned over the years are most effective. But there's nothing I can do except move forward. And maybe I shouldn't have started this entry this way, maybe I should have just written it out and let my words unroll the way events did today. It's one of those days where I feel every one of my choices was a bad one.

I only slept a few hours last night because I was up so late writing, but they were restful hours despite the thin mattress, and Kasselen fed us a good breakfast. (I don't think I wrote that Jeddan and I stayed in his house. He was an excellent host.) Even so, I felt lazy, so we took our time packing our things—Jeddan has a backpack with essentials, including shaving tackle, and he makes a ritual out of shaving I'm sure will become annoying when I'm in a hurry, but today it didn't bother me—and then visited a few stores in the village.

I found someone to buy one of Audryn's hair clips, only one because it occurred to me Castaviran money would do us no good in a Balaenic town, so I saved the other to sell later. It's not a lot of money, but it's enough for an emergency. Erael is a pretty town, as pretty as Jeddan's village, and it makes me angry that they're probably going to destroy each other because they don't have the good sense to make common cause.

We were about to head out of town when we heard horses coming toward the village from the south. That is, Jeddan heard the horses, and pulled me to one side of the road to put us behind a stack of boxes displaying the last vegetables from someone's kitchen garden. I resisted, and he said, "We haven't seen any horses around here, just mules and oxen. And that sounds like quite a few horses. I don't like it."

I was impressed with Jeddan's paranoia, so I stood with him behind the boxes and watched. By this time a lot of people had heard the approaching riders, and it was clear they weren't happy about it. Mothers dragged their children off the street, storekeepers shut their doors, and soon the street was empty except for about twenty or twenty-five people lounging casually in doorways or on hitching rails. Their seemingly relaxed stances did a poor job of concealing tension. Some of them were standing near posts or hammers or pitchforks, things that could become weapons under the right circumstances. A few had rifles concealed against their legs or at their feet. All of them looked like people who expected a brawl to start soon.

It took only a minute or so for the riders to come into view, and by then we could also hear the ominous sound of a lot of marching feet, thudding echoes in perfect rhythm that to me screamed "soldiers." Sure enough, six men (or women, I couldn't tell at that distance) rode at the head of a double column of thirty or so soldiers. They were fully armed and armored, down to the chicken helmets, but their long-sleeved linen tunics were green instead of black and they wore short green surcoats bearing the falcon emblem over their steel mesh shirts.

The man in the lead had black stripes sewn to the cuffs of his shirt, three or four of them, and for some reason he was carrying his helmet in the crook of his arm instead of on his head. The other riders' tunics and surcoats were white, and each carried a very familiar wooden board in his hands. (His and hers. Two of the mages were women, I eventually discovered.)

They rode right down the middle of the street, ignoring the villagers, who turned to watch them go but otherwise didn't move. The leader raised his hand in a gesture that meant "stop," and they did, right at a point where they were surrounded by villagers. I have no doubt he did that on purpose, and I can see why he thought he had the upper hand. Poor bastard.

He said, in a loud voice that carried the length of the street, "In the name of the most benevolent God-Empress Renatha Torenz, greetings. God requires that all Castaviran subjects contribute to the support of her army, which protects her subjects against enemy incursions. You will provide five hundred measures of wheat, four hundred measures of oats, two hundred bales of hay, and twenty casks of beer, all to be collected in three days' time."

"We need that food to survive the winter," a man called out. He stood a little ways behind the leader (captain?), arms folded, leaning against a post as if he were entirely relaxed. His long black beard quivered in the brisk, chilly wind that had risen as the soldiers approached, as if in warning, or in omen.

"Your duty to God will bring blessings. She will not permit her servants to starve," the leader said, not turning around.

"We went hungry last winter 'cause of her demands," the man said. "We won't do that again."

"If you refuse to give willingly, it will be taken by force," said the leader. He gestured, and the soldiers began spreading out, drawing swords and choosing targets.

"Your choice," the black-bearded man said, and to my surprise lightning forked out of the clear sky and struck the ground at six equally spaced points surrounding the soldiers, hitting some of them and making them fall. The bolts that didn't strike targets radiated tendrils of electricity, making the other soldiers fall back.

I looked up to see where the lightning had come from and saw Lineta, leaning out of an upper window with her board and scribbling rapidly. She screamed as fire circled her, and dropped back inside the room. Then everything was chaos. Villagers leaped to the attack with their makeshift weapons, or took swords from dead soldiers. As the lightning faded, battle was joined.

I had just enough time to realize the battle mages had entered the fight—villagers began collapsing, gray-faced, or screaming through flames—when Jeddan shouted and ran past me, throwing himself at one of the battle mages' horses, and then through it. The terrified animal reared up, dumping the battle mage on the ground and knocking his board from his hands.

It shook me out of my stupor. I feel bad that I didn't think to attack first, but the truth is I'm used to fighting from the shadows, protecting myself from discovery so I could live to fight another day, and attacking simply didn't occur to me. Then I lashed out with the fire-summoning pouvra, which I've gotten very good with; it engulfed another battle mage, who also fell off her horse, screaming and beating at herself. I didn't take time to admire my handiwork, just bolted from my hiding place and ran straight at the leader, wrapped my arms around his leg, which was all I could reach of him, and worked the concealment pouvra on both of us.

I was hoping it would have the same disorienting effect it had had on the God-Empress's soldiers back in Colosse, but I wasn't able to look around to see because I was too preoccupied with not being shaken free by the leader. *He* was disoriented enough that he dropped his sword and leaned down to beat at me. I squinted hard and exerted all my will to see him, his arm flailing around, and switched my grip to his wrist and let myself go limp.

I had about half a second to realize this was a bad idea before he tumbled off his horse and landed atop me, knocking the wind from me and making me lose my concentration and turning us both visible again.

Terror at being pinned and helpless gave me the edge I needed to recover first, and I shoved him and scooted away only to have him grab my upper arm and pull me back. We struggled for a bit, but he was a lot bigger than me and soon he had me pinned again. "What are you?" he said, breathlessly.

I'd like to say I came up with something clever like "Your worst nightmare" or "Retribution," but all I did was stammer out, "None of your business" which sounds even stupider when I write it. He scowled and said, "I think the God-Empress will want to know about you. Thank me for sparing your life."

"Oh, she already knows about me," I said, "and you're a fool if you think I'm in any danger from you." (See, I *can* be witty and clever. Sometimes.) Then I spun out a string of fire and looped it around his neck, crossing it in back like a garrote and drawing it close enough to singe his skin. He started to jerk away, came up against the fire, and froze. "Let me go," I said, "or I tighten the noose."

He wasn't stupid. He let go of my arms and knelt in the street, holding perfectly still. I rolled to the side and stood and looked around. To my surprise, the fight was nearly over—and the Viravonians had won. They'd taken losses, but more soldiers than villagers lay dead in the street, a couple of women were controlling the horses, and Jeddan was coming toward me, limping a little but otherwise unharmed. "I didn't know it could look like that," he said, nodding toward the line of fire.

"It took a lot of hard work," I said. Then I returned my attention to the leader, who looked furious now. "Is the God-Empress with the army?" I said. He ignored me. I tightened the noose fractionally. "You know, that fire will burn a long time before it kills you," I said. "Besides, think of this as a chance to brag about how she's going to bring her army down on this village and burn it to the ground."

"This village is *nothing* in God's eyes," he grated out. "She has greater conquests to make."

"Really? What conquests?" I said.

"She is God. She will rule this land, Castavirans and invaders alike. You think you've won today, but you have only delayed the moment when she drags every person in this village into the street to peel the flesh from their bodies and feed it to the dogs." He looked as if I would be first and he would hold the knife.

"That does sound like something she'd do," I said. "Where is she now?"

He glared at me. I said, "Fire. Neck. Lots of pain." (I was bluffing. I've only just been able to bring myself to burn flesh, and I don't think I could do it in cold blood. But I'm a really good liar and he didn't know I wasn't serious. I feel sick thinking about it now, like I was a child playing at war without understanding what it meant.)

He clenched his jaw, then said, "There is an invader city some three days northwest of here. It is to be her first conquest."

I briefly considered my mental map. The only "invader" city anywhere near here was Calassmir. That scared me. Calassmir is on a couple of major trade routes, and the Royal Road and the southern trunk route both converge on it. If the God-Empress could take Calassmir, she could move her army easily through Balaen—I mean, along the Balaenic highways to any Balaenic city and probably a few Castaviran ones.

"What's the size of her army?" I said. He clenched his teeth harder and looked away from me. "Talk," I said, but he said nothing, and I had to either make good on my threat or give in. So I gave in. I dismissed the fire and shoved him toward Jeddan, who held him fast as easily as if the man had been a kitten. Jeddan's got shoulders like a lumberjack. He might *be* a lumberjack. I still don't know what he does for a living.

I hadn't really thought about the God-Empress until then—too busy surviving. When she'd disappeared in Colosse, we had no idea what had happened to her, though as I wrote before I was fairly certain she wasn't dead. So whatever that th'an was she did at the end there, it seems it took her to Viravon, to her army. All I know about the army is it's about a third of the combined Castaviran armed forces, but since I don't know how big that is, it doesn't really tell me anything. On the other hand, if she's attacking Calassmir, her army has to be fairly big, because Calassmir isn't a small city. I wonder if she has any war wagons, or if Vorantor gave them all to Aselfos?

I'm stalling, aren't I? Because I really don't want to write what came next. Maybe I'd feel different if I were Viravonian, because I know some of what the army has done here, the atrocities they've committed against helpless people, and even if the Viravonians don't want revenge (which they do, true God help them) they have to be ruthless to survive. But I'm not Viravonian, and I can't kill a man in cold blood, so when the black-bearded villager took the leader's sword and drove it into the man's stomach, I turned away and threw up. I am never going to forget the look on that man's face for the rest of my life.

Jeddan came to stand next to me, thankfully not saying anything inane like "are you all right?" and held my shoulders so I didn't fall down. I vomited until I was wrung out and empty, then I wiped my mouth and stood up straight. None of the villagers would meet my eye. That's small comfort.

I walked away down the street so I wouldn't have to see more killings. Jeddan followed me, still silent. He's good at quiet, which makes him a comfortable companion. I think we might become friends, even. At some point, I stopped, and looked into one of the shop windows, though I don't remember what I saw, and then I said, "Let's go," and we walked away from Erael without looking back.

We had to dodge Jeddan's village on the way north. I asked him if he wanted to get anything, and he said no, so we just kept going. Around sunset we stopped and made a fire; it's starting to get cold at night, and I wish we'd thought to equip ourselves for sleeping outside, but not enough to go back. We ate, and then I started writing, and Jeddan asked about the book and was satisfied with the answer I gave him, which is that it's a record of my journeys. Eventually he fell asleep, but it's been another hour or so since then and I'm still not done.

The truth is I've been thinking about the God-Empress, and Calassmir, and the army, the whole time we've walked today. Calassmir does have an army detachment, because it's only another fifty miles to the southern border of Balaen and there's always been a lot of bandit activity down that way, what with the trade caravans traveling from the jungles where they harvest medicinal plants. But I don't think their army is very big. If the God-Empress came on them unawares (and why wouldn't she) they might not be able to put up much of a fight. And, as I wrote, capturing Calassmir puts her in a position to drive deeper into the heart of the combined countries.

The southern trunk route leads to Garwin, where the Myrnala branches south and west, and the Royal Road is named that because it goes all the way north to Venetry, the capital city. Either highway would put her in a position to conquer more Balaenic cities, and I have no doubt her ultimate goal is to rule the new world.

I just don't know what to do. Time for a list:

1. I could warn whatever city is her next target. Both Garwin and... actually, I guess Hasskian would be the next city north of Calassmir... anyway, they're both defensible and have military presences.

2. I don't know what her next target is. If I guess wrong, it would be catastrophic.

3. I could keep going to Colosse. Those cities *are* defensible and they probably don't need my warning.

3a. i.e. I could take the cowardly, selfish way out.

4. I could find out what her next target is and warn them.

1 and its corollary 2 aren't sensible options. If I guess wrong, I'd be wasting my time in addition to risking catastrophe. And much as I want to run to Colosse as fast as I can, I'd hate myself for taking option 3.

But 4...I'd have to sneak into the God-Empress's camp, and hope to find some kind of drawing or plan because I can't read Castaviran, damn it, and that's incredibly dangerous even with the pouvrin. And I certainly can't ask Jeddan to risk his life over this, so I'd be doing it alone. And even if I did succeed in learning the God-Empress's plan, I'd still have to find a way to convince whatever city she's attacking next that they're in danger from someone they've never heard of, at the head of an army they've never seen.

So that's settled. I'm going west to Calassmir. And I'm hoping the God-Empress's army isn't so enormous they'll have taken the city before I get there.

CHAPTER FOUR

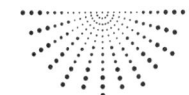

21 Coloine

To look at him, you wouldn't think Jeddan was very restless. He's so big and calm that he looks stolid, like nothing moves him. But when I explained to him this morning what I'd decided, he said, "We should get started, then, if it's three days away."

"You don't have to come," I said.

"What else is there for me to do?" he said. "Go back to my village, back to a life of hiding what I am, never able to learn anything new? Travel somewhere else, alone, and get hopelessly lost because I've never been farther than twenty miles from my village? I'm afraid you're stuck with me. At least until you teach me those pouvrin."

I thought about protesting further, but I discovered the idea of traveling alone again, after being surrounded by friends for so many weeks, made me feel incredibly lonely. So I just said, "You understand it's dangerous and we could be killed."

"I know," he said, "but I've been in danger of being killed for years. This is just a different kind of fear. And it doesn't seem so terrible. Maybe that's crazy, but it's how I feel."

It was crazy. And I completely understood. I've taken so many risks for the sake of my magic over the last ten years that the idea of risk, in general, doesn't frighten me. I'm not deterred from acting just because something bad might happen. Not that I'm terribly reckless; I like living, and I carefully consider my actions before I take a wild leap. Mostly.

Anyway, we packed up our few things and headed west. I think we made good time. It's been a while since I've been this far south, and while I know I kept us on the right course, I wish I had a map. We're going to run out of food by the time we get there, so there's something to add to the list of things to do in Calassmir, if we can. It's going to be a busy trip.

We talked about pouvrin while we walked and discovered we perceive them very differently. I see pouvrin as three-dimensional shapes given form by memory and sense. Jeddan says to him it's more like *being* shaped, as if he's altered to be something that can, for example, walk through walls. The only thing we both agree on is you have to bend your will to meet the pouvra, that force does nothing but make it slip from your grasp.

We discussed the walk-through-walls pouvra a lot. Since we can both do it, there's a chance each of us understanding how the other does it will be the key to learning from each other. Jeddan's intelligent and comfortable to be around. I wonder if the other mages are like him? I hope we don't all have different ways of understanding pouvrin, because it could take forever just to be able to speak the same language.

22 Coloine

I dreamed of Cederic last night. It was a very *intense* dream, so much so that when I woke up to nothing but bare ground it was so disorienting I had to go for a walk so Jeddan wouldn't see me cry. I'd resolved to stop dwelling on the possibility that something bad has happened to Cederic and all my friends, to be strong instead of weak and tearful, but I could feel his arms around me and his lips on mine, actually feel it, and when he wasn't there.... I hope I don't dream like that again.

Today there was more walking and more talking about pouvrin. Sometime around noon, after we'd eaten and rested for a bit, Jeddan said, "I'm going to go insubstantial for a bit. I want to try something."

I nodded, and watched him go in and out of that state. It's hard to tell someone is insubstantial, actually, because it's not like they turn misty or pale or resemble any natural object that's capable of slipping between things. It's more in the way they move, as if parts of them get to places before the rest of their bodies. Jeddan can hold that state longer than I can, longer even than I think he's capable of holding his breath, but we haven't talked about that so I don't know how he does it. He can't talk while he's insubstantial, though, and he does start to fall through things if he stands still long enough, though again it doesn't happen as soon as it does to me.

After about half an hour, he stopped walking, went solid, and leaned over to put his hands on his knees and breathe deeply. "I got dizzy," he said.

"That's happened to me when I use that pouvra too often," I said. I waited for him to rise, and then we walked on, though I was impatient to find out if he'd learned anything, or even what the point of that exercise had been.

"There's definitely a shape there," he finally said. "It's like…a cage, maybe? Or a mold for iron or bronze? But I'm on the inside, not on the outside as you seem to be."

"Can you describe the shape?" I said.

He shook his head. "Eventually, maybe," he said. "I just think discovering we are doing things the same way is important. I was afraid our magic was too different for us to learn anything from each other."

"I think Castaviran magic is easier in some ways," I said, "since each th'an is clear, and you know when you're getting it wrong because it just doesn't work."

"But you said you'd learned to create a pouvra using th'an," he said.

"Yes, but I don't know enough th'an to make that a practical method of learning magic," I said. I did the binding pouvra then, with no results—I practice it occasionally, hoping to work out what it's for.

"If the two countries can learn to coexist, maybe you'll have the chance," he said.

"Do you think that's possible?" I said. It was something I'd been thinking about, off and on, between wondering what we'd find at Calassmir and what the God-Empress's next target might be.

"It's either that or the strangest civil war anyone's ever seen," he said. "Two countries invading the same piece of land at the same time."

"But maybe war is inevitable," I said. "Balaen and Castavir can't remain autonomous; their lands overlap too much. One of them has to come out on top."

"Just so it isn't your God-Empress," he said. "You're lucky she didn't have you killed."

"I know," I said, and then we both ran out of things to say for a while. With Jeddan, that's not awkward or uncomfortable; he's good at quiet, and so am I, so we went a couple of miles before I picked up the topic of pouvrin again, this time talking about things I thought might be possible. We went back and forth coming up with ideas until it was time to camp for the night, and now I'm sitting by the fire across from him. He's watching the logs. I wonder what he thinks about.

23 Coloine

Another dream, more intense this time. This had better not be a pattern, because I won't be able to bear it if it keeps happening, night after night.

We reached the edges of the God-Empress's army about an hour before sunset. It's big, but not as big as I feared, and while there's smoke coming from Calassmir, there's none of the noise you get when a city is being overrun. I can't explain the difference, but I think of it as being more...terrified, I guess. That could just be me putting my own interpretation on it, but that's how I see it. There *was* a lot of shouting and screaming, though, and occasionally we heard these deep thunderclaps I didn't recognize, but they couldn't be anything but battle noises.

So the army is clearly attacking, but we don't know more than that because we decided to rest and come at the problem fresh in the morning. The good news is Calassmir doesn't appear to be in immediate danger of falling. I hope I'm right about that.

24 Coloine, noonish

I didn't get far scouting the army this morning. For one, Jeddan wasn't happy about being left behind, even though he had to agree I'd move faster if I didn't have to hold his hand to conceal him. For another, there are still a lot of people in the camp even though the siege was going strong, and I had to depend as much on my stealthiness as the pouvra to keep from being detected.

It looks like the Balaenic military camps I've seen in my journeys —lots of dull canvas tents, lots of cookfires where people were having breakfast, lots of people grousing about the bad food and the bad weather (it was drizzling a bit, typical southern winter weather). I guess there are only so many ways you can organize an army and still have it be effective. The only unusual thing, to my eyes, was the presence of female soldiers as well as male. The Balaenic Army is entirely male. I don't know what goes into that kind of decision, and I don't really care.

The point is, despite those problems, I was able to infiltrate the camp deeply enough to find their command center, and that's where I ran into different problems. That's why I'm back here and writing while Jeddan is hunting for our lunch (we ran out of food this morning, and decided he should try to gather more while I was gone, just in case).

It was easy enough to identify the command center, since it flew the falcon flag from its highest peak, and just as easy to sneak into the tent with the walk-through-walls pouvra, and easy to stay concealed, though at that point my fingertips were pretty numb. It's big, though not the biggest tent in the camp—that honor, naturally, goes to Her Godliness Renatha Torenz—but bigger than any I've ever seen before. It has several tent poles holding up the roof and they put rugs down to cover the ground so it doesn't get muddy.

Even so, military tents are all the same no matter the size: lots of uncomfortable-looking stools, the smell of whatever greasy meat was for dinner, and the dim wavering light of camp lanterns, always lit no matter the hour, so it wasn't as if it was luxurious. The God-Empress's tent, on the other hand—well, I should tell this in order, so more on that later.

So it was easy to get inside undetected. The problem was the tent is almost always occupied, and I couldn't see any of the information we needed lying out in the open. And there's no way I can rifle through the papers spread out over the tables without someone noticing. There were always three or four officers there, going over paperwork and writing out orders, and it seemed just as one left, someone else came in.

I wandered around the tent for a bit, in case something changed, but the officers just talked about how the siege was going and a lot of technical stuff about strategy and tactics that didn't mean anything to me, given that I don't know much about besieging a city. Nothing useful. So after about half an hour, I gave up and left.

Only I didn't return to Jeddan immediately. There was, as I said, an even bigger tent nearby, also flying the falcon flag, but with a difference: there were angular symbols printed beneath its beak, the God-Empress's personal sigil. There was no way I'd leave the camp without investigating her tent. I circled around to the back and went through the wall.

This was luxurious. It also had rugs on the ground, but they were plush and soft and looked as though they'd come from a palace guest room. The lamps hanging at intervals from the tent poles shed a warm, bright light over the space. And she'd brought actual furniture, a four-poster bed and dresser and a little table next to a deeply upholstered armchair, and even now I can't imagine how she managed that. I suppose if you have enough manpower, you can do almost anything. The place smelled not of greasy, stale food, but of her sweet-citrus scent that made me gag because I associate it so strongly with the deaths she's caused.

The God-Empress wasn't there, and I was confident no one would enter the tent without her permission, so I dismissed the conceal-ment pouvra and poked around for a bit. She'd even brought useless knickknacks to decorate her dresser. I thought about stealing one, not because I'm desperate to own an abstract pink marble sculpture of (I think) a woman giving birth, but because it might have been a disruption for the God-Empress to believe one of her soldiers had stolen from her. But I realized she wouldn't hunt down the perpetrator; she'd just pick some random person to blame and have them executed on the spot, not slowing down the attack at all. And even though it could probably be justified as an act of war, I couldn't bring myself to cause some innocent person's death. So in the end, I just reflected on how insane the God-Empress is, then came straight back here to our "camp," such as it is.

I told Jeddan what I'd learned and we discussed options:

1. I go back alone after dark and look for more information. I was in favor of this, but Jeddan is increasingly worried we'll get permanently separated. This is reasonable, but I'm not sure it's worth the risk of going in together. The real problem with this is military camps never entirely sleep, and there's a chance the tent will *never* be unoccupied. So I'd risk being caught again for nothing.

2. We go back together now and try to distract the officers so we can get what we need. Jeddan's plan. If we can get the officers out of the tent, we can quickly search for their plans. The problem here is creating the right distraction when we don't know what would be effective.

3. We capture an officer and interrogate him or her to learn where the army's going next. The most effective plan, but dependent on too many variables, and what would we do with the officer afterward that wouldn't reveal our presence?

4. We give up on learning anything, wait for the siege to end, then see which way the army goes and try to beat them to their destination. I hate this plan, but it's our last resort, because even though we can move a lot more quickly than the army, we need the best head start we can get.

So it looks like 2 is our best bet. Jeddan just came back with an armful of apples, only a little worm-eaten, and we'll have lunch and then make a more detailed plan.

CHAPTER FIVE

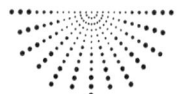

25 Coloine

It shouldn't have worked. I think the true God is watching over us, because there were so many places where the plan should have failed, and luck saved us.

The first part of the plan involved stealing uniforms. This was harder than it should have been because Jeddan is so damned big. By the time we entered the camp, almost everyone was gone to the front, and we almost didn't need to conceal ourselves to avoid being noticed. We searched tents and found a uniform for me almost immediately, minus the chain shirt, but I'd seen soldiers without them and judged I wouldn't look too wrong. Those leather pants are uncomfortable and stiff, and they make me walk funny, but I'm keeping them in case we need to impersonate soldiers again.

I was more worried that I didn't have the sword and knife, but we didn't see a practical way of getting them, and in the end it was just another risk we had to take. I hate that kind of risk. Normally, if I were doing something like this, I'd spend a couple of days mapping out the camp, stealing pieces of the uniform until I looked right, then walk all over the camp making sure I'd fool people before making my theft. But we don't have time for that.

It took us nearly an hour to find something to fit Jeddan, during which time I became increasingly anxious. We were nearly spotted twice—I love the concealment pouvra, but it's not perfect, and all it takes is for one very observant person to look in the right direction and then you have to run for your life. But finally we were properly outfitted and could come out of concealment and walk openly.

I'd instructed Jeddan in some of the basics of sneaking around in plain sight:

1. Move confidently.

2. Don't keep looking around to see if someone's watching you.

3. Meet people's eyes and nod when you pass.

4. Be prepared with a believable response if someone wants to know where you're going.

That last had me worried, since Jeddan doesn't speak Castaviran. We decided I'd speak for both of us and hope no one addressed him directly. But no one did. We passed any number of people and none of them wanted to talk to us or tell us to do something. It was so easy I became even more tense and had to calm myself. Bad to become complacent when it's easy, but worse to be so on edge to overcompensate that you make mistakes.

Then we nearly did get caught. Someone called out, "You there!" I didn't think he was addressing us until he repeated himself and added, "Don't ignore me, soldier!" So we stopped and turned around, and I subtly positioned myself so the officer would direct his attention at me.

"Yes, sir?" I said. The man was probably in his fifties and had the kind of florid complexion that comes from a too-rich diet with too little exercise. My heart was pounding as I thought of all the possible mistakes I could make, starting with not knowing how to salute him. I went back over what I'd observed earlier that day and settled for what seemed to be the all-purpose gesture, right arm crossed over chest, right fist pressed to shoulder, sharp nod. It was acceptable and he didn't draw his weapon and attack us.

"Where are you going, soldier?" he said.

"The front, sir, to join our unit," I said.

"Why aren't you there already? Malingering?" he said.

"No, sir, Weylan here was vomiting this morning and I was told off to wait with him until he recovered," I said, bluffing with all my heart, "then escort him, just in case he wasn't as well as they thought."

The officer looked at us narrowly. "I want you to take a message to General Burris," he said. "He's to send a squad to wait on God at the pavilion."

"Yes, sir," I said.

"And move it along," he said, then turned to Jeddan and said, "Big man like you, it's shameful you should let illness interfere with the performance of your duties."

"Yes, sir," Jeddan managed in Castaviran, and I was impressed at his lack of accent—though it's not hard to pronounce just a few words properly. Even so, it was good. This time, he joined me in saluting the officer, who (fortunately for us) turned and walked away without waiting to see where we went. Since he hadn't told us how to find whoever it was, we were clearly expected to know, and walking off in the wrong direction could have been disastrous. We waited for him to move out of sight, then proceeded toward the command tent.

It was a lot busier than it had been that morning. Jeddan and I separated; he walked casually around to the rear of the command tent, and I turned and made a wide loop that took me to the far side of the God-Empress's luxury abode. As I walked past, not looking at the tent, I set it on fire.

It was only a little fire, since I didn't want it to look suspicious, but that meant I risked having someone see it when it was still small enough to be easily extinguished. So I set a few more fires at different places, and *then* I screamed, "Fire! God's tent is on fire!"

That caught everyone's attention. People came pouring out of the command tent, soldiers came running from every direction, and everyone was squawking and calling out conflicting orders. Someone brought a swath of canvas and began beating at the nearest fire, so I started another one above her reach, all the time shouting and pointing.

I'd half hoped the God-Empress would be in her tent, just to add to the panic, but she didn't appear. Probably a good thing, because she would certainly have recognized me if she'd seen me. More people arrived with buckets of water, which helped—would have helped more if some crafty person hadn't kept starting new fires in place of the old. Hahahaha.

"I've found it," Jeddan said in my ear, startling me. "Let's go."

"Wait," I said. "There's one more thing we're going to do."

We strolled away from the fire—easy enough, everyone was no doubt preoccupied with terror over what insanities the God-Empress might rain down upon them for letting her things be ruined—then went directly to the quartermaster's tent. Tents, I should say. It takes a lot of food and supplies to run an army, and I'd seen (from a distance) supplies being brought in by a long train of wagons, supplies probably looted from Viravonian and Balaenic villages.

We went through the back of one of the supply tents that was divided in half, and though we could hear someone moving around in front, the back was unoccupied. We discovered it contained food, so I left Jeddan there to fill our rucksacks and I hunted around until I found a tent where I could get bedrolls, blankets, a pot and some utensils, and a heavy ground cloth I had trouble fitting into yet another pack, but it makes winter outdoors so much more comfortable. No tent, unfortunately, but I was heavily laden at that point anyway.

I concealed myself and sneaked back to find Jeddan, we distributed the load better, and hand in hand we walked off, practically invisible and ready for a long trip. We came out on the southern side of the camp, the far side from both our potential destinations. Jeddan said, "I found a map of the area. I didn't recognize any landmarks except the river, but the marks on it say they're heading north next."

"Hasskian," I said. "And then Venetry. Well."

"I think she knows where the capital is," Jeddan said. "I saw what I think was a map of Balaen. She must have taken it from one of these towns. Even if she can't read Balaenic, the way it was marked, even I could tell which were the big cities. And there was one up in the northwest with a triple star over it, like on the flag."

"She has to eliminate Calassmir as a threat, or have them dogging her heels all the way north," I said. "And they can probably hold out for a while. If we can get to Venetry quickly enough, they can send out the army to meet her, and from what little I saw, they outnumber her even without the forces at Calassmir."

"Then let's go," Jeddan said, and shouldered his pack. He can carry about twice what I can, and I hate to think how rough I'd be living if I didn't have him along. Plus, I like him, and not just because he's the first mage like me I've ever met. He's good company.

We took a long route around the camp, then struck out northeast, following the Arinz River even though it took us in the wrong direction; the ground next to it was clearer, so we made good time, and having a source of water helped us stretch our provisions. Though we'll still need to find food long before we reach Hasskian—it's about nine days' travel from Calassmir if you take the direct overland route, so even longer for us, but I don't think we'd make it through The Forest on the provisions we have.

We walked a good ways before camping for the night, and I feel that buzzing, elated feeling you get when you've pulled off a good theft without dying. I think we both also feel more confident: we have direction, we have a plan, and we had a hot meal tonight. Nice not to have to rely on matchlighters to start a fire.

26 Coloine

Less cheerful today as the aftereffects of our infiltration of the God-Empress's camp sank in. We did a lot of walking, and talked about pouvrin on the way, but mostly went in silence. I'm starting to see relations between pouvrin—not between his and mine, but between my own, specifically the concealment pouvra and the walk-through-walls pouvra. That was unexpected, since the concealment pouvra was developed by a Castaviran madman, and I've always thought of it as more angular than the others. But the more I look at them both, the more I can see similarities.

I asked Jeddan to experiment with the pouvra for seeing inside things, since he said it was a variation on the walk-through-walls pouvra. If there are categories of pouvrin, if some of them are related, then it could be possible to learn, or even create, new pouvrin based on your familiarity with one of its companions.

27 Coloine

We came out of the forest mid-afternoon and turned north to follow the foothills. That was a shock. This part of Balaen is, or was, all forest—it doesn't even have a name, just The Forest. But now there are low hills covered in scrub interspersed with the trees, and the weird thing is it doesn't look torn up the way you'd expect if the worlds were mashed together. It looks as if the landscape has been this way forever, thick forest growing right up to where the hills begin, then clumps of trees here and there between the hills and none growing on them.

I'm starting to worry about my ability to recognize landmarks. I know there's a town near here, right where the Royal Road enters the forest, but with the hills, I'm not sure where it is anymore. I hope it wasn't destroyed by the landscape changing, though Cederic did

Just writing his name struck me with the most awful heartsickness. It's not like I want those dreams to persist—I've never had sex dreams before, and I feel so embarrassed to think Jeddan might see and know what's happening—but they feel like a connection to him I don't want to give up.

We're traveling farther from Colosse every day, every step, and that breaks my heart more. If he knew where I was, he'd have come after me, done some kathana to bring me back, which means he doesn't know and is suffering as much as I am—more, because he has no reason not to believe the convergence kathana killed me. I wonder what he does to keep his mind off it. I at least have Jeddan to talk to and pouvrin to think about, and when we stop for the night I'm so weary I don't have the energy to worry about Cederic. And then I dream.

No. I'm writing this down so I don't fall into despair. Pouvrin. Today I tried to isolate the similarities between the walk-through-walls pouvra and the concealment pouvra. Though I'm not sure what good it will do. I need a third companion pouvra to those two for more points of comparison. Possibly it's time to get Jeddan to teach me the see-inside pouvra. And I need to apply more logic to our studies. I'm used to learning from books, so this is new and uncertain, but I see no reason Jeddan and I can't learn from each other.

28 Coloine

I don't know how I'd make sense of things if I didn't have these books to lay it all out on paper. Would I remember everything differently? Or start misremembering? On days like today, though, what I'm most grateful for is how writing forces me to look at events...not dispassionately, or critically, but at enough of a distance that I can learn from them and not simply be overwhelmed by whatever emotion is attached to them. I don't know if that's good or not. Maybe it makes me too distant from my own life. But I don't think so. This is me putting it all down in a way I hope will still make sense to me when I come back to it, months or even years from now.

We came upon a village just as we'd eaten the last of our stores, as if we'd timed it that way. It was the town I remembered, the one on the Royal Road that caters to hunters and trappers who ply their trades in The Forest. We were cautious in approaching it, since we had no idea if they'd had contact with their new Castaviran neighbors or what that contact might have been like. At the time, my fear was they'd react the way the people in Jeddan's village did. I had no way of guessing what we'd actually find.

It's a sprawling little town, with farms on the outskirts, and we passed a lot of stubbly, harvested fields without seeing anyone. That wasn't so odd, since no one would be working the fields at this time of year. What was odd was how the place continued empty even as we came nearer to the town proper. There were houses with tiny yards and thatched roofs with their doors hanging ajar or completely open, and not a single person in sight. It was as if everyone had simply walked away. We were the only living things on the road.

I moved closer to Jeddan and said, "I don't like this."

"Me either," he said. "But we need food. If the whole town really is empty, maybe they've left supplies behind. It wouldn't be looting."

"Not exactly looting," I said. Then I saw movement up ahead, and I grabbed Jeddan's arm and pointed. "There."

"I don't see—wait." We both stopped and stared at the corner of a house where we'd seen something run behind the building. I scanned our surroundings—tidy little houses, and a widening street, and up ahead there were buildings that didn't look like houses, despite being as low to the ground, maybe shops. Still no other movement.

"Let's see what it is," Jeddan said.

"It could be dangerous," I said.

"An even better reason not to leave it at our backs," he said, and I had to agree with his logic.

We went slowly toward the house, wary, trying to look in all directions at once. The house was, like the others, a single-story building with white plastered walls and a thatched roof and two windows flanking the door that made the house appear startled, as if we'd succeeded in sneaking up on it. Still no movement.

We went around the side, turned the corner, and something growled at us, making us both take a few steps backward. It was just a dog, crouched against a shed; it looked like it was favoring its front paw, and it continued to snarl even though we'd stopped advancing on it.

Jeddan held out his hand, and I said, "Don't. It's in pain; who knows what it might do?"

"You're right," Jeddan said, but he looked regretful as we turned and left the animal to its solitude. We came out from between the house and its neighbor, and suddenly I was picked up off my feet and thrown against the side of the house, pinned there by some unseen force. I couldn't even turn my head to see what had happened to Jeddan, but I could hear him cursing, and I guessed he was in the same predicament as me.

"There's no point in fighting," a man said, then he came to stand where I could see him. He was younger than me, maybe twenty. He had a lean face that looked as if it had gotten that way through malnutrition rather than nature and, not at all to my surprise, green-gray eyes set deep in his face. "We're prepared this time."

"No point talking, Baltan, she don't speak our language," said a woman.

"I do speak Balaenic," I said, or tried to say; my jaw was as fast held as the rest of me. Jeddan said, in a somewhat muffled voice, "We're Balaenic, you idiots. Let us go."

"Could be those bandits," Baltan said, "sending people in to suss out what we got."

"We're not bandits either," Jeddan said, sounding more annoyed by the minute. I was fairly irritated myself, and not thinking very clearly, because it hadn't connected that these were mages like us (I realize that makes me sound stupid, but it all happened much faster than it takes me to write it). So I retaliated with fire, looping it around his body in a thick rope the size of my wrist. He screamed, and I fell as his mind-moving pouvra released me. I got up quickly and said— this was when it all fell into place—"We're Balaenic, and we're mages like you, so let Jeddan go so we can talk!"

There were actually three of them, two women and the man Baltan. One of the women, short and with gray-streaked hair, had her hand stretched out toward Jeddan, as if she needed the gesture to work her pouvra. The other woman, who was young and pretty, stood a little ways back and hadn't done or said anything, so I didn't know if she was a mage or not, but she, like the other woman, had green-gray eyes, so I figured the odds were good.

I realized Baltan was still screaming on the ground, so I dismissed the pouvra and, after a second's thought, extended a hand to help him rise. He ignored it and scrambled to his feet. "What did you do?" he said in a hoarse, terrified voice. "That wasn't scribbling."

"Let Jeddan go," I repeated, and flicked fire at the woman, not to burn her, just to nip at her feet. She squeaked, and Jeddan fell. "I told you. We're Balaenic and we can work magic the way you do." Then I realized what he'd said about scribbling, and I added, "Did some strangers come this way? People who don't speak our language, and work magic by writing?"

"They're with them, Baltan, how could they know that?" the woman said.

"No, Gismara," the other woman, the one who'd been silent, said. She came forward and laid a hand on Gismara's arm. "Didn't you see? They're like us." She took a few more steps forward, extended her hand palm out, and said, "I grant you the freedom of my name, which is Nanissa. Be welcome here."

I placed my palm against hers in greeting and said, with no hesitation, "Sesskia. And this is—" I caught myself before I usurped Jeddan's right to privacy. I've decided that, for good or ill, we mages have something very personal in common, and I want the connection sharing praenomi gives, but that doesn't mean I can make that decision for Jeddan. But I think he reasoned the same way I did, because he said, "I'm Jeddan," he said. "Thank you for the welcome, Nanissa." Then I had so many questions I didn't know how to begin, but Nanissa began for me.

"You've got a lot of control, for only having a couple of weeks to learn," she said. "Fire...that's frightening."

I exchanged glances with Jeddan. "Maybe we should have the rest of this conversation indoors," I said, and not because the wind was picking up and I was cold. If they assumed we'd only been mages for a few weeks... I started going over possibilities in my head, all of them tangled and confusing.

Nanissa gestured down the street toward the rest of the town, and I realized we had an audience. Men and women and children peered out from practically every doorway, some brave souls even venturing onto doorsteps. Nanissa called out, "It's all right, they're not dangerous."

"That's not a given," Baltan said, glaring at me. (He was so antagonistic he almost made me regret my decision about praenomi.)

"I'm sorry I burned you, but I didn't feel like hanging there all day until you realized we're not a threat," I said. He glared harder.

The other woman, Gismara (poor woman, I bet she's been teased all her life—or maybe that story isn't as widely known as I think) said

"We can't trust them on the basis of all of us having the same kind of magic."

"You're right," Jeddan said, surprising her. "We could still be enemies. But isn't it worth that risk to learn more about yourselves?" Gismara tightened her lips and said nothing more. It was frustrating they were so suspicious—I know, Jeddan was right that even if we were the same kind of mages, we might still want to do them harm, but with Balaen in general being so fearful of magic, don't we have a...maybe an obligation?...to band together? Or is that me indulging in a rare fit of optimism? I don't know.

Nanissa took us to a tavern and asked the woman behind the bar if we could use the private room. She looked at us skeptically, but nodded, and we all went into this dark, low-ceilinged room that probably would be more cheerful in summer, when the small windows let in a brighter sunlight. Just then it seemed dreary. Nanissa sat down and said, "What can you do?" to Jeddan even before he'd taken a seat.

He blinked at her abruptness. "I can pass through things," he said, "and see inside things."

Nanissa's mouth fell open. "You have two magics," she said. "How is that possible?"

I put my hand on Jeddan's wrist to keep him from speaking. "First I have to ask you a couple of questions," I said.

"We get to do the talking," Baltan growled.

"All of this will make more sense if you just answer two questions," I said. "Please. Then we'll tell you anything you like."

Nanissa hesitated, then nodded. Baltan rolled his eyes and sat back in his chair. Gismara, to my surprise, looked like she was actually listening instead of stubbornly resisting anything we might say.

"First question," I said. "There was an...event...about two weeks ago, 15 Coloine or so. Felt like being pulled hard in different directions. Did you develop magic when that happened? Or right afterward?"

Nanissa looked puzzled, but nodded. "We all did. But you already know that, if it happened to you, so I don't see the point of that question."

"You will," I said. "Second question. Did something else happen to each of you, something *other* than the con—the pulling? Something traumatic, like being trapped in a burning house, or almost drowning?"

Nanissa looked at the others. "No," she said. "Why?"

"So it was the convergence that did it," Jeddan said to me. "How? Or is it 'why'?"

"Time for you to talk," Baltan said. "No more stalling."

"All right," I said. And before Nanissa could start asking questions, I told them everything.

I explained how Jeddan and I had become mages well before the convergence and that we'd been studying pouvrin for years, which is why we had several. I explained about the worlds coming together and how the convergence had triggered something in them that woke up the magic—something related to the color of their eyes.

(It's getting harder to deny the eye color is related to magical ability, even though it sounds so stupid. Such an insignificant thing on which to hang such power. And poor Terrael. If he's lost his magic...it makes me want to shout and scream at whoever or whatever set up this stupid rule—one of the four false Gods, maybe? Or is it just the way the world is? I still hope I'm wrong.)

Lost track—okay, I told them the reason each of them only had one pouvra is that when the magic wakes up inside you, it has to take shape somehow, and that shape is a pouvra that meets your need. After that you have to learn to bend your will to the magic if you want to gain more pouvrin.

I hope that wasn't a lie. It was just something I realized after remembering my own experience, and hearing Jeddan's story, and watching Cederic sweep the God-Empress's soldiers across the room, and knowing each of these "new" mages only had one pouvra... anyway, it feels right, but I'll keep looking for more proof. And we showed them our pouvrin, as many as we could. Baltan and Gismara both have the mind-moving pouvra, and Nanissa has the walk-through-walls pouvra.

By the time I was finished (I probably told them more than that, little things I've forgotten now) they were all staring at me like they'd been slapped in the face by a slab of rock. Jeddan said, in a low voice, "I think you overwhelmed them."

"They deserved to know," I said, feeling stung.

"True," he said, "but it's a lot to take in, all at once."

I nodded. Baltan said, no longer antagonistically, "How many more of us do you think there are?"

It was such a logical question coming from someone I'd pegged as hopelessly irrational that it caught me off guard. "I don't know," I said. "Your town doesn't have more than a thousand people, does it? And there were three of you."

"Nanissa and I came here from other towns," Gismara said. "I frightened so many people in my home town I had to leave or risk being torn apart by a mob. I feel lucky to have found this place."

"So one out of a thousand," I said. "Though that might not be normal."

"Are there any other people with those eyes in this town who *didn't* develop magic?" Jeddan said.

"No," said Baltan. "I'm the only one."

"And I found maybe ten people in my journeys with those eyes," I said. "Ten people in ten years. Granted, I wasn't interacting much with others, but that's not many."

"We're just guessing at this point," Jeddan said.

"True," I said. But I was thinking of Venetry, which has a population of over a million people, and wondering how many of those were green-eyed mages now. Even a tenth of a percent of that population was an unbelievably high number. The city might not care about an invasion; it might already have torn itself apart. But Jeddan's right, and that's all guessing. It's not like we can do anything about it.

"It sounded like you've had attacks by strangers who don't speak our language," Jeddan said. I think he was intentionally changing the subject.

"Yes," Nanissa said. "There's a town about two miles from here that wasn't there before the convergence. They've sent fighters against us, and some of their scribbling mages, four times now. The first time they hurt a lot of people before we drove them off. We're better prepared now. We don't know what they want. It's not as if we've done anything to hurt them. *They* came after *us*."

"Remember from their perspective, you're the ones who appeared out of nowhere," I said. "Not that I'm excusing their behavior, but they might just be afraid of what you might do to *them*."

"Or they have someone in charge who's aggressive. Or thinks he or she is justified in defeating you on the God-Empress's behalf," said Jeddan.

"Who's the God-Empress?" Baltan said. So I had to explain something about Castaviran politics, and the coup, though I didn't say my husband is a Castaviran mage—no sense giving them more questions to ask—and I didn't go into any detail

Oh no. I'm such an idiot. That town is right on the Royal Road the God-Empress's army is going to take once they've conquered Calassmir. They're all going to be slaughtered.

We have to go back.

CHAPTER SIX

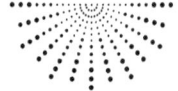

29 Coloine

I'm so sick of talking to people. I'm no diplomat and I'm sure as hell no leader, but I've done more talking in the last two days than any human being should be expected to do. And we've delayed our journey by a day, which has made me tense and irritable, but what else could we do?

It actually wasn't as hard as I'd feared to convince the three mages the God-Empress was an imminent threat. And once I did, they started coming up with plans on their own—setting up a semi-permanent camp in the nearby hills, sending people to observe the siege of Calassmir who would return when they saw the army move in their direction so they could evacuate—and they seemed confident, like this was something they could handle.

What I wasn't sure they could handle was a possible attack by Castaviran villagers while they were in their camp, which was meant to be secluded rather than defensible, given that there's no way they can keep the army from overrunning them if they're found. So once we were sure they understood the situation, we bade them goodbye and headed straight for that Castaviran town.

Like I wrote, I'm sick of talking to people. And I'm even sicker of the unrelenting fear and suspicion both countries are displaying toward each other. I realize it's a normal human reaction, but really, is *everyone's* first reaction to encountering the strange and unknown going to be violence? People can't take a moment to learn what kind of strange and unknown thing they're facing? This is the way the world is now, Balaen and Castavir lying cheek-by-jowl with one another, and it's not going away, damn those long-ago mages and their arrogant belief that they had the right to make decisions for everyone around them.

Last night I lay awake, sleepless, not thinking of Cederic for once but of the possibility that our civilizations are going to destroy each other and the survivors are going to claw their way out of the wreckage *and still go on fighting each other*. It made me so angry I finally had to go for half an hour's walk before I could calm down enough to sleep.

Anyway, the point of all of this is Jeddan and I marched across the fields (there's no road to the Castaviran village, not yet, maybe not ever) out where anyone could see us, no trying to hide. It's a walled town, so a little bigger than...I don't know what Nanissa's village is called. I can't believe it never came up. Anyway, the farms outside the walls were all deserted the way they'd been in that village, and when we were close enough we could see the defenders huddled up at the gate, not sure what to make of us.

The minute I could see the boards two of them were clutching, I let loose with a huge sweep of fire, bigger than anything I've ever managed before, made it circle them without burning (yet) and shouted "*Drop your weapons!*"

It took them a second or two, but drop them they did. "*Boards too!*" I shouted, and the two mages were much quicker to respond. One of the boards cracked in half when it hit the frozen ground. I kept the fire going until we were about twenty feet away, then dismissed it and stood facing them with my arms crossed over my chest.

"Who speaks for this town?" I said. I scared even myself at how angry I sounded, but I was tired and frustrated and heartsick and afraid we wouldn't reach Hasskian in time, and I didn't much care if I frightened anyone, because we didn't have time to waste.

"Our mayor," said one of the women.

"Get him," I said, and waited for the woman to duck past the growing crowd and run for the mayor. Why he wasn't with the defenders—no, I know why he wasn't with the defenders, he's a coward and a bully. But it doesn't matter now. We stood there, waiting, watching each other. The mages looked like they might go for their boards if I gave them a chance, so I sent a couple of fierce glares their way. We waited some more. I started to feel the anger wearing off, replaced by anxiety. They would only stay cowed by my display of magic for so long. If that mayor didn't return quickly...I didn't know what I would do next.

But the woman came back in less than five minutes, bringing with her a tall man who moved more slowly than she did, trying to exert control over the situation and, by extension, over me. "How dare you threaten us?" he called out when he reached the front of the crowd. "We haven't done anything to you. Leave now before we kill you."

The men and women around him looked nervous at that. Well, he hadn't seen the fire-summoning pouvra. "That was just to get your attention," I said. "I want to talk to you about the village about two miles down the road."

"The invaders?" he said. "What about them?"

"You need to stop attacking them," I said, trying to be reasonable even though his tone of voice irritated me. "They haven't done anything to you and they're only interested in living in peace." That was mostly true.

"They are foreign invaders and represent a threat to the Castaviran Empire," he said. "It's our duty to eliminate them."

"They are inhabitants of the shadow world, joined to ours again," I said. There was no point explaining the convergence to this fool. "The world belongs to both of us. You don't need to conquer them any more than they need to conquer you."

He examined me and sneered. "I know what you are," he said. "They've played a clever trick, choosing someone who looks Viravonian and somehow teaching you our language. But you're one of them. Kill her."

No one moved. "Kill her!" he screamed. One of the mages bent to pick up his board, so I set it on fire and he flinched away. The crowd muttered and backed up. "Cowards!" the mayor shouted, and snatched a sword from the ground and ran at me. That was unexpected, and I had barely begun to respond when Jeddan stepped in front of me, grabbed the mayor's sword-wielding arm, and used the man's own momentum to wrench it behind him so painfully he gasped and dropped the weapon.

"Thanks," I said to Jeddan. He nodded, and gripped the mayor by the back of his neck, holding him tightly. He flailed at Jeddan with his free hand, and I grabbed it and worked the walk-through-walls pouvra to slide my hand through his, making his face go white and the rest of him go limp.

"Listen to me, you idiot," I said in a low voice that didn't carry any farther than the three of us, "you can either be a hero in this, or I can make you look so foolish no one will obey you ever again. This is the new world. That village is not a threat to you. They are *allies*. Now, here's what's going to happen. You're going to...open diplomatic relations with them. You're going to start learning their language, or teach them yours—doesn't matter which way that goes. You're going to trade with each other.

"And in a while, I don't know how long, an army is going to march down that road, and you are going to help keep that village from being overrun. You're going to do all of this because what you want, more than anything in the world, is respect. Up until now you've been getting it because you're a bully, but I think you've just learned that only works until a bigger bully comes along. If you want respect for a lifetime, help people get what they need. Right now, they need direction. It's a new world and everything's different. You get to choose what happens next."

(I cleaned all that up and made myself sound more eloquent than I actually was. A lot more eloquent, actually. I was getting angry again, which makes me stammer, and when I tried to regain some self-control, I stammered more.)

"What are you?" he said.

"I'm a mage of the shadow world," I said, "and I'm the wife of a Castaviran mage, and I don't want both my worlds destroyed. *Please* see sense."

I knew the moment he decided to disregard what I said by the way his lips thinned and his eyes narrowed. "Hold him," I told Jeddan, and while the mayor thrashed around trying to get away from someone a foot taller than he was, I walked slowly toward the watching villagers. I felt so weary then, all the anger gone, leaving nothing but cold sorrow. "Hi," I said. "Sorry about the fire. I really was only trying to get your attention. Can I ask you one question? Who struck first, you or the, um, invaders?"

They looked at each other, mute. "Just tell me," I said.

"We did," said one of the men. He looked ashamed, and that lifted my spirits a tiny bit.

"And you all thought that was okay? Because they were strangers, didn't speak your language, and were mysterious, and that frightened you?" I said. I looked at the man who'd spoken, and said, "What's your name?"

"Aiden," he said.

"Aiden, was it right, what you all did?" I said.

He raised his head to look at me directly. "No," he said in a loud, carrying voice. "It wasn't right. And I knew that, and went along with it anyway, because I was afraid. And I'm ashamed of myself."

"Thanks, Aiden," I said. "What do you think you all should have done, instead?"

He shrugged. "Try to talk to them. Find out why they're here."

"Did you all hear that?" I said. A lot of nodding happened. "Do you agree with Aiden?" Murmuring, all of it agreement. I felt even more relieved. "Then this is what you're going to do," I said. I repeated what I'd told their mayor, but since I was calmer it came out more reasonable-sounding and I'm sure it was more effective. "It's going to be hard," I said. "But winter's coming and I think you can both use all the help you can get."

"We're experienced at fading into the hills," Aiden said, "and we'll help the newcomers do the same."

"You're both newcomers," I said, "and you shouldn't forget that." I glanced back over my shoulder, where the mayor hung unresisting in Jeddan's hands. He didn't look unconscious, just like he'd given up. "But I think this town needs new leadership," I said. "Aiden, I'm appointing you mayor. I think you'll do a good job for the immediate crisis. Then you can have an election, or however it is you choose your town leadership, and maybe they'll keep you, or maybe it will be someone else, but it had better not be *him*." I jabbed my thumb over my shoulder.

"You don't have the right to do that," someone said.

"Really? How would you like to go about it?" I said. "Because I'm interested in your suggestions."

The voice subsided. No one else seemed inclined to speak. "Then that's settled," I said. "We'll go back and tell the Balaenics what you've decided, so they won't attack you when you visit them. Make peace. Make friends. You might even make marriages. I did."

That was all there was to say. Jeddan let go of the ex-mayor and gave him a kick to the seat of his pants to propel him on his way. I pretended not to notice. We went back to the Balaenic village and explained the situation, which took far too much time because they had all these irrelevant questions they wanted to ask, but eventually we were back on the road and, coincidentally, ended up camping in the exact same spot we did last night.

Huh. I was done writing, but I want to put this in too. I was about to curl up in my bedroll when Jeddan said, "I wish I'd been able to understand what you were saying back there."

"Maybe I should teach you Castaviran," I said. "It's less difficult than Balaenic."

"Not so I could follow along," he said, "because I could guess the content. But I've never seen anyone control a crowd just with words before."

"I did nearly set all of them on fire, you know," I said.

"That just got their attention. Whatever you were saying...they knew you meant it. If you'd told them to follow you to Hasskian, they'd have done it."

I thought about that for a while until I had to get up and write it down because it was keeping me from sleeping. I've never been a leader. Haven't had anyone to lead, for one thing, and leaders stand out, which I've tried not to do my whole life. I think Jeddan is wrong.

And yet...talking to those people, even talking to that idiot mayor, I felt...I'm not sure what. Rightness, maybe. As if I'd touched on something true and had the power to show that truth to everyone around me.

I wonder if that's how Cederic feels. I only know a little of what leadership means, from watching him, and it seems more a burden than a blessing, all that responsibility. But it comes so naturally to him, how he listens so carefully to what people say, and sees solutions where other people see only problems. How he can command a room without saying a word. It reminds me of the day Vorantor was killed, just before the convergence, and Cederic held everyone together even though I'm certain he was just as afraid as anyone because we still didn't have the right kathana. I miss him so much.

I hope I dream of him tonight.

30 Coloine

It's been an awful day. I suppose I shouldn't have expected anything less; 30 Coloine has been a terrible day for me every year for the last six years. Fortunately, it ended well—quite a surprise, actually. I think I might be able to sleep tonight.

We're making good time now we're on the Royal Road. Balaen's King is erratic and hedonistic, our government is sometimes guided more by vanity and greed than by good sense, and the nobles play vicious games with lives, part of why my family lost its status I guess, but we've got an excellent road system. I don't know if that's down to the current Chamber Lord who has jurisdiction over transportation (lady, actually, Debarra Jakssar, the only woman in the Chamber) or if it's something she inherited, but the major roads are well-kept and smooth. Of course, that's going to benefit the God-Empress too, but there's no point worrying about that.

That wasn't the awful part. The Balaenic village hadn't had much food to spare, and we forgot to ask at the Castaviran village, so we're running low on supplies. Jeddan's good at setting snares, but now we're out of The Forest—there are still trees surrounding the road, but it's not heavily overgrown—there aren't as many places for animals to shelter, and I think the convergence's upsetting of the landscape has caused many of the animals to flee. So when we saw signs we were approaching another village, I cheered up.

It makes me sick when I remember that now, because as the road curved out from beneath the trees, we saw smoke, a lot of smoke, and heard screaming, and there was far too much movement in the streets. Jeddan and I looked at each other, then I took his hand and concealed us, and we ran toward the village.

It was carnage. Men and women were fighting in the streets, some with blades, others with whatever weapons they could find. Bodies lay fallen everywhere, some of them crumpled where they'd managed to crawl away a bit before they died. As we watched, a handful of men burst through a door with their arms full of—I don't know what, boxes and piles of cloth, whatever they thought was valuable. Half of the main street was on fire, and I saw a woman climbing out of a second story window and dropping to the ground; by the way she landed, it looked like she broke her leg. The tingling numbness of the concealment pouvra seemed to spread through my body, making everything around me seem unreal.

Jeddan tugged at my hand and we turned around and left. There wasn't anything we could do. I know, I have all this magic, I should have been able to think of *something*, but I was too numb to think. No, even now we're well away from it, I still don't know how I could have made a difference. I wonder what started it. Not that it

I was going to write "not that it matters," but it does, because if we can understand what made Balaenic clash with Castaviran, and Castaviran with Balaenic (and I can't imagine it was anything else that caused that horror) maybe we can stop it next time. Maybe. I'm depressed enough right now all I can picture is that now-familiar image of both worlds going up in an epic conflagration, and the survivors clawing their way out of the wreckage and *still* being unable to create a new, common world.

We made camp and ate a scanty meal, then sat staring at the fire. Jeddan said, "We probably…"

"I thought of that too," I said. "But I couldn't bear the idea of taking advantage of that calamity to stock up on food like some looter."

"Me neither," Jeddan said, and we both went silent again. I know I've said I like being alone, and silence doesn't bother me, but right then I thought I might scream if I had to listen to the emptiness one minute longer. So I said, "How old are you?" Then I wished I'd thought of something else, it sounded so inane, but he said, "Twenty-four."

"I'm twenty-seven." And that was when I understood what had been niggling at me all day. "It's my birthday today," I said. "I'm twenty-eight."

He smiled. "I wish I had a candle for you to light," he said.

"I wish I had a gift for you," I said. It's been years since I had anyone I cared enough about to gift on my birthday. It was a surprise to discover I like Jeddan that much—he's just comfortable to be around, and we have so much in common. I definitely think of him as a friend, almost as good a friend as Sovrin or Audryn, but in a different way.

"You could tell me a little about yourself," he said. "That's like a gift."

So I did. Not much—he may be a friend, but we're not close enough yet for me to tell him all my secrets. I told him about Dad and Mam and growing up in Thalessa, but not about Bridie or Roda, told him about traveling and learning pouvrin, but not about how the magic woke up inside me, told him about Castavir and how we'd come up with the kathana to save the worlds.

I couldn't talk about Cederic—I'm trying not to think of him at all, it hurts too much—but I did tell him about the God-Empress, and made him laugh at the story of my failed wedding to Aselfos, which in hindsight is pretty funny. Jeddan is a good listener, and when I wound down, he said, "Thank you for the gift, Sesskia. And good fortune on your day."

"Thanks, though that seems a wish that didn't get fulfilled, given the day we've had," I said.

"We didn't get caught up in the disaster," he pointed out. "We still have food and shelter. We're only ten days from Venetry—fourteen at worst. By my standards this has been an excellent day."

"Your standards seem low," I joked.

He shrugged and bowed his head. "I've been outcast for a long time," he said in a low voice. "I did a good job looking like I fit in, but I knew I was different, and so did they, and the strain of pretending—you know what I mean. I should have gone traveling like you did, but I was too afraid to leave the village. But it was getting harder, all the time, to be normal, especially when I discovered the second pouvra and started thinking about learning more. Being with someone else like me...it's like there was a rock pressing down on me, all these years, and now it's gone. I hope that doesn't sound too...I don't know. Too sentimental."

It did feel a little sentimental, but I was so moved at his willingness to share something so personal I didn't feel embarrassed. "I feel the same way," I said. "The Castaviran mages are friends, and it was good to be around other mages, but there was always a gap I didn't know how to fill because we couldn't really understand each other's magic."

"You and I can't understand each other's magic either," Jeddan said, smiling.

"But we're getting there," I said. "Tomorrow I want to work on learning the see-inside pouvra. And then I'll teach you how to see in the dark. It occurred to me today that that pouvra alters the body, which is what you said happens to you when you work magic. Maybe that will make it easier for you to learn."

"Then don't stay up all night writing in that book," he said, and climbed into his bedroll. So I'm finishing this, and then I'm going to sleep, and tomorrow will look better.

CHAPTER SEVEN

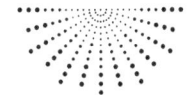

1 Nevrine

I'm frustrated because I felt so close to understanding the see-inside pouvra today, and just couldn't make it work. Jeddan's more patient than I am, because when we sat down to eat, and I complained, he shrugged and said, "Tomorrow, then."

Tomorrow, unfortunately, we have to do something about food. We've got enough left for one meal, and the terrain here is all plains, no more forest to shelter delicious edible animals. I think Hasskian is another five days' travel north, but it's been about seven years since I took this road, so I'm not sure. We'll have to find a town before then.

2 Nevrine

Snowed today, not much, but enough that I wished I had a heavier coat. We shared a hunk of dried meat I found at the bottom of my rucksack. Still very hungry.

3 Nevrine

So much warmer tonight, even if it is just a shed. We came to a little town, a Balaenic town, well off the main road at sunset. They were fortified as if they expected an attack and had an elderly rifle they pointed at us when we approached. It took both of us talking in our most reasonable voices to convince them we weren't Castavirans scouting their town in preparation for a raid, which apparently happened a few days ago. The town's mayor was on edge; I think the townspeople blamed him for letting it happen, though that's probably irrational fear rather than any failing on his part.

We tried to explain about the convergence, but it only confused them, so I settled for saying the Castavirans didn't speak our language and were as confused as anyone. They didn't believe me. I wish I knew why the Castavirans attacked. Fear, probably, but fear of what? The unknown? I know I wrote this before, but I have trouble believing *everyone's* first reaction in this situation is going to be violence. Yet that seems to be true.

We bought food and a tent—it took way too much of our money, and I know I'll have to steal before we reach Venetry—and the mayor let us sleep in a shed, which sounds callous, but it's more of an outdoor porch for sitting in on summer evenings, very pretty even though it was inadequate for winter weather. I think they were all still suspicious of us. I think they also thought Jeddan and I were a couple, since there was no offer of separate quarters. Just as well, because Jeddan gives off plenty of body heat and the shed is quite comfortable.

4 Nevrine

I'm snuggled up against Jeddan's back right now, too overwhelmed by the events of the evening to feel self-conscious. He's a good friend, but he's also a man, and...I don't know why that makes me feel awkward, because it's not as if I expect him to attack me, and he doesn't behave as if he's attracted to me.

Not that I'm all that good at picking up on those cues. I had no idea Cederic loved me until he told me, but I know now he'd felt that way for weeks without giving any hint of it. (He said he was waiting to tell me until the convergence was over, when things would be stable, so I'm almost glad he lost his temper at me because it gave us those two weeks of happiness together.) He's so self-controlled it makes sense that I wouldn't have observed anything, but there were moments that in retrospect were obvious, like the day he made me tell him about the collenna master's murder. He used those th'an on me to make me sleep, but when he was done he brushed my cheek with his fingers, so lightly, and I knew it wasn't a th'an but I was too ignorant to know a lover's touch when I felt it.

I'm so glad I remembered that just now. It makes me feel so much less awful about myself. It's snowing heavily now, which makes everything feel quiet and distant, and I'm sure it's insulating the tent, so even though the ground is cold, I think I'll be able to sleep. Just as soon as I write all of this down.

Most of today was uneventful. More walking, more discussion, more me almost but not quite managing the see-inside pouvra. We passed a few more Balaenic villages (this is a Balaenic road, so that makes sense) and saw a Castaviran one in the distance. There's a marked visual difference between the two that gives us a warning as to what kind of behavior we should exhibit.

One of the Balaenic towns sat astride the road, and the people there acted as if nothing were wrong, with kids waving at us and women chatting with their neighbors with barely a glance our way. It was unsettling. Jeddan and I tried to talk to their leaders, to warn them about the God-Empress's oncoming army, but no one we spoke to took us seriously. They all had these expressions like they thought we were crazy, and not in a harmless, funny way. A couple of them put their hands on weapons, or things that could be weapons, while we were speaking. I was afraid to use magic to convince them, and Jeddan came to the same conclusion. We were both relieved to leave that town behind.

By the time the sun set, we'd entered another forest, not heavily overgrown, and with the trees mostly bare it didn't feel confining at all. We found a place off the road to camp, a little natural clearing, and lit a fire and had something to eat. Jeddan talked about setting a few snares, so I said I would write while he did that. But after he left, I didn't feel like getting my book out. Some of that was because I can see the pages diminishing, and there's *really* no chance of me finding a new blank book out here. Some of it was just tiredness. So I sat next to the fire and let my mind go blank.

I don't know when I realized the thrumming sound wasn't the

blood rushing through my ears, but something external—hooves, and a lot of them. I jumped up and put the fire between myself and the road, not thinking, then I woke out of my stupor and concealed myself. I knew whoever the approaching riders were, they'd already seen the fire, because the bare trees weren't very good concealment, so there was no point trying to hide the camp. It was possible the riders wouldn't want to harm me, but that wasn't a chance I was willing to take. I hoped Jeddan, wherever he was, was safe.

The noise of the hooves grew louder, then stopped nearby. I heard people dismounting, the sound of harness jingling and the whiffle of a horse at rest. Then three men came into the clearing. They were roughly dressed, unshaven, with heavy coats and broad-brimmed hats, and their boots struck the frozen ground with loud clumping sounds. One of them approached the fire and kicked dirt at it, desultorily, not trying to put it out. Another ducked into our tent and started making noises like he was going through our things.

The third circled the little clearing, peering past it as if he were looking for someone. I had to move silently out of his way, praying he wouldn't look in my direction, because he had the air of someone who didn't miss much.

"They can't have gone far," the first man said.

The second man emerged from the tent carrying our rucksack of food. "They've got bugger-all worth taking," he said.

"Gather it up," the third man said. "Elssan and Nattas are searching the woods for them. Might have their goods on them."

He turned to walk back the way he'd come. I took another step away, silently, I thought, and his eyes came around and met mine, and saw me. I tried to run, nearly fell into the fire, and his hand went around my wrist and jerked me back. "What's this?" he said, and shook me so hard I lost my concentration. "A woman." He said it as if there were something inherently wrong with being female.

"Let go," I said, which was stupid, because why would he let me go just because I told him to? I almost used the walk-through-walls pouvra on him, but realized in time escaping his grip wouldn't get me past the other two men, and I could only dodge them for so long before running out of breath. And I didn't know where Jeddan was, and the only place he would know to look for me was by the fire. So I held still and examined my other options.

But to my complete surprise, he let me go! Before I could react, I was stunned again when a long, fat rope of fire rose up from nowhere and wrapped around me, close enough it started to singe my clothes, but not enough to actually burn me. I gaped at him, then said, "You're a mage."

"Don't know that word," he said. "My people always called it witchcraft. Or did before I burned the town to ash."

That shut my mouth. I'd been about to say something excited, something about us having so much in common, but now it was clear we didn't. Then he smiled, and it was a nasty, leering smile that made me feel cold and afraid. "Didn't expect to find a woman traveling the roads," he said. "Where's your friend?"

"Who says I have a friend?" I retorted. The fire was starting to hurt. I wish I knew how to dismiss someone else's fire pouvra, not that that would have made a difference.

"Two bedrolls says you have a friend," the second man said.

"So where is he? Or are we twice blessed, and it's a she?" the mage said.

"Gone where you won't find him," I said.

"Oh, I don't think he'll leave you to us," the mage said. "Who knows what we might have in mind?"

That made me mad. Even if I hadn't been nearly raped once, I'd still be furious at any man who thought he had a right to take what wasn't willingly given. "How sweet," I said, and lashed out with my own fire, turning him into a greasy pyre. He screamed, and the rope of fire disappeared, and that was when Jeddan burst out of the forest and bore the second man, the one with his hands full of our things, to the ground.

The mage shook like a dog, and fire flew off him like water. "*Bitch*," he screamed, and fire wrapped me again. This time I went insubstantial and jumped away from it, which made his eyes and mouth go wide. He flung fire at me again, and again, and I let it pass through me, or dodged it when I had to breathe, and lashed out at him with my own fire, which he dodged in turn.

The other man, the one Jeddan wasn't wrestling, turned and ran from the clearing, shouting to people I couldn't see. I didn't have much attention to spare either for him or for Jeddan, because I was trying to come up with a way to end the little dance I was having with the increasingly maddened mage. He didn't seem to be tiring at all, but I was becoming light-headed, and at some point I would have to stop going insubstantial, and that would be it for me.

Maybe it was the light-headedness. Maybe it was the hours of practice finally coming together. But as I went insubstantial one final time, I could see the shape of the pouvra as if it were rods and curves spun from spider's silk, as insubstantial as I was, and then it shifted and I saw a new shape that emerged from the old one. Without stopping to think, because I could never have done it if I analyzed it, I bent my will to the new shape.

It was as if—I've thought about this a lot since then, thought about it to avoid thinking about other things, and it was as if the world blinked, and when its eye opened, I could see everything differently. It was so strange I forgot I was fighting for my life. I was about five feet from the mage at that point, keeping my eyes on his chest because its movements told me where he was going to fling fire next, and it seemed the most natural thing in the world to turn the pouvra on him.

Thinking back on it, I don't know why the pouvra's revealing his innards didn't disgust me. I must have been more light-headed than I thought. Mostly I was fascinated by what I saw, heart and lungs pulsing, arteries and veins quivering as blood flowed through them.

I was too distracted, I suppose, because he was able to grab me in a moment of solidity and shake me so hard I couldn't summon fire. "I am going to enjoy killing you, burning the skin from your body an inch at a time," he snarled, and that woke me up. I tried going insubstantial, but I was too tired and breathless, and I couldn't burn him without burning myself, and his innards were pulsing queasily inches from my face.

I could see his heart throbbing, rapidly because he'd exerted himself as much as I had. I remember thinking how strange it was that all the blood went in and out through those few slender vessels, and again in that dreamlike state I reached out with the mind-moving pouvra and crushed all of them until they twisted and broke.

Nothing happened for a moment. Then the mage released me and clutched at his chest. His expression was so surprised, so normal, it was hard to believe he'd been trying to kill me seconds before. I stepped away and watched him collapse. He didn't move much, just twitched as his face went ashen. Then he was dead, and I stood over him, breathing quietly. It still didn't seem real. Even the memory, as I look back on it now, seems unreal, like I'm remembering someone else's life.

Jeddan must have said my name several times before I heard him, but what I remember next is him putting his arms around me and holding me close, his chin resting on the top of my head. "What did you do?" he whispered.

"I killed him," I said. "It was easy."

Jeddan didn't push me away, or make sounds of fear or disgust. "He would have killed us both," he said.

"I know," I said. "But it was easy."

Then he let go of me to hold me at arm's length, and I was startled at the intensity of his gaze. "You're not a killer," he said. "I've never known anyone less callous about human life than you are."

"Okay," I said, which was so inadequate, but was there anything I could have said that would have made things better? Then I turned away and went rummaging through the mage's clothes. I remember thinking if I was going to kill someone, it should at least be worthwhile, and if he had money on him, we could use that. Jeddan didn't say anything else, and I was grateful more than ever that he has a gift for silence. I know he doesn't understand how I feel, but I know he realizes talking about it now will only make me feel worse, and he won't push. So grateful for such a friend.

The bandit had a little purse with fifteen crowns and a handful of smaller change, and a fire opal pendant that looked too feminine to be his, and wore a gold ring on his left hand. I left the jewelry, but Jeddan collected it, along with the other bandit's purse; Jeddan hadn't killed his man, but he wasn't going to wake up any time soon.

Then we struck camp and moved on down the road, though it was so dark we almost couldn't see to find another campsite, even with the see-in-dark pouvra. There weren't any horses when we emerged onto the road, so I think the bandit who escaped probably warned the others the mage had referred to. I almost wish we'd been able to take a couple of horses, even if we can't ride; how hard can it be to point a horse's nose in the right direction and hang on to the saddle? But there's no sense worrying about it now.

It started snowing as we put up the tent, then Jeddan guided me inside and told me, "Lie back to back," so I did. I waited for him to fall asleep before I started writing, in case I was going to cry, but I don't feel tearful. I don't feel much of anything except overwhelmed.

I used a pouvra to kill a man—not by accident, the way I did when I worked the fire pouvra for the first time, but deliberately, consciously choosing that man's death. It's fitting, in a way. I'm already a thief, and it seems I'm now an assassin, because what else can you call that kind of pinpoint, fatally accurate attack? I know my mind-moving pouvra is never going to be as powerful as Cederic's, but then he can't manage the kind of delicate movements I can. The kind that can crush blood vessels and—true God help me, I can't stop thinking of the possibilities now.

It scares me that I can so coldly consider ways I might turn this combination of pouvrin to my benefit. And the worst thing is I don't dare swear never to do it again. What if using the pouvra that way meant saving someone I love? Meant bringing Balaen and Castavir together in peace? I wouldn't even think twice about it.

I can't write anymore, and I don't think I can sleep. I'm glad Jeddan's here. I wish he were Cederic.

4 or 5 Nevrine, don't know

Dreamed again, dragged myself out of it before it was embarrassing. Finally cried.

5 Nevrine

Now that we have two pouvrin in common, it's easier to find common points for discussion. We're inventing a whole new vocabulary of "bends" and "flexion" and "beadery" and "star-rods" and other words meaningless except as they pertain to the pouvrin. After dark, I tried to give Jeddan the shape of the concealment pouvra, and while it didn't work, he said he understands it and it's just a matter of learning to bend his will. Based on what he's said during all these conversations, I get the feeling bending his will is what Jeddan finds most difficult to do.

We should reach Hasskian tomorrow sometime. When we weren't talking about pouvrin, we've been talking about how to warn the city. We certainly don't look like anyone of importance, and least of all like Balaenic soldiers—too bad our uniforms are Castaviran, since that would get us attention of the wrong sort.

The last time I came through here, Falak Endolessar was Lord Governor of Hasskian, but that was several years ago, so it's possible he's been ousted. But I don't think so. He's a clever politician, good at keeping just enough of his promises to stay in power, and I think in a twisted way he really does care about Hasskian's well-being, insomuch as that reflects well on him as their beneficent ruler.

Hasskian's prosperous enough, and the nearby towns benefit from being part of its economy. I stayed here last time just long enough to pick up the trail of a book I needed, and I liked the city all right, though I wouldn't want to live there—the walls are oppressive.

At any rate, I can't think of anything we could do to draw Endolessar's attention that wouldn't also get us tossed in a cell. So my plan, if you can call it that, is to enter the city and see what happens. At least I'm confident they won't arrest us just for walking through the gate.

6 Nevrine, late
Nothing went the way we expected. I was going to write about it all, but now that I've got pencil to paper I realize I'm too exhausted to think. Tomorrow.

CHAPTER EIGHT

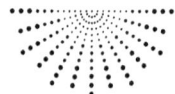

7 Nevrine

We camped early tonight because we found a place where this river—more of a stream, I guess—runs through a copse of trees near the road, and we were so tired we decided it was better to stop here than to push on until nightfall and risk not finding anywhere good. The fire is so comfortable, and I'm full, and I wish all of that physical comfort meant emotional comfort too, but I'm still not sure we made the best choice last night, and that's not a good feeling.

I wish I had Jeddan's confidence. Once he's made a decision and acted on it, he doesn't keep revisiting it and worrying he did the wrong thing. When he frets, it's about much more serious, life-altering things, like death. Me, I can't stop thinking about possibilities —like, what would have happened if I'd chosen differently, or how can I analyze a situation to know whether this decision would be right in other circumstances. I have to live with the consequences of my actions, and I'm fine with that, but I'm always looking to a future in which I'll have to choose again, and worrying I won't learn from my mistakes. Especially when those mistakes hurt other people.

I keep getting ahead of myself. I think it's because, by the time I get to writing, since all the events are in the past it's hard for me not to look over them and draw conclusions and think about what it all means. And that's interesting, but I wonder if it doesn't color the "story" I'm telling in these pages.

So this begins early yesterday morning. We started before the sun had fully risen so we'd have plenty of time to explore Hasskian and work out a real plan that wasn't "let's see what happens," which is my least favorite kind of plan. We passed a still-sleeping Balaenic village that lay right on the Royal Road, then made the turn that leads to Hasskian, which is about ten miles off the main road.

There's another town—small city, really—called Debressken near that junction, and we were nearing it when Jeddan said, "That's a Castaviran town over there." He pointed, and I saw the distinctive pointed roofs off to one side, maybe a mile away from Debressken to the south. It also looked quiet.

"I think we should visit them," I said. "See how they've fared. I don't like how close they are to these towns."

Jeddan nodded, and we set off across the fields—not cultivated fields but the untamed lands between towns, full of tall, dry grass and small animal burrows. It was going to snow, which made everything dim even though there was a small bright spot to the east where the sun was peeking over the horizon, showing Hasskian, even at that distance, as a black blob low to the ground. Our footsteps swishing through the dead grass were the only noises anywhere.

"Don't you think we should hear people waking up?" Jeddan said.

"Yes," I said, and started walking more quickly. Jeddan sped up as well. We reached the first of the outbuildings, a barn, and looked inside. It was fully stocked with bales of hay, and fitted with the pails and other necessities of a dairy farm, but there were no cows, nothing living at all. It was eerie.

We turned around and went toward the farmhouse, where the back door hung ajar and swung slightly in the cold wind blowing a storm toward us. After exchanging glances, I pushed the door open and we went inside.

It had been ransacked. The kitchen we entered was strewn with pottery shards, drifts of flour and sugar lay across the floor, chairs were knocked over, and the tablecloth puddled on the floor beneath the table. The fear choking me subsided when I realized there were no bodies, but there were so many other rooms... Jeddan and I spread out and searched the house. Everything had been torn apart. There were no bodies, and no living creatures anywhere.

"I wonder where they went," Jeddan said, stopping inside the front door, which had been smashed. He scanned the ground. "A lot of people came through here, not that that's news. But I can't see any indication of people being dragged away. And only two or three people other than us went out the back."

"They had to go somewhere," I said.

"I'm just saying I can't tell where that is," Jeddan said. He went through the door and stood for a moment, looking toward the rest of the town. "Do you want to look further?"

"I think we have to," I said.

I wish we hadn't. We found the first bodies, all men, about a hundred yards from the farmhouse. They'd been dead for a while—Jeddan said probably a week. I don't want to know what he's seen that he knows that so precisely. There weren't many bodies, but we didn't look very hard for them.

It didn't take long for us to establish what had happened: the town had been raided, the villagers and their livestock rounded up and taken somewhere, those who fought back were killed. We both agreed it was likely soldiers had done this, Jeddan based on the nature of the dead people's wounds, me because I've seen mobs and I've seen raids and I can tell what kind of damage is caused by which. I wish that weren't true.

It sickens me that the Balaenics just left the bodies there to rot. They saw the Castavirans as enemies, true, but that was like they didn't think they were human. I have to stop thinking about it if I want to keep my meal down.

After about an hour we'd had our fill of the destruction and decided to move on, since there was nothing we could do. We were both depressed, I think, and I was nauseated by all the death, so we decided we'd hurry through Debressken so we could finish our business in Hasskian and get back on the road.

It only took a few minutes for that plan to go to hell. It was full light when we left the ransacked village, and we were no longer the only travelers on the Hasskian road. No one we passed seemed inclined to speak; most of them kept their heads down and ignored us. Or maybe they were just huddled up against the cold. Either way, it's not that unusual for travelers to keep to themselves, because you never know if the person who wants to be friendly is actually looking for a victim. And we were just as happy not to talk to anyone.

So it was surprising when we were hailed in an unfriendly voice and told to stop where we were. I hadn't been paying attention—was hunched into my coat like everyone else, blinking away the tiny cold motes of snow blowing into my face—so when I looked up I was surprised to see an armed guard pointing at us. Another guard had accosted one of our fellow travelers and had a rifle, not military issue, held in a way that suggested violence was definitely an option.

Jeddan and I looked at each other, and he shrugged, which I took to mean "let's try to avoid trouble, but we can overcome him if we have to." We walked over to the guard, trying to look innocent, though if the man was as suspicious as he sounded, he probably thought Jeddan was a threat because of his size. Jeddan no doubt felt the same way, because he trailed behind me so I could do the talking.

"What's your business in Debressken?" he said. He wore a fur-lined cap and a heavy coat, and his nose was red and drippy. I saw smears on his gloves where he'd swiped the back of his hand across it. Lots of smears. It made me feel like my own nose needed wiping, though it didn't.

"None," I said, going for politeness. "We're on our way to Hasskian. Just passing through."

"Fine," he said. "We'll give you an escort."

"Why do we need an escort?" I said.

"We aren't taking any chances, not after we been attacked," he said. "You could be foreigners in disguise."

"Do you think foreigners could possibly speak Balaenic this

well?" I said.

He shrugged, and said, "Not taking any chances."

"Looks like you took care of the foreigners well enough," Jeddan said. "If that was their village we saw a ways back."

The guard looked as if he wanted to find something suspicious in this statement, but couldn't. "Brought it on themselves, trying to attack us," he said. "Lord Governor sent out the troops and took them all away."

"It's not a small town," I said. "Where did they take them? Far enough away to keep them from attacking honest Balaenic folk like you, I'm sure."

He grinned. It wasn't a nice grin. "Put them in a camp northeast of Hasskian," he said. "Nobody's sure what to do with them. Can't let them attack us, but we won't kill women and children no matter if they're foreigners. Lord Governor's still thinking about it. He's a good ruler, even if he is touched."

"Touched?" I said, because I'd never heard anything to suggest Endolessar wasn't mentally stable.

"Touched by the magic," the guard said. "One of those who rose up after the calamity to work magic. Lord Governor Endolessar can move things without touching them."

"I'm surprised he wasn't lynched," Jeddan said.

"We're not small-minded people," the guard said, and I had to pretend I was coughing to cover my laughter. "Nothing wrong with magic if you use it for good. We had a bunch of people changed like that, all of them swearing to use their magic to benefit their city. I almost wish it was me." He looked more closely at my face. "You've got the eyes," he said. "Are you..." Despite his words, he looked afraid. A reasonable fear, since he'd been harassing us.

"We are," I said, and on a whim did the water-summoning pouvra almost in his face. I'm most comfortable with fire, but I didn't want to scare him further—that's not true, I *did* want to scare him, but it was an ignoble desire that would have done nothing but satisfy me. Jeddan, for his part, passed his immaterial hand through the man's arm, making him look as if he were going to be sick. I know Jeddan did that because it's the only overt pouvra he has, but I'm sure he got as much satisfaction out of doing it to the man as I would have from fire.

"I'm sorry," the guard said, "I didn't—I wouldn't—but you're not going to Venetry, then?"

"After Hasskian," I said, puzzled. ~~If we'd~~ (I was going to write "if we'd asked him more questions, we might not have gone to Hasskian at all" but that's not true, we still would have needed to warn Endolessar even if we'd known about the king's summons.)

"Well, safe journey, then," the guard said. "If you stop at the sentry post inside the Hasskian city gate, and tell them you're magickers, they'll take care of you. Sorry about the misunderstanding."

"That's...all right," I said, and we went on down the road. Off to the left, another guard was turning away a traveler who presumably didn't have a good reason to be there, and there was a line forming at the city gate.

Debressken grew up around us, made of stone hauled from the quarries to the west, cheaper than timber in this place, and the people were surprisingly friendly. Or maybe it wasn't surprising, if they knew their guards were turning away "undesirables" before they could get this far. The snow was falling more heavily, still tiny specks, but they drove into my eyes and nose, and I turned up my collar and pulled my hat down over my eyes.

"They took them northeast," Jeddan said. "What's northeast?"

"Nothing that I know of," I said. "Nothing special, anyway, unless the convergence changed the terrain. More plains, more towns. A forest, not a big one. Maybe that's why it's special—they can round up hundreds of people and there's no one to make a fuss about it."

"What can we do?" he said.

"Us? Nothing. What do you think? We can't walk into Venetry trailing a village's worth of Castavirans and their cattle," I said. I wiped my nose with the back of my hand, then thought better of doing it again.

"It just doesn't seem right," he said, but he fell silent and we walked the rest of the way to Hasskian without saying anything. Not much point, when we were both thinking the same thing and neither of us had a solution.

For the last mile or so we shared the road with a dozen other travelers, all mounted, who came up from behind and then passed us. Apparently they met the stringent Debresskian code of acceptability. We watched as, one by one, they were stopped at the gate, a big iron-barred door a good ten feet tall that had a rusty portcullis drawn up above it.

Hasskian is a good distance from the Fensadderian border, and it's been almost seventy years since Balaen came under attack from the west, but the last time, the enemy got this far, and Hasskian held the defense for fifteen days before the army could arrive to repulse the invaders. So its gate, and the black stone walls circling it, are there for a reason.

I'm sure they don't realize the irregularity of the stones make the walls easy for a determined person to scale, and the spacing of the three gates means there are places where said determined person can get inside the city without anyone noticing. I've been to Hasskian half a dozen times over the years, even though it's been a while, but this was the first time I've gone in via the gate.

When it was our turn, the guard, who was better armed and armored than the Debresskian and had the hard look of a man accustomed to hurting people, said, "Name and business?"

"Rokyar Axe," Jeddan said—I didn't know the name of his village until that minute, and it was nice to see my surmise about his occupation proved correct.

"Thalessi Scales," I said, "and we have been touched by magic and would like to see the Lord Governor on a private matter."

"All magickers are to see the Lord Governor upon entry," he said. (I still think "magickers" sounds stupid. I wonder who came up with it.) "Follow me."

That was easier than I'd expected. We went through the gate and into a tiny round room at the base of one of the towers flanking the portcullis. Most of it was taken up by a table on which lay a stack of official-looking papers, a shallow dish of ink, and a wooden stamp stained dark with use. The guard scribbled our names on two of the papers, stamped them, and handed them to Jeddan and me. "You know where the Citadel is?" he said. I nodded. He didn't need to know how well I knew the Citadel, at least certain very well guarded rooms of it. "Show these to the majordomo. He'll make sure you see the Lord Governor."

We thanked him and set out. Hasskian is an old city, older than Venetry, and its age shows in the narrowness of its streets, which are worn slick from the passage of hundreds of thousands of feet over the last five hundred years, and the narrowness of its houses, built right up against one another, some of them sharing common walls. It was cleaner than I remembered; I think they finally put in modern plumbing sometime in the last seven years, because no one was dumping chamber pots out the windows. Another one of Endolessar's plans to improve the lives of his citizens and make himself look good at the same time. I wonder how much it cost. Well, we weren't in the slums, so maybe those were as smelly and dangerous as I remembered.

The people of Hasskian didn't look as if they were afraid of whatever danger the foreign "invaders" might pose. They were as friendly as city-dwellers ever get, which is to say they're happy to nod in greeting, but they have an air about them that says they won't intrude on your business and they expect the same courtesy from you. I like that about cities. The streets were full of people going about their business, but not so full that we had trouble getting from the gate to the Citadel.

The grand-sounding building is actually just a manor in a part of Hasskian that was razed about a hundred years ago so the rich could build larger, nicer, more solitary houses than were available in Hasskian at the time. It looks like a tiny castle, with turrets that couldn't possibly have full-sized rooms in them, whitewashed stone, a little front door that's a replica of Hasskian's gate and, unbelievably, a moat. Endolessar's great-grandparents built it, and people actually travel great distances to see it. I guess some people are so bored they'll do anything for entertainment.

There was a guard standing at attention outside the gate (standing open, tiny portcullis raised) but we showed him our papers and he waved us through without even examining them. Inside, the Citadel looked even more like a castle. Our footsteps echoed off the twenty-foot-high stone ceiling, ribbed with more stone, and tapestries hung on every wall.

Opposite the door was an arched opening through which I could see a long, long table and an equally long fireplace holding what appeared to be most of an oak tree, ashy with the residue of past fires. A stone staircase with no handrail ran up one wall to a gallery high above. It was hard to imagine anyone being brave enough to use it. Well, *I* would, but even I would think it was pointless.

A man emerged from the dining hall, straightening his over-robe. "Papers," he said, extending a hand. He had dark gray hair swept back from his forehead and the pinched look of someone who'd smelled something unpleasant. We handed our papers over and he scrutinized them as the guard had not. "What magic have you?" he said.

"I can—" I began.

"Show me, woman, don't talk me to death," he said, which made me want to set his over-robe on fire. It was elaborate brocade shot with gold, and his fussiness about it made me want even more to set it on fire, but I controlled my impatience and again summoned water. I admit I could have chosen any pouvra to demonstrate, but I opted for the one that would be the most annoying, and it worked. He took some quick steps backward to avoid the splash and said, "How dare you!"

"You did tell me to do it," I pointed out, and he subsided, growling. Jeddan was more circumspect and put his hand through the nearest wall, which impressed the man more than my display had.

"Very well," he said, and removed a little book from inside his robe, which reminded me I *really* needed to find a new book soon. He flipped through the pages, took a tiny pencil from a loop of fabric near the spine, and said, as he wrote, "Come back in two weeks and the Lord Governor will see you."

"What?" I exclaimed. "We can't wait that long! We have urgent news for the Lord Governor."

"Don't they all," the man said, snapping his book shut and returning it to his hidden pocket. "Two weeks."

"I—all right," I said, sizing the man up and liking the conclusion I came to. I've had to talk my way in and out of situations since I was twelve, and the first thing you learn, when you have to live that way, is to judge what kind of person you're bluffing. Some people, it's just a waste of time. Others will believe anything you say. This man was in the middle somewhere. I felt reasonably confident I could get him to bend my way so long as I kept a straight face and didn't let up on the pressure. And, at worst, he'd kick us out.

"That's a good policy," I said, "since I've heard he's a very efficient man who hates wasting time."

"True," the man said, though he looked wary at how reasonable I'd suddenly become.

"What's your surname, please?" I said.

He analyzed this for traps. "Messkala," he said.

"Good name. Easy to remember. Don't you think it's easy to remember?" I said to Jeddan.

"I know I won't forget it," Jeddan said.

"Me neither. All right, Messkala, we'll come back in two weeks and give our news to the Lord Governor then. Which news, I promise you, is not only important but timely. I'm pretty sure he's going to be furious when he finds out we waited so long to pass that news along to him." I leaned right up into Messkala's face. He was starting to look uncertain. "And at that point, he's going to want to know *why* it took so long. And it's going to be no trouble at all for me to tell him your name. I wonder what he'll think of that?"

"You're bluffing," Messkala said. He didn't look certain.

"I could be," I said, "that's true. But you should consider whether it will be worse for you if I'm telling the truth and you *don't* get me in to see the Lord Governor, or if I'm lying and you *do*."

"You'll have no proof," he said.

"He knows who arranges his appointments," I said. "He'll know you had *something* to do with it. And he'll be angry enough I doubt he'll care about investigating very much." I took a step back, easing up on the pressure just enough. "Look, Messkala, he must see, um, magickers every day. I imagine he counts on you to keep track of all that. So he won't have any idea we were supposed to come in two weeks. Letting us in now won't hurt anyone, least of all you. I guarantee you'll be glad you did."

His look of pained superiority was gone, replaced by uncertainty. I gave him my most appealing smile. (I hope. Like I've said, I haven't ever been in a position to look much at my own face.) Finally, he said, "Come with me."

We trailed along after him, giving him plenty of space so he wouldn't feel intimidated by Jeddan's muscular frame. "That was impressive," Jeddan whispered.

"It was luck," I said. "I much prefer—never mind." I'd been about to say "sneaking in at night" but realized Messkala might be listening.

We went along some wide passages made of stone and freezing cold, then up a spiral staircase and into a narrower hall floored with planed wood that felt much warmer. Messkala opened a door on the right and entered without waiting for us. "My Lord Governor, two magickers to see you," we heard him say as we followed him into the room, which was as brutally hot as the downstairs passages had been cold.

"Thank you, Messkala," the Lord Governor said, "you may leave," and Messkala retreated at a pace that wasn't quite a run.

The heat came from a fireplace about half the size of the one downstairs, which meant it was still far too big for the room. Everything in the room was too big for it, the chairs built as if for giants, a cupboard against the wall opposite the fireplace so tall it looked as if it had been wedged into the space between floor and ceiling. The windows, on the other hand, were tiny and square and let in very little light, though that could have been the snow, which was falling heavily. I tried not to feel intimidated, since I was sure that was the intention. It took some effort.

"Welcome to Hasskian," the Lord Governor said. If I'd seen this room before meeting the man, I'd have guessed he was as oversized as everything else. But no, he was no taller than average, neither fat nor thin, with longish blond hair the same color as mine and, of course, the same green-gray eyes. He approached us with his palm out, and we each saluted him; the skin of his palms was hot and dry, probably from his proximity to the fire. My own skin was starting to feel parched.

"Please, sit down. Thank you for joining me," he said. We put our packs next to the door and sat down. My feet dangled. Jeddan looked as if he belonged in the oversized room. Endolessar looked beyond us, and shortly a pitcher and a couple of glasses came bobbing past, unsupported by anything but his pouvra. Impressive, if he'd only had it since the convergence. He poured water for us, again with the pouvra, which I tried not to gulp. "What are your surnames?"

"We don't have surnames," I said. "I'm Thalessi Scales, and this is my companion, Rokyar Axe."

"Thalessi, Rokyar, welcome," Endolessar said. "May I ask your magics?" He looked eager enough I almost forgot why we were there in my shared enthusiasm.

"I can summon water, and Rokyar can walk through things," I said, since Jeddan didn't seem to mind me speaking for both of us.

"I have never heard of summoning water," Endolessar said. "Would you show me?"

I summoned a little blob over the pitcher so it fell inside without splashing. Endolessar looked thrilled. "Wonderful," he said. "I'm sure we will find a use for you."

"I'm sorry?" I said.

"In the defense of Hasskian," he said. He sounded as casual as if he'd pointed out it was snowing.

"Then—you know about the invasion?" I said, which was stupid, because how could he possibly know? But I was so preoccupied with delivering our warning and getting back on the road I wasn't thinking clearly.

"Of course," he said. "We discover more of these excrescences every day, more foreigners intruding on our territory. We must eliminate them."

"The village," Jeddan said, because he was quicker on the uptake than I was.

"We are making this territory safe for Balaen," Endolessar said.

"No," I said, "the villages aren't a threat. It's the invading army you have to worry about."

He frowned, and said, "What are you talking about?"

So I told him about the convergence, and about the God-Empress's army, though I didn't call it that because that would have revealed I have far too much knowledge about Castavir for someone who doesn't speak the language, and ended with a plea for him to leave the Castaviran villages alone. "You need to put all your efforts into defending Hasskian's lands, and the towns dependent on it," I said. "That army has many, many battle mages who are far better trained at warfare than your mages—your magickers—are, and if your efforts are divided, who knows what might happen?"

"Interesting," Endolessar said. He got up and walked toward the fire. I half expected to see his hair start to frizzle from the heat. "Then you will fight with us?"

"We have to go to Venetry," I said.

"Surely their summons is irrelevant, with this news," he said. "They couldn't possibly expect us to give up our only advantage, though I'm not sure how much use dropping water on someone is."

"What summons?" Jeddan said.

"You haven't heard?" Endolessar said. "The King and Chamber have summoned all magickers to the capital city to help in its defense against the invaders. But as Hasskian is going to meet this army before it reaches Venetry, I'm certain the King will understand your refusing the summons."

"We have to warn them of the threat from the south," I said. "We're only two mages. You don't really need us, and as you said, I won't be of much help."

"I can send messengers," Endolessar said. "You'll stay here." He took two steps and grabbed my arm, painfully tight. I tried to pull away with no success.

"You can't keep us," Jeddan said.

"I can't keep *you*, certainly," he said, "but I'm counting on you being unwilling to abandon your companion, and *her* I can most certainly confine."

I glanced at Jeddan, who gave me the briefest nod, then I went insubstantial briefly and stepped out of Endolessar's grasp. "No one said I had only one magic," I said to Endolessar's astonished face, then we ran for the door, awkwardly scooping up our packs on the way, and dashed through it, not bothering to open it first.

We went substantial and pounded down the corridor to the stairs. "Where now?" Jeddan said.

"Out," I said, "then we need provisions, and then we get the hell away from Hasskian before anyone finds us." Behind us, we heard Endolessar shouting for his guards, and a stirring below told us someone was responding to the call. "Be ready," Jeddan said, and we came out of the stairwell into the cold stone hallway, and made it almost all the way back to the entry when half a dozen guards poured out of it and headed in our direction.

"*Now,*" Jeddan said, and we worked the walk-through-walls pouvra and kept running. I fell behind Jeddan, since I still can't pass comfortably through flesh and had to dodge the guards, but even so it didn't take long for us to leave the screaming behind and tear across the moat and down the road back into the city.

There are still two pages left in this book, but this feels like a good place in the story to switch to the new one. I'm glad I thought to steal it before leaving Hasskian. Sort of steal it, that is. I'll miss writing in this one; it's all I have of Cederic right now.

Huh. It never occurred to me, in all this time, that he must have bought this for me because he loved me. That this was a gift of the heart. And it has so much of him in it, from the night he told me he loved me to his final goodbye. When we're together again, I'll read it to him. I think he'd like that.

PART II
BOOK EIGHT

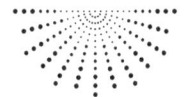

CHAPTER NINE

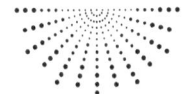

7 Nevrine, continued

This new book feels strange, probably because the cover is thick, stiff paper made of many layers pressed together and not beautiful blue leather. All that matters is that it's a book, I know, but it's hard to look at it and not think how much better a job I'd have done making it.

We ran, for a while, without paying attention to where we were going, getting as far away from the Citadel as we could. Eventually, we were breathless and hot even in the cold weather, and I had a stitch in my side I kept trying to bend into, hoping that would make it go away, so we stopped and went to walking at a normal pace. "I don't think they'll find us," said Jeddan.

"Two anonymous strangers who don't look different from anyone else, in a city this size?" I said. "You're right."

"We do look a little different," Jeddan said, pointing at our shadowy reflections in a shop window (dozens of little glass panes, very modern). Our images were crisscrossed with the black leading of the windows, but I could see his point: we looked travel-worn, and our coats and hats looked incredibly provincial, and I was still wearing my Castaviran uniform boots, because they were warm and waterproof. In the window, I saw someone passing behind us give us a skeptical look.

"We can either get new clothes, or find somewhere to hide," I said.

"We could do both," Jeddan said. "My shirt is getting ripe."

"We don't have a lot of money," I said, "and we should buy food. And we ought to do it quickly, in case somebody here has a locate-person pouvra."

"We'd have to kidnap that person, if that's true," Jeddan said, making me laugh. I wish there were such a pouvra. I have so many friends I wish I could find. Even a prove-someone's-alive pouvra would be nice.

"All right," I said, "let's walk," and I linked my arm with his so we looked like a couple of sweethearts out for a stroll. I didn't really know where to go. The only places I was ever familiar with in Hasskian were the noble manors near the Citadel (probably not a good idea to go back there), the slums (dangerous unless you were very familiar with them, which I wasn't after seven years' absence), and the industrial district (because nobody wants to pursue a thief through an abattoir). And none of those were exactly what I wanted. But the place we were in now was too upscale for our business. So I took us in the direction of the slums, and hoped we'd find something in between.

To sum up, because it was boring by comparison to what came next, we found a neighborhood where we could not only purchase cheap, clean clothing, but they let us change in the back of the shop and gave us a discount in exchange for our old clothes. I like my new trousers; they're old-fashioned, so they have deeper pockets than the last, perfect for keeping my books in.

Then Jeddan bought food, and I stole this book and a new pencil —true, we had money enough for it, but I was feeling reckless and felt like giving myself a challenge. Then I felt guilty and left some money on the counter when the store owner wasn't looking. I don't think I've ever stolen anything except out of need, because I know what it's like to have almost nothing and then have that snatched away from you. Anyway. I have it now, and it's a nice fat one that should last me for a while, unless we keep having adventures like yesterday's.

We were watching over our shoulders the whole time we were in Hasskian, but never saw a single guard. I'm worried Endolessar didn't take our warning seriously, given that we "betrayed" him and ran away. I hate to think of these people being crushed by the God-Empress's army. But we've done what we can, and now it's up to them.

Despite not being pursued by the guards, we went through the northeast wall, between two of the gates where the industrial district is. It was every bit as smelly as I remembered, what with the tannery and the butchers and all the other unpleasant things no one wants to think about that civilization needs to move smoothly. We passed through, concealed—this was about mid-afternoon—and hugged the wall, circling the city until we could strike out toward the road.

The snow had stopped falling for the moment, but I could still smell the storm in the air, waiting to start dumping on us again. I felt pretty good in my fresh new clothes (used clothes, but cleanly laundered) and almost cheerful about getting on the road again.

Then Jeddan said, "It's not right. We have to do something, Sesskia."

"What's not right?" I said.

"The Castaviran villagers," he said, "the ones they took from their homes. We can't just leave them there."

I stopped and turned to face him. "What do you propose we do?" I said. "Even if we could sneak them all away, they can't go back to their homes. And we can't go to Venetry trailing who knows how many Castaviran refugees."

"You think those people give a damn about the comfort and safety of foreign invaders?" he said, hotly, which surprised me. "They're penned up in some camp somewhere, probably without enough food and inadequate shelter, and that camp is going to be their home for months, and with winter coming on they're going to start dying. That's assuming someone in Hasskian doesn't decide they're too much trouble and orders them all killed."

"They wouldn't do that," I said.

"They already think of them as dangerous outsiders," Jeddan said. "Leave them there long enough, they're going to start thinking of them as not human. And nobody thinks twice about squashing a spider that might be poisonous."

I thought about it for a minute while he watched me, silent. We were both right, unfortunately. The Castavirans were in danger no matter how you looked at it. But there were too many of them—one, or two, or a dozen we might have been able to help escape, but a whole village? I cursed myself, but I could see we only had one choice.

"Let's find the camp, and investigate," I said, "and make a plan from there. We won't abandon them unless there really is nothing we can do, all right?"

"Agreed," Jeddan said.

We retraced our steps and circled back along the walls to the northeastern gate. The guard outside Debressken had said the camp was to the northeast, and it seemed logical that anyone going to or from it would leave by that gate. I thought about walking wide around the city, but I didn't want to risk missing the path to the camp and maybe getting lost, so we stuck close to the walls, holding hands to stay concealed.

We had to conceal ourselves for longer than I liked, staying hidden from the guards at the gate, but eventually we were far enough along the road we could walk openly. There weren't a lot of travelers, and if we'd been sane people, we wouldn't have been on the road either, because the snow had started falling again, and now it was big wet clumps that stuck to everything and dampened the shoulders of my coat.

"I think this is it," Jeddan said. He'd been watching the road carefully, and now he stood next to a smaller road, more of a large track, that branched away more northerly than the main road. "The snow is packed down the way you'd expect if a lot of people had used it, but there are only a few faint footprints. They set up the camp and then had a couple of men traveling between it and the city, or several men but only a few at a time."

"All right," I said, and we took that side road and trudged on. It was getting dark, and I tried not to be resentful of the Castavirans for getting us into this. I reminded myself we'd still be out in the wet and cold even if we weren't heading into who knew what kind of trouble. I shook like a dog to get the snow off me and kept trudging, watching the road ahead so we didn't run into a patrol, or something.

Specks of light ahead grew into lanterns, barely visible in the snow, and I grabbed Jeddan's arm to slow him down. We crept along, watching dark shapes emerge—walls thrown together from boards and rope, poles where the lanterns were attached—and then one of the shapes moved, and I worked the concealment pouvra on both of us as a guard bearing a rifle walked past, circling the camp. The moment he was gone, I dismissed the pouvra, said "Wait here" in Jeddan's ear, and ran to the wall, concealed myself again, and ducked through it.

It was pretty bare beyond. There were lots of tents, heavy dark army tents, and more lights, lanterns with their tiny flames holding back the dark. There were so many of them that if it hadn't been snowing, everything would have been bright as midday. I saw no guards. I ran back to Jeddan and the two of us went inside, then quickly ducked under the nearest tent flap.

It was as dark inside the tent as it was bright outside. A woman screamed, and then there was a lot of movement. "No, no, we're friends!" I said, "stop or they'll want to know what's going on!" The scream cut off, as if someone had muffled the woman. "Sorry to startle you," I said, "but we saw your village, and heard you'd been taken away, and we came to see..." My voice trailed off because I wasn't sure how to end that sentence without sounding like their suffering was nothing but entertainment for us along the road.

My eyes adjusted to the dark—I'd thought about using the see-in-dark pouvra, but I wasn't sure if we'd need to pass quickly through the brightly-lit space between tents—and I saw people huddled together, most of them wrapped in blankets. A baby coughed, then wailed, and its mother shushed it. "Who are you?" said someone in the darkness.

"My name is Sesskia," I said. I felt so sorry for them it felt like an affront to distance myself by using my placename. "Is there anyone who speaks for all of you?"

More shuffling. "Carlen Liskesstis, I suppose," said the same man.

"Is he here? Can you get him?"

Silence. "Carlen's a girl's name," the man said. "You ought to know that."

I cursed myself. "I didn't know, because I'm Balaenic. One of the, um, foreigners. But I speak your language, and I want to help," I said.

Nobody said anything for a long, long moment, in which I wondered if a week's captivity was enough to weaken them enough so they couldn't attack us. "I'll get her," the man said. He came forward, glancing at me briefly—he had dark hair, and dark eyes, which was all I could see of him—then left the tent, keeping low to the ground.

Jeddan and I waited. I felt awkward. I don't know what Jeddan was thinking. I couldn't come up with anything to talk to these people about; polite small talk would have been ridiculous, and I started worrying we'd been truly stupid to come here at all. There was nothing we could do for them but raise their hopes and then smash them.

The man came back through the door, making me step out of the way. He was followed by the shortest woman I'd ever seen, her hair silvery in the dim light. She, too, was wrapped in a blanket, and I realized I hadn't seen a single coat on any of these people. Suddenly I was so furious I wanted to kill every guard in the place and burn my way through Hasskian until they learned to behave like human beings.

"Who are you?" the woman said. Her voice sounded like a flute, not at all creaky the way I'd expected.

"Sesskia. This is Jeddan. We—" I didn't know what else to say. I couldn't make these people any promises. I couldn't do anything useful except be angry, and that wasn't useful at all.

"We saw what happened," Jeddan said. "You're in danger here. If we could get you out, is there somewhere you could go?"

"Jeddan, they don't know what you're saying," I said.

"Then tell them," he said.

I sighed inwardly, but repeated his words. Liskesstis's expression didn't change. Slowly, she raised a hand, twitched her fingers, and amber light outlined a th'an just before the same amber light coursed down the poles of the tent, filling it with a warm light. "You don't look like a fool," she said.

"We can get you out," Jeddan said, and I started to protest, then shut my mouth because even as I'd been about to say "We can't promise that," an idea had blossomed into life inside my head. I didn't know what Jeddan had in mind, but I knew him well enough to believe he wouldn't make that promise if he didn't have some idea of how to do it. "Tell them, Sesskia."

"You're the enemy," Liskesstis said. "He can't even speak our language. You will only bring us death."

"We're mages, Balaenic mages," I said, "and even though we do magic differently, it's still magic." I grabbed Jeddan's scarf from around his neck, making him squawk, wadded it into a ball and tossed it in the air, and set it on fire. That got a lot more noise, and then shushing, and the burning scarf fell to the earth (bare earth, no rugs for the evil foreigners), where I stomped on it to put it out.

"No th'an," Liskesstis said, staring at the remnants of the scarf.

"It's how Balaenic mages work their magic," I said. "I swear we mean you no harm. And I think we can get you out."

She looked skeptical. Worse than skeptical—she looked *disdainful*. I said, grasping at anything, "Master Liskesstis, I promise you in the Kilios's name we can free you, if that's something you think will help. I know you can't go back to your village, and I don't know where else you can find shelter, but you will certainly start dying if you stay here. I bet some of you, the sickest and the smallest, have already succumbed. Please let us help you."

She sneered. "I know the Kilios. Who are you to make promises in his name?"

"I'm his wife," I said.

That changed her expression completely. She said, "Cederic Aleynten has no wife."

"We were married two weeks before the convergence," I said. "You know him? How?"

Her eyes narrowed. "What hand does he cut his meat with?"

"His left," I said, "even though he's right-handed, and before you ask, he cuts all his meat, even chicken legs, and it's an impressive feat of agility."

"Which of his ears is pierced?" she asked.

"Neither, though his right ear was pierced a long time ago. You can still see the mark," I said, trying not to think about what we'd been doing when I made this observation.

"That only proves you've been close to him, not that you're married," she said.

I wished at that moment I could raise one eyebrow like Cederic does. "I could give you any number of corroborating details," I said, "but then we'd have to have a very...intense...discussion about why you happen to know what he looks like naked."

To my surprise, she laughed. "No need," she said. "You're exactly the sort of young woman Cederic would marry, if he had any sense, which he does." I don't know why I blushed at that. I'm putting it away somewhere to consider later.

Just then we heard footsteps outside, and hands grabbed me and Jeddan and pulled us into the crowd. Someone pounded on the tent pole in the door opening with what sounded like a big stick. "Shut up in there, damned traitors!" growled the guard, and everyone held still until he went away. After a long, long time, Jeddan and I were released, and Liskesstis came to stand before me again. "We will not survive this," she said in a low voice. "They have already raped a few of us. And our children...we will risk anything for a chance at survival."

"We can't free you unless you have somewhere safe to go," I said.

"There's a town about ten miles east of here, or was. No reason to believe it's not still there," Liskesstis said. "We can walk that far, or die trying, but at least we'd die on our own terms. And I don't think we'll die."

"How many mages do you have?" I asked.

"Only one, in addition to me, and she is barely more than a child," she said. "I am the only Darssan mage here. I thought my retirement would be peaceful." She laughed.

"You should gather anyone the people will listen to, and begin planning your journey," I said, "and Jeddan and I will work on helping you leave this place."

"We can't just walk into the snow! We'll wander until the storm kills us!" a woman said.

"Have faith," Liskesstis said. "We've kept you warm so far, haven't we? Hidden the most vulnerable? These two have offered their help, and I think they can deliver on their promise. They will open the way, and we will walk out of here. Or would you rather wait here for that pretty daughter of yours to be snatched up? Twelve, isn't she?"

The muttering subsided. I said, "Will you have any trouble bringing everyone together?"

"We've been moving secretly between the tents ever since arriving here," she said. "You worry about your own problem. I imagine it's more difficult than ours."

I shrugged, then repeated the conversation to Jeddan, quickly. "I had an idea, but I was wondering what you'd thought of," I said.

"Let's see how many guards we're dealing with, then plan," he said. "I'll go outside the camp, where the snow will help conceal me, and you can look around in here."

It took us about half an hour to feel confident we knew what we were facing. There was a tent, well-lit and comfortably warm, where ten or twelve guards sat, clearly uninterested in going out into the cold, though one of them made a desultory loop between several of the prison tents while I watched.

Seven other men patrolled the outside of the camp, though none of them were very alert. It was clear they all were counting on their rifles and the weather and the barrenness of their surroundings to keep the prisoners penned in, because anyone could have knocked the "fence" over and walked away. We met back up in a corner between the prisoners' tents to confer. Jeddan was grinning far too broadly for someone facing an impossible challenge.

"I was nearly caught," he said, "and look what happened." He wavered, flickered, and I suddenly had to look away, my eyes watering from trying to see past the concealment pouvra. "It's the strangest experience."

"Do you think you can use it on someone else?" I said.

"I don't think so. I'll try. But at least I can sneak up on those guards and overpower them. If we can clear them away, can the Castavirans walk out of here?" he said.

"There are far too many of them not to attract attention," I said. "They'll make too much noise. And we can't get rid of all the guards I saw in that tent at once. But...I have an idea."

"Can you set the tent on fire?" Jeddan said.

"I could, but that wouldn't be a long-term solution," I said. "I was thinking of doing it the old-fashioned way."

Which is how I ended up sneaking into the storage tents and stealing about forty rifles, five at a time (I could carry three and use the mind-moving pouvra on two at a time, which means I'm getting stronger), and passing them out to some Castaviran volunteers with some quick instruction in how to hold them. (The Castavirans had never seen rifles before. I don't know why they don't have them.) It was extremely dangerous because the storage tents were adjacent to the guards' main tent, so they could watch them, and the more trips I made, the more often I had a chance of being caught.

But the guards were all making a lot of noise playing some card game that involved penalty drinking—take a drink every time you lose a round, or play the wrong card—and were well on the road to inebriation. My Castaviran warriors were getting impatient by the time I brought the last armful, but I told them, "There's one more thing I need to do, or some of you might get hurt or killed. So be patient. Half of you need to go back to Master Liskesstis—*quietly*—and the other half wait here for your part of the plan."

It was going so perfectly I should have known something was

about to go wrong. Just as I'd sneaked inside the main tent, intending to start gathering the guards' rifles (there were six or seven of them, all propped against the tent wall or lying next to camp stools) one of the men stood up, stretched, and said, "I'm gonna go take a piss," and headed unstably for the door. I was on the wrong side of the tent and there was nothing I could do except watch in horror. He was going to step outside and find himself facing two dozen armed Castavirans, they would shoot him, and then everything really would go to hell.

But nothing happened. I had one gun clutched to my chest and my other hand resting on another rifle, preparing to turn the conceal-ment pouvra on it, and felt as if the pouvra had turned me to stone. No shots, no screams, not even the thud of an unconscious body hitting the ground. I slowly concealed the rifle and picked it up—might as well finish the job, since I was there—and eased my way out of the tent. There was no way I was going back for the rest. It would have to be enough.

I went around the tent to where I'd left the prisoners, and found them huddled up, I thought against the cold. But no, they'd surrounded the guard and completely immobilized him, gagged him with somebody's scarf. He looked furious and terrified all at once. "Take him somewhere, and bind him. Use the tent rope if you have to. You won't be coming back here."

Three of them dragged him away, and I told the rest, "Just a few more minutes. And remember, you can't kill any of them."

"We'll do what we like to the bastards," said one of the men. I recognized him as the one I'd spoken to first.

"I don't care what you do to them, myself," I said, though I quailed inside at the thought of them murdering even such vicious brutes as these guards no doubt were. "But if you kill them, Endolessar will have to hunt you down or risk looking weak. Then all of this will be pointless. Please. Leave your vengeance behind, at least for now."

None of them looked convinced, but they did as I asked. I don't care that it's skipping ahead in the story to say that. I was so worried, at the time, that their anger would get the better of them, and I honestly couldn't blame them for wanting revenge. I have no idea what it's like to have your homes destroyed and your families brutalized in that way and I couldn't tell them they shouldn't be angry. But I was risking my life for them, and if they were all killed because some of them let that anger overcome them, it would've been a pointless risk. So I was so relieved when everything else went as planned. More or less.

I went to find Jeddan, who'd subdued four of the guards. I told him I was impressed and he rolled his eyes. "Somebody really did believe these Castavirans were too weak and afraid to fight back," he said. "I hardly needed the concealment pouvra to get close enough to choke them unconscious. Are you ready for your part?"

"Are you sure it's safe, with three guards still out there?" I said.

"There's nothing more I can do," he said. "The last one made some noise, and when the next sentry went past, he looked a lot more alert. They'll have to take their chances."

I nodded and went to find Liskesstis. She was waiting at the door of her tent, peering out into the snow. "This is not the best weather," she said, "but it's not snowing heavily anymore and I think in a few hours it will be clear."

"Are you sure you want to do this?" I said. "If you can't find that town, you'll wander until you freeze to death."

"It's better than dying in captivity," she said, "and we'll have a guide." She moved her fingers, stiffly, and did it again, and then a globe of red light about an inch across hovered level with her nose. "It should lead us to our destination," she said, "if those who know this area are capable of using it. I'm not entirely certain it will work, but it's a better chance than we had before."

"Did you teach Cederic that?" I asked on a whim. "The writing on air?"

She laughed. "He taught me," she said, "some eight years ago, in exchange for some knowledge I gave him. The key to certain kathanas he needed to master to become Kilios. Why are you not with him?"

"We were separated during the convergence," I said, "but I'll find him, or he'll find me. I'm certain of it."

"I wish I could tell you where he is," she said, "but the locator kathanas no longer work, no doubt because of how the convergence brought the physical worlds together. The magic...you could say a locator kathana recognizes the world around it and identifies a person within that landscape, and of course much has changed now. But don't worry about it. Cederic Aleynten is stubborn and has never given up on a problem before he's solved it."

"I know," I said, and saluted her the Castaviran way. "You'll know when to move. Good luck."

I went back to join my "soldiers" and said, "Take your places around the tent. They probably won't think to grab their weapons. And remember, don't attack. Unless it's your life or theirs." Then I took a deep breath and summoned fire in a great swoop, spiraling around the tent from the ground to its many peaks.

Shouts and screams spilled out of the door, followed by guards who came up short when they discovered how many rifles were pointed at them. "Drop to the ground," I shouted, "or we shoot."

A couple hit the ground immediately. One looked like he was thinking about going back into the tent, but men were still spilling out and tangling themselves with the ones on the ground. "On the ground!" I shouted, and poured more fire into the conflagration.

Then one of the guards, who was either less drunk or had more presence of mind than his comrades, raised his rifle. Without thinking I bent my will to the shape of the walk-through-walls pouvra without touching him and saw the rifle fall through his hands, making him scream and fall backwards into the fire. Too shocked to think, instinctively I grabbed his feet and dragged him to relative safety, where a couple of Castavirans immobilized him. I told the Castavirans, "Tie them up, securely, and let's put them inside that tent over there."

By the time we were finished, Jeddan arrived and said, "They're moving. Your men need to come now."

A steady trail of Castavirans was exiting by way of a new hole in the fence that had Jeddan's work stamped on it, literally, because I could see the shape of his boot where he'd kicked the so-called wall down. I saw two soldiers wriggling in their bonds just inside the wall. "Where's the third?" I said.

Jeddan looked grim. "He got away," he said.

"Then they need to move more quickly," I said, taking a few steps toward the line. Jeddan put a hand on my arm.

"He didn't get far," he said. "I...killed him. Accidentally. Went through him, and he spasmed and fell down. I didn't know it could do that."

"Time to think about it later," I said. "Where's the body?"

"I hid it where no one will find it until the spring thaw," he said. "Are we done here?"

He sounded weary, and sad, and I wished I knew what to tell him that would comfort him. I remembered what he'd said to me the night I killed the bandit, and said, "You're not a killer. You couldn't bear the thought of these people being left here to die and you made me see the truth of that. If you didn't care about people, it wouldn't matter to you what happened to that guard. Right now, that doesn't feel like comfort, but eventually it will. You showed me that too."

He glanced down at me in the darkness, and said, "I think we should go," so we trudged back around the camp, leaving the line of Castaviran refugees behind. Liskesstis was right, the weather was starting to clear, but only Jeddan's ability to find his way outdoors kept us on the track leading back to the road, and the city, and then Debressken and the Royal Road. Then we kept walking until we found a place well off the highway to camp, and fell unconscious for maybe ten hours. We ate, and walked, and made camp again, and after writing all that I feel as wrung out as if I'd experienced it a second time.

I keep seeing that line of travelers, stretched out like ants following a sugar trail, their heads bent against the snow. I don't know if we sent them off to their deaths or not. I realize it was their decision, and it was a risk they wanted to take. I know we couldn't have left them there without finding out if there was something we could do to help. If they don't make it...I shouldn't feel responsible, but I do. I guess it's because I feel their fates are tangled up with mine now, and I wish I could go with them, to help along that journey. I think that's what I feel guilty about—Jeddan and I started them on that path, then couldn't follow it to the end.

I need to sleep again. We're about six days' journey from Venetry, unless something else happens to slow us down. I just want to get this over with. Talking about Cederic with Liskesstis made me miss him more. Venetry, report to the king—oh, damn it, he's summoning mages, he won't want to let us go. Report to the king, sneak away, and go east to Colosse, which Cederic's probably already left, looking for me. We might go across this new world and back fifty times and never find each other.

I'm going to sleep now, and pray the true God everything looks better in the morning. Jeddan hasn't said anything since we left the Castavirans but what's necessary to set up camp. I hope he's coming to terms with that death. I hope I'm doing the right thing by not making him talk about it. I'm so glad I'm not alone on this journey.

CHAPTER TEN

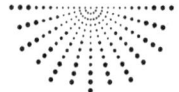

8 Nevrine

Jeddan was back to normal today, or at least he was able to talk about normal things as we walked. We discussed pouvrin, mostly our mutual unexpected discoveries. Jeddan showed enthusiasm when he told me, in more detail, how he'd mastered the concealment pouvra. "You're right," he said, "it's not the same as the others. It felt sharp, somehow, like a knife blade pressing against my skin."

"Yes, to me it feels more angular than the Balaenic ones," I said. "I wish I could talk to the mage who invented it. I wonder what he thought he'd discovered. He put everything in terms of th'an, even though Cederic said there was no way it would have done anything if someone tried to write it. But he knew *something* about pouvrin. Not the way we both do, but even so, maybe his knowledge would help us."

"You said he was insane," Jeddan said. "I'm not sure how useful that would be."

"True," I said, and sighed. "What I'd like to know is how I managed to do that with the walk-through-walls pouvra. It happened so quickly I'm not sure I can do it again."

"I think you should practice as we go," Jeddan said. He took a few steps off the road and wrenched a thick branch from a tree; it was dry, and snapped off easily. "I'll hold it, and you make it fall."

"I guess it's something to do," I said. So we did that for a couple of hours, with no success. I feel like I'm groping for something I've only heard about, even though I can remember a little of how it felt. ~~It was~~ I don't want to lie. After hearing what Jeddan did to that guard, I was feeling uncertain about using the walk-through-walls pouvra in any way. We haven't discussed it, but neither of us has any idea why, after all the times Jeddan has dived through people, this one died of it. So my heart wasn't in my efforts. I'll try again tomorrow.

9 Nevrine

It worked this time. It feels *really* strange. I've been thinking of this pouvra as a single thing, but with this new...technique, maybe? I've realized it's three separate pouvrin: turning myself insubstantial, turning that on someone else I'm touching, and extending that to work on something I'm not connected to. And they look...I've been thinking about it all day, and all I can say is it's like they're made of the same fabric, but assembled differently. Like a pile of twigs used to make a bird's nest and then a woven mat. I don't know what it means yet, but it feels important. If I could find more related pouvrin, or find another way to

It took me about twenty minutes, and I don't know if that's fast or if I'm slow, but I've confirmed that the fire pouvra as a mass of fire is different than as a rope of fire, and concealing myself and turning it out on someone else are different. Not as different as the walk-through-walls pouvrin are from each other, so I'm not surprised I didn't see it, but I'm still shocked.

So I've created four new pouvrin without the help of books—or maybe they exist somewhere and I just discovered them independently. No way to tell. I still don't know what it means, though! And it's hard to analyze the pouvrin while we're walking, so the only time I have is in the evening, and then I'm usually so tired I have trouble bending my will to anything.

I feel even more urgency, now, to get to Venetry, deliver my message, and then...would I really want to stay there for a few days just to study? I would. I'd apologize to Cederic, but I know he'd do the same. We're both infected with the disease that drives us to learn. He might even be annoyed I let my desire to rejoin him interfere with my becoming a better mage. He's going to laugh when I tell him about this.

10 Nevrine

We've decided I should try to teach Jeddan the mind-moving pouvra. I actually suggested teaching him the other walk-through-walls pouvrin, but he went very stiff and very silent, so I didn't say anything else. I hope he doesn't give up on using the pouvra entirely. It was his first, the one that made him a mage, and...maybe it's not the same for him, but even though I don't use fire often in comparison with some of the others, I know I'd feel like part of me was missing if I stopped using it. But it's not my right to tell him how to use his magic, so we're concentrating on the other pouvra, and it's true that the mind-moving pouvra is the most generally useful, at least to people who don't have to sneak around on a regular basis.

It's been not quite three months since I learned that pouvra, but it took me more than twice that long to understand it. I've written before about how I learn a pouvra, how it's about learning the figurative language the mage who created it used to describe it, then understanding the shape that arises from that language, and finally bending your will to meet the pouvra so it manifests through you.

Since I've already done all the work of interpretation, Jeddan and I will use our new vocabulary to give him the shape of the pouvra, and the rest is up to him. That's the idea, anyway. We've never done this before; it's possible no one's ever done this before, given how solitary mages have had to be thanks to Balaenic society. So I *hope* it will take less time, but we both know there's no use making assumptions where magic is concerned. I would have sworn the mind-moving pouvra was for small, finicky movements, and then I saw Cederic knock half a dozen soldiers across the room with it. I wonder if he uses it often, or if he's so used to th'an it never occurs to him to try. I wonder if he's figured out any more pouvrin.

Anyway, today we mostly just refined our vocabulary, made sure we meant the same thing when we used a word or image, and I practiced making things insubstantial. I have no idea what use that might be. Hah. I felt the same way about being able to turn the concealment pouvra on another person, but using it on the God-Empress saved the lives of my friends. So maybe there will be a crucial moment that depends on someone dropping their weapon, or something like that. It's fun to speculate about.

We're going to need food soon again, and we've almost used the last of the bandits' money. There aren't any large cities between here and Venetry, and I really, really don't want to steal from people whose lives depend on the food they have stored for the winter. But I also don't want to starve. We'll have to think of a better way.

11 Nevrine

I'd completely forgotten Jeddan took the mage bandit's pendant and ring. We found someone this morning willing to take the ring in exchange for five days' worth of food, more than enough to get us to Venetry, which is only two more days away. It was worth a good deal more than what we got for it, and part of me wishes we'd waited until I could sell it in Venetry, but the rest of me, the part that doesn't like going hungry, shouted that little part down.

Our learning technique works, and it doesn't. That is—and I shouldn't have done this—I had this unreasonable expectation I'd be able to pour the structure into Jeddan's head, so to speak, and he'd get it immediately and then it would be just a matter of his flexibility of will. And that didn't happen. But we're making a *lot* more progress, more quickly, than I did, so in that sense, it works. Jeddan's enthusiastic about it. Still won't talk about what happened to that guard, and I'm starting to worry that maybe I need to bring it up, and I don't know how to do that. I don't want to make things worse. So I'm going to leave it alone, and hope, if he needs someone to talk to, he'll feel comfortable turning to me.

We came across the strongest evidence of the convergence's destruction this afternoon. There was a place on the Royal Road where a Castaviran highway intersected with it, or would have if the convergence didn't destroy every structure that overlapped with another. So the Royal Road comes to a crumbling halt, and then there's a big roundish space where everything's been obliterated, and then it starts up again. It was eerie, and we detoured around it even though we assured each other it was harmless. Castavir's roads aren't as well-kept as ours, and they don't have the new procedure that keeps ruts from forming, but then we don't have self-cleaning chamber pots, so I think they win.

12 Nevrine

Nothing important happened today. Jeddan's still working on the pouvra, but we're both distracted wondering what's going to happen in Venetry tomorrow. Some of our food turned out to be rotten. Wish I could steal that ring back.

CHAPTER ELEVEN

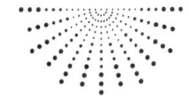

13 Nevrine, after curfew (hah!)

I've decided to keep these books hidden now we're among the mages. Not that we've met any of them yet; it was late when the King's men brought us here. So they might all be friendly and intelligent and committed to learning—in short, like the Darssan mages. But I'm not counting on that. No telling what someone might make of these records...all right, that's a lie, I have a very good idea of what someone might make of these records, which is that I'm a traitor to my country on any number of grounds, not least of which is being married to a high-ranking mage from the "invading" world. The fact that I've done all of this to save *both* worlds would be lost on anyone who was stupid or fearful or had a grudge against me, though I hope there isn't anyone here who falls into the latter category. Making enemies is the worst kind of being noticed, and I've spent my life trying to avoid *that*.

It stopped snowing early this morning, but it was still gray and depressing and Jeddan and I were impatient to get to our goal, so we didn't stop except once to relieve ourselves, ate on the way, and spoke little. When we approached Venetry sometime late this afternoon, there was a crowd milling about on the road outside the gate, not aimlessly, but with the erratic movements of a lot of people in one place, all wanting to be somewhere else.

We hung back, observing, and realized that rather than being an incipient mob, which has a much tenser, higher note to it, these were all people waiting their turn to get into the city, which was strange. I've been to Venetry often, and yes, I did use the gate, and nobody stops travelers unless they're carrying trade goods. But we could see a lot of armed soldiers stopping people and having long conversations with them before letting them inside. It made me nervous, and I suggested we enter the city by another way.

"We're mages. The King wants us here. It's not like we'll be turned away," Jeddan said.

"They're making people put their names on lists," I said. "I don't like that."

"But we have to get the King's attention somehow," Jeddan said. "Being on an official list will help with that. And these soldiers will send us to wherever the mages are supposed to go, and that's got to give us better access to King and Chamber than going through the wall will."

I scowled, and said, "All right, but if this goes wrong I'm blaming you."

"If this goes wrong, neither of us might be around to do any blaming," he said cheerfully.

We fitted ourselves into the loose line of travelers and inched forward with everyone else. It was boring, and cold, and I wished we'd gone through the wall. Jeddan had the glazed-eyed expression that said he was working on the mind-moving pouvra. I'm not sure he'd thought about what might happen if he succeeded in the middle of this crowd and knocked someone over. At least it would be exciting. The whole thing made me realize I haven't stood in line for anything in at least five years. I vowed it would be another fifteen before it happened again.

"Name?" said a soldier, and I realized we'd reached the front of the line while I was daydreaming.

"Thalessi Scales and Rokyar Axe," I said.

The soldier wrote our names in a little book, along with the date and time (there are about fifty big clocks in Venetry, none of them in agreement with each other, and one of them is just above the main city gate where we were. No one knows why some long dead ruler, or Chamber, thought people entering the city ought to know what the time was. At least that one doesn't toll the hour) and had us initial the entry. "Purpose?" he said.

"We're mages," I said.

"What's that?" he said.

I rolled my eyes. "Magickers? People touched by magic? With the eyes?" I pointed at my eyes in emphasis.

He peered closely at me, then at Jeddan, and I realized he was very nearsighted. "Papers?" he said.

"We don't have papers," I said. "We heard about the summons in Hasskian, but no one said anything about papers."

"Then you'll have to prove yourselves," he said, and pointed at another soldier, standing just inside the gate. "Talk to Nessan there. Curfew is nine p.m., no carrying weapons in the streets, no loitering, watch for the off limits signs, and if a soldier tells you to do something, you do it without question."

"Curfew?" I said. "I've never known Venetry to have a curfew."

"Martial law," he said. "City nearly tore itself apart after the calamity, what with magic happening and the earth shifting. Things still aren't back to normal. Move along."

Jeddan and I went to where the soldier Nessan was standing. He was older than the first, his hair graying and his eyes deeply lined at the corners as if he'd spent thirty years staring at the sun. He also wore a different uniform I didn't recognize as either regular army or city guard. "Magickers?" he said when we approached.

"We're called mages," I said, which was pointless, but I was feeling edgy and annoyed and wanted to get the whole thing over with.

"You can call yourself nasturtiums for all I care," he said. "Over here, and let's see what you can do."

We stepped out of the way of traffic into a little guard room empty of everything except a couple of chairs, a chest with a couple of warped drawers, and some smoked-glass lanterns, lit against the dimness of the windowless room. Jeddan put his hand through the wall and didn't seem afraid or upset or anything but calm, so I hope that means he's coming to terms with what happened in the camp. I settled on the fire pouvra, the ropy version. Nessan wasn't impressed by either of us. "You're to go to Fianna Manor for instructions," he said. "You know where that is?"

"I've been to Venetry before," I said, which was a non-answer, but he understood the way I meant it.

"But we have to deliver a message first," Jeddan said. "An urgent message from the army at Calassmir."

"Go ahead," Nessan said.

"It's for the King and Chamber," Jeddan said. We'd worked out he should bring the message, in case anyone wondered why a woman had been entrusted with military intelligence.

"Of course it is," Nessan said sarcastically. "And I'm supposed to take you to the King on no more proof than the say-so of some backwoods lumberjack."

I opened my mouth to speak, but Jeddan cut across me with, "What exactly do you think I'm going to do? You think I've traveled all the way from Calassmir just because I feel like wasting the King's time? I'm tired and I'm hungry and if I could deliver this message to just anyone, I'd tell you and my work would be done. But this message is for the King himself, because he's the only one who can decide how to act on it. So find someone to take us to him, or we'll wait here until you change your mind or carry us off to jail."

I was impressed. And terrified. Nessan hadn't struck me as the sort of man who can be bluffed, but Jeddan wasn't bluffing. I'm sure he meant it when he said they'd have to haul us away. And Nessan knew it too.

Nessan tapped his finger against his lips for a few seconds, then opened one of the drawers, took out paper and pen and ink, scrawled something on the paper, blew on it and folded it. Then he walked around us to lean out of the guard room and call to someone passing nearby. "They're to see the King," he told the young soldier who answered the summons, and handed him the paper. "Urgent military business. Five minutes."

That made me nervous; he might have written our execution sentence, and I wished he'd had better penmanship so I could have read it while he wrote. But there was nothing we could do about it except follow along.

The soldier saluted, and we trotted after him through the wide streets of Venetry. In the late afternoon, everything looked dismal, what with the slushy, filthy snow peppered with frozen horse turds shoved to both sides of the road, making a frozen barricade between the passing horses and the pedestrians. I made note of landmarks as we went, updating my mental map of the city.

Not much had changed in the thirteen months since I'd been here last. All the traffic from the main gate funnels through the center of the city, where everything is new and modern and enticing to the eye of the visitor to Venetry. But that's just the center. As you spread outward from that wide main avenue, you enter much older, dirtier places, some of which aren't safe for anyone after dark, even their own denizens. I'll have to see about renewing some old acquaintances there. Derria's shop is probably still open, and she might give us a good price on that opal pendant. But that will have to wait.

We trotted along for a good while, through the city center and into the wide spiral that leads up to the top of Venetry where the rich manors are. One of those manors used to belong to my family, according to Mam, but I've never cared enough to find out which one. No point mooning over the past. I don't even know what our surname used to be. I guess I'd be more interested if I didn't feel like it was betraying my Dad to care about our past, when he set out to make a new life after he'd been ejected from his old one instead of clinging to what was. If I ever think about it, I mostly get mad over the injustice of it all, though I don't even know if it was injustice. I know my Dad was a wonderful man, so he couldn't possibly have deserved to lose all that.

But I'm getting off course. We went all the way to the top of the city, which has an amazing view, maybe not as nice as Colosse, with all those white walls and colored roofs, but still amazing. You can see the whole city laid out in tiers below, and beyond that, the plains, but the best part, the part that actually brought tears to my eyes, was a distant lumpy smudge off to the west I recognized as mountains. Mountains that hadn't been there before. The Arabel Mountains, in fact, under which lay the Darssan.

It struck me then as it hadn't before that the land had changed; the desert we'd traveled through to reach Colosse was gone, but the mountains remained. I wonder if Cederic will want to reopen the Darssan, when things have settled down and the God-Empress's threat has been eliminated. Thirty years from now, probably. No sense worrying about it at this point. We still haven't even met our fellow mages. Magickers. There's no way I'm calling us that. I'll just have to change everyone's minds about it.

The royal manor—one of them, there are several throughout Balaen—anyway, the one in Venetry is called Janeka Manor. (I've never understood why so many of the wealthy manors are named after women, especially since women haven't had much of a role in government until the last fifty years.) It's a beautiful old house, built in the style of 150 years ago, with lots of windows made up of grids filled with thick glass bricks you can barely see out of and steep, shingled roofs that meet each other at odd angles. The gardeners had put the beds to sleep for the winter, which gave the manor a bare look, its harsh stone walls unsoftened by the hedges that would bloom in the spring. The ivy that used to grow on the walls all around the front door was gone, adding to the harsh look.

Two more soldiers stood at attention at the front door, and our guide saluted them, told them his errand, and they let us pass. I thought that was lax behavior until we came through the narrow hall, almost a tunnel, that led into the main hall of the manor, and came face to face with ten more soldiers, all of them standing where they could easily attack an intruder, all of them with the humorless faces that characterize the really good warriors. I tried not to let them make me nervous. This time, at least, I was here legitimately.

Our guide took us the wrong way at first, and I had to remind myself I was a newcomer and a country girl and of course had no way of knowing where King and Chamber meet. He corrected himself without any slips that might suggest he'd made a mistake, which I approved of, and soon we were in the southwestern wing of the manor and stopping in front of a large double door banded in red-painted iron. Two soldiers stood there. They didn't look as awe-inspiring as their brothers in the entry hall, but they clearly took their job of standing and staring into space seriously.

"Messengers to speak to the King. They get five minutes," our guide said, handing over the note.

"They're in session. No one goes in," the soldier on the left said.

"How soon?" our guide said.

"No idea," the soldier said. "They can wait if they want."

Our guide turned to us and said, "You can see the King when the session's up. It shouldn't be more than an hour or so." He nodded at us and went back the way he'd come.

I glanced at Jeddan, who shrugged. We were both thinking another hour's delay wasn't going to matter, and it wasn't as if we could do anything about it. So we waited. I leaned against the wall, surreptitiously examined my surroundings, and plotted a way to draw the guards away so I could enter the chamber. Then I remembered I was now capable of assassinating the King with magic, which would be the only reason for me to sneak into that chamber, and it made me feel sick.

So instead I counted stones, made lists, daydreamed about what it would be like when I found Cederic, and went over the see-in-dark pouvra for possibilities of companion pouvrin. I didn't have any success on that last one, but I haven't given up. It does make me impatient to rejoin the Darssan mages and practice turning th'an into pouvrin. Which reminds me I haven't practiced the binding pouvra for a while. No sense, when it doesn't do anything, and we've got so many other interesting things to pursue.

I don't know how long we waited, but it was a lot longer than an hour before some signal imperceptible to me led one of the soldiers to throw open half of the chamber door and say, "Your Majesty, my Lords, these messengers beg five minutes of your time." No one said anything in reply, but he advanced into the room, out of sight, and Jeddan and I looked at each other, wondering if we were supposed to follow.

I'd almost decided to stop hesitating when the soldier came back and said, in a low voice, "Approach to the edge of the carpet, go to one knee, and keep your head lowered until you're told to rise. Address them all as "Honored" and don't say anything until you're spoken to. Say your piece and wait to be dismissed." He gave Jeddan a little shove. "You first," he said.

So Jeddan went through the door, and I followed him, which means my first view of King and Chamber was obscured by his massive shoulders. I knew what the room looked like, of course: it's not big, and windowless, I've heard for security reasons.

The walls are covered by the Lessareki tapestries, which are so valuable no one could put a price on them. Their value comes not from their materials or their subject matter (the life of a minor Queen of Balaen from maybe two and a half centuries ago) but because they were created by Balaen's most famous artist, whose placename is still one of the most popular girls' praenomi in the country. I've never had time to admire them properly, and of course today wasn't the right moment. But it was exciting to be in their presence.

There's a square black rug in the center of the room, and five chairs are set in a circle on it, all of them identical as a reminder that in this place, King and Chamber are equal in the service of Balaen.

Hahahaha.

Anyway, I didn't actually see any of this until Jeddan stopped and knelt, and I took a quick step to the side and knelt next to him and bowed my head. That only gave me a quick glimpse of four men and one woman, all of them looking at us. Then the King said, "Deliver your message." (He has a distinctive voice that sounds like it's coming from the back of his head and gets pinched a little on the way out. It's not a voice you forget, even if you've only ever heard it while you're hiding in a cupboard listening to him grouse at his valet for not ironing his nightshirt properly.)

Jeddan didn't raise his head, which was probably the right decision. "Honored," he said, "we come from Calassmir, where an enemy army has attacked the city as its first move in invading Balaen." I hated saying it this way, because it wasn't going to make the King more friendly toward the Castavirans who weren't the God-Empress's pawns, but explaining the Castaviran sociopolitical situation and the consequences of the convergence would just have confused everything.

There was silence. I'd expected a least a couple of gasps, but no. Then, "Rise," said the King, "just you, young man," and I had to keep kneeling, which annoyed me. "You're not a soldier," he said.

"No, Honored, we're both just loyal Balaenics who were in the right place when it mattered," he said. "We were traveling here to look for other mages like us, and meant to stop in Calassmir for provisions, and nearly got caught by the foreign army. It looked impossible for our soldiers to get a message out, so we figured we ought to take it ourselves, just in case."

"Foreign army meaning these invaders who have appeared among us in the last month?" said another man. He had a rich, strong voice, and if I hadn't known who the King was I'd have thought this man was him.

"I think so, Honored," Jeddan said.

"Then this puts a new light on their tactics in the north," he said, half to himself. "How long before they arrive?"

"I don't know, Honored, I'm no soldier," Jeddan said. "We were there 24 or 25 Coloine and based on what the surrounding villages said, the attack had only started a couple of days before that."

"You took too long about it," said a woman. Debarra Jakssar, Chamber Lord of Transportation. Her voice was nearly as deep as the other man's, but more gravelly even though it was still clearly a woman's voice.

"We're truly sorry, Honored, we came as quick as we could, but we were on foot," Jeddan said.

"You should have requisitioned horses," said a third man, this one sounding very old, so I guessed he was Jarlak Batekessar, Chamber Lord of Agriculture. I've worked enough harvests to know he's disliked by farmers, particularly the ones with the big estates, because of the demands he puts on them. "This is far more important than anything else you could do."

"We can't ride, Honored, and we didn't have any proof we were what we said we were," Jeddan said. "The soldier Nessan at the gate showed great insight when he passed us through."

"That's his job," the rich-voiced man said. "How many insurrections did you pass on your way here?"

"I beg your pardon, Honored, but I don't know what you mean," Jeddan said. My knees were starting to ache. I have no idea how Cederic manages to hold that position indefinitely.

"The other invaders. They were causing disruption in preparation for their army to attack our cities, hoping to weaken us?" he said.

"Ah, no, Honored, we didn't see anything like that," Jeddan said. "Most of those invader towns kept to themselves. And a lot of our people were, um, subduing them themselves."

"Good initiative," said the last man, whose voice had a bit of a whine to it, a whistling sound like he was speaking through a blocked nostril. "We ought to send another decree, commending their patriotism and encouraging them to stand strong against invasion."

"I don't want civilians interfering in military affairs, Lenssar," the rich voice said. "Self-defense is one thing, but vigilante action is dishonorable."

"I didn't mean we should tell them to take up arms," Lenssar said. Lenssar is Chamber Lord of Commerce and I don't remember his first name. I don't know much about him at all.

"Any encouragement could be seen as just that," the rich voice said, and I realized he had to be Caelan Crossar, Chamber Lord of Defense. He's got a reputation for cleverness and has maintained the army at full strength even though Balaen hasn't been at war since forever, which says a lot about his influence over King and Chamber. I don't know if he genuinely believes Balaen is in danger of invasion, or if a strong army increases his political power, but either way it's due to him that Balaen could repel such an invasion if it came.

"I'm more concerned about us being overrun," said the King. "Shouldn't we draw the army back to protect the city?"

"I'll send word to General Tarallan for his analysis," Crossar said. "He knows the tactical situation better than we do."

"I don't want the army wasting time pacifying an enemy city just to have this one captured," the King said, whining.

"Your Majesty, we will make the decision that will best keep *Balaen* safe, and that includes this city," Crossar said. "How many magickers do they have?"

It took us both a second to realize he was talking to us. "Um," Jeddan said.

"Seven squads of ten each," I said, thinking fast. The only thing I knew was battle mages were, in fact, organized into squads of ten, and that each squad had its own standard, with a unique emblem and a red and black border. In reconnoitering the camp, I'd seen at least seven battle standards. What I *didn't* know was how many of those battle mages had retained their powers. I'd been told once that the green-eyed mages tended toward academia and private service, so I'd guess the military would have fewer than their counterparts from the Darssan, a third of whom had green-gray eyes. But that didn't tell me anything certain. So I gambled that they'd have more squads than I'd observed, but fewer functional mages within those squads, and it would come out to roughly the same number either way.

"You were not addressed," Crossar said.

"I'm sorry, Honored, but I'm the one who went into the enemy camp to learn where the army was going next," I said. I was tired of being ignored.

"Were you?" Crossar said. "Rise."

I stood, feeling wobbly, and got my first look at King and Chamber. The King I've seen before; he's an average-looking man, not someone you'd peg as a leader, and has the slightly flushed cheeks and pouchy expression of someone whose diet is too rich.

Batekessar looks as old as he sounds—I think he's in his seventies

—with unpleasantly pale skin and deep grooves carved into his face, dragging his mouth into a permanent frown.

Jakssar is a lovely woman with a matronly, comfortable figure, but she has a mannish haircut and wears robes and trousers like the men instead of a formal gown, which makes me wonder about her position on the Chamber, if she feels she has to act like a man to get respect. I felt sympathy for her, if that was the case.

Lenssar gave me a bit of a shock, because he looks so much like Cederic—long dark hair, high cheekbones, crooked eyebrows. He's about ten years older than Cederic, though, and shows it, and he's got dark, deep-set eyes that are nothing like my husband's. Even so, it threw me off balance enough that Crossar had to repeat himself. "I said, you were in the enemy camp?" he said, rising and coming to face me.

"I was, Honored," I said. Crossar doesn't look anything like his voice. Not that he's ugly; he has silvery-dark hair, and a short beard, the kind that only goes around his mouth and chin, but he's incredibly thin, and his nose is sharply pointed, and his lips are narrow, and between that and the hair he reminded me of a needle. I won't deny he made me nervous, because I couldn't read him at all.

"Daring work, for a woman," he said.

"I've always been good at not being noticed, Honored," I said. I put that "for a woman" remark aside to be angry about later.

"How were you able to identify the enemy magickers?" he said.

I was really glad he'd asked that question, because I'd forgotten for the moment I wasn't supposed to be able to speak Castaviran and thus couldn't have learned anything by reading or overhearing it. Crossar is clever enough that if I slipped up, he'd know it.

"I saw some of them working pouvrin, Honored," I lied, "and the ones I saw wore special uniforms. I was there long enough to observe that they were organized into groups, and I counted those to learn how many they had. Though it's possible there were more squads somewhere closer to the city, because I wasn't able to explore the whole camp."

"Did you see their leader?" he asked.

"I...think so, Honored," I said, concluding rapidly it might be good for them to know who their most important target was. "There was a finely dressed woman who seemed to be giving orders. All the officers bowed low to her, and it looked as if they were explaining the strategy to her and waiting for her instructions."

"A woman at the head of an army," Lenssar said with a frown.

"Something to keep in mind, at least," Crossar said. "You have served Balaen well, both of you. What are your names?"

"Thalessi Scales and Rokyar Axe. Honored," I said, almost forgetting the politeness ritual in my worry that I'd done wrong in speaking for Jeddan, since they clearly thought him more important because he was male. Bastards.

"I ask the honor of your praenomi, for Balaen to honor you," the King said. He sounded peeved that Crossar had taken the role that should have been his.

I looked past Crossar, and said, "Honored, my name is Sesskia."

"And mine is Jeddan," Jeddan said.

"And you are both magickers," the King said, coming forward and having to push past Crossar, who paused the tiniest fraction of a second before moving away. Crossar's eyes, which are nearly as light as his silvery hair, stayed fixed on me, and I wished I dared hide behind Jeddan again. I dislike being the focus of attention of anyone who has the power to make me disappear in the night. Which is probably all wrong, and Crossar is actually a good man who's committed to the defense of Balaen.

Hah. Unlikely. People in power don't get to be that way by being nice to others. He might have Balaen's good at heart, but there's no way he cares anything for me, or for Jeddan, except for how useful we might be to his plans. I wish I believed being a known mage was somehow a protection.

The King came to stand right in front of us, examining our eyes. I let mine go unfocused so I wouldn't go cross-eyed at how close the tip of his nose was. "Those with your peculiar green eyes are magickers," he observed, inanely as far as I was concerned.

"Yes, Honored," Jeddan said.

"And will you demonstrate your magics for us?" he said.

We did our usual tricks—it was starting to feel as if we were performing animals—and received the usual reaction, which was to say, nothing at all. They've probably seen any number of mages in the last month. What I don't understand is why everyone in Venetry seems to have adjusted so quickly to the idea of magic, when it's always been feared and hated before. Something else must have happened to change everyone's mind.

I guess it's possible that seeing the Castavirans work magic might have convinced a few key people that maybe Balaen should encourage mages of their own, but it would have been days after the convergence before anyone encountered a Castaviran mage to learn about magic at all, and some of these pouvrin aren't exactly subtle in their manifestation. I'd think a lot of mages would have been killed in those early days, so to go from executing people to being blasé about magic seems unlikely. One more thing I want to ask about. It's frustrating, really, because I keep finding reasons to delay leaving Venetry, which means it's all my fault I'm still here.

I'm getting off course again. We did our pouvrin, and then we were standing there wondering if we could leave, and was there some politeness ritual we had to follow, when the King said, "I invite you to dine with me, Jeddan and Sesskia. I feel it is my duty to understand the plight of my southern subjects, and you will tell me of your journey and of magic. We have magickers who have become conversant with two or even three magics, you know!"

I gave him the wide-eyed stare of amazement he was angling for, and his smile broadened. "Come, you will be provided with the wherewithal to bathe, and new clothes, and you needn't be overawed, I'm just a man, after all!" He clapped his hands together delightedly and left the room by a tiny door to our left.

"Of course he leaves it to us to handle the details," muttered Lenssar, then in a louder voice he said, "You are indeed favored highly among your class. I hope you will show proper appreciation for his Majesty's condescension."

"Yes, Honored," Jeddan said. "Where should we go?"

Batekessar rose and walked past us without a word. The others didn't seem to think there was anything strange about this. "I'll summon a servant to take you to the guest wing," Jakssar said, though she didn't rise, just sat there looking at us with the same intent expression Crossar had. I was starting to feel twitchy.

"It makes one wonder," Lenssar said, and I had to avoid looking at him because that whiny whistle coming out of a face so eerily familiar was too disconcerting, "how society will be shaken up, all these nobody magickers coming up from nowhere."

"Be polite, Lenssar, you're talking about our guests," Jakssar said, and now she did stand. "You went into the invading army's camp, young woman? How thrilling. Whatever prompted you?"

"I wanted to help our country, Honored," I said.

"I don't know many people who would take such a risk simply to help their country," Jakssar said. She came to stand in front of me, looking down—she's not hugely tall, but taller than me—and I had this strange feeling I was in front of the God-Empress again. They're nothing alike physically, and Jakssar strikes me as sane, so I'm not sure what I was responding to. I've decided to be very careful if I have to interact with her again. She may seem friendly, and I have sympathy for her position, but she's still a Lord of the Chamber and every bit as ruthless as her peers to hold that position.

"It wasn't much of a risk, Honored, the enemy has female as well as male soldiers," I said.

"Really?" said Crossar, more interested now than before, which made his needle-sharp attention even more acute. "What else did you see?"

I'm embarrassed that my first reaction was to tell him nothing, so I wouldn't betray Castavir. Then I felt stupid because, for one, it was the God-Empress's army and even Castavir wanted her defeated, and for another, I was still a Balaenic citizen and wanted my people to have every advantage when it came to war.

Then I told him as much as I could remember about the number of troops, the number of generals, the way they organize themselves, and how well supplied they were. I also told him about the God-Empress, including some details I pretended I'd learned in the camp that I'd actually learned from personal observation.

"I don't speak their language," I said at the end, "but by the way they reacted when her tent burned, I think half her officers are afraid of her. Honored." I'd realized about halfway through my speech that some of that information I could only have gotten if I understood Castaviran. I hoped no one noticed the inconsistencies. I have got to be more careful now we're among Balaenics exclusively.

"This is excellent information," Crossar said, and I saw him close his lips on a sibilant that was almost certainly the first syllable of my name. He had permission to use my name, as I'd been maneuvered into giving it by the King, but it was still a presumption on a relationship we didn't have, so his choosing not to felt like more of an honor than the King's dubious request. Naturally, this made me even more suspicious of him: was he trying to gain my, if not allegiance, then my good will? Because basically I don't think someone like Crossar ever does anything without an eye to his political future. And I'm certain he wants something from me. I really don't trust him.

We answered questions for a while, the kind of questions people of high rank ask of their inferiors that show they have no idea how anyone manages to live without a hundred thousand crowns' income a year, then Jakssar finally did summon some servants, who took us away to be washed and clothed appropriately. The clothes are nice, but too ornate for my taste, and I don't know where they took my old clothes. Probably burned them, so it's lucky I smuggled these books behind a curtain instead of wrapping them in my clothes. Too bad, because I liked that shirt. These new clothes are going to make sneaking around Venetry difficult.

Then we had dinner with the King, who asked the same equally foolish questions as Chamber had, though he did manage to stay focused on our trip and what we'd seen along the Royal Road. He also wanted to know about magic. We told him the truth about pouvrin, which made his eyes glaze over, but didn't say anything about our having more than one. At some point we'll have to reveal ourselves, probably tomorrow when we meet the mages, and I'm not looking forward to that. The King said "two or even three" like that was really impressive, so I'm certain walking in there tomorrow with twelve is going to disrupt whatever power structure they've got in place. Time enough to worry about that when it happens.

Dinner was very, very long, with so many courses I ended up taking nibbles off some of the dishes I liked most because I'd incautiously eaten too much of earlier ones I didn't care for. I hope they give what we couldn't eat to the servants. Some of those dishes were delicious. We ended with after-dinner drinks, which I only pretended to imbibe, and finally the King yawned, and told us someone would take us to Fianna Manor, and left before we could finish saluting him.

We didn't see much of Fianna Manor in the darkness. I'd like to say it's the same as all the other manors up at the top of the city, but none of them share any similarities aside from having walls and windows and roofs. Sizes, construction materials, floor plans, all of those are unique to each manor, which is a fun challenge for a thief.

I've never stolen from Fianna Manor, so I didn't know what to expect, and I still don't, because we went through a side door down a narrow corridor, up stairs that had to be servants' stairs, and into a wider, low-ceilinged corridor lined with plain wooden doors. These also are probably servants' quarters, which makes me wonder if someone's already trying to prove a point by pushing us to the side. If I were planning to stay, I'd care more about that. It's still a nice, sizable room, though, with a pretty rug and matching counterpane, and a water closet, and furniture that all matches (heavy old oak, and I wonder how they got it up those stairs).

Jeddan's across the hall from me and his room is almost identical, except for the rug and counterpane being in different colors. I was tired enough that all I did was strip down to my underwear and cuddle up in the bed to write all of this. It's a good, comfortable bed, too. It makes me wonder what kind of luxury some of these mages might be living in.

I wonder what tomorrow will bring. I'm planning to stay three days and then head out for Colosse. I haven't asked Jeddan if he wants to come with me—that's part of what the three days are for, to see what happens with the mages and whether Jeddan would rather be part of whatever they're doing. I'd miss him if he stayed, but I know too well what it's like to crave learning to be disappointed if he did.

CHAPTER TWELVE

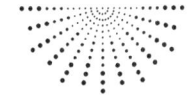

14 Nevrine

I feel like I begin a lot of these entries with variations on "I wonder if I made the right choice." I used to pride myself on being decisive. Not rash or reckless, but when your actions can potentially get you killed, waffling about them is a big mistake. So I always try to think things through, and go over all the possibilities, and then, when I've decided what to do, I do it without revisiting every last detail. (That's not the same as changing plans in midstream, which happens frequently, but is a response to the situation changing, not my analysis.) It's like I'm swimming out of my depth all the time, not having enough information but having to act anyway, worrying that if I knew more, I'd see whatever decision I'd made was the wrong one.

In this case, however, despite having not even close to enough information, I know I made the right choice. I just wish it had been the wrong one.

The day started, for me, with a knock on my door, and when I called an invitation, a woman entered with a steaming tray and set it down across my lap with a bow. It was scrambled eggs and bacon and apple juice and hot, black coffee, which I don't care for but smells divine, and all the little condiments to make the meal perfect, and it was the first hot breakfast I've had in over a week, so I fell on it like I was starving and was really grateful no one was around to see my lapse of good manners.

The woman left me to my breakfast with another bow, and I ate my fill, then set the tray on the floor and got up to dress. I wish I'd had my own clothes, because the ones the King forced on us gave the impression that Jeddan and I are somewhat higher class than we are, certainly people who deserve a surname and a home with two servants. Not what I wanted these mages to think of me, and I certainly couldn't blend in very well in that getup, but there was nothing I could do about it except consider finding a servant's room and stealing something more practical. I'd leave money, naturally.

Anyway, I dressed—at least the clothes look nice—and then waited for a few minutes before remembering I'm not the sort of woman who sits passively waiting for things to happen, and I didn't care if wandering through the manor was against the rules. So I crossed the hall to Jeddan's room and knocked, then entered on his invitation. He was sitting on the edge of the bed, dressed in his own too-nice clothes. "So what do we do now?" he said.

"Explore," I said. "I want to meet these other mages."

"Have you decided what you want to do about the pouvrin?" he said. "Or, for that matter, telling everyone they're called pouvrin, because I doubt that's knowledge they got when they became mages. Especially since somebody came up with 'magickers.'" He made a face.

"I've been going back and forth on that all night," I said. "On the one hand, if we go in there claiming one pouvra, then have to reveal more later, that makes us seem untrustworthy. But if we manifest several, who knows what kind of balance that will upset, if none of them have more than three? On the third hand, I'm leaving soon, and don't care if they think I'm trustworthy. So I've decided to say I've got just the one, and see what happens from there. My least favorite kind of plan, but I don't know enough to do better."

"That's the conclusion I came to," Jeddan said. He made a motion that encompassed all of him. "People see me as a threat because I'm as big as I am, and having several pouvrin will only make that worse. Better to find out what the people are like, and then reveal everything."

"Then let's see if we can find our colleagues," I said, "and maybe we're being too paranoid. Maybe we'll be able to share what we know and learn from them."

"Or maybe it will be as bad as I know you think it will, and we'll both be leaving this place at a run," Jeddan said.

"I'm trying to learn optimism," I said. "You're not helping."

We retraced the route we'd taken the night before, down the narrow stairs, and went down the corridor only to discover ourselves outside. So we turned around and went the other way, through a small door into a tall-ceilinged hallway half-paneled in light maple, with skylights high above that made the place look cheery. There were two or three doors opening off the hallway that led to empty rooms with the same paneling and bare wooden floors. None were occupied.

At the end of the hall, another hallway, this one wider, intersected ours. More doors, more skylights. We investigated each one: these were furnished, mostly sitting rooms, but also a music room and a formal dining room with a table that could seat forty diners. We saw not a single living soul in all this time, not even servants. I think, now, all the other mages are used to a leisurely morning, like we used to have in the Darssan, but while that does appeal to me, it certainly wasn't how I was going to behave when there were so many things to explore.

We finally found a staircase, a big one with an ornately carved railing and thick carpeting with brass stair-rods, and climbed to the next floor. That one had hardly any doors at all, and we were almost all the way to what I gauged was the north end of the house before finding anything worth investigating. That hallway terminated in the most beautiful window made of two enormous sheets of curved glass, one framed above the other, and it looked out over Venetry and the view was just breathtaking. Cities are beautiful, if only from a distance.

We looked at it for a while, then decided to try the door on our left, which was a big three-paneled thing. It looked like three doors in the same frame, but only the outer two opened, and the middle was just a wood panel. We figured couldn't possibly lead to someone's bedroom, which was what had kept us from trying the other doors on this level so far.

The room it led to was *enormous*. The ceiling was two stories tall and capped with a dome of glass so clear it looked as if it wasn't even there; the silence, as opposed to the birdsong of early morning, was the only thing that dispelled that illusion. More tall windows lined the walls on two side at regular intervals, with rose-painted panels dividing them. The floor was a glossy parquet of wooden squares of different sizes and colors, like a mythical giant's puzzle, and sunlight reflected off it to cast a glow over the other two walls, which by contrast had been covered to a height of about twelve feet with rough oak planking that was scarred and burned everywhere.

I took a few steps into the room and turned in a slow circle. "Those light fixtures above the windows would turn night into day here," I said. "I think this is a ballroom, or was."

"There's a patio over here," Jeddan said. He'd crossed the room and opened one of the tall windows, which turned out to be a door. "It's a sheer drop fifty feet down, but you can see most of Venetry from it. Very pretty."

"I'm guessing we've found at least one of the places where the mages study," I said, summoning a rope of fire and flicking it like a whip at the paneling. It made a mark paralleling an old burn scar. I tried again and managed to overlay the old mark entirely. Very satisfying.

"How did you do that?" said a dark-haired man who entered just as I struck my target. "I've never seen anything like that kind of control."

"Um," I said. I could see my plan start to fray at the edges. "It was a lucky stroke, I guess. I'm Sesskia. What's your name?"

"I—" He looked embarrassed. "I don't think I've earned the right to your praenoma."

"We've met several mages in our travels," I said, "and given how different we are from other people, it felt like kinship. My placename is Thalessi Scales, if you're more comfortable with that."

"No," he said, "no, you're right. I didn't think of it that way. Kinship." He brightened. "I'm Davik."

"And I'm Jeddan," Jeddan said, coming forward to exchange salutes with him. "What magic do you have?"

"The fire rope, same as Sesskia," he said. "Did you say 'mages'? I haven't heard that word."

"Everyone in the south uses it," I lied—though it wasn't exactly a lie; I'd pushed that terminology hard everywhere we'd been—"and we think it sounds more dignified than 'magickers.'"

"I wonder if Norsselen will like it," Davik said, mostly to himself. "But I'm serious about your ability with the fire rope, Sesskia. I don't have nearly that much control."

"Well, I might be able to show you," I said, then remembered I wasn't going to be here long, and he didn't have the right vocabulary, and added, "Have you all had much success learning each other's pou—magics?"

"Learning each other's—that's not possible," Davik said. "Some people have acquired more than one magic, but that just happens as you get better with the one you start with."

Jeddan and I glanced at each other, and Jeddan gave the tiniest shake of his head. I agreed with him. This was not the time to contradict this man's assumptions. I wondered about this Norsselen he mentioned (now, of course, the name makes me scowl) and why his liking anything would matter.

"Well, I can try showing you what I've learned," I said, and directed him to take up a solid stance, which I don't think is necessary but is something the Darssan mages find critical in scribing certain kinds of th'an, and I figured the focus might help him. Then I broke down the steps of the pouvra and tried to walk him through it, which led to us having to stop to discuss how it felt to wield the magic at all. Davik isn't terribly bright, but to my surprise this made things easier; he was compliant instead of argumentative, and we'd almost come to common ground when a couple of women showed up, and then another handful of people, and they were all curious about the newcomers.

We kept introducing ourselves by our praenomi, explaining of course no one should feel obligated to return the favor, and only about a quarter of the mages declined the honor. Interestingly, they all stuck together in their own corner, like a gang of toughs in the street who were dismissive of anyone not in their group, even down to a sense of low-grade menace. I kept an eye on them, just in case. Now I've met their "boss" Norsselen, I'm even more cautious around them. If I can't predict what he'll do, I certainly can't predict what he might ask of his minions.

So we met people, and demonstrated our pouvrin, and I was more careful this time not to look like I had tremendous control over my magic. It turns out to be difficult to pretend to be less capable with pouvrin than you are. I was glad I'd chosen one I really am less experienced with. Jeddan had no problem downplaying his pouvra. At least he's using it, though I have a feeling he's never going to go immaterial through flesh again, which is fine by me.

Nobody seemed to think we were remarkable, and things were going well, when another man came through the door and said, "Ah, you must be our new members! I hope everyone's made you feel welcome." He was blond, white-blond, and had a long jaw and freckles that made him look younger than the thirty-plus I guessed his age to be. He also reminded me so much of Vorantor, with his broad smile and his "I'm a great leader" pose, that I choked back nausea, remembering my last sight of Vorantor collapsed across the kathana circle with his throat slit.

"My name is Norsselen," he said, "and my magic is fire. And you are?"

"We choose to offer our praenomi in a spirit of kinship," I said, "but if you'd prefer, my placename is Thalessi Scales." I said this because despite what I avowed, I had no desire for this man to use my praenoma. I'm still not certain he won't turn out to be an enemy.

"Thank you, Thalessi, I would prefer to maintain formality at the beginning of our acquaintance," Norsselen said, extending his palm to me, then to Jeddan.

"Rokyar Axe," Jeddan said, not even pretending to offer kinship. "I can move through things."

"And my, um, magic is the fire rope," I said.

"Good, good," Norsselen said. "I take it we haven't demonstrated our magics for you? Everyone, let's show our new friends what we can do."

The next part was impressive, and I have to give Norsselen credit for being able to point all these people in the same direction, even though I disapprove of both his methods and his motives. Everyone went to what looked like pre-determined spots in the room to form small groups. Then, exactly as if they'd practiced (because of course they had) each group took turns demonstrating a pouvra.

Norsselen (I guessed this, and it was later confirmed) had done the organizing, and he'd at least worked out the fire mass and the fire rope were different pouvrin. There were a lot more people doing the former than the latter, which made sense to me, given how hard it had been for me to learn the rope. The largest group did mind-moving—I forgot to mention there were stacks of all kinds of things all around the room, bricks and short planks and hard rubber balls and things like that. None of them were capable of using the mind-moving pouvra on the same level as Cederic, but all of them seemed stronger than me. I'd feel inadequate about that if I didn't remember crushing that bandit's heart, and I try not to remember that.

There was another small group who could walk through things, and then, excitingly, a woman who flitted from one side of the room to the other in the blink of an eye. I'm still trying to figure out how to justify taking her aside and making her teach me.

A couple of people, no more than ten, moved from one group to another to demonstrate a second or even a third pouvra. Norsselen has three—fire, mind-moving, and see-in-dark, though he not so modestly told us this later since of course he couldn't demonstrate the last. There are another five who have that one, and three who can see through things. No concealment, obviously, no see-inside, and I don't think any of them can turn their pouvrin on other people. They're all pouvrin you'd expect someone to develop first based on some trauma, even though we established (through some quiet questioning) none of them had experienced anything unusual but the convergence.

Norsselen wanted us to be impressed, so we made appropriate noises. Then he said, "You've seen which groups you'll work with. They'll explain the techniques we're studying, though of course everyone's equal and you're free to make comments of your own." The look on his face said he didn't consider himself anyone's equal. He was really starting to annoy me, despite my resolve not to be drawn and my constant reminders to myself I wasn't going to be here long enough to worry about what he did. But I couldn't help saying, "You must be experienced, to be in charge."

"I live in Venetry, so I was the first to respond to the King's summons," Norsselen said, "and I've gained new magics faster than anyone, so everyone agreed I was the logical choice. I like to think I've been able to organize us efficiently. Of course I don't think of myself as better, and I'm certainly not the best at everything. But someone has to take charge, and I'm pleased to do so."

"Not everyone agrees with that decision, Norsselen," said a woman who was just then entering the room. She had black hair, and brown eyes, and was so nondescript I felt a pang of jealousy, because with her looks I could go anywhere and never be noticed. Then I remembered Cederic thinks I'm beautiful the way I am, and the jealousy passed. (It was stupid, I know, but I still think of myself as a thief first and a mage second, no matter how many pouvrin I learn.) "And not everyone believes we are pursuing the right course."

"Phellek," Norsselen said, "it's good to see you. You see we have new members." He really did sound genial, not at all offended by her remarks, and when I observed him he didn't show any signs that he was concealing a different emotion. I think this was because he doesn't see Relania as a threat and therefore is genuinely unmoved by her disdain for him.

"Of course I see that," she said, and extended her palm to Jeddan, who was nearest her. "Welcome," she said. "I'm Relania Phellek."

"I offer you my praenoma in a spirit of kinship between mages," he said. "My name is Jeddan."

"And mine is Sesskia," I said, "though—"

Relania gasped, and instead of laying her palm against mine, gripped my hand so tightly it pinched the skin. "Sesskia," she said. "I know you. I've been following the trail you left for two years. Did you ever learn the mind-moving pouvra?"

I was so shocked I couldn't pull away. This was no new-made mage. I'd left clues, here and there, for other mages to follow, but I'd never actually believed anyone would find them, much less be able to use them. So I'd signed my praenoma to all of them, more as a gesture of defiance at an uncaring world than to brag. "How long," I began, realized that was a pointless question, and changed it to, "You found my clues?"

"Excuse me," Norsselen said, but Relania overrode him.

"About two years ago, I stumbled on the cache outside Durran," she said. "The one that has the see-in-dark pouvra. And you'd left that note about some of the secondary materials in the book, pieces that were incomplete, and that you were going off to find more of it. I never was able to make sense of it, myself, but did you?"

"Phellek, I've told you we aren't humoring your desire to complicate magic with foreign words," Norsselen said, though he looked at me as if he wanted to ask me questions but didn't know which ones. "Or your claims of seniority."

"Shut up, Norsselen," Relania said. "This woman has even greater seniority than I. You should be asking *her* to teach *you.*"

This was where I regretted more than I ever have not having enough knowledge in advance to make the right plan. Not that I blamed myself. I couldn't have guessed an...well, an old mage, in contrast to the new mages, even though Relania is younger than I am. Anyway, there was no way for me to know an old mage would find her way here, and not only an old mage, but one who'd used the same resources I had.

I couldn't have guessed she and Norsselen had been fighting for over a week over Relania's insistence that she had more experience; in the arguing that followed, I learned Norsselen didn't believe Relania was any different than the rest of them and was dismissive of her pouvrin, since two of them were the invisible sort (the see-in-dark and see-through pouvrin). Not only that, he thought she was delusional and interested in stealing his power.

Relania, for her part, not only persisted in her story (because it was true) but was resistant to the idea of using pouvrin in the service of war. What the rest of the mages thought...well, the gang of toughs were Norsselen's men (all men), and about a quarter of the others were willing to let him boss them around, and a handful of the rest sympathized with Relania, but covertly, since Norsselen seemed to have all the power.

All of that came later, though. At the moment, Relania was looking at me with something akin to worship, Norsselen was looking at me with suspicion, Jeddan was expressionless, and we were gathering an audience of people who probably were used to Norsselen and Relania butting heads and considered it good entertainment. And I had no idea what to do. I mentally cursed Relania for putting me in this position, and cursed Norsselen for needing to be in charge, and then I said, "I don't want to interfere with the system you have in place. It seems to be functioning well."

"Do you know her, Thalessi?" Norsselen said.

"No," I said, and Relania made a sound of outrage. "We've only read the same books."

Norsselen smiled one of those smug, self-impressed smiles that made me want to slap it off his face. "Another delusional," he said in a low voice. "I suppose you're going to claim you learned your magic from those books?"

"I'm not sure I understand, Norsselen," I said in my sweetest, most reasonable voice. "How do you know that's not possible?"

"We all have magic because of the Event," he said, and I could hear him pronounce the capital E. "None of us needed books to become magickers, because magic is something inherent to each person. No one can teach magic any more than someone can change their hair color by thinking. It's not possible."

I'm a thief. I've survived all these years by not standing out, by not causing trouble, by not letting my emotions get the better of me. And my first reaction to Norsselen's smugness was to do just that. It didn't hurt me that he was ignorant and power-crazed. I was leaving in a few days and it didn't matter what he thinks of me. So I was going to let him keep his delusions. It would crush Relania's hopes, but I wasn't responsible for her emotional well-being. And it would give Jeddan the opportunity to choose whether he'd align himself with Relania or continue to conceal his abilities.

Then I looked around the room at everyone, and at this point it was everyone, watching our encounter. Norsselen had spoken loudly enough everyone had heard him. I looked at their faces, and I realized Norsselen was going to deny every one of them their magical heritage. Who knew how many of them were capable of learning more pouvrin? Who knew how many of them would discover ones I'd never heard of? I could keep quiet for my own sake. Or I could speak out for theirs.

So I said, "Norsselen, how long have you been a mage?"

"A magicker," he said.

"Almost exactly a month, isn't it?" I said, ignoring him. "And yet you are awfully quick to say what is and isn't possible." I took a step back and raised my voice. "I've been a *mage*—" I couldn't help stressing the word—"for over ten years. Jeddan here has been a mage for four. I learned my first pouvra when I was sixteen, and in the years since I've developed eleven more." That got a reaction. I let them murmur for a few seconds, waited until Norsselen opened his mouth to speak, and overrode him. "You're all young by my standards," I said, "and you all came about your magic differently than I did. But there's no reason you can't learn new pouvrin the way I did. More easily, maybe. So let me show you what I can do."

I took a few steps toward the scarred wall and summoned the long whip of fire the way I had minutes before. Then I brought up a huge swathe of fire (I admit I was showing off there), summoned water and tossed it into the center of the blaze, raising a huge cloud of steam. I worked as many pouvrin as were easily visible, saying "I can't show you how I can see in the dark or see inside things, but I can do those too," and ended by working the concealment pouvra and making all of them, except Jeddan, exclaim in fear or wonder.

Norsselen looked stunned and furious. I took a few steps toward him and dismissed the pouvra, making him curse and stumble away. "Sorry," I said, though I wasn't very. "You learned three pouvrin in a month, Norsselen. That's impressive. I mean it. You're a remarkable mage."

"You dare come in here," he said in a low, vicious voice I had to step close to hear, "and try to take over, as if you had any authority?"

"I don't want to take over, Norsselen," I said. "You've got these people working together, you seem to understand what the military needs from us—they look to you for leadership. But I know more about magic than you do. I just want to help everyone learn more. I want us to work together."

Norsselen glared at me. He was breathing heavily, and he looked both angry and afraid, and that made me afraid also, because it was the sort of situation that turns on a knife edge, balanced between sanity and violence. I hoped Jeddan was nearby, because if I had to turn a pouvra on Norsselen to protect myself, the room would erupt into a full-out magical war, with who knew how many sides. I kept my eyes fixed on Norsselen's, willing him to see sense.

Finally he said, "I don't think any of us realized magic existed before the Event. Or that...mages...from that time might have been able to survive the prejudice and hatred that dominated society before the King proclaimed magic to be good rather than evil. I think we all have a lot to learn."

His little speech made everyone else relax, but my gaze was still locked with his, and there was neither humility nor friendliness in it. If Norsselen could manage it, he'd make me disappear. One more reason he reminds me of Vorantor: he's dangerous because he hides his true nature behind a façade of cooperation and amity, and even if you know not to believe the façade, there's still no way to tell where he'll attack from until he's already launched himself at your throat.

"I know Jeddan and I have much to learn about how to use magic in the service of the army," I said, hoping Norsselen would accept the bone I was throwing him and not toss it back in my face. "Will you let us work with you in mastering more pouvrin, and you teach us your military strategies?"

Norsselen nodded once. "You've seen what we can do," he said, "and we've seen your abilities. I think it would be best if all of us were capable of fire, or of moving things; those will be useful in attacking the foe. Which do you judge will be easier?"

Jeddan said, "I've almost mastered the mind-moving pouvra. I could teach that and you could teach fire, Sesskia."

"Either way, we have to begin by teaching everyone to understand what it is they do when they work magic," I said.

"That's what I've been saying all along," said Relania. "That it's all about giving the magic shape. But they can't understand."

"It takes time," I said. I'd seen Norsselen bristle when Relania spoke, and I couldn't exactly blame him. She'd been vindicated, and from what little I knew of her I was fairly certain she'd rub Norsselen's face in it. That would destroy any hope I had of getting Norsselen to cooperate.

"Remember how hard it was to learn the second pouvra?" I said, hoping her experience matched mine. "How everything seemed counter to sense? It's not really fair to these people to expect them to understand more quickly than we did, I think."

Relania's gaze flickered to Norsselen's face for a second. "You're right, Sesskia," she said. "But then, of course you'd know best." (Side note: Relania uses my praenoma ALL THE TIME. As in, every sentence she directs at me. I think she's trying to show we have a special connection due to our having read the same books and therefore share some magical genealogy. And she doesn't have much in the way of social graces. Huh. As I write that, I realize that being as isolated as both of us have been makes it logical we'd lack social graces. Which means me having them at all is what's unusual. I don't have the heart to tell her to stop, but I'm worried she'll try to boss people around on the strength of her imagined connection to me.)

"Thanks, Relania," I said. "Norsselen, you know everyone's strengths. Could you direct them to gather in groups based on what pouvra they're best at?" I hoped I didn't sound as patronizing as I felt. Either I didn't, or Norsselen was pretending to be cooperative, because he started directing people into their groups, and I could take a few seconds to think rapidly back over what Jeddan and I had been doing for the last month.

As I write all of this, I realize how quickly everything happened—too quickly for me to think beyond the moment. It's cold comfort to realize that even if I'd had time to consider the implications of what I was doing, I still would have made the same choices. Though maybe I would have been happier, making a conscious choice rather than feeling, as I do now, as if the choice was made for me.

So we sat everyone down, and I talked about pouvrin, and asked people to explain what they felt when they used their magic. It's remarkable how easy it is to see the connections when you have enough mages in one place, all talking their way through the process of manifesting pouvrin. Where Jeddan and I had been initially frustrated by our different experiences, I was heartened to discover that in this group of forty mages, instead of forty different ways of perceiving pouvrin, there were three.

So I rearranged everyone into new groups and told Jeddan to handle the mages who learned the way he did. Relania and I fell into the second group, and, somewhat reluctantly, I asked her to work with them. That left me talking to the third group, whose experience was completely alien to me and, naturally, included Norsselen and five of his minions.

It didn't go well. Norsselen's group was resistant to any suggestion I made, and my efforts to teach them the vocabulary of pouvrin were mostly met with confusion. At the end, frustrated and tired, I resorted to bald-faced flattery. I pulled Norsselen aside and said, "You see magic so differently from me I'm not sure I can help you. But I think anyone who could learn so many pouvrin so quickly can certainly figure out how to teach them to other people. And I think Relania isn't experienced as a teacher. So it would be best if you'd take over here so I can work with that other group."

It worked. Good thing for me Norsselen is either not as smart as he thinks he is, or is motivated by a lust for recognition and honor. And maybe I'm wrong, and he'll be able to analyze his perception of magic so learning new pouvrin will come more easily to him. But the real point is this gives him something to do when we aren't learning battle tactics and, I hope, keeps him from causing trouble. I don't want to write about the tactics. I don't understand about military strategy, but the thing is, I don't think Norsselen does either. He's got us drilling in ways I think would be useless in combat, but there's no point me saying anything, both because it's Norsselen and because, as I said, it's not like I really know anything about it. So I'm going to skip that part.

It was a long, difficult day, and the only bright spot in it was that my group, and Jeddan's, learned some of the pouvra vocabulary, enough that they could start comparing notes with each other, and it was amazing how cheerful everyone was about it. Not that this is a morose bunch. They all seem not to have any reservations about using magic, none of the fears we old mages lived with all the time, but I think knowing that learning new pouvrin is not a matter of luck made them all feel confident in the magic they already have.

Lunch was brought to us in the ballroom, cold meats and cheeses and hunks of bread, but dinner was an elaborate affair in the large dining room (I was wrong, the table seats fifty) and Jeddan and I chatted with some of the other mages and learned something of how they'd come to Venetry and what things had been like in the first few days. Though no one wanted to talk about that last subject, and when bringing it up blighted the conversation for several minutes, Jeddan and I didn't press.

I gather that here in Venetry, at least, most of the mages created by the convergence were killed, and the survivors were lucky enough to either have had hidden pouvrin or people who cared about them to keep them concealed. I'd like to ask Norsselen what happened to him, but the odds of my carrying on a civil conversation with him are low. So we danced around that subject, and ate too much, and now I'm in my room, and I'm so tired I can barely think.

But I don't need to be able to think to know I'm not leaving Venetry any time soon.

I honestly didn't realize this for the longest time. Not when I was organizing mages or coddling Norsselen's ego, not when I was deep in enthusiastic discussion with my group (after gently relieving Relania of her duties; she's not a good or patient teacher), not even when I was consulting with Jeddan on how he thought his group was doing (very well, though his group is also smaller than the other two).

No, it wasn't until we were at dinner, and somebody said he wanted to learn the see-in-dark pouvra, joking that he wanted to be able to sneak into the kitchen for a late night snack, and I joked back and said something like "That will take at least a week" that I realized I'd committed myself. I'd acted all day like someone who'd made a long-term plan and was going to see it through. So the first thing I did upon returning to this room, before writing anything, was fling myself on my bed and scream into my pillow and beat my fists on the mattress. Because *I don't want to do this.*

I'm not a leader. I don't know anything about what the army wants its mages to do. I was barely able to teach Jeddan anything about magic, and he's got actual experience with learning it, something none of these people have. I shouldn't be here. I should be with my husband, learning to blend Balaenic magic with Castaviran, surrounded by my friends and working to bring our countries together, something I've got no power to do here. I should pack my things and walk out of here tonight, walk through Venetry's wall and keep walking until I find Cederic. This isn't my problem.

Except that it is.

I keep remembering how they all looked, listening to Norsselen talk about how impossible it was to learn magic, and how they believed him because they had no reason not to. I remember becoming a mage, and how the desire to learn more filled me so completely it was like a pouvra itself, compelling me onward, and I *know* every one of these men and women has that same feeling. And Norsselen was telling them that feeling was wrong, that it was impossible to satisfy. I couldn't let them go on believing that.

And once I'd proved to them it *was* possible, I couldn't walk away. I have to teach them, even if all I can teach them is how to learn for themselves. I still don't know how those ten mages learned more pouvrin spontaneously. It could be becoming a mage via the convergence alters how you acquire pouvrin. See? Even now, even as I'm railing against fate, I'm making plans for what I'll do with the mages tomorrow, and the next day, and so forth, indefinitely. I'm stuck here, and I did it to myself.

I hope, in the morning, I'll be better resigned to my fate. Right now I'm going to put this book away and indulge my petulant, spoiled self whose only desire is to find the man she loves and curl up in his arms for the rest of forever. Tomorrow, everything will look different.

CHAPTER THIRTEEN

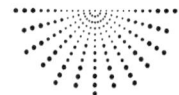

15 Nevrine

We were more organized today. Had the mages practice their pouvrin as a warm-up before breaking into groups for more theory. My group is moving along quickly, though not as quickly as Jeddan's. I think their understanding of pouvrin, that sense of being shaped by the magic, is easier to comprehend than seeing it in multidimensional shapes the way I do.

I also think it's why Jeddan has so much trouble learning to bend his will to meet the pouvrin; he's used to thinking of it as something that makes him change and doesn't have experience letting himself change. So their progress will almost certainly slow down once it comes to learning an actual pouvra. Jeddan also told me he still hasn't mastered the mind-moving pouvra and wanted to work on it privately, so we're doing that first thing in the morning.

No idea how Norsselen's group is faring. They sit together, and talk a lot, but there's nothing to see at this stage. I regret putting him in charge, because I'm less certain he's willing to accept my explanation of how magic works. And he has a point, given that he didn't need all this talking to learn more pouvrin. What I'm hoping is that he took my demonstration of pouvrin to heart, believes people can be taught pouvrin, and is trying to figure out how he learned them so he can teach the method to others and spit in my eye. As long as he's successful, I don't care what method he uses.

16 Nevrine

More progress. I hope. Three new mages arrived. Norsselen led everyone except me and Jeddan in the pouvra performance. He hasn't invited us to learn it.

17 Nevrine

Bad news. A couple of mages from Norsselen's group approached me to complain. He's been "teaching" by way of spouting meaningless but inspirational-sounding platitudes that boil down to "if you practice magic hard enough, you'll be given more of it." Basically what he was telling them before, only now (according to the mages) he's backing it up by explicitly referring to his greater skill with magic. And those mages have been talking to friends in other groups who really are learning to understand magic, and they realized they're being cheated.

So we went out on the patio with our lunches, and I had them do their best to explain how they perceive magic. I didn't understand fully, but it took a while for Jeddan and me to come up with a shared vocabulary, so I wasn't expecting to. It seems where Jeddan and I see pouvrin as existing shapes, me observing them from the outside and Jeddan feeling as if he's on the inside, this third group sees magic in pieces that shift until they reach the right configuration. Their explanation was more detailed than this, and "right configuration" isn't accurate, but at least it makes a kind of sense.

I told them I would talk to Norsselen and that his approach wasn't necessarily wrong, since it had worked for him. I felt bad about lying to them, but I'm still working out how best to handle Norsselen, and challenging his authority isn't the way. Yet.

More progress. The new mages are surprisingly quick to learn, or maybe it's just that Jeddan and I know which paths are dead ends and avoid those in our teaching. Jeddan managed the mind-moving pouvra this morning and turns out to be as weak at it as I am. Hope that's not a result of my teaching. He doesn't seem to mind—asked me how hard it is to learn to pick locks. I said with the see-inside pouvra it's not even a challenge. Neither of our doors has a lock, so we'll have to search around for one so I can show him.

I miss the days when it was just the two of us on the road, though not the cold ground and the bad food and the small-minded, bitter, xenophobic people. Jeddan says he's also working variations on the see-inside pouvra at night. He's more dedicated than I am. At night I barely have enough energy to keep my record up to date before I fall into bed.

Dreamed of Cederic again last night. That was the first time in a long time. I'm embarrassed to admit that, having some privacy now, I didn't try to wake myself up when things got really good. I miss him. I hope he's safe and well, and that he and the mages are making progress in bringing our cultures together, because I know that's what would matter most to him. That, and finding me.

18 Nevrine

Another new mage showed up today. Jeddan and I amuse ourselves by trying to predict which faction the new people will attach themselves to. Most of the factions are just groups of like-minded people, the kind you get in any large group where you're looking for people who share your interests so you don't feel lost in the crowd, and therefore aren't a problem. But there's still Norsselen's people, some of whom are causing trouble in Jeddan's group (I try not to feel too grateful that none of them are in mine), and to my surprise there's a small contingent who think we're doing the wrong thing by turning our magic to the service of war. I'm sure if the King hadn't made this a royal decree, backed up by threat of force, they wouldn't be here. Relania heads this group, and while none of them resist the lessons they're receiving, they're all quick to point out the non-military applications of their pouvrin. (None of them have fire pouvrin. I don't know if that's relevant.)

We've got a few people in each group who are ready to move on to learning pouvrin. I feel stretched out, I have so many things to do—teach the pouvra vocabulary, teach pouvrin, wrangle Norsselen, suppress Relania's tendency to give orders in my name, corner Jerussa (the mage who can flit from place to place) to get her to teach me her pouvra. It's limited to range of sight, which is still impressive, but imagine a bunch of mages who can flit from Venetry to Thalessa in less time than it takes to say "Venetry to Thalessa." That's a three and a half week journey! I'm not giving up on that possibility, but I have to learn Jerussa's pouvra first.

19 Nevrine

Norsselen is becoming a problem. I've had more and more of his mages (the ones in his group, not the ones who follow him) come to me asking me to take over their group. It's about to come to a confrontation, and I don't see any way around it. I wish I could use what I learned seeing Cederic keep Vorantor in check, but in that case they had a common goal, even if Vorantor's main motivation in achieving that goal was to bring himself glory. Norsselen doesn't want the same things I do; from what I'm hearing, he doesn't actually want these mages to learn new pouvrin because he's maintaining his authority by virtue of having so many, and having tied gaining pouvrin to purity of character, he's made it seem like he's intrinsically a better person than they are.

Wonderful. Now confrontation is not only inevitable, I'm starting to think I should be the instigator. I have to make it clear Norsselen's approach is wrong on every level. But he's got maybe twelve mages who look to him for guidance, and if it comes to physical conflict, that's a lot of people to fight. And even if that fight goes my way, what am I going to do with thirteen belligerent, bitter mages who are required by royal fiat to be here? I need some way to get them on my side. Damn it. I wish Cederic were here, because he understands these things. I can only fumble along and hope I don't screw up too badly.

20 Nevrine

I could have killed Norsselen today. That's not metaphor. It still makes me sick when I think about it. And the thing is, I had the same feeling of rightness I did facing down those Castaviran villagers who were attacking Nanissa's village, as if I could see the right thing and make everyone else see it too. I won't know until tomorrow what

Norsselen's reaction will be, but what makes me ashamed is I couldn't find a better solution than being a bigger bully than he is, just like in that village. I never thought I'd use these pouvrin to frighten people into submission. I'm afraid of who I'm becoming.

It was in all other ways a typical day. Jeddan and I decided not to start teaching the new pouvrin until we have more "students" ready to learn. That left us with a handful of people who had nothing to do, until it occurred to me to have them start helping with instructing the rest. It was only mostly a good idea, since they kept coming to me for guidance anyway, but it still means faster progress, and I like the camaraderie it builds when they're communicating with each other instead of just listening to me talk. But it meant I was too busy with my group to realize something was going on with Norsselen's until one of the mages in that group stood up and said, loudly but not quite shouting, "I think you're wasting everyone's time, Norsselen."

Norsselen looked up at him and said, "If you're not capable of learning this, Kesse, I don't think it's my fault."

"It is if you're not teaching," Fanion (that's Kesse's praenoma) shot back. "Telling us to embrace our inner magic is useless. I don't think you have any idea of how magic works. I'm going to join Sesskia's group—at least they're making progress."

"Sit down, Kesse, you're making a fool of yourself," Norsselen said. Fanion turned on his heel and walked away. And Norsselen circled him with fire. He cried out and stood motionless.

"Stop it, Norsselen," I said, taking a few steps in his direction, and to my shock Norsselen repeated the trick on me. I was so surprised I just stood there in my ring of fire. It was tall enough I couldn't step over it, and I couldn't dismiss it so long as he was controlling it, so I had no choice but to stand there and listen to him.

"I'm tired of playing this game, Thalessi," he said. "You've tried to usurp my authority for long enough. I don't care how many magics you have, I'm in charge here and I say what we do. And what we do is stop wasting our time trying to find structure in something that arises naturally out of who we are. So why don't you go back to playing with your magic, and let me teach these people how to fight, which is what we're all here for."

I couldn't believe it. I'd had no idea he'd so insulated himself in his own group he didn't realize the mages were actually accomplishing anything. "Norsselen," I said, and then I couldn't think of anything to say that would make a dent in his self-centered ignorance.

"Norsselen!" shouted a mage on the far side of the room. She was one of those who could work the walk-through-walls pouvra and nothing else, a mage in Jeddan's group. She came forward until she stood next to me, showing no fear of the fire. "You think we're not learning anything?" she said, and pointed at the far wall. Two bricks and a handful of rubber balls came floating jerkily off their respective piles.

Norsselen and I both goggled at her. "I can do this because I understand the shape of the magic," she said, "not because I gained some kind of...of mystical insight, or because I practiced really, really hard with my first pouvra. And I think you should shut up and start listening to Sesskia."

Norsselen's face went livid. He raised his hand (I don't think I've said he's taught all these people to use big gestures when they work pouvrin, the idiot) and pointed at the woman, and Jeddan started moving forward, and I shouted, "Everyone *stop!*" And everyone froze in place except Norsselen, who grinned evilly at me. "You have no power here," he said, and actually set the woman on fire.

Everyone screamed. And I did something I don't think I could repeat if it weren't a matter of life and death—I turned my fire pouvra inside out and used it to dismiss Norsselen's fire before it could do more than frighten the woman. Then I worked the same pouvra on myself and Fanion. And then I took several running steps and used all my weight to knock Norsselen to the floor.

Before his goons could react, I'd looked inside his neck and found a couple of key veins, held them closed long enough to knock him unconscious, and between working those pouvrin I surrounded his followers with fire. It was exhausting, and I was breathing heavily both from exertion and from fury. I panted for a bit, hands on knees, then straightened and walked with slow, deliberate steps toward the corner where I'd pinned Norsselen's men.

"I don't want to fight you," I said, and I put the fire out. It was harder that time. I'm going to have to figure out how I did that, but later. Much later, probably. "You've been listening to Norsselen because—I don't know, I could be wrong about this, but I think he's saying things you want to hear. Things that make you feel special. But you don't realize being able to work magic already makes you special. Not better than other people, of course, not more worthy of respect, but you've got something only a handful of people have. And you have the chance to learn more, and be more, and I don't understand why you don't want to take that chance. Think about it. If you don't believe what I've been saying, fine. But please don't interfere with all these other people who do."

They were huddled into their corner, staring at me, not exactly afraid—more stunned, I think. None of them said anything. They kept casting glances at Norsselen; I realize now they thought I'd killed him, which probably worked in my favor as far as keeping them under control went. Then Norsselen groaned, and shook his head, and looked up at me as if he didn't remember who either of us was. It took him a while to come to his senses. Then he got to his feet, shook his head again to clear it, and ran at me with his fists raised.

Again, I didn't even stop to think about the potential dangers. I just went insubstantial and let him run right through me, which made him stumble and go to his knees. Then I was terrified I'd killed him, and that fear turned into anger. Fury. Here was this man who had so much magic potential, had learned so much in a way I'd never thought possible, and all he could do was cling to his so-called power and bully others and tell them, essentially, that they'd never be as good as he was. And that infuriated me. It was a good feeling, a clean feeling, and I knew what to do with it.

"Jeddan, get him up," I said. Jeddan hooked his hands under Norsselen's arms, hauled him to his feet, and turned him to face me. Norsselen fought him, and shouted obscenities at me, until I got right up into his face and looped fire around his neck. That made him shut up fast, though he was still furious. I didn't care anymore about what he felt.

"Listen to me, you idiot," I said, loudly enough for everyone to hear. "I am sick of your posturing and your insistence that everyone defer to you because of some fantasy of power you dreamed up. I think you got lucky in developing several pouvrin and you don't want anyone else to match you. How you manage to reconcile that fact with Jeddan and me working far more pouvrin than you all day long is a mystery I don't care to unravel. But I'm not putting up with you any longer.

"If you can humble yourself, you're welcome to learn with the rest of us. I'll be happy to teach you. But if you persist in behaving as if the true God dropped you on the throne of Balaen to rule over the rest of us, I will turn every pouvra in my power on you until you are nothing but a puddle of weeping flesh. This is not a threat. This is a promise of the future. Drop him, Jeddan."

Jeddan did so as I released the noose of fire. Norsselen looked up at me, and it makes me sick, now, to remember how much his expression of fear satisfied me. "If you can't subordinate your pride to learning magic," I continued, "get out. I'll take responsibility for it to King and Chamber. I think they'll understand when I tell them you were undermining our ability to defend Balaen. Now, which is it going to be?"

I thought about relenting a bit, telling him how much we needed his unique abilities, which was true as far as it went. But it didn't go past an idle thought. I can't believe how much pleasure I took in bullying him.

Norsselen got to his feet. He was shaking. Then he turned and left the room without saying a word. I realized I was shaking too. I said, "I think we're done for today. I don't know what you do for entertainment, but we all need to relax. I'll be here in the morning, and anyone who wants to learn—" I glanced at Norsselen's mages—"can join me and Jeddan." Then I went to my room and sat unthinking for a while. And then, as I always do, I wrote.

Now that I've gotten that out of the way, I can think about the consequences of what I did. I don't know where Norsselen went. I think he's probably gone. I guess I'll find out come the morning. He might try to strike back at me, but right now I can't think about that. I can't think about anything except how afraid he looked at the end, and how much it satisfied me. It was wrong, and yet

There. I took about ten minutes to think it through, to calm myself. Because I don't know that I was wrong in what I did. I've known a lot of people like Norsselen, and most of them don't respond to anything but violence. I just never thought I'd be that person, the one facing them down. I feel like a stranger to myself today. Me, Sesskia, who's spent a lifetime staying out of the way and not making waves, giving orders and facing down bullies and making speeches, true God help me. That's not who I am. Except now it is.

I never wanted to be this person. I was happy with who I was. But it seems this is what these mages need, and I can't abandon them. I just wish I hadn't taken such joy in tearing Norsselen down. I wish I had someone to talk to about it.

I tried telling Jeddan, but he just said, "The bastard had it coming, and everyone in that room knew it. The worst I can say is they probably shouldn't have been so relieved it wasn't them doing it, which is cowardly, but maybe none of them could. I think you've been their leader since we came through the door, Sesskia." And that wasn't helpful. I don't want to

Oh, hell. I've just received a letter—it was directed to Norsselen, but nobody could find him, so they brought it to me. The army's back. And it seems I've nominated myself as the mages' official liaison to Mattiak Tarallan, Commander General of the Balaenic Army.

CHAPTER FOURTEEN

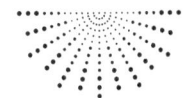

21 Nevrine

I think I like General Tarallan. He's not what I expected, after meeting Crossar. For one thing, he's young to be Commander General of the entire Balaenic Army—I don't think he's more than forty. He's got the fair coloring of a northwesterner, light blond hair and pale eyes that I think are gray rather than blue, and is ruggedly handsome. He's not noble, but he behaves to King and Chamber as if he's their equal, and they treat him with respect. I can see why. He's got the same air of competence about him Cederic has, the charisma of a born leader. I've heard he came up through the ranks and has earned the respect not only of King and Chamber, but of all the men under his command. And he's kept the army strong even though Balaen is at peace, which is pretty remarkable. He's interesting, and I think we might be able to become friends.

Though I wouldn't have said that earlier this morning, when we first met. I was escorted back to Janeka Manor, grateful for the first time the King had pressed these fancy clothes on me, and brought to a different meeting room than the one I'd been in before. This one had a long table, and ornately carved armchairs with heavily stuffed seat cushions, and was hung with portraits of famous Kings of

Balaen, all of whom looked the same despite not being contemporaries. I wondered if they'd been painted from life, and concluded not, since they all seemed to be by the same hand. So who knows if that's how those men actually looked?

Anyway, the room was empty when I arrived, and I wasn't ushered to a seat, so I wandered the room and looked at the portraits, and peeked out the windows, which faced north and therefore showed nothing of interest. I waited for several minutes, trying not to become bored or angry at how my time was being wasted, until a different door opened and a black-robed servant came in, a steward I think. He stood like he had a rod shoved up his ass and announced, "His Majesty Garran Clendessar, King of Balaen. Lord Jarlak Batekessar, Lord Caelan Crossar, Lord Merdel Lenssar, Lady Debarra Jakssar."

The King and Chamber filed in in the order they were announced and took seats around the table. I still wasn't invited to sit, but I hadn't expected to be, so I didn't mind. Lenssar said, "Tarallan should be here already."

"He has many duties," Crossar said. "We may excuse him some tardiness, I think."

"And who's the woman?" Lenssar said, jabbing his thumb at me.

"Lenssar, pay attention," Jakssar said. "We met Sesskia the other day. She entered the invading army's camp and brought us information about their forces."

"I knew that," Lenssar said, flushing. "I meant, why is she here?"

"Yes," Crossar said, "why are you here? I summoned Corrmek Norsselen. Did he think a summons from the Chamber is something lightly ignored?"

"Um, Norsselen isn't with us anymore," I said. Norsselen was gone this morning, as were three of his minions. I was surprised it was so few, but I didn't have time to do more than ask Jeddan to reorganize Norsselen's former group before I had to attend this meeting. "He became incapable of performing his duties. I've, um, taken his place."

"I don't think a woman ought to hold a military position, even one as irregular as organizing those magickers," Batekessar said querulously.

"Why not?" Jakssar said. "I'd think it was more important that a leader of mages should have magical ability. Sesskia, I assume you're qualified."

"I have the most pou—magics of all the mages," I said, "and the most experience in using them. I don't know that I have any knowledge of military matters, but I understand we'll be directed by someone who does." I was relieved none of them seemed inclined to pursue the issue of why Norsselen was gone. Despite what I'd said to him, it wasn't a conversation I wanted to have with the rulers of Balaen.

The door I'd entered by opened, and a man said, "My apologies, your Majesty, lords and lady, there was an unexpected issue I had to deal with." He sat down near me, several seats away from King and Chamber, without being invited. He didn't look at me, which annoyed me, but again, it didn't matter.

"General Tarallan, welcome back," the King said. "Are you prepared to defend this city?"

"We will be, your Majesty," Tarallan said. "I've sent scouts to investigate the enemy position and we're evaluating a strategy now."

"What happened at the foreign city?" Crossar said.

"You know we had to abandon the siege," Tarallan said. He sounded angry. "I don't think they'll send their troops after us, but I left a couple of battalions concealed near Brekner Pass to ambush them if they do. It's a risk, leaving an enemy force where it can come upon our flank, but more risky not to try to meet the main army on our own terms."

"It's far more important that you protect Venetry," the King said, once again sounding petulant. "We can't afford to have the capital overrun by foreign invaders."

"I don't think it will come to that, your Majesty," Tarallan said, a little too smoothly, I thought, like cosseting a child. But then I'm not sure anyone who knows him respects the King, poor man. Though I don't know why I pity him. He's responsible for protecting every Balaenic, which is a big responsibility, and I don't think he takes it seriously. So I guess I don't respect him either.

"Well, you're going to have help," the King said. "We're training... Sesskia, you call yourselves mages, correct? We're training mages to counter the magics of the foreign invaders."

"I know that, your Majesty," Tarallan said. "I intend to speak to Corrmek Norsselen this morning to learn how their training is proceeding."

The King looked confused. "I thought you were in charge of the mages, Sesskia," he said. "Isn't that what you said?"

Tarallan turned in his seat to look at me. "You?" he said. He sounded incredulous, as if there were something innately wrong with me that made my appointment to that position too strange to believe.

"Yes, General," I said. I refrained from adding *and yes, I'm a woman.*

Tarallan looked at the King. "I'm not comfortable with this," he said. "Norsselen and I had a good working relationship, and I don't think it's a good idea to change that when we are so close to conflict. I'm afraid I'll have to insist he be reinstated."

"Excuse me, but I don't think you understand the situation," I said, not caring that it might be out of line for me to address Tarallan directly without being invited. "Norsselen wasn't removed from his position. He chose to leave. Reinstatement isn't an option."

"I'm the one who decides how my army runs," Tarallan said, once again sounding angry. "You don't get to tell me what I can't do."

"Enough," the King said. "Commander General, Sesskia has my full confidence. You will work together to make our army stronger so it can defend this city. Sesskia, how are the mages coming along?"

"Well enough, Honored," I said. "They're all learning offensive magics to turn against the enemy."

"Good, good," the King said. "I'm confident you're all doing your best. We will come to observe your progress tomorrow morning."

My throat tried to close up. "Tomorrow morning, Honored?" I said.

"Unless that's a problem," the King said, with an expression that told me it had better not be a problem.

"Of course not," I said. "We look forward to your visit." I'm still not sure what's going to happen tomorrow morning. After I met with King and Chamber, and had that long conversation with Tarallan, I went back and got everyone working on flashy pouvrin that would satisfy the King's need to see *something* that would convince him he would be safe. But that was later. At that moment, I just stood there, wondering what else they wanted of me and why they'd needed to call a special meeting just for a status report. I still don't know the answer to that.

Crossar said, "General Tarallan, I'll speak with you and your chiefs of staff at one o'clock this afternoon. Right now we'll leave you to confer with Thalessi on the role her mages will play in the war. Thank you both for coming." He stood, followed quickly by the King, who glared at him for once again usurping his role, and he and the rest of the Chamber filed out of the room, leaving me alone with Tarallan.

He'd stood when King and Chamber did, and now was leaning against the table, his palms spread flat in a gesture I'd seen Cederic use a dozen times before. When Cederic does it, it means he's thinking hard about something. I don't know what it means to Tarallan. Possibly that he's trying not to lose his temper, because after several seconds of silence in which I tried to think of ways this conversation might go, he said, "No offense to you, but I don't think this is going to work out."

I pulled out a chair and sat down. "Now, how could that possibly be offensive to me?" I said lightly. "Other than implying I'm too incompetent to be of any use to the military?"

He stood upright and his light-colored eyes came to rest on me. "I don't know you, I don't know your capabilities, and I don't think the army is a place for women," he said. "I'm telling you this because I think we should be honest with each other."

"I don't know if the army is a place for women," I said, "but you didn't know Norsselen once, and you grew to trust him. Though I don't know why, since he's an incompetent braggart who's more interested in personal power than in serving his country."

Tarallan's eyes widened. "Bold words," he said. "I trusted him because I saw his magics and they were powerful. I'm not a fool."

"I don't think a fool would have the reputation you do," I said. "And it's true Norsselen's magics are powerful. He just didn't understand how they worked." I was also thinking *If powerful magics are all it takes to gain your trust, General, you and I are going to become best friends.*

Tarallan's eyes narrowed. "And I suppose you do," he said.

"Yes," I said. "Norsselen developed magic a month ago, during the con—the Event. I developed it over ten years ago."

"Impossible," Tarallan said. "Magic was a thing of children's tales until the Event."

"No, General, mages were just very good at staying hidden," I said, "and that makes sense, don't you think, since they risked death if their power became known?"

"Impossible," he repeated, but without the vehemence of his earlier statement.

I stood. "General Tarallan, why don't you come meet your mage auxiliaries?" I said.

It turned out Tarallan had never seen the mages perform, since he'd been in the field almost the whole time since the convergence and Norsselen had told him it would "interfere with their training" if he did. The mages were able to do their performance without Norsselen's guidance, and looked as impressive as ever. Tarallan watched silently until everyone was finished, then said to me, "I didn't see anyone make lightning, or create black fog."

"We don't know those pouvrin," I said. "I take it you've seen the enemy mages do those magics? They'll be capable of things we aren't, but there are things we can do they can't." I worked the concealment pouvra and grinned as he struggled to keep me in sight. Astonishingly, he wasn't fooled for long. I get the feeling he doesn't miss much in general.

"Now *that* would be useful," he said. "How many of you can do it?"

"Just Jeddan and me," I said. Tarallan eyed Jeddan speculatively.

"You might be too big for infiltration," he said. "Concealment from sight is one thing, but if you're too noisy..." He looked at me, and I could see conflicting emotions battling across his face.

"That's right, General," I said. "I'd be perfect for whatever it is you have in mind. Especially since it's not the first time I've had to sneak into places. *And* I'm a woman."

He shook his head, and smiled. "I'm going to have to adjust my thinking," he said. "But I don't need concealment nearly so much as I need something that will remove those enemy mages from combat. Fire is good. Raining stones down on them is good. What range do you have?"

"I don't know," I said.

"You ought to know. That's important to our strategy, Thalessi," he said.

"I know, General. Can we walk out here?" I said. We went onto the patio, I shut the door, and said, "I admit I know nothing about military strategy. All I can do is train these mages. If you can tell me what you need them to do, and how you'll use them, I can—I hope—produce those results for you. But we'll have to work together."

Tarallan nodded once, slowly. "You're not what I expected," he said, "but I think we can do that." He extended his hand to me, and I pressed my palm against it. His skin is warm and dry, but not unpleasantly so.

We talked some more about what he needed, and I told him something of what Castaviran mages are capable of, pretending I'd learned it in my exploration of the enemy camp, though I'm still not sure what battle mages can do that's different from ordinary mages. Lightning, I suppose, and the fog Tarallan referred to, and fire.

I felt guilty about doing this, because there's no guarantee the "good" Castaviran forces won't come into conflict with Balaen's, and then I'd sort of be a traitor. Not that I know for sure that there are any "good" Castaviran forces. Even if Aselfos was able to control the army, he might be as bent on conquering Balaen as the God-Empress is. But I have so many friends among the mages I can't help feeling as if I'm betraying them. Even so, right now the threat is the

God-Empress, and we're going to need every advantage I can give us.

Tarallan was impressed at how much I'd learned and that I'd used the concealment pouvra to such good advantage. I could almost see him generating plans for espionage missions behind enemy lines. We'll see if I decide to go along with them.

After he left, I explained what he'd told me to the mages and we yet again rearranged how we're doing things. Jeddan's dividing his time between teaching his group to understand the structure of pouvrin and helping those who've passed that stage learn to work the mind-moving pouvra. I was right that that's taking them longer than did understanding how pouvrin work, but we have at least two mages achieve it every day.

I'm doing the same with my group, except we're learning to manifest fire; I have a couple who are ready to learn the fire rope as well. Relania, who still isn't a good teacher, is at least experienced enough with the see-in-dark pouvra to help those who have that one use it more efficiently. A couple of the more experienced mages volunteered to help those who've mastered the mind-moving pouvra improve their strength and dexterity with it.

I feel protective of our little army, which is trying so hard even though I doubt any of them has any idea what war is like, or what they'll be doing. It worries me that I have no way of knowing if any of the fire mages will be able to burn flesh, or if the mind-movers could crush someone's skull, and I won't know until we're in a position where it's their lives or the other man's at stake.

Just before dinner I got Jerussa to work with me on the flitting pouvra. She's not good at describing what she sees, and I think it's going to take forever before I learn it, but I've gotten glimpses—it's fluid, constantly in motion, unlike most pouvrin, and smells like lilac or possibly wine grapes, which I realize aren't at all the same kind of smells.

After dinner, Jeddan and I conferred about the war. Jeddan said, yawning, "I feel like things are coming together, don't you?"

"I feel less like I'm scrambling all the time," I agreed. "I just wish we knew when the God-Empress's army will be here. I have all these plans, but I don't know if there will even be time for them. Imagine, for example, someone being able to flit next to a key officer and stab him through the heart, then flit away?"

"I can't imagine any of these people stabbing anyone in the heart," Jeddan said.

"I know. But it's an interesting tactic, don't you think?" I said.

"I think you're bloodthirsty," Jeddan said. "Good night."

I'm so tired, but I'm having trouble sleeping. I'd go explore the house, but I've already been all through it, and sneaking places is less fun if there's no chance of being caught. Derria's shop is too far from Fianna Manor, and it would be after curfew by the time I got there even if I left now, and she'd be closed. I think I'll go sit on the patio rail and look out at the city. It looks different now I'll be defending it instead of stealing from it.

CHAPTER FIFTEEN

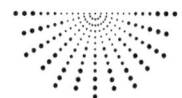

22 Nevrine

List of what I still need to do:

1. Work out who knows which pouvrin to make our training more efficient. The goal is for every mage to learn the fire and mind-moving pouvrin. They'll have to be the foundation of our defense (offense?) even though it means we lack flexibility. I don't know any other pouvrin we can turn against the enemy, and there's no time to discover more.

2. Start teaching the concealment pouvra. If we can be hidden as we work pouvrin, the enemy mages won't be able to find us to strike back. I hope. This assumes we can also teach these mages to maintain concentration on one pouvra while working others.

3. Practice Tarallan's tactics. It's easier to understand the theory than I'd imagined. Not so easy to put it into practice. He wants a lot of simultaneous attacks, which means teaching the mages more of the organized movements Norsselen taught them, and that takes time. Like everything else.

4. Learn the flitting pouvra. This may be selfishness on my part, but I can't help thinking it could be useful to us. It's still not coming together, though.

Not only the King, but the entire Chamber and Tarallan showed up at the manor around mid-morning without having bothered to give us any warning of their arrival. Fortunately, we knew he'd be here sometime, so nobody was too flustered, or at least not flustered enough to be unable to perform. They all went through their rehearsed demonstration while Jeddan and I stood near King and Chamber, then Jeddan and I showed off the walk-through-walls and concealment pouvrin.

The King was delighted by all of it. I think he hasn't realized our magic has anything to do with the war and thinks it's all for his personal amusement. Batekessar looked sour, more sour than usual I mean, and Lenssar looked bored, but I think he was covering fear. Jakssar watched everything carefully, as did Crossar, but where Jakssar seemed to be formulating questions to ask, Crossar seemed to be analyzing our strengths and weaknesses. Which makes sense, if he's Chamber Lord of Defense, but it felt uncomfortable, like he was doing it so he'd know how to defeat *us* if that became necessary.

And when he turns his attention on me, I feel as if he's doing the same thing, as if he's trying to figure out what use he can make of me. I don't like it, but what can I do, other than try to stay out of his way and remind myself that if he ever physically attacked me, which I don't think he'd do, I can defend myself.

After we'd shown off everything we could, Tarallan said, "Do you have any questions, your Majesty, my lords and lady?" I felt as if that was something *I* should have asked, but he's our commanding officer, so I guess we're his responsibility.

"Sesskia, how is it you know so many magics?" Jakssar asked, overriding whatever the King had been about to say. "You seem so young to be so formidable."

"I did almost nothing but study magic for ten years," I said. "It's something that matters to me. And the better I understood how it worked, the more magics I was able to learn."

"Magic was illegal all that time," Batekessar said. "You brag about breaking the law openly to your King?"

"Magic has never been illegal, Batekessar," Crossar said, "just feared. Thalessi was brave to risk death for the sake of magic. I'm not sure I would have done that."

"I've seen enough," said Lenssar. "We should leave them to their training."

"I have more questions," the King said, whining. He whines a lot. "Most of these magics seem useless in our defense. Why do you even have them?"

"Honored, each of us developed a pouvra when we became mages," I said. His tone of voice really gets under my skin and makes it hard for me to be patient with him, sovereign or no. "We didn't choose which one. So even though we're all learning pouvrin we can attack the enemy with, some of us still have other magics we need to practice. And studying one pouvra makes it easier for us to learn others."

"It's good that you can all produce fire," the King said, proving he once again hadn't been paying attention. "That was impressive."

"Thank you, Honored," I said. "Would you like to know anything else?"

"I want to know if you can take over someone else's body with that going incorporeal magic," the King said. "Make them do what you want."

The idea made me sick. "No, Honored, and it's extremely dangerous to pass through living flesh, for both of you," I said. "We don't do that."

"Implying that you can," Crossar said.

"And we don't," Jeddan said. "We can't 'take over' anyone else, either. Honored." He sounded dangerous, and the King looked nervous.

I said, "But General Tarallan has some ideas for how it can be useful in other ways, Honored."

"Intelligence gathering, mostly, your Majesty," Tarallan said. "Combined with the concealment pouvra, we could have spies capable of entering enemy strongholds and retrieving valuable information without being noticed."

"Or men and women capable of stealing anything they wanted,"

168

Crossar said, again turning that needle-sharp gaze on me. "Am I right, Thalessi?"

"I suppose that's true, Honored," I said, "though I don't think a mage is any more likely to be a criminal than anyone else." Which was a non-answer to the question he was really asking, but if he wasn't willing to come right out and ask *Are you a thief?* I didn't feel obligated to give him an open answer.

"Well, keep up the good work, everyone," the King said, addressing the room. "I'll probably come back and watch you work sometimes. I think it's important for a King to be aware of what his subjects are capable of." Without noticing how all our faces blanched at the idea of being under royal scrutiny, he turned and left the room, followed immediately by Batekessar and Lenssar.

Jakssar said, "You're setting a remarkable example, Sesskia," before following them herself. I think she might see me as a figure-head for female empowerment. She certainly seemed to be scruti-nizing the women mages carefully. (I don't think I've said we have more female mages than male, though not by much. With fewer than fifty mages in all, it's impossible to say if that means anything about the mage population in general.)

Crossar stayed behind to talk to Tarallan. It didn't seem like a private discussion, but I didn't think it had anything to do with me, so I was about to excuse myself when Tarallan said, "Nessan tells me all mages have the same eye color. Is that true?"

It took me a minute to remember where I'd heard that name before—the soldier at the gate. "It's true," I said. "Nobody who doesn't have those eyes developed magic after the event."

"Fortunate for you no one knew that until recently," Crossar said. "You would have found it much more difficult to stay hidden."

"I'm grateful for that, Honored," I said.

"So would it be worth seeking out more like you?" Tarallan said. "Rather than waiting for them to come forward on their own?"

"We don' t actually know whether everyone with those eyes devel-oped magic. If they aren't already mages—if they haven't already developed a pouvra—I don't know how to give them that," I said. "So

I'm not sure it would increase our numbers any faster. It would depend on how many resources you have to put toward doing it, identifying actual mages before sending them here."

"Then we'll focus on training the ones we have, and spread the word of the King's summons more widely," Crossar said. "But I don't know how much time we have."

"They've laid siege to Hasskian," Tarallan said. "If we leave immediately, we might be able to trap them against the city before it's overcome."

"Hasskian can hold out indefinitely," Crossar said.

"Not against the weapons this army has," Tarallan said. "Not only those battle mages, but weapons we've never seen before. They seem to work like rifles, but they fire shot the size of a man's head that fractures when it hits its target. My spies tell me Hasskian's walls are starting to look like lacework."

My stomach churned at the thought of Hasskian and all its inhabitants being overrun. I wondered if those mystery weapons could be the war wagons. The God-Empress couldn't have many of them, could she, if Vorantor had transferred most of them to Aselfos's troops? *Idiot, who says that room you saw was the only one she had?* I thought. I considered telling them about the war wagons, realized I couldn't without giving away knowledge I shouldn't have, realized further there was nothing I could tell them they didn't already know, and held my tongue.

"I don't have the power to order the army away from the city," Crossar said, "and the—" He seemed to realize I was still there, listening, and turned a frown on me. "Excuse us, Thalessi," he said, and I nodded and walked away.

It's strange that the Chamber Lord of Defense doesn't have power to maintain the kingdom's defense, since he can't order the army to move. I guessed the King, frightened of Venetry being overrun and himself being taken or killed by the God-Empress's army, insisted the army make their stand here. I don't know enough about strategy to understand what the best battleground is, but I'm sure Tarallan, and probably Crossar, do, and it's not in the area surrounding Venetry. My respect for the King, never great, is diminishing.

Tarallan and Crossar talked for a while longer; I watched them covertly as I worked with my group. Finally Crossar exchanged farewell salutes with Tarallan, looked at me in a way that told me he knew I'd been watching, and left the room. Tarallan also looked my way and nodded to indicate I should join him.

"You heard enough to know what the problem is," he said without preamble.

"I guessed the King doesn't want the army to leave Venetry," I said.

"Not a single division of it," Tarallan said. "Even though the enemy has divided her own forces somewhat. Hasskian's the only city of any size in that area, but she's spreading out to take over all the smaller cities surrounding it, taking provisions and killing the inhabitants. If she can afford to do that and still smash Hasskian's defenses to powder, she's a formidable threat."

"Does that affect what the mages are doing?" I said.

"Only in the sense that the more of you we have, the better," he said. "Hence my question about searching out mages rather than waiting passively for them to arrive."

"They still come in, a few at a time," I said, "and about half of them already know the offensive pouvrin. I just wish I could be sure they can use them, um, offensively."

"No way to know until we come to that point," he agreed. "I'd like to discuss more of the tactics I want you to use, but I don't have time until evening. Let's meet over dinner."

"All right," I said, and we arranged a time. Then he left, and I went back to working with the mages. Two more came in that afternoon, both fire mages, both in my group (interestingly, the majority of my group started with the fire pouvra, and most of Jeddan's knew the mind-moving pouvra first, and the third group is primarily the see-in-dark pouvra. Something for me to study *if I had any time which I do NOT*). This gives us a total of forty-nine mages. We're going to need another dining room soon.

Out of forty-nine mages:

1. Thirty-six know the fire pouvra, and fourteen of those can do the fire rope.

2. Twenty-five know the mind-moving pouvra. All of them except Jeddan and me can lift weights of at least five pounds, all the way up to Saemon at several hundred, and I think he hasn't reached his limit.

3. Twenty of 1 and 2 combined can do both pouvrin.

4. Eleven mages have three pouvrin, and all of those except Relania have fire and mind-moving as two of theirs.

5. The remaining eight are all, probably not coincidentally, Relania's pacifist friends. They're all good at seeing in the dark and walking through things. I haven't told them yet this makes them perfect spies. I'm saving that in reserve for if Relania gets too smug about her pacifism.

I've spent the last few nights going over what I can remember the Castaviran mages doing, wondering if there's any way I can build a pouvra to replicate those things. I have a good memory, but I don't

Oh. The shield. Cederic's shield kathana. Tarallan never said anything about the God-Empress using it, and I think Cederic only taught it to the Colosse troops. But—no, it's impossible. It was so complicated, I can barely remember half of what he did.

22 Nevrine, half an hour later

I'm confident I can reproduce twelve of the th'an Cederic used. Damn it, if I had that hypothetical memory pouvra...I would still not have any idea how to turn the th'an into a pouvra. I guess that's not entirely true; I remember how the binding th'an came together into a pouvra, and I know that pouvra works even if I don't know what it's for. But this is a lot more th'an than the binding had, and I don't think I can keep all the pieces in my head at once, let alone practice arranging them into a pouvra. I need an alternative. But not tonight. I'm so tired now.

I forgot to write about dinner with Tarallan, so I guess I'm not going to sleep yet. He's set up his headquarters in one of the manors about a quarter mile from ours—*not* in Janeka Manor, which I think makes a statement about the army's relationship to the king—but it's surprisingly non-martial in feel, at least the part of it I saw. Probably he's turned most of the ground floor public rooms into offices. But we had dinner in a nice dining room, not a huge one like ours but small, with just the one round table, and it was a good meal. I wonder if his cook goes with him when he's out campaigning. I have trouble imagining anyone, no matter how good a cook, producing meals like that one over a camp stove, so probably not.

Anyway, we ate, and discussed tactics. Tarallan wants us to practice extending the range of our pouvrin, so we can attack more distant targets. Apparently the God-Empress's battle mages can do damage from a great distance, and we're intended to neutralize them (Tarallan's word) rather than use our magic on the army itself.

Tarallan told me about the Castaviran city they'd been besieging when they were summoned back to Venetry thanks to our information. Our side didn't know exactly how it all started, but Tarallan thinks when the city appeared (from our perspective) their ruler decided to start conquering territory by running over all these towns that lie along the highway between Venetry and Durran. I felt sick listening to Tarallan's description of what they'd done to those Balaenic towns, even though he didn't go into much detail. They'd managed to claim a good chunk of Balaen before King and Chamber learned about it and dispatched the army.

Tarallan pinned down their forces, making them retreat to their city, and the siege had been going well until they were forced to withdraw. Tarallan is bitter about that, but he puts a good face on it because it's not the King's fault the God-Empress is marching on Venetry.

I asked him more about the army staying at Venetry rather than advancing south, and he said, "Position is important. By leaving immediately, we have a chance to choose our ground. If we wait here long enough, we'll be fighting a defensive battle, and in this case that's a mistake. I want to catch the enemy when they're weakened from fighting a hundred little battles around Hasskian, not when they've had time to regroup and rest and, not incidentally, cut us off from some of our support."

"Are there more troops in Balaen you can call on?" I asked. "I assume they've already eliminated the forces at Calassmir."

"Unfortunately," Tarallan said with a frown. "Our forces are already divided. I had to leave troops to watch that enemy city, in case they decide to emerge and go back to sacking and looting the countryside, or, true God forbid, nip at our heels. There are several divisions at Barrekel, but we haven't regained contact with them, and for all I know they're fighting off more enemy invaders and aren't able to join us. Hasskian doesn't have much more than a token force these days, and Denderiss has its hands full dealing with Fensadderian refugees and maintaining the border defense. It sounds as if Fensadderis is falling apart more rapidly now than it was before, which means it must be in utter chaos."

"I wish people could be told what really happened," I said. Jeddan and I had explained a bit about the convergence to King and Chamber, claiming to have learned it because we are such gifted, experienced mages, but I'm not sure how much they believed. The King got it into his head everyone in this world had a counterpart in Castavir and kept asking, worriedly, what we were doing about his double. Tarallan, on the other hand, understood it quickly and had asked a lot of questions at the beginning of the meal. After dealing with King and Chamber, it's refreshing to talk to someone so intelligent and quick-witted.

"I don't think it matters," Tarallan said. "It's unfortunate, but people will always be afraid of things, and people, they don't understand. Conflict is inevitable."

"But it shouldn't have to be, if we try to understand each other," I said, but I remembered how afraid and suspicious I'd been of the Darssan mages before Terrael gave me their language, and knew Tarallan was right. It left me feeling discouraged, thinking once again of the destruction of both our worlds not by the convergence, but by each other.

"What's troubling you?" Tarallan said. Did I mention he's observant as well as intelligent?

I cast about for something to say that wouldn't implicate myself as a Castaviran sympathizer and came up with, "I'm worried about my husband. We were separated during the convergence and I don't know where he is."

"I...didn't realize you were married," Tarallan said, sitting back in his chair. "Where were you when you were separated?"

"Near the Myrnala River, several days' journey north of Garwin," I said. "The middle of nowhere, or at least it was. Who knows what kind of Cas—of invader cities might have appeared there?" Like, for example, their strife-ridden capital.

"It's a dangerous place these days," Tarallan said. "The messengers we sent in that direction returned with news that the whole area has been occupied by the enemy. I hope your husband is unharmed."

"I'm sure he is," I said. "I was traveling to find him when the trouble at Calassmir, and the King's summons, brought me here."

"Just as well," he said. "You might have been killed, and the mages would be leaderless, and this dinner would have been a good deal more boring."

I laughed, and said, "The mages wouldn't lack for leadership, they'd still have Norsselen."

"Really?" Tarallan said. "You make it sound as if Norsselen's leaving was a response to your presence."

"I, um, that's a *little* true," I said. "We had some differences of opinion, and he chose to, um, go elsewhere to use his talents."

"I think you may be prevaricating," Tarallan said, but with a smile. "However, you seem extremely competent, and the mages seem happy, so I'm willing to accept your version of events. And I admit I enjoy your company."

"Thank you, General," I said. "I enjoy yours as well."

"That's fortunate, because I'm going to require you to bring me a report every evening on your troop's progress," he said. "I want to know when new mages arrive, what progress they make on learning pouvrin, and I especially want to know how those ranges are extending. A verbal report will be enough, and I expect to see you between six and six-thirty every evening."

"Yes, sir," I said, pretending seriousness, which made him laugh.

"Keep in mind I'm still your superior officer, Thalessi," he said, "and you're to show respect." He smiled at me to show he wasn't entirely serious. Which is to say, I know he believes respect is key to good discipline, but he's not so stiff as to have no sense of humor.

"I certainly intend to, but *you* should keep in mind I'm not military and I don't always know how to be properly respectful," I said in the same light tone.

"I'll let you know if you overstep," he said, still smiling, and rose to indicate the meal, and the meeting, was over. And now I truly am exhausted. I wonder what I'd be doing if I were with Cederic instead of here in Venetry. Not sleeping alone, for one.

CHAPTER SIXTEEN

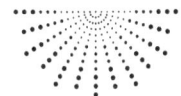

23 Nevrine

The good news: everyone with fire or mind-moving pouvrin can work their magic at a distance of 100 feet, which is from one side of the ballroom to the other. The bad news: we're pretty sure everyone's actual range is a good deal farther, and we can't practice finding the real distance without dropping fire or stones on the heads of people in the lower city.

In order to have that kind of practice area, we'll have to go outside the city—at least a mile outside the city. And transporting all of us is a logistical nightmare. We lose too much work time in transit. But I don't dare suggest we set up a camp outside the walls, out in the cold and snow (it's been snowing heavily for two days, on and off), or I'd have a mutiny to deal with. So as frustrated as I am, I've had to accept the situation as it is.

So tomorrow morning there will be many, many carriages to drive us to our new practice grounds. All of us, including those who don't have an offensive pouvra, and Relania's group tried to pitch a fit about that until I said they would be learning new tactics that did not involve doing violence to anyone. I guess we'll see tomorrow whether espionage falls under their rules about non-violence.

I wish there were three of me. I have two, maybe three mages who are almost capable of taking over the fire pouvra instruction, and when that happens I can focus on—well, it's not exactly "focus on" if there are three things you're splitting your attention between. I'm excited about teaching my pacifist mages thief skills, seeing if any of them take to it naturally. I was, after all, a thief before I was a mage, and I'm proud of those skills.

24 Nevrine

Unbelievable. Once we got access to a nearly unlimited space to practice, it became clear a lot of these mages had power nobody dreamed of. We went north of the city today, where there isn't anything but fallow land stretching all the way to the northern forests a hundred miles away, and spent the morning marking off distances. The farthest marker was at two hundred yards, which I thought was optimistic, but better to have marked off too far than too short, right?

We marked too short. I was able to start a fire *five hundred yards* from our starting mark without even straining. Daerdra reached nearly as far. Hasseka and Saemon were so nearly tied for mind-moving things at five hundred and fifty yards' distance we spent half an hour watching them compete for first place. That contest is still undecided. The fire-rope is limited in distance; no one could manifest it farther than fifty feet away, even me, but that's a one-on-one "weapon" so that makes sense.

Once we'd extended the markings on the field, and I'd demonstrated the kind of exercises I wanted everyone to do, I left Jeddan in charge and had a handful of mind-movers help me set up the things I'd brought in a very large, very heavy wagon pulled by a team of placid horses whose shaggy winter coats made them look warmer than we were. At the end, we had a couple of "houses" that were just prefabricated walls jammed into the ground at right angles to each other, no roofs, a lot of sticks standing upright with ropes strung between them to make a path, said ropes being hung with little brass bells, and another wide stretch of empty field marked off at ten foot intervals.

Relania's group watched all of this curiously—they don't have the fire or mind-moving pouvrin, so it was either watch me or watch the great clouds of steam that went up wherever someone set a fire in the snowy field. When I was finished with my preparations, I called them to me and said, "You haven't made any secret of the fact that you don't believe we should be using magic for violence. Now, I don't know if that means you don't want to be here at all, or if you wish there were something else you could do. What I *do* know is King and Chamber see us as key to fighting the, um, invading army, and they are extremely unwilling to let any advantage slip away. Which means unless you want to make the kind of stink Norsselen did, you're stuck here."

"If you're trying to make us feel bad, Sesskia, it won't work," Relania said. "We're all committed to principles of non-violence."

"Believe it or not, I agree with you," I said, "mostly, anyway. I've spent most of my life trying not to get into fights." Of course, my reasons for doing so weren't that I believe violence is always the wrong way to handle conflict—sometimes it's the only way—but that I'm too small to be an effective fighter. But that was irrelevant. "So I'm not going to train you to be fighters. I'm going to train you to be spies."

That got them talking all at once. The voice that won out over the rest wasn't Relania's, but Tobiak's. He's about fifteen years old with terrible acne, poor kid, but he's got the kind of self-confidence you usually only see in really attractive people. "How is that any different from making us fight?" he said. "We're still advancing the cause of the military."

"Tobiak," I said, "what is the purpose of pacifism? In your opinion."

"To oppose violence as a tool to make people do things," he said. "To prevent people from being hurt or killed."

"Sesskia, that's not what—" Relania said.

"I know it's not as accurate a definition as you'd like, Relania," I said, "but the point here is to establish what exactly all of you want to accomplish by refusing to use pouvrin in the war. Am I right that you don't want to be responsible for people's deaths?"

They looked at each other, then began nodding, some vehemently, others as if they still weren't sure. I pushed forward so I wouldn't lose momentum.

"I know you don't like it, but this war is happening whether you fight with us or not," I said. "I don't like it either. I think it's idiotic that our people and their people can't figure out a way to live in peace. But the army that's advancing on us is commanded by a madwoman who doesn't give a damn how many people die in her conquest of both countries. She doesn't even care how many of her own people die. General Tarallan is working to stop her before too many people are killed. To do that, he needs information. And that is what spies are for—to minimize losses and end wars more quickly."

Most of them looked confused, but to my surprise, one or two people had looks on their faces that said both that they'd never thought of it that way, and that now they *had* thought of it, it made perfect sense.

"So you need to consider this," I said. "I'm not going to make you learn those offensive pouvrin. I'm not going to make you do anything that violates your principles. If you want, you can sit this out in Fianna Manor—I won't even let the General know I'm not sending him all my mages. And you will have absolutely no effect on stopping this war. *Or...*you can learn to gather information about our enemies, give it to people who know how to use it, and maybe keep hundreds or even thousands from dying. It's up to you."

And I walked away and went back to watching mages argue over how to bring boulders here so people could practice their lifting as well as their distance. And that is almost exactly word-for-word what I said. It felt right, again, only better because I wasn't making a speech to bully someone. I can't even say I learned it from watching Cederic, because he doesn't make speeches. I don't know where it came from. It felt good, the kind of feeling I usually only get when I'm doing magic. I think I felt like an actual leader for the first time today.

Anyway. I let them talk quietly among themselves for a while, maybe ten minutes, and then I went back and said, "Well? What do you think?"

Relania stepped forward. "You make a good point, Sesskia," she said. "We're not just opposed to violence because we think it's inherently wrong, though most of us do. We're opposed to it because we care about human life and the preservation of it. And we think it's not enough to sit back and not participate. So we're ready to learn."

"Some of us also want to know why you're qualified to teach us to spy," one of the mages said, grinning so I'd know he was teasing, and everyone laughed, myself included.

"Well, Keonn, the truth is I've had to do a lot of things in the course of learning magic, and one of those things is sneaking in and out of places," I said. "You'll be learning the concealment pouvra as part of this, but you have to remember it's not invisibility, and you can't rely on it to protect you. You also can't rely on the walk-through-walls pouvra unless you think passing out is a good way to not be caught. So in addition to practicing those pouvrin, we'll be learning how to move quietly, and how best to investigate an enemy's home— or camp—and some other skills that will be of use in that. But first —" I waved my hand at the marked-off field—"we're going to see how fast you can run."

The rest of the afternoon was actually fun. I lined them up along the field and had them go insubstantial and see how far they could get before shortness of breath stopped them. Then I had them go inside the "houses" and practice putting their faces through the walls, trying not to expose themselves too much. And *then* I set them to walking the narrow, curving path I'd made with rope and bells. They couldn't go insubstantial, and they couldn't make the bells ring or I'd make them start over.

"You all know you can't stay insubstantial forever," I said when they complained. "You have to learn to move quietly, and you have to learn to pass obstacles. Yes, if this were a real camp, you'd work the pouvra and walk through the whole thing, but you can't always count on being able to do that. Tonight we're going to do this in the manor, with the see-in-dark pouvra. Think how much of an advantage that will be."

They're all more enthusiastic about it than I thought possible.

And Rutika is a born thief, not that I told her this. She can't stay insubstantial as long as some of the others, but she walked the rope course perfectly the first time, and she has a good sense for how far she can go through a wall to examine her surroundings without revealing too much of herself. I already have some special training planned for her.

I told most of this to Tarallan that evening when I "reported" to him—not the bit about Rutika being a good thief, but that she was going to be an excellent spy. He was happy to learn how far a range most of us have, and pleased about the budding spy corps. I think he might have made a good thief himself, because he thinks about problems sideways the way I try to, and he appreciates the value of intelligence.

Our conversation went long enough that he invited me to eat with him again, and I accepted. This time we talked about other things as well as the war, mostly him telling me about his family, and me talking about my Dad—I don't know how we got on that subject. He seemed interested in the loss of our surname, and said, "So you don't have any idea who your family was?"

"None, and I don't really care," I said. "From what I've seen of the upper classes, there's nothing inherently wonderful about being part of them. And it's not like I could regain our status even if I knew what the surname was."

"I'd think it would be uncomfortable, not knowing if I had a connection to one of these families," he said. "Suppose Lenssar was your uncle, for example."

I shuddered. "Sorry, I don't mean to disrespect Lord Lenssar, but—"

"—it would be like being related to a weasel," Tarallan said.

I laughed. "A little. But the only thing I know is our family line was completely lost, so it's unlikely I'm, for example, the King's long lost heir."

"Too bad," he said. "That is, the King having an heir would almost mean more to Balaen than winning this war."

"Why is that?" I asked. This was the first I'd heard of the King not having an heir.

"Obviously the King has no offspring, since he's not married, and he hasn't designated an heir," he said, "which means if he were to die, the noble houses would go to war, so to speak—or maybe literally, I'm not sure—over who would take the throne. I'm not privy to their machinations, but I imagine the Chamber Lords have an edge over the others, and there's no question they're building support for themselves even though the King is relatively young and quite healthy."

"One more reason not to belong to the upper classes," I said, and we parted on that note. I like him. He's interesting, and clever, and never makes me feel stupid when I say something that shows I know nothing about military science. I think we might become friends.

Time to go teach my spies about moving silently in the dark.

25 Nevrine

More practicing. Hasseka and Saemon still fighting it out for greatest distance with the mind-moving pouvra. My spies are getting better at navigating the rope course. Last night was funny. The see-in-dark pouvra makes moving around at night easier, but they don't have any experience with moving quietly, and were all caught completely off guard when I flung open the door to a well-lit room in their faces and made them cover their eyes and cry out in pain. Not that I took pleasure in that. Well, maybe a little.

26 Nevrine

Mattiak—Tarallan offered me his praenoma tonight at dinner and asked the honor from me, and I do feel like we're friends—is worried about the advance of the God-Empress's army and the fact that we're still stuck here in Venetry. He won't come out and criticize the King, even behind his back, even privately to me, but it's clear he's frustrated at not having the power to do what he's responsible to do, which is defend Balaen. Not protect the King, not protect Venetry, but defend our country.

The God-Empress is still besieging Hasskian, from last reports anyway, but it takes so long to get a messenger from there to Venetry we won't know if she's taken the city until it's already happened.

Mattiak showed me how they'd attacked the Castaviran city to the north with the utensils and condiments on the table, and I didn't understand the details, but I think it made him feel better to have something concrete to focus on.

He also told me a few more details about the conflicts to the east that are centered on Colosse, not that he knew that, and asked if Cederic and I had a plan for finding each other. Of course we don't, and that made me depressed, but Mattiak reassured me the best chance we had of being reunited is for only one of us to do the searching, that my remaining in Venetry was the smart thing to do. That made me feel better, as did the thought (which I couldn't share with Mattiak) that Cederic and the mages are too powerful a force to simply have been destroyed no matter what had happened in Colosse. But I'd feel happier if any of Mattiak's men would return with more specific information.

More progress. We set up some practice dummies from the archery range and worked on setting them on fire and smashing them with stones or bricks. I don't like how excited everyone was about destroying them, because it feels like they're not taking this seriously—when we face the enemy, we're going to do it to actual people who scream and die. That's what war is.

I'm afraid some—maybe a lot—of these people won't be able to use magic on living targets, but there's no way to test that. I'll have to ask Mattiak what soldiers do to become inured to killing people. Or maybe they don't. Something else I can ask him.

Funny, that reminded me of some of my entries in the sixth book, where I was going to Cederic for everything and never realized I was falling in love with him. Not that I'm falling in love with Mattiak. I like talking to him, but I'm not attracted to him and he's far too old for me. It's just that we often end up talking about Cederic, so I come back from our dinners remembering things about my husband, especially memories that look different when I realize he was secretly in love with me. That trip by loenerel to Colosse, when he was always the one to come for me when it was mealtime, and I thought it was because he was trying to give me privacy to keep my book hidden, but it was actually because he was attracted to me and trying to work out how he felt.

Damn it. Now I'm crying. I thought I was past doing that.

My spies learned quickly from their first lesson and none of them were blinded last night. Rutika even managed to duck inside a wall when I "caught" her. Tonight I'm going to have them retrieve their first piece of "information"—a vase I borrowed from one of the sitting rooms and concealed in an unused bedroom. Oh! That reminds me, that bastard Norsselen claimed the best rooms for himself and his cronies, which is why we ended up in the old servants' quarters. We're not moving, of course, but it still makes me mad.

27 Nevrine

1. Forty-two mages with the fire pouvra, minimum range 155 yards, maximum 600.

2. Thirty-nine mages with the mind-moving pouvra, range 729 yards (way to go, Saemon!), minimum weight 65 lbs. "maximum" 425 lbs. (This number increases every day.)

3. Eight mages being trained as spies, minimum time insubstantial 1 min. 48 sec., maximum 3 min. 26 sec. Still working on the non-magical skills. Rutika continues to need greater challenges. I don't know if she realizes how good she is.

4. Two mages with the flitting pouvra. It's incredible. It feels like flying.

Dinner with Mattiak again. He wasn't as excited about our progress as I thought he'd be, but then I learned he'd had an argument with King and Chamber today about moving the army toward Hasskian that had ended with the King accusing him of disloyalty and Mattiak storming out without being dismissed.

I expressed my concern about what the King might do to him, and he said, "I'd have to attempt to assassinate him before he'd do anything truly punitive to me. They don't have anyone else who can command the army. Not that it takes much skill to tell soldiers to sit on their asses and do nothing."

"Is there any more news of the G—the invading army's progress?" I said.

"Hasskian must have fallen by now," he said. "I expect a messenger tomorrow. And there's nothing I can do about it but continue to press my case and try to convince the King moving the army will do more to protect him than having it camp outside Venetry's walls."

"It's too bad there isn't a way to get news instantaneously," I said, remembering Lineta and her talk about the "Firtha thanest" communication.

"Are you sure there's not?" he said, and I laughed before I realized it was a serious question.

"Sorry," I said. "It's like I've told you before, Mattiak: there could be pouvrin to do anything we can imagine, but nobody knows how to create one. We have to depend on people either spontaneously manifesting them when they become mages, or finding them in old books. And there's just no time for study."

"I know," he sighed. "I don't want you to think I'm not grateful for what you *can* do, Sesskia. It's hard for me to do nothing, and I start groping for *anything* to keep myself from feeling helpless."

"I understand that feeling," I said.

"It must be difficult for you, unable to continue your search for your husband," he said.

"Well, you made a good point about it being easier for him to find me if I stay put," I said, "much as it makes me impatient."

"I'll keep you informed about the situation to the east as I receive information," he said, "which I realize isn't much, but it's all I can do at the moment. It's dangerous out there right now."

"I appreciate it," I said. I really do. If the God-Empress has captured Hasskian, and is on the move again, our communication with the east will be entirely cut off. And, as I told Mattiak, I am so impatient, all the time. I throw myself into training so I'll be too exhausted to think about what might have happened to Cederic and my friends. I wonder if Terrael has come to terms with the loss of his magic. I wonder how he and Audryn are bearing up under what must be the terrible stress of her still having magic when he doesn't. I wonder if anyone's trying to fix the locator kathanas.

186

Time to meet with my spies. Mattiak sent Nessan back with me after dinner. That strange uniform he wears? It means he's a member of an elite military force, the White Squads, that are trained for infiltration and assassination. Nessan is going to put the spies through the training course his force uses. I'm afraid he might kill them by accident, but with the knowledge that the God-Empress is advancing, I think the time for coddling them is past.

CHAPTER SEVENTEEN

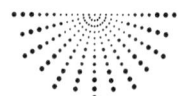

28 Nevrine, dawn

I didn't realize, when Nessan said he'd be putting the spies through the training course, that he was including me in the group. I hadn't even thought about it, hadn't really thought about what I'd be doing when it comes time for combat, because so much of my efforts have been directed toward teaching the other mages. But the truth is I'm still a better thief than I am at any of the individual pouvrin; despite my range with the fire pouvra, my skill seems to be my ability to learn pouvrin quickly and, if the binding pouvra is any indication, I might be good at creating them from th'an. None of which is as useful to the military as my ability to sneak into places where people might try to kill me.

And the course is *brutal*. Nessan believes in treating every exercise as if it's the real thing—smart, I think, at least in principle. In reality, it makes for painful training. I had to use every trick I know and the flitting pouvra to keep from being caught by his traps. The pouvra surprised him, and I think he would have called it an unfair advantage if he believed in such things. He's more suspicious and paranoid than I am, squeezes every ounce of advantage out of whatever situation he's in, and I really like him, the sneaky bastard.

My spies weren't so lucky; all of them were caught at some point, though Nessan approves of Rutika, or at least that's how I interpret his being harder on her than the others. They've all learned things, and what I'm happiest about is knowing they won't ever be caught by those traps again. Other ones, that's a different story. I'm satisfied with their ability to move quietly, though Nessan's not going to let up until they can walk across five feet of dry leaves with hardly a crackle. (I wouldn't bother doing it stealthily. I'd make it sound like I was a harmless squirrel.)

When we were done, Nessan just grunted and walked away, saying over his shoulder, "Tonight again. Don't eat so heavily, you were all moving like pigs in wallow." I think that means he doesn't completely despair of us, or he wouldn't come back. So that's something, anyway.

I'm going to have to figure out a way to get more sleep, if I'm going to be training mages all day and training spies all night.

28 Nevrine, night

Mages doing very well. I wish the army would move out, because we're getting to the point where they're going to lose their edge if they don't have some new challenges. Jeddan and I have been trying to figure something out. Asked Mattiak for suggestions, and he said maybe it was time for them to train with the regular army. Maybe not tomorrow, but the day after; tomorrow I have to get some sleep, even if it means staying behind while they all go practice.

Dinner was tense. Mattiak still fighting with King and Chamber. Says Crossar is speaking in favor of Mattiak's strategy, but Jakssar doesn't want to interfere and the other two are as scared as the King. Hasskian fell on 25 Nevrine and the God-Empress's army is on the move. I asked (obliquely) what would happen if Mattiak ordered the army to move out, and he said, "If I survived the conflict, I'd be executed for treason."

"That seems unfair, if you saved the country," I said.

"An army more loyal to its general than its King is Garran Clendessar's worst nightmare," he said. "With the control I have over the army, I could easily take the throne, and if I went against the King's express command, it would be a sign that that's exactly what I had in mind. It wouldn't matter that I have no interest in ruling Balaen. The King would have to send a message to anyone else who might think to do the same thing."

"But he's in *more* danger if we wait until the invading army is at our door," I said. "Why doesn't he see that?"

"He doesn't understand how warfare is conducted, and he is afraid," Mattiak said. "And that's all I can say on the subject, Sesskia." I knew his abruptness covered his frustration at not being able to speak freely words that would also be considered treason, so I didn't take offense, but it made everything awkward between us, and I was glad to escape early, with Nessan's grueling instruction as my excuse.

I have about twenty minutes before I have to join the others, so I'm going to talk to Jeddan for a few minutes about tomorrow's training schedule, which I won't be attending because I need to sleep eventually. I almost wish I had Cederic's ability to survive on four hours a night, though I doubt he does that when the fate of the world isn't in the balance. I hope not, anyway. I don't think I'll enjoy sleeping cold for half the night, once we're finally reunited.

30 Nevrine

Nothing happened yesterday. I slept for a while, then practiced the flitting pouvra to go to the practice field and back. It's disorienting. I can flit a few hundred yards, but then I have to pause to find a new point to aim at. Jerussa says it gets easier with practice, but for now I won't be doing any flitting into enemy territory.

Today we drilled with the army, though not for very long, all together, because the soldiers were all so fascinated with our magic they kept stopping to ask questions. I had some questions of my own for Mattiak, first of which was "why isn't everyone terrified of us?" It's starting to be common for me to have dinner with him, partly because I always report at the right time and also, I think, because Mattiak likes having someone to talk to who isn't a subordinate or interested only in military matters. The story he told me was so long, I've only just now gotten back—it's nearly nine-thirty in the evening, half an hour or so before Nessan arrives, so I'll have to sum it up:

The convergence hit Venetry hard, about as hard as Colosse was hit—physical shocks as well as the pulling everyone felt, and a lot of people thought the world was ending. Then the mages started appearing, and the manifestation of their pouvrin was taken by many to be a sign confirming the apocalypse. A few illogical people concluded if they killed the mages, the destruction would end, and others were just afraid of magic, and still others were victims of the pouvrin (don't know if those were intentional attacks or not), and that's how the slaughter began.

More than three hundred mages were killed that first day. Some mages were sheltered by their families, and others fought their way to safety outside the walls, and the killing became more indiscriminate as society fell apart. It took three days for the city guard to pacify the mob, during which time any other mages who manifested did their best to hide. There weren't any more mage killings, at any rate.

It was several days later that the reports from the north, where the Castaviran city had appeared, started to arrive. The news that the invaders also had mages threatened to send Venetry into another cataclysm of violence against anyone suspected of being a mage. The explanation for what happened next was Mattiak's supposition, because no one knew how it started, but the rumor went around Venetry that Balaen's mages had been sent by the true God to defend the country against the enemy's mages.

Mattiak thinks the rumor was started by a group of people, maybe several mages, because it spread too quickly to have started in only one place, *and* it reached King and Chamber faster than could be explained even by the speed of gossip. The King latched onto the rumor and decreed mages were to be protected, and all mages were to come to Venetry to assist in Balaen's defense.

That was when the *second* rumor started, which was that the new mages had magic that was different from what everyone had feared, good magic that couldn't harm anyone who didn't have evil in their hearts. Not as many people believed that one, but between them, and families who couldn't believe evil of their own relatives just because they were now mages, and the pragmatists in government who saw mages as a weapon, the majority of Venetrians either aren't afraid of mages or hide their fear well. And the soldiers we trained with today have seen Castaviran mages in battle, so they see us and our magic as allies.

I still think it's odd. Maybe I'm just having trouble forgetting ten years of fear and secrecy, but I think that kind of change of heart is unlikely. Or maybe the city guard is cracking down on anti-mage sentiment harder than I realize, and the people are still afraid of mages but more afraid of what the military can do under martial law. Or *maybe* I've been wrong about the level of fear of mages in the country at large. I don't know. What I do know is this doesn't change anything as far as I'm concerned; I'm still not going to flaunt my magic in the city if I can help it. The soldiers do seem genuinely unafraid of us, though, so I could be wrong.

Anyway, Mattiak set up a drill that was a lot of fun in addition to being a good new challenge. He handed out marked helmets to a bunch of soldiers, then set everyone to practicing swordplay outside the walls. Then he put our mind-movers on the wall and had them fling sponges soaked in paint at the marked targets. The idea is to learn to target specific individuals in a crowd and knock them out without hitting any of our soldiers who might be nearby.

It was almost too fun, as the soldiers ducked and ran in ways they wouldn't on the battlefield, and the mages were laughing so hard they sometimes couldn't control the sponges at all. I wish we had enough colors of paint we could assign one to each mage, to more clearly see how each individual does, but I don't think there are thirty-nine colors of paint in the world. We have enough to divide the mages into teams tomorrow. I still have reservations about treating this like a game, but Mattiak says there'll be time enough for them to realize how serious it is.

Nessan's divided the spies into two groups; he does stealth training with one while I teach the concealment pouvra to the other, then we switch. He hasn't had me go through the full course since the first time, which I hope means he doesn't think I need it. He *has* had me demonstrate a few techniques, like memorizing the contents of a room to be recalled later, and doing that made me realize how much better my memory has gotten since I started writing all those conversations I had with Terrael and Audryn and Cederic and the others. Though I still think a memory pouvra would be useful.

Time to join Nessan. I think Relania is close to mastering the concealment pouvra; she's got the mental flexibility I think all the "old" mages have, or at least that Jeddan and I have as well. Rutika's not as close, but she's coming along so quickly in Nessan's training it almost doesn't matter. I wonder if I should give them all a talk about not using their new skills to steal things, but it's possible I'd just be giving them ideas.

31 Nevrine

I met with King and Chamber this morning in what I think of as the audience room, the room Jeddan and I saw them in first. This time, I was escorted by a pair of armed soldiers, which would have reminded me uncomfortably of being taken to see the God-Empress all those times if I hadn't known both of them from our drills. So we made conversation the whole way there, quietly so no one would think they were being unprofessional, and they handed me off to the guards outside the audience room with unsmiling faces.

After a few minutes of mutual silence, the guards outside the door escorted me into the room and all the way to the black rug. One of them had whispered, before we entered, "Go to the center of the rug and face the King. If you're addressed by someone else, turn and bow your head briefly before answering. Don't forget to address them as Honored." I'm grateful for that guard. In fact, all the ones I've met, even Nessan, have been polite and respectful, and I don't think it's because they believe I can kill them with a thought. I'm sure there are venal and corrupt soldiers in the army and the city guard, I just haven't met them, thank the true God.

I did as I was instructed and went to face the King. He didn't have the slightly vacuous smile I'd always seen him wear. Today he looked tense and restless, with his leg crossed over his knee and his fingers thrumming on the arm of his chair. "Sesskia," he said, "are the mages prepared to fight?"

I was about to give him an honest answer—they're never going to be *fully* prepared, there's a lot they can still learn—but realized in time he wanted reassurance, not facts. "They're ready, Honored," I said.

"As I assured you, your Majesty," Crossar said, sounding faintly exasperated, nothing the King could take offense at, but still a clear statement of disapproval.

"They're a slender thread to hang a strategy on," Batekessar said. He was more querulous than usual. Even Crossar, beneath his exasperation, had sounded on edge.

"You've opposed that strategy from the start," Jakssar said. "Reactionary measures aren't going to defeat this enemy."

"Don't you call me a reactionary, woman," Batekessar said. "Not placing our fates in the hands of magickers who'll turn on us when it suits them is a sound strategy. Balaen's survived worse than this without the help of magic." He said "magic" like he might have said "filth."

"This is much worse," Crossar said, now audibly exasperated. "Their mages are powerful and experienced. We need magic to counter magic."

"How well do you think our mages will stand up to the invaders' magic?" Lenssar said, sounding almost as querulous as Batekessar. "They've been training less than a month. They'll be destroyed, and we'll be where we started. Might as well not bother."

"Sesskia, you've seen the enemy's mages fight," Crossar said. "What is your assessment?"

I turned, bowed slightly, and said, "Honored, the Chamber Lord of Commerce is correct that our mages are inexperienced. However, they have advantages over the enemy mages. One is that our pouvrin can be worked anywhere, without the need for the boards our enemies use, which means we are as fast or faster at responding to attacks. Another is that we know pouvrin they don't, that they can't defend against easily. And we've been training to act in concert, something the enemy mages don't do. Most importantly, they believe we don't have *any* mages, and will be unprepared for our attack."

"You see?" Crossar said. "We will be able to stop the invading army, but we need to strike soon, to prevent them ever reaching Venetry at all. It is time to send the troops out."

"I agree with Crossar," Jakssar said. "If we wait for them to reach the city, who knows what kind of advantage they'll gain?"

The King said nothing. I didn't dare turn to look at him. Finally, he said, "Sesskia, what is your opinion?"

I turned to face him and tried not to show how alarmed I was at his question. "Honored, I'm not qualified to speak on military strategy," I said. "You should ask General Tarallan."

"Tarallan has his own motives," the King said darkly, which made me afraid for Mattiak. "I want to know what *you* think."

I swallowed to moisten my suddenly dry mouth. "I think taking the fight to the G—the enemy is a good idea, Honored," I said. "Like Lady Jakssar says, they could gain advantage if we give them time to advance. And it might also give them time to learn of our mages' existence."

The King was expressionless now, and I feared I'd said something offensive that might earn me death. But he said, "The army goes. The mages stay here."

"Your Majesty!" Crossar said, and I almost joined him in that expostulation. "The mages have been training to enter battle! This will cost the army its greatest advantage!"

"We can't leave Venetry completely unguarded," the King said, still expressionless, but with that whine in his voice that made me itch to slap him.

"Then we will leave a detachment of the army here," Crossar said.

"Not good enough," the King said.

"Honored, excuse me for speaking out of turn, but could you not do both?" I exclaimed. "Keep some soldiers and some of the mages here for the city's defense. Then the army will have that advantage, and you—I mean the city will be protected."

"I make the decisions, Sesskia, and if you speak out of turn again I'll have you imprisoned," the King said, and I almost went insubstantial right there to remind him he didn't have the power to keep me locked up. In the next second I realized I might need that advantage, so I kept quiet.

"It's a good idea, your Majesty," Jakssar said. "With the mage auxiliaries, the army might be able to stop the invaders before they reach Venetry at all. And if they don't, we have defenses in place."

The King looked past me, I think at Crossar, then back at me. "Very well," he said. "Sesskia, choose half your mages to remain here. The best mages, you understand."

Crossar made a choking sound. I said, "Of course, your Majesty," wishing I dared slap him. I think he'd be the better for regular slappings.

I bowed to each person there, then left the manor and flitted to where everyone was practicing to talk to Jeddan. Then we cancelled practice and gathered everyone in the ballroom to explain what was happening. They knew how long the army had been waiting to march out, so they were all relieved it was finally happening, but when I got to the part about half of them staying behind, there was an uproar.

I let it go on for a minute or two—let them relieve their feelings— then said, "This is going to be hard, I know, but you need to remember the point is the defense of Balaen, and it doesn't matter where you personally make that defense. Those of you who are staying behind have what I think is the more difficult task, because you have to stay ready to fight at all times, and that's wearying and dangerous. You risk losing your edge. And those of you who are going will face bloodshed and possibly death. But I believe every one of you is ready for those challenges. So Jeddan and I are going to discuss it, and we'll tell you our decision in the morning. The rest of the day is yours."

The discussion about who to take and who to leave was intense, especially when we realized Jeddan was going to have to stay in Venetry to command those mages. He was not happy about that, but we both knew my extra pouvrin might become necessary, and there was a chance I'd have to sneak into the God-Empress's camp again— the spies are coming along more quickly than I'd anticipated, but they're still amateurs. *I'm* not happy about it. I trust Jeddan with my life, and throughout all this we haven't been separated, so it feels strange to know he won't be there when the fight begins. So I'm even more furious with the King than I was this morning.

The rest of the discussion was just as difficult, because neither of us knew what criteria we should use for dividing our forces. Jeddan didn't want me to take both Saemon and Hasseka, which might leave the defenders underpowered as far as the mind-moving pouvra went, but I argued if the God-Empress's mages were as experienced at the mind-moving th'an as Cederic's abilities suggested, having that extra edge was worth the risk.

I showed Mattiak our decision at dinner and he suggested a few changes, but otherwise approved. He also wasn't angry about the King's decree, saying he was just glad the army was finally moving and at least would have *some* mages. "And you'll be coming along, which relieves my mind," he said with a smile. "I'd miss our conversations, and I think the mages need someone they trust to give them orders."

"They trust you," I said.

"They hardly know me," he said. "You're the one they look to. You're a natural leader."

I felt horribly uncomfortable. "I don't think so," I said.

"You only feel that way because staying in the shadows has kept you alive all these years," he said. "You have a knack for getting people to listen to you and you can back that up with experience and talent. Use it. Don't be afraid of it."

I remembered threatening Norsselen and enjoying it. "I think it's a dangerous ability," I said.

Mattiak shrugged. "That's up to you," he said. "Now, let's talk about something else." And he turned the conversation to the latest news from the east, which distracted me enough that I could finish eating. But I'm still thinking about what he said.

I don't know if I'm a natural leader—I think he's wrong. Even so, he's right that the mages look to me, and I don't feel awkward about that. Afraid, sometimes, that I'll make the wrong decision—more afraid now that the wrong decision could get people killed—and worried I'll use intimidation to achieve results that could be better reached through other means, but the idea of me leading people doesn't seem so unlikely anymore. It's unexpected, and unnerving, because this is nothing like who I was before. And yet I can't say it isn't me.

Enough introspection. I'm going to ask Nessan what he thinks we should do about the spies. Leaving any of them behind is pointless, because there won't be an enemy to practice their skills on, unlike the others who can drill with the soldiers, but if I take them, I have to leave several of my warrior mages—ooh, I like that phrase, I think I'll start calling them that—behind, which could weaken our attacks. He'll have a better idea than I do of how necessary their skills will be to Balaen's army.

CHAPTER EIGHTEEN

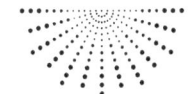

1 Seresstine

A new start to a new month. I'd like to think it's auspicious, but the King came to Fianna Manor first thing this morning, and he's not an early riser so I was afraid he was going to tell everyone he'd changed his mind. But no, he wanted to see the mages who were staying behind perform their pouvrin and prove I'd chosen the best for ~~his~~ the city's defense. Since he has no way of knowing what "the best" would look like, it didn't matter how good they were, but the truth is Jeddan and I divided the mages so each group had a balance of more- and less-experienced mages.

So the King watched the performance, and then he wanted to know why they didn't have uniforms. He wanted them to wear special armor and surcoats with a distinctive emblem. We explained this was so they wouldn't stand out for the enemy to target, at which point he got this petulant look on his face and said, "We're not ashamed to use magic in this fight, Sesskia."

"No, Honored, but the whole point of this strategy is to protect the mages," I said.

"Soldiers wear uniforms. The mages are soldiers. I want everyone to know they're unique," the King said. "I've had uniforms designed for them and they will wear them."

"All right, Honored," I said. It's too bad you can't beat sense into royalty. I feel sorry for the King, as much as I can when I don't have any idea what it's like to rule a kingdom. Probably his fears are grounded in fact. But he doesn't seem to trust his advisors, which tells me he's alone, and that makes it hard to make good decisions. I wonder if he knows how everyone around him feels that he hasn't ever married, or had children, or named an heir. Well, he's the King, and the truth is despite my feelings about him, I'll still fight to protect him and Balaen.

We didn't get far today, but Mattiak says he didn't expect us to. It takes time to get an army moving, and striking camp took longer than usual because it had become semi-permanent and therefore had things that had to be packed up and left behind. That gave Jeddan and me time to shop for some more suitable clothes than the fine garb the King had presented us with. Even though Jeddan wasn't leaving with the army, he was just as tired as I was of looking like some palace functionary's idea of a mage, especially the silk shirts; they're pretty and soft, but easily damaged, and Jeddan's was scorched from where a mage's fire whip had gotten out of control.

I'm not sure where the money came from, but since it's ultimately from the kingdom's treasury, I had no trouble accepting it. I bought nice, well-made shirts and trousers with big pockets that were completely nondescript, as well as a gray wool coat with a hood lined with the fur of some animal even Jeddan couldn't identify, and managed to pack it all up so I could carry it with me easily if it turned out I needed to run away. We said our goodbyes at the store so we didn't have to do it with all those mages watching. I'm really going to miss him.

I didn't realize how much like a small town an army camp is. Balaen may not have women soldiers, but there are women who follow the army, even a few wives, and they're all as accustomed to the life as the men are. They have their own society and didn't look as if they welcomed us, not because they're afraid of mages (which many of them are, surprisingly) but because we're of such different classes as far as the army is concerned. Not that we were looking to fraternize. The soldiers were willing to train with us, but now we're on the road it's clear they consider us somewhere between the non-commissioned officers and Mattiak's general staff, and therefore off limits.

(This doesn't stop some of the soldiers leering at our women, which is hard because I've told everyone not to use magic against our own men unless defending themselves against physical threat. I don't want soldiers to start thinking of mages as evil or dangerous again.)

We have tents near the center of camp, and (to my surprise) servants to care for our belongings and make our meals. I told Mattiak we didn't need to be waited on, and he said, "You're expected to focus your efforts on being ready to fight, and that means not wasting time cooking or cleaning up. Just tell the mages not to take advantage of the service. These are soldiers, and they see this as contributing to the cause—don't insult them."

I have my own tent, which feels strange since the last tent I slept in was a two-man shelter little more than canvas draped over a couple of poles, and I was sharing it with Jeddan. It doesn't have much more than a bed and a folding table and camp stool, where I'm writing this before lights-out.

I wish we had some way to communicate. The Castaviran mages do, or did, so I'm sure we could too if we had time and space to figure it out. I don't like not knowing what's happening back in Venetry. And I'm used to being able to go over the day's events with Jeddan. I can talk to Mattiak, and do, but it's not the same because he doesn't understand magic, just as I'm sure he feels I'm not the best conversational partner when it comes to warfare. These days we mostly talk about other things, like our childhoods—his childhood—and my travels.

I wish I hadn't lost those other books. I feel as if I kept my memory in them, as if by writing them down I've made it impossible to call those events to mind. I wonder if I will ever find them again. Do locator kathanas work on objects, or just people? Cederic might be able to help me find them, unless they were destroyed in the convergence; the Arabel Mountains did more or less appear on top of that barn where I left them.

Having Cederic here would make things so much better, if only because if he were here, the war would be over. I can't imagine even Mattiak being open-minded enough to let the most powerful mage of Castavir roam freely through a Balaenic military camp if we were still enemies. If I miss having Jeddan to talk to, I can't express what I feel at not being able to tell Cederic everything that's happening, or get his opinion on training the mages or creating new pouvrin.

I try not to talk about him much to Mattiak, because I don't want to bore him, but sometimes Mattiak brings him up, I think to try to cheer me even though we still don't have word from the east. He assures me as soon as things are more settled, he'll send messengers specifically to hunt for Cederic. It's a sweet gesture, and I feel bad about not being able to tell him why they aren't likely to do much good. I don't know what he'd think if he knew my husband is a Castaviran mage. Still, he's a good friend, and it makes me feel warm inside to know he cares.

I wonder why Mattiak isn't married. Maybe he thinks he has too many responsibilities in the army to be a good, attentive husband. I don't think he's attracted to men, and he doesn't have a woman in the camp, but whatever his reason, it's a mystery I won't pry into.

Time to put the light out. Tomorrow the army separates into divisions, I don't know why and it doesn't matter to me, because the mages stay with the main army instead of being dispersed. We ride in wagons because walking all day would exhaust us, and only a handful of us can ride horses. I don't think I've said that a couple of our mages are upper class, though not noble, and they've been as quick to follow orders as anyone, but they did bring their own horses and like to tease those of us being carried.

I suggested maybe I should learn to ride, that it might be more dignified since I'm the leader of my own "division" and all the division commanders ride, but Mattiak said riding for seven hours every day is not the best way to begin. So I sit in the wagon and we practice pouvrin, or I work on flitting to improve my recovery time between flits.

It really is the most amazing feeling. It's like the walk-through-walls pouvra, except there's no uncomfortable sensation of bones and muscles sliding through matter, more like becoming air shifting through air. I think I'll start teaching it to the other mages; Jerussa stayed behind, and she's teaching Jeddan. I don't think the Castavirans can do it any more than they can become immaterial, which means it's one more weapon we

I can't believe I thought that. I'm turning my pouvrin against the God-Empress's army, yes, but this is the first time I've thought of a pouvra as a weapon first and magic second. I wish this war were over already. I want to get back to studying magic for its own sake instead of figuring out how I can use it to kill.

1, possibly 2, Seresstine, very early

Nessan woke me an hour ago and said, "Time for practice." He's far more diligent than I am, but he's right, we need to practice. He took three mages elsewhere in the camp while I worked with Tobiak, who still hasn't mastered the concealment pouvra.

Nessan told me, when we were dividing our mage army, to leave half the spies behind, then he told me which ones were coming. I didn't argue with him, even though I'm concerned about Tobiak's skills in general and not just his lack of the concealment pouvra, because Nessan has many years' experience in training intelligence officers and his instincts are excellent.

So I have Rutika, Relania, Tobiak, and Alessabeka, and I have no idea what use Nessan will make of us. I don't even know what he had the others do. But Tobiak is almost there, and I think if we work on it tomorrow he'll be able to work the concealment pouvra by nightfall —just in time for Nessan to drag him (and possibly me) off to some training exercise. I'm almost looking forward to it.

2 Seresstine, very late (or very early)

Nessan's idea of a training exercise is to put objects into sleeping soldiers' tents without disturbing them and without being insubstantial except during the time it takes to enter and leave through the wall. This strikes me as dangerous, considering four of the five of us are women, and a soldier roused unexpectedly from sleep might assume the worst (or, from his perspective, the best) of intentions from a woman sneaking into his tent at night. Nessan said that was the point. I think if he could find a way to make these exercises life-threatening, he would.

When I asked him if there was a purpose to this (I made it sound less accusatory than I did just there) he said, "I won't know until we see the enemy what use to make of you. So we're going to behave as if you might face anything. Tomorrow they'll be stealing things and then putting them back. And I'll have a special challenge for *you*, since I doubt you need any practice stealing things."

He grinned as he said that. He has very white teeth that shine in the moonlight, so he looks like he's nothing but a canine smile. It's eerie. I don't know what about my performance during these exercises told him I'm a thief, but it's comforting to have his professional respect, one sneak to another.

Nobody got caught, though Relania came close because she came through the wall into someone's cot and panicked at passing through flesh. *I* panicked a little when she told us about it, remembering Jeddan's experience, but nobody died, and we all went to bed tired but triumphant. I wonder what Nessan's got in mind for me.

3 Seresstine

I have no idea if we're making good progress or not. We also don't know where the God-Empress's army went after leaving Hasskian. Our scouts say it looks like she turned east, which fills me with dread; suppose she decided to go to Colosse instead of Venetry? It's already chaos out there, and her army might be able to plow through the countryside and take Colosse unawares. If we have to chase her eastward...I don't know what that would mean, strategy-wise, but assuming Aselfos managed to solidify his claim to the throne of Castavir and controls the army, I can't imagine he'd be happy to see the Balaenic army thundering down on Colosse behind the God-Empress. He might even think we're her allies.

It's been snowing all day and everyone is miserable. You'd think riding in a wagon would at least be better than walking, but we all get cold because we're not moving, and the wagon has no roof. Paddrek had the idea of spreading a thin layer of fire to cover our heads, melting the snow before it reaches us, and we've been taking turns maintaining it, but it creates this fine mist so we're all damp *and* cold. Better than being soaked by snow melting on our hats and coats.

Mattiak talked enthusiastically about strategy at dinner tonight, and I nodded and tried to keep up with him. Eventually he figured out I wasn't fully committed to the conversation, laughed self-consciously, and said, "Sorry. I sometimes get carried away."

"I don't mind," I said. "I understand something of the individual units' roles, I just don't see how it all fits together."

"You have other skills," Mattiak said, "and what matters is that you understand how the mages' pouvrin can be used in this fight."

"I don't know how I feel about that," I said, and told him what I'd been thinking about the flitting pouvra (which is hard to use in a snowstorm) and magic as a weapon, and how uneasy it made me. "I see the necessity, because the invaders want us dead, but I don't like it," I concluded.

"Nobody sane seeks out war as the first option," Mattiak said. "I hope I don't seem callous in my enthusiasm for planning strategy. Sometimes we lose track of the fact that these marks on the map represent men, and the strategy is meant to kill them. But I've seen too many soldiers fall to ever completely forget the purpose of war is achieved through death." He took my hand and squeezed it briefly. "I don't think you're a killer, Sesskia."

That reminded me of the bandit mage, and I couldn't help shuddering. "I hope you're right," I said, but now I'm back in my tent I can't help wondering if assassinating the God-Empress might be the best use of my talents. I could get close enough, though I might not be able to get back out—so would I be willing to sacrifice my life and my soul to end this conflict?

I can't. I just can't. I know what I wrote earlier, about if I had to use those pouvrin to protect the people I love, I'd do it, but I just can't. I'm weak and selfish and I've been trying to comfort myself by saying the God-Empress has generals who won't abandon their course of action just because she's dead. If Aselfos was interested in becoming Emperor, I can't imagine there aren't more high-ranking officials who've thought the same thing. So killing her wouldn't solve anything.

I'm going to lie down and try to calm myself while waiting for Nessan to come. A good challenge is exactly what I need right now.

4 Seresstine

I'd meant to write about Nessan's exercise when I finished it, but it was nearly dawn when I did and I barely got back without being spotted. I met him well after midnight, and we ran the perimeter of the camp, dodging our sentries a little too easily—Nessan was annoyed about it, and when we were finished, he said, "I'm going to do something about that. Here." He handed me a knobby sack and said, "You have three hours to put these back in the exact places where they belong. Same rules as before—insubstantial only to walk in and out of things, bonus points if you don't use the pouvra at all. If you're seen, you fail."

"What's the penalty if I fail?" I said.

"I mock you for the rest of the week," Nessan said. "Your three hours started one minute ago. Move."

The sack contained five objects I'd noticed many times before around the camp and one I couldn't remember seeing before. I considered not using the walk-through-walls pouvra just to show off, but realized as I was about to return my first item (General Drussik's pipe with the enormous carved bowl) I should use every advantage I had, and the extra challenge was one of Nessan's tricks to distract me from my goal. I set the pipe on Drussik's table and was off with the second item.

It took me about half my allotted time to place the five objects I recognized. Then I had to find a hiding place so I could examine the sixth. It was a pocket watch on a silver chain, complete with fob that wasn't much more than a lump of silver; expensive materials, not very good workmanship. I examined it more closely. No, it was made to look plain, but a lot of effort had gone into achieving that effect. There were no initials on the case or inside it, no engraved sentiment. The owner had had it for a long time, judging by the fine scratches on the case that indicated ordinary wear over the years. I opened it and looked at the innards again. Very old work. No, this was a family heirloom.

It *was* familiar, and Nessan wouldn't have given me anything I hadn't seen before, though his definition of "seen before" might encompass a wide range of observations. I thought about what I could surmise about the owner. Male. Someone who had enough wealth to use this daily as opposed to keeping it safely out of harm's way, as a poorer man would. Someone not interested in drawing attention to that wealth. This was narrowing down the possibilities quickly. Probably not noble, because almost all noblemen marked their jewelry with their names or personal sigils as an anti-theft measure. Hahahaha.

That left me with about seven members of the general staff, plus Colonel Ivalys, but he and two of those staffers were off with other Army regiments. Five men, all of whom I'd seen regularly since we started training with the army, none of whom wore pocket watches. So which of those men would bring along a valuable watch and then not wear it?

It took me ten minutes to reach Mattiak's tent and then stop in dismay, because a tiny light was burning inside. Sneaking past him would be almost impossible; he was observant enough that he'd seen through the concealment pouvra, something even Cederic had trouble doing. And he was awake. And I wasn't sure where he normally kept his watch. I checked that watch and discovered I had less than an hour before I'd have to endure Nessan's taunts for the rest of the week. Then I concealed myself again and went as quietly as I could over the snow to the side of Mattiak's tent, and peeked inside.

Mattiak was seated at his table with his sleeves rolled up, writing something in a book. I think it might have been a personal record, like this one, and I was seized with a tremendous desire to read it.

Then I was ashamed. I would hate it if he read this book, so was it fair to read his private thoughts?

I set the desire well to one side and surveyed the room. He has a bed and table and chair that aren't more ornate than mine, so either he's a humble man or our furnishings reflect the highest standard of living the army can provide. There's a trunk at the foot of the bed and a totally incongruous skinny coatrack next to it that holds his uniform jacket. The light came from a small lantern that swung above his head.

As I watched, he laid the pen down, stretched, and began unbuttoning his shirt. I withdrew quickly and moved around to the front of the tent, near the trunk, and waited for the light to go out. Then I waited some more, hoping he was quick to fall asleep. I had half an hour left when I finally poked my head back into the tent, then dropped to my knees and crawled, so slowly, toward the trunk.

Mattiak doesn't snore, but I can tell the difference between someone who's actually sleeping and someone who's faking it, so I kept crawling until I was right next to the trunk, where I stopped to take a few deep breaths. I worked the see-through pouvra and took a look at its contents. A note read BRING THIS BACK WHEN YOU'RE DONE.

It amused me so much I let out an incautious snort, and Mattiak stirred in his sleep, rolled over, and then sat up. I sat perfectly still as he looked around, then went to light the lamp and looked around again. I was running out of time. With the pocket watch in my left hand, I carefully slid my arm inside the trunk, not looking at Mattiak—I've written before I think if I meet someone's eyes, the pouvra won't be able to conceal me against them. So I had no idea whether Mattiak had seen me or not, except if he had, he probably would have grabbed me.

Insubstantial, I couldn't burrow between Mattiak's neatly folded clothes to hide the watch, so the best I could do was open my hand and let the watch fall out of it, becoming substantial as it did. Whatever noise it made was muffled by the wood of the trunk and the clothing inside, and I carefully turned Nessan's note insubstantial so it wouldn't rustle and withdrew, a little too rapidly because I was starting to feel lightheaded.

Mattiak moved then, walking toward the tent flap, and I could only kneel there and pray he wouldn't try to open the trunk, because he'd walk right into me. But he just stood there, so I quietly shifted toward the wall—and he spun and reached to grab me as I threw myself backward.

I scrambled to my feet and sidled along the edge of the tent where the snow hadn't fallen so I wouldn't leave footprints for him to follow. Seconds later he burst out of the tent and rounded the corner, scanning the ground for those footprints I wasn't leaving, but I'd already reached the far end and was bolting through the camp back to where Nessan waited. I slapped the note into his hand with three minutes to spare.

"You weren't spotted?" he said.

"Almost," I said, "but what matters is I wasn't caught."

"You plan to tell the General it was you in his tent?" he said.

"I plan to make him believe it was his imagination," I said. "I take it the spies are all safely asleep in their tents?"

"With plenty of witnesses to say they were there all night," he said. "Nice work."

"You don't even know I put everything back correctly," I said.

"Don't have to," he said. "If you'd failed, you'd have told me." He started to walk away, then stopped. "Could you kill a man in cold blood?" he asked.

"I don't know," I said.

"Think about it," he said. "You may have to."

It felt as if he knew my secret ability, even though I know he doesn't, no one does except Jeddan. I think Nessan isn't training me to be a spy. I think he's training me to be like him, and I'm certain Nessan wouldn't think twice about assassinating someone. I feel even more of a stranger to myself than ever.

I couldn't convince Mattiak it was his imagination, because he said, "My watch was missing, and now it's back. Did you decide you couldn't sell it easily, all the way out here?" He was smiling so I'd know it was a joke.

"Why would I steal from you?" I said, with calculated innocence.

"I'm sure you'd have some reason," he said. "And *someone* was in my tent last night, I'd swear to it. Is that a habit your husband knows about?"

"What, sneaking into men's tents? Which I would never do," I said.

"I hope not," he said. "You might give someone the wrong impression."

That flustered me, and I had to change the subject, which he let me do with a look that said he knew I was doing it on purpose. I hope Mattiak doesn't think I'm the kind of woman who'd go looking for male companionship simply because she was missing her husband. Damn Nessan and his training exercises.

It was, in fact, a very long day of travel. By dinner time, Mattiak seemed to have forgotten last night's incident and we talked as usual about our progress and where the invading army was. One of the army's divisions has headed almost directly east and we're getting messengers back, reporting on forests that weren't there before and a lake they had to skirt, but no sign of an army passing. We're continuing south tomorrow.

CHAPTER NINETEEN

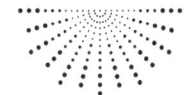

5 Seresstine

We're camped near the destroyed crossroads where the Royal Road intersects with that Castaviran highway, and you can feel the excitement, because we picked up the God-Empress's trail. It's excitement tempered with anger, though, because the news came from men who escaped the slaughter near Binna, and Mattiak looked grim when he found out about it.

I wasn't there when the soldiers arrived, but Mattiak sent for me to come to the command tent before he let the soldiers tell more of their story than the basics: their division, the one that went east, encountered part of the God-Empress's army, there was a vicious battle, and our division was routed, though not without inflicting terrible casualties. The soldier who repeated all this for me looked terrible. His head and left leg were bloody, and he and his two companions were filthy and exhausted. All three of them were sitting on camp stools looking like men who'd been defeated, which they had been, but it was more than that—they looked completely demoralized.

"Start at the beginning now, Corporal," Mattiak said. "When did you first see the enemy, and where?"

"We'd just passed Binna—Major only stopped long enough to talk to the elders and see if they'd seen anything of the invading army. Which they hadn't," the corporal said. "Then our outriders found theirs. They ran, and we followed, came over a rise and saw them. The invading army."

"So they were headed west when you encountered them?" said Mattiak.

The corporal nodded. "Captain said we were in a good position and we outnumbered them, and our company was going to move around to the north to attack their flank, try to circle them." He coughed, hard, looked like he wanted to spit but swallowed instead.

"Our front line crashed into theirs—they don't fight like we do, got strange swords and knives 'stead of fighting with sword and shield, no rifles—but we were doing all right. And then..." He shuddered. "That was when the fire started. Lots of big fires, actually, all over the place, but mostly in a line that cut our front lines off from the rear. Then the officers' horses started screaming and rearing up like they was being stung all over by horseflies the size of a man's head. Lot of officers fell. Some of 'em were crushed underfoot. Signalman sounded the advance for us, and I swear, General, we didn't back down."

"I believe you," Mattiak said. "Go on."

He coughed again, and I reached around for a flask of water and gave it to him. He was so miserable he didn't even react to my having used the mind-moving pouvra to do it. He swallowed, passed the flask to his comrade, and said, "We cut into their flank pretty deep. They're fierce fighters, but they depend on that knife to do the killing while the sword keeps the other man busy, and they didn't know what to do with our shields. So we were thinking their evil magic wasn't enough to save them...

"I heard Captain shout something that was cut off in the middle, and I looked up because he was right near and saw his face was gray and he had his hand to his throat, like he couldn't breathe. Then he fell. And more of our officers fell. Then a man next to me...I couldn't do anything for him. We were still fighting, but now they had the advantage, and there wasn't anyone to tell us what to do. It was down to my sergeant, and he told us to fall back toward the main army just before he went down too."

"Did you see what happened to the rest of the army?" General Kalanik said.

The soldier shook his head. "Not until they were running too. We didn't know what else to do. Can't fight magic. The fire, and the choking, and big rocks flying through the air to sweep a line of men and smash them to bloody pulp. We couldn't do anything else." He was pleading, and I wondered if he was afraid he'd be in trouble for escaping what sounded like an impossible situation. But Mattiak didn't look like he was in a mood to blame anyone but the Castavirans.

"You did right, Corporal," he said. "No sense all of you getting killed and leaving no one to pass the word. Thank you all for your service. Go see the camp surgeon now."

The three men saluted (the Balaenic salute is two fingers to the forehead and a bow at the waist, deeper the higher the rank of the man you're saluting) and left the tent. Mattiak sighed and said, "That's not the way I hoped to find our enemy."

"They're headed this way, sounds like," General Drussik said. He waved his pipe around, gesturing the way he did when he was feeling some strong emotion. "But where's the rest of their army?"

"Could be that division was coming here to slow us down while the main army rips eastward through Balaen," General Kalanik said.

"But there's nothing there," General Bronnok said, sounding frustrated. "Garwin's much farther south and Barrekel is four weeks east across nothing but plains. And they'd have to cross the Myrnala."

"What if they're going to one of their own cities?" I said, unable to be more specific, but thinking *If they overrun Colosse* and then being unable to finish that thought.

That made them all look thoughtful. "Could be anything there," Kalanik said. "And we haven't gotten news from the heartland for six weeks. If they've got more troops out there...."

Mattiak stood to pace. "We have to pursue," he said. "If they have more forces out east, we might not be able to defeat their combined army. We have to catch them before they get too far."

"We need more information," Drussik said. "We might be running into a trap."

"We can't afford to wait that long," Kalanik said.

"I can find out," I said.

All four of them looked at me. Drussik looked annoyed. He's about eight hundred years old and is suspicious of me because I'm both female and a mage. Kalanik and Bronnok, both reluctant supporters of the mage auxiliaries, looked skeptical. And Mattiak frowned at me. "Sneaking is one thing," he said, "but we need someone who can move quickly."

I shrugged, and flitted from one side of the tent to the other. "Is that quick enough for you?" I said.

Everyone but Mattiak recoiled when I did it. Mattiak's frown deepened. "Gentlemen," he said, "leave us." They glanced at each other, then at me, and filed out. "Sit," he told me. I sat.

He sat down opposite me. "You can't go farther than you can see," he said. It wasn't a question. I nodded, wondering where he was going with this. "You get disoriented when you...I don't know what you call it. Arrive. Yes?"

"True," I said, "but—"

"We don't know how far ahead the invaders are," he added. "So we don't know how long it will take."

"I'm still going to be faster than any of your runners," I said.

He put his hands on his knees and gripped hard, like he was trying to keep himself from standing and pacing again. "So, to sum up," he said, "you can't go straight there, you're defenseless at the end of each of these leaps, you don't know where you're going, and you don't know how long it will take."

"That sounds right," I said.

He shook his head. "I can't allow you to risk yourself like that," he said.

"I'm a soldier, aren't I?" I said.

"You are *not* a soldier, and I don't give a damn what the King thinks about it," he shouted, startling me. "Who else is going to direct those mages if you don't come back? You think those invaders are going to be gentle with you if they catch you? This is not a risk worth taking!"

"So we should wait to see if we run into them the way that division did, unprepared?" I said. I managed not to shout at him in return. "Or send a runner who might be captured and killed because he can't escape the way I can? We're not—"

"Out of the question," Mattiak said. "You want to be a soldier? I'm making that an order."

"I misspoke," I said, still remaining, if not calm, at least outwardly so. "I'm not a soldier. I'm a spy. And this is what spies do."

"Not you," Mattiak said. "You—" He stood and turned away. "You're not replaceable," he said.

"Elleria and Ryenn are both capable of directing the mages, and Rutika is almost as good a spy as I am," I said. "I'd be a poor general if I were actually irreplaceable."

He shook his head, but said nothing. I went on, "This isn't as dangerous as you think, Mattiak. I haven't told you even a third of the things I've done over the years that were more dangerous than this. Mostly because you might think you should hand me over to the authorities." I smiled so he'd know I was joking, but that was wasted because he still had his back to me. "I'll be careful. Remember, I can't flit farther than I can see, and I'm sure I'll see the enemy long before I get that close. Then I'll come back. I won't go into the camp or anything like that."

"I wonder if you'll be able to help yourself," Mattiak said.

"Of course I will. As if I'd risk myself like that when the point is to tell you where the army is," I said.

His shoulders slumped, then he turned around to face me. "I hope I never meet your husband," he said. "There's no telling what he might say to me for letting you do this."

I remembered all the times Cederic had told me not to go wandering, but with that look on his face that said he knew I couldn't help myself. *My instinct is to protect you, but that instinct is wrong. You would not be who you are if you were not willing to risk yourself,* he'd said, and the memory made me smile, because everything he felt for me had been in his eyes at that moment. "He knew what I am when he married me," I said, "though he'd sympathize with you having to deal with my recalcitrance."

"I know exactly how your husband feels about you," he said, turning around to smile ruefully at me. "You go, you come back, and if you spend one more second than you have to in the field, I'll devise a whole new set of punishments just for recalcitrant mages."

"Yes, sir," I said, saluting him. "I'll need to explain what's happening to the mages, and then I can leave immediately."

"In the morning," Mattiak said. "You might be able to see in the dark, but not as well as you can see in the daytime, and I don't want you missing any evidence if they've turned well aside from where our men met them. And you should be rested. I'll speak to those soldiers again and see if I can get you at least an initial direction." He took my arm as I was about to leave the tent. "Be careful," he said, and he looked so serious it made me shiver. I nodded.

So I've had time to pack some essentials, food and water and a blanket in case this takes longer than a day, and I'm doing what I always do to calm myself, which is write. I'm more excited than afraid. ~~I'm sure I can keep away from~~ I'm not going to write that. Too superstitious. Let's just say I feel confident in my abilities, and I'm going to be careful, just as I promised Mattiak.

Though I feel...it's probably nothing, but—the way Mattiak looked at me suggested he was concerned about me as something more than a friend. But he wouldn't, would he? He knows I'm in love with my husband—I talk more about Cederic with him than anyone else, and he even encourages it, so would he do that if he had a romantic interest in me? I suppose attraction doesn't care if the object of your interest isn't interested in you, but why would he...

No, I'm being stupid. He's far too old for me, and he's not the sort of person who would let himself fall in love with someone who's unavailable. And he certainly wouldn't use a friendship to build that kind of connection when there's no chance of it going anywhere.

Besides, I'm really bad at picking up on those kind of cues, so I'm almost certainly mistaken. There was a night—the last night before the convergence—where Cederic and I lay in his bed and made each other laugh at how we'd misunderstood each other so often. I'd told him how I'd thought of him as Smug Git before I could understand his language, and he'd said every time he'd come to my room in the palace to say goodnight, he'd thought about sweeping me into his arms and kissing me and couldn't believe I had no idea how he felt. I teased him about being as blank-faced and unemotional as a statue, and he started tickling me, then kissing me, and that led to more interesting activities no statue ever dreamed of doing.

I have this fantasy—well, lots of fantasies—but this one is that I'll flit all the way to the army, and it won't be the God-Empress's, it will be the army from Colosse, with Cederic at its head, and we'll be able to clear up all the misunderstanding and bring peace to two countries so we can go off and live our lives somewhere far away from anything remotely political. I'd settle for just finding Cederic again.

6 Seresstine

I feel so stupid. And I don't know what to do. So I'm going to write this all out and hope by the time I get to the end, I'll have figured everything out. Unlikely, but with war bearing down on us, I'm trying to remain optimistic.

Just after dawn this morning, I took my first bearing, then flitted off before Mattiak could change his mind. I can now go about three miles at a time, and despite what Mattiak thought, I only experience about two seconds of disorientation between flits and it takes another second to take my next heading. I know that doesn't sound like much time, but a lot can happen in three seconds, and I had no intention of flitting into the middle of a division of Castaviran soldiers. I wish I'd been able to take the Castaviran highway, but the God-Empress's forces, the one our people had run into, had been ten or fifteen miles north of it, so that's where I went.

I managed to go about fifty miles before I ran into a forest that wasn't there the last time I came this way. I think it's the same forest that runs north-south near Hasskian, the one the Castaviran refugees were going to lose themselves in—not lose *themselves*, of course, but disappear into. It's not that thick, but thick enough that flitting was a bad idea; I'd get less tired if I just walked between the trees. Flitting isn't exhausting really, but it seems related to the walk-through-walls pouvra because it's not instantaneous (takes maybe two seconds) and you can't breathe. So flitting rapidly leaves you light-headed and breathless. Even so, it took me less than two minutes to get that far, and I felt smug. Just a little. Not enough to become overconfident.

I walked east for a while, took a rest to eat something, wished I'd brought something more interesting than trail bread and jerky, then walked some more. I made a lot of plans about flitting for when everything was over, calculated how quickly someone could flit from one side of Balaen to another and how much of a load someone might carry. Or—carrying another person? There are so many *non-military* possibilities.

It was about noon when I came out of the trees onto the plains that make up much of Balaen's heartland. These, at least, looked the same, but they're wide enough there might be any number of changes outside my visual range. I stopped at the tree line and took a look around. Snow had fallen heavily here, but the wind had blown it around so it was deeper in some places than others. I saw animal tracks, but no evidence of an army passing and nothing on the horizon.

I took a bearing and flitted away. Ankle-deep snow falling into my boots, melting uncomfortably, more animal tracks (I don't know how to recognize anything but the difference between a bear and a deer. Jeddan could probably have told me what sex they were) and still no army. So I flitted again—and this time found myself in the middle of snow trampled by thousands of boots.

I checked my location by the sun's position and figured they were either going southwest or northeast. I guessed it was the former, based on what the soldiers had said, but realized I shouldn't make assumptions. So I flitted back the way I'd come in short steps until I came to the edge of where the army had passed and looked for outliers. It took me about half an hour to be certain they were going southwest—more south than west, actually.

This was where I had to be careful. I didn't think it was breaking my promise to Mattiak to follow the army's path until I found them, because we needed as accurate a position as we could get. But I didn't want to flit into the middle of a bunch of the God-Empress's soldiers. So I looked as far ahead as I could see, determined there was no army on the horizon, and flitted away. Then I did it again, and again, still finding nothing. It was almost twenty miles on before I saw the black smudge of a body of marching soldiers, two miles beyond where I stood. That was when I realized I had no idea where I was.

Well, I had *some* idea. I knew if I went west far enough, I'd run into the Royal Road, and from there I could find the Balaenic Army. But it would be hard for me to give a position for the God-Empress's troops without finding some landmark or other. *It's a good thing Mattiak isn't here*, I thought, concealed myself, and set about flitting my way to the front of the God-Empress's army.

It was definitely the division that had routed our soldiers, and those soldiers hadn't exaggerated when they said they'd done some damage. The army marched raggedly, as if they were a fishing net with holes torn into it. Missing soldiers. A *lot* of missing soldiers. Not many mounted officers, either. I counted ten white-coated battle mages, but didn't know if that represented all the ones they'd started with. They make themselves conspicuous twice over, between the uniform and the horses; I don't think we'll have any trouble targeting them. And there's no way in hell I'm making my mages wear the King's uniform. He's not likely to find out, and if he does, he's unlikely to do anything to me if I come back with a big enough victory, which I intend to do.

But I'm getting sidetracked. I got as close as I dared to the front of the division and took a look at it. It wasn't a big division, and I think I miscalculated the number of feet that had made that path. But it was still big enough that, along with those mages, it could take a large chunk out of our forces. Those soldiers had been fortunate that division didn't have any war wagons, assuming that's what destroyed the walls at Hasskian. Or maybe they only use them against cities and not people. I don't know.

I decided to assume they weren't going to change course and flitted forward along their line of travel. Clouds were coming up, covering the sun, and it was starting to get cold—colder, anyway. I had to remind myself not to rush even though I was starting to feel a desire for a fire and a hot drink.

Three flits later I took a look around and saw I'd gone about five hundred feet past a wide, unfamiliar road. I went back to look at it and realized it was that mystery Castaviran highway. It made sense they'd want the nice wide road to travel along, and since they were cutting west instead of east, it also made sense they were planning to continue westward. The question was, as before, where was the main army? Because even though I hadn't gotten that close, I'd only seen two battle mage pennants (interesting, two pennants but only ten mages?) and not the big battle standard or the God-Empress's personal banner. So this was not the main army.

I looked westward down the road, then eastward. I still don't think I was breaking my promise to Mattiak by continuing to explore even though I'd found the "invading army" I'd been sent to locate. So I started flitting east. There was no reason to believe I'd find the God-Empress's army along that road, but as I wrote, it's a good way to move an army, and I was certain we'd have found it if it were farther west than where I stood.

And my—not even a guess, more like a whim—was right. I found the God-Empress's army not thirty miles away, camped outside a size-able Castaviran city. They didn't seem like they were planning to move any time soon, but I don't know much about armies except what I've observed in my travels and over the last ten days. But there were the banners, and the big tents, and I stood some distance away, concealed, just in case, and watched them for about an hour, wrestling with myself. Because I was seriously considering breaking my promise to Mattiak, going into the camp, and killing the God-Empress.

I think I could have done it this time.

The more I think about it, the more convinced I am the world would be a better place without her in it. Maybe I'm right that her generals would go on fighting even without her leadership, so maybe her death wouldn't stop the war. But it would have to have *some* effect. No more focus for worship. No more insane demands.

What stopped me, in the end, was the realization that I didn't know who would take over after her death. She's got no heirs, which was why Aselfos could be so confident about being able to rule Castavir in her place. But it would almost certainly mean civil war in Castavir, and that would leave them open to conquest by Balaen. And much as I feel loyalty toward my country—though not much, mostly loyalty to Jeddan and the mages—I don't want *either* of these countries subjugating the other.

So I realized it was a bad idea, then felt guilty that deciding this made me feel relieved. I have pouvrin that would make killing the God-Empress easy, not only easy but safer for me than for anyone else. So if I'm the only Balaenic who knows why she's dangerous, and I have the capability of ridding the world of her, shouldn't I do it? Even if the idea makes me sick? That's what I was thinking at the time, at least. After my talk with Mattiak, I changed my mind. About a lot of things.

Anyway.

I eventually worked through all of that and turned around to leave, flitted once—and landed squarely in the middle of a group of Castaviran soldiers. I can't believe I was so careless. I was also startled, so startled I waited too long and one of them grabbed me and said, "What the hell are you?"

"None of your business," I gasped, which sounded stupid then and still sounds stupid now. I wonder if there's ever a time when that sentence sounds strong and defiant rather than like a whine.

"It's God's otherworlder, the one who was going to marry Aselfos!" one of them shouted, which disoriented me further. Not that I expected to be able to identify any of the anonymous soldiers who'd stood guard during that bizarre ceremony, but that anyone in this mass of people could identify me was preposterous.

I went insubstantial and stepped away from my captor, went substantial long enough to say, "Tell your mistress I said hello," and flitted away. Not far, because I was breathless from the walk-through-walls pouvra, but far enough that none of those soldiers could reach me before I flitted again. And again. I was thirty miles down the road, back to where I'd started, before stopping to catch my breath. It might have been stupid to let the God-Empress know I was somewhere nearby, but—well, I hadn't done it on purpose, and being defiant was something she'd expect from me.

I flitted back to our camp, slowly, because I was starting to feel achy—I don't know if that's just from the flitting, or from the walking, but I figured I had time—and reached the Balaenic Army camp about an hour before sunset. I walked into the command tent without announcing myself and dropped onto a stool, and said, "I could use a drink. Not of water."

Somebody put a blanket around my shoulders, which I appreciated, even though I hadn't realized how cold I'd gotten, and someone else handed me a flask of something that burned all the way down and warmed me up beautifully. Mattiak said, "Thank the true God you're back."

"I was perfectly safe," I said. Of course I wasn't going to tell him about running into the God-Empress's soldiers, and I definitely couldn't tell him about how they'd recognized me, since Jeddan's the only Balaenic who knows the truth about me and the Castavirans. "It just took longer than I anticipated. Let me tell you what I learned."

"Rest first," Mattiak said, putting a hand on my shoulder.

I shook my head. "You need to know this now," I said, "because I'm not sure how much time you have." Then I told them everything I'd discovered, and marked on the map the positions of the main army and the division that had routed ours, as well as the Castaviran city. "I don't know how fast they're going to travel," I said, "but I think it's safe to assume that division sent messengers to tell the main army what happened, and I think—sorry, I know I'm not military, but I think that division is coming this way to investigate how large a force we have and then return to join the main army."

General Kalanik said, "That's likely. If they keep on that heading, they'll join that highway far ahead of the main army. They're probably the advance force."

"Which we will overrun," General Drussik said, "if they're as reduced as you say." He looked as if he questioned my veracity or, possibly, my intelligence.

"I think," said Mattiak, tapping the place on the map where that smaller division was, "it's possible they've underestimated the size of our army. There's no other reason to sacrifice an entire division." But he looked uncertain, as if he were weighing other possibilities. I thought it was possible the God-Empress had simply decided they should be sacrifices to her, but held my tongue.

"Very interesting," Mattiak said. He tapped the spot again, then said, "We'll move out in the morning, after our staff meeting. We'll discuss strategy then."

We all filed out, but Mattiak took my arm and said, "You look exhausted. I was about to eat dinner when you arrived; would you care to join me?"

I nodded. Food sounded so good just then. We went to his tent, where a meal was already set. It looked like it might have gone cold. "Don't worry about it," Mattiak said after calling a servant to bring another plate. "It's not that cold, and I've eaten worse."

We ate in silence, me because I was too hungry to spare any time for words, Mattiak because he seemed preoccupied with his thoughts. As I was mopping up the last of the gravy with a chunk of bread, he said, "You weren't telling us everything, were you?"

"I didn't risk myself," I lied—well, it was only sort of a lie; it was an accident that I'd nearly been caught, not a result of my being reckless.

"I know," Mattiak said, which made me feel bad about abusing his trust in me. "But something happened that disturbed you. I was hoping you'd tell me what that was."

I started to deny it, but instead found myself telling him what I'd thought as I looked over the God-Empress's camp and wondered if I should kill her. "I've seen the way everyone behaves around her," I

said finally. "They're afraid of her, and with good reason. I've seen her
—" I hesitated only briefly before realizing he wouldn't know when
I'd seen this. "I've seen her have someone murdered just because she
spoke to her on the wrong day. I can't imagine what kind of a ruler
she is to her own people, and she wants to rule Balaen too. Our
government isn't perfect, but it's a hundred times better than that."

"And you think her death would solve everything," Mattiak said.

I shrugged. "Maybe not everything," I said, "but it would have to
have *some* effect."

"Then I suppose the real question," Mattiak said, "is if her death
is your duty."

"I seem to be ideally qualified to kill her," I said, trying to keep my
tone light.

"That's not the same thing," Mattiak said. "I know half a dozen
men more qualified than you are, starting with Nessan, and that's
only if I thought this woman's death would make a difference on the
battlefield, which I don't."

"None of those men can slip through walls or walk invisibly
across an enemy camp," I said.

"But all of them have something you lack, Sesskia," Mattiak said.
"You're not a killer. I think taking a human life is as far beyond your
abilities as walking through walls is beyond mine."

"That's not true," I blurted out, then realized my mistake and
went silent. Mattiak leaned forward, and my eyes met his. "Tell me,"
he said.

Maybe I should have realized what was happening at that point,
or maybe not; I was preoccupied with my feelings of fear and guilt,
and right then I needed...I don't know what I needed. Comfort?
Absolution? Whatever it was, I told Mattiak about killing that bandit
mage, about watching him go gray and rigid from what I'd done. I
knew Mattiak wasn't going to be horrified by my story, because he's a
soldier and he's seen and done things as bad or worse, but I wasn't
prepared for him to say, when I was finished, "You're right. That
would make you an ideal assassin."

I felt like he'd slapped me. That was when I realized I'd wanted

reassurance that I *wasn't* evil, not more condemnation. I stood to go—
I don't know how I looked, but I felt numb—and he grabbed my
hand and made me sit. "I'm not finished," he said.

"I'm not sure I want to hear the rest," I said.

He shook his head, and he had that serious look again, the one
that made me uncomfortable. "Sesskia, you can do things I can
barely comprehend," he said, "but what I do know is that none of
them force you to be anything you don't choose to be. That fire-
summoning pouvra doesn't make you burn everything you see. And
much as I joke about you being a thief—even though I know some of
those aren't jokes—you aren't forced to use the mind-moving pouvra
solely to pick locks, or the walk-through-walls pouvra only to secretly
enter my tent at night." He grinned at me, and I had to smile, though
I was also trying not to redden with embarrassment.

"The truth is, you choose how to use what you've learned," he
went on, "and I don't give a damn how many killing applications you
come up with, because I maintain *you aren't a killer.* And that makes
me happy." He took a deep breath. "Everything about you makes me
happy, Sesskia."

His grip on my hand had loosened, become something gentle,
and his thumb stroked the back of my hand. I stared at him. I still
don't know if I should have seen that coming. I feel stupid and
embarrassed. I liked him. I thought we were friends, but apparently
that's not how he felt. I don't—I have to write the rest first.

I just stared at him. It didn't even occur to me to pull my hand
away. "Sesskia," he said again, "I know you're waiting for your
husband, but even you have to admit he's almost certainly dead. You
know as well as I do what kind of chaos central Balaen is in right now.
If he hasn't found you by now, he's not coming."

"No," I said, but came up once again against the fact that I
couldn't tell him my husband is a powerful Castaviran mage who is
absolutely still alive, wherever he is. "I know he's alive," was what I
came out with, but it sounded weak even to me.

He pressed my hand, gently again, and reached across the table to
brush his fingers across my cheek. *This* time I knew that touch for a

lover's caress, and it sent a shiver through me, though I had no idea what emotion had prompted it. "I understand," he said. "It's one of the things I love about you, your strength of spirit. But *you* should understand something, too. At some point, you'll realize the truth, and when that happens, I will be here for you."

I retrieved my hand and said, "I think I should go," and walked away before he could say anything else. I went straight to my tent and curled up, fully clothed, on my bed. I lay like that for about ten minutes, then got up to write. Which brings me to now.

I'll admit there was a fraction of a second in which I considered a reality where I returned his love. It didn't last long, and I don't feel guilty about it; it was as if I looked at a shirt that belonged to someone else and wondered how it might look on me, but never considered actually wearing it. I love Cederic, and that's not going to change just because an attractive, interesting man told me he cares about me.

But—it's like what happened when I learned Cederic had loved me for weeks before I knew it, and I thought back over that time and saw so many things I'd missed. In hindsight, Mattiak's interest in me was obvious. Every time he brought up Cederic's name, it was always accompanied with some comment about how dangerous things are in the east, or something reminding me we were separated and how it would be so long before he was found. He's been trying to drive a wedge between me and my husband that would let him fit himself into the space between. And it makes me feel sick, because I thought we were friends. I thought I could trust him. But all he wanted was to steal my affections.

I feel stupid for not realizing. And I don't know what to do or how to behave toward him. I have to be polite and friendly, and I can't avoid him because I'm technically on his general staff, but I can't have dinner alone with him anymore, knowing what he's thinking when he's looking at me.

There's no one I can tell, either; I'm not close to the other mages in that way, and the only other person I have more than a casual relationship with is Nessan, and this isn't something I can share with him. I wish Jeddan were here. I wish *Cederic* were here. Hah. I wouldn't have this problem if he were, because much as I'm angry with Mattiak right now, I don't think he's the type to make a play for a man's wife with the man actually standing there. Clearly he has no problem doing it when the man is absent.

It's far too late now. I have to meet with the general staff in the morning, where we'll learn what Mattiak has decided. I hope it's that we're moving east to attack the God-Empress's army. I might not be a killer, but right now I could happily burn swathes through the enemy line.

CHAPTER TWENTY

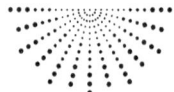

7 Seresstine

We struck camp and moved east this morning. The strategy, as I understand it, is to intercept that weakened division so it can't rejoin the army. It should be easy to defeat and will give our mages practice before we face however many dozens of mages the God-Empress has in her camp. I'm glad to be moving. Mattiak estimates we'll encounter them sometime tomorrow morning, and after we defeat them, we'll reevaluate our position with regard to the main army. "After we defeat them," his exact words, which makes me wonder if he's really that confident or just good at optimism.

He invited me to eat with him tonight and I declined, saying I was going to eat with the mages so we could talk about what they might be able to do. He smiled, and said, "Another time," and the look in his eyes told me he knew what I was doing, and he wasn't offended. It made me angry, that he was so confident of winning my heart he could humor my coldness toward him. Nothing I can do about it but endure. At least he won't attack me—I'm certain he won't be happy unless I come to him voluntarily.

We're going into battle tomorrow. All the mages are nervous and excited, but none of them seem afraid, or worried about being able to perform. We've talked about tactics, and I've told them something of what the Castaviran mages can do, and how to recognize them—they're usually mounted, to give them a better view of the battlefield, I think. And I've made it clear that disabling them is not enough; we can't afford to have them coming back to attack our troops. They all *say* they understand, that they can kill if they have to, but it's not the sort of thing you know until you're at that point.

The spies are the most relaxed, probably because we're not sure they'll have anything to do in this battle. Nessan joined us after dinner and said the same thing. He's going to scout ahead tonight; I volunteered to help, but he shook his head and said, "This isn't something I can hand off to you," and then he was gone. I wonder what Mattiak told him.

Sleep, now, and we'll see what the morning brings.

8 Seresstine

I've just come back from the surgeon's tent. He'd told me Paddrek wasn't going to survive, but I hoped he was wrong. Why is there no pouvra for healing? I even tried the binding pouvra, but it did nothing. As usual. Though I suppose if that's what it was for, the Castaviran mages would have known.

I've been trying to tell myself it could have been worse. He's the only mage who died and only three others were wounded, none of them seriously. But Paddrek wasn't a number, he was a man, and a friend. It was so stupid—he'd gotten out of formation, concentrating on maintaining fire, and our unit of defenders let some of the God-Empress's soldiers through. They didn't get any further than Paddrek, I saw to that, but that wasn't much comfort with him screaming and clutching his stomach to keep his intestines from sliding out. I guess I should be glad he's not in pain anymore, but I'd rather he was alive.

We struck camp early so we could reach a place Mattiak's scouts, i.e. Nessan, had described as a good place for us to stage our attack. There had been a lot of discussion about where to put the mages, mostly about whether it was better they stay on the ground where they didn't look like anyone else, or be in the wagon where they could have a better view of the battlefield but also be more exposed.

In the end, we decided on the ground, mainly because of my repeated insistence that we have no shield pouvra (I still can't work out what Cederic did, damn him for being so brilliant. He's going to teach me that when we're reunited) and are better off being slightly less effective at fighting if it means being better protected. So we were assigned a unit (as I mentioned above) to keep us from being overrun by the God-Empress's army and sent to where we'd be out of *our* army's way.

Then we waited. Not very long, though. We saw them approaching, of course, long before they reached us; one of the good features of our position was that it was just over a low rise, which gave Mattiak a view of the whole battlefield and put him in a position to dictate changes in strategy. He doesn't do much of that. His officers are bright and are good at understanding how they fit into the army, and altering their tactics accordingly. Not that I have any idea what those tactics are—that's just something Mattiak told me over dinner. The memory of all those dinners is sour now.

Anyway, the mages didn't have anything to do until we could see the army clearly. We could tell it was a lot smaller than ours, of course; I don't know what we would have done if the entire army had come marching down the road. I was straining to see the mages, and half-listening to a conversation Rutika and Ryenn were having, and then there was a cry, and the sound of trumpets, and the front of our army surged forward and met theirs with an enormous clash of sound that rippled over our heads. Fire blossomed here and there along their line and arched from the battle mages to fly into our army, making spots of fire the soldiers shifted to avoid. I grinned because I knew they wouldn't be able to do what we could.

"There, left of center—oh, and right, too," Elleria said. "They're spread out in a line like their range is limited."

"They aren't outside our range," Ryenn said. "Shall we attack?" He's one of our upper class mages and his language sounds elegant no matter what he's saying.

"Let's give them a surprise," I said. "Count of three, and let's see if we can hit all...yes, there's ten of them." I counted off three, and said, "NOW!"

A wall of fire sprang up where the battle mages were, burning hot and yellow, and then there was a *lot* of screaming, not just from the mages—there weren't enough of them for us to hear them over the noise of the battlefield—but from the several ranks of soldiers in front of them who turned to see where the heat came from, then stumbled in their haste to get away from it. The mages' horses thrashed about, and burning bodies fell to the earth and out of our sight.

"Dismiss it, and let's see what's left," I said, and the fire flickered out. Not a single mage was still mounted. Crazed horses bucked and ran, trampling more soldiers and making the rear of the enemy army look like a riptide had torn it apart. The effect was spreading forward as more soldiers turned to see what was going on, until it reached the place where our soldiers were fighting theirs, and even I could see the tide turning against the enemy.

More fires erupted, smaller this time. "Find your targets, and attack independently," I shouted, and then rocks and even small trees were hurtling through the air toward the enemy mages. I couldn't see much of anything except a glimpse, now and then, of a scorched white robe, but it seemed the other mages didn't have the same problem. The fires went out. No new ones arose.

"Take a rest," I said, and we all sat down for a minute. Still no new fires. "Time for new targets," I said. "Remember what the General said—mages first, then the officers. Let's see how well they do when they don't have direction." I felt a wicked pleasure at doing to them what they'd done to us, but didn't have time to indulge it, because I had to follow my own orders.

That was when it got long and brutal. My instructions were to continue attacking until we were too exhausted to manifest pouvra or they started running, and neither of those things happened for a while. Paddrek was wounded somewhere in the middle there, and I had to force those soldiers back with fire because everyone else was either focused on their own attacks or waffling in a corner—no, that's unfair, the spies weren't trained for combat, and what could they have done that wouldn't get them killed? They made sure we had plenty of water, and helped with the wounded, and took Paddrek to the surgeon's tent, and I'm glad they were there.

Then the sound of the battle changed. I haven't been in many battles—well, no battles, really, but I've been close enough I could tell the moment when one side starts to flee. That was our signal to sit down and rest while the soldiers pursued the enemy. Not far, I think, because we weren't sure how far the main army had come and nobody wanted to run into them. I think I fell asleep, because it only seemed like seconds before I was being prodded to get up and return to camp.

The soldiers were making a lot of noise, shouting and cheering, with women's voices rising above theirs. It felt like a celebration, but one I was on the outside of. Not that I wasn't happy we'd won, I just felt worn out and empty. I think most of that was having used so many pouvrin in so relatively short a time, but it also felt a little like how I feel after I learn a new pouvra, flat, as if nothing interesting will ever happen again.

But I smiled and accepted congratulations. All of us mages were heroes today, especially among those who'd seen the destruction outside Binna and those who'd been on the periphery of the enemy mages' attacks. I didn't tell them we'd been successful largely because they hadn't known to expect us. Many of the enemy soldiers escaped to run back to the God-Empress and would certainly tell what they'd seen, and even if the Castaviran mages didn't know what to expect from us, they'd definitely know to be prepared with defensive kathanas.

That makes me sound more discouraged than I am. The mages worked well together and independently, and didn't panic when they saw they'd killed someone, and the spies had been useful, and much as I grieve over Paddrek, it's true our casualties could have been far worse. Everyone else was just as cheerful over dinner, cheerful enough that I didn't give them the "let's not celebrate too soon" speech I'd been working on. Time enough for that tomorrow morning.

I just got back from talking to Mattiak, who behaved exactly as if nothing awkward had ever happened between us. He congratulated me and the mages, said something about how effective they'd been, and then said, "It's going to be harder next time, you know."

"I know," I said. "When will that next time be? Soon?"

"We'll encounter the main body of their army in a day or so," Mattiak said. "But there may be conflict sooner than that if they have more divisions coming up from the southeast, flanking the army. We have four companies spread out in that direction with instructions to send runners back if they encounter the enemy."

"Will they attack if they do?" I said.

"Better for them to retreat and draw them out, away from the security of the other troops," he said. "If we have to fight a battle on two fronts, which I think we won't, we'll want to crush one of those forces quickly and see if we can't turn that attack back on them. If that happens, your mages are going to be key to that defeat."

I said, "They'll be ready. Even the spies."

"I may have a different purpose for them this time," he said, "depending on what news Nessan and his men bring back."

"You could have sent us to spy on the G—the enemy's forces," I said.

"Time enough for that," he said cryptically, and that seemed to be the end of the conversation. I wanted to hurry away before it became intimate, so naturally I tripped over my stool and fell. Mattiak helped me up with a smile that said he was thinking about flirting with me again, which flustered me, and I almost ran out of his tent and to my own.

I thought I was going to be able to handle him, but that was when I thought all I had to worry about was an attempt at physical intimacy, which I still don't think he's going to try. No, it's those intimate glances, the meaningful smiles, everything he *doesn't* say that nevertheless speaks volumes. It makes me feel so uncomfortable because he wants something from me he's never going to get, and I wish he could understand that. I wish we'd never become friends. A professional relationship would be so much better for both of us.

9 Seresstine, noonish

We've found the God-Empress's army. It's not nearly as big as I remember it being from Calassmir. That could be because they're bunched up along the highway and not spread out, and of course they've lost that division we scattered, and there might still be a division or two south of here, though the companies Mattiak sent that way have been reporting in regularly and haven't seen any sign of enemy soldiers. Our soldiers seem confident of our chances, I hope not overconfident.

The mages are...not subdued, exactly, but they're not as eager for battle as they were yesterday. Paddrek's death hit us all hard. I didn't realize he and Neomae were moving toward a relationship, not that I would have since I just don't pick up on those things, and she's been despondent over things she never had the chance to say. I know how she feels, a little, though at least I'll have the chance to say them to Cederic someday.

They're far enough away, and it's late enough in the day, that we're going to look for a good position and wait until morning. Though they aren't advancing either, so maybe we'll move again tomorrow. I wish—no, I don't wish I understood military strategy, it's just that I feel at sea, not knowing what's best for us to do, or what Mattiak's going to want from his mage spies. I haven't seen him at all today, not that I was looking for him, but *he* generally finds a way to be near *me*, so it was a relief not to have his eyes on me all the time. I suppose there's nothing to do now but wait.

10 Seresstine, too early

I'm so tired I can barely see to write, but I feel obligated to record everything that happened, for Rutika's sake if nothing else. After I finished my last entry, I sat with the mages and talked tactics, and had dinner, and it was all pleasantly boring. Especially since Mattiak didn't send for me.

But as we were finishing our dinner, Nessan showed up and

grabbed my arm and marched me away. I slid free and said, "What the hell are you doing?"

"You didn't tell me you'd been in the enemy camp at Calassmir," he said.

"Why would you care?" I said.

"Because we've found something we don't understand," he said, "and you might be able to explain it."

I felt a moment's irrational fear that I'd been discovered, then reminded myself he couldn't be talking about my secret knowledge of the God-Empress. "What is it?" I said.

"Come with me," he said, and walked away without either grabbing me again or waiting for me to follow. I had to jog to keep up with him.

We went to his tent—not his personal tent, the place from which he directs his spies. It's dark and smells of mildew and the roof leaks, and it's the most slovenly tent I've seen in the Balaenic Army camp, but he seems to like it. He's got a table that's as elderly as the tent that's always covered with scraps of paper, some of it dirty, but what he showed me was a charcoal sketch on clean white paper. "Did you see any of these in Calassmir?" he demanded.

I nodded. It was a war wagon, if somewhat distorted and out of proportion. "I've heard they're like giant rifles," I said.

"Right. Some kind of projectile, anyway," he said. "They shoot balls that fragment on impact and turn everything in a five-foot radius to paste. And their range is beyond even what your warrior mages can reach, which makes them safe from fire or mind-moving. The bastards have fifteen of these they're going to turn on us as soon as they get them into position. Looks like they weigh more than a ton, and they don't have horses pulling them."

"How do you know that?" I said.

Nessan crumpled the paper and tossed it at the wall, where it rebounded and fell into a dirty patch (no rugs for Nessan, he'd probably think them a sign of weakness). "That they'll attack?" he said. "We can't fight in the dark any more than their soldiers can, but those weapons are like a drunk man swinging a club—doesn't have to be accurate, just has to be close. So they can mark a target spot before the sun goes down and keep lobbing those projectiles into our camp. If they start pounding on us with those things, we either have to advance or retreat, and they're counting on us not wanting to advance into true God knows what kind of nighttime combat. So they're going to force us to retreat, which loses us our position, gives us no chance to rest, and puts us in a weakened position when morning comes and they can pursue us."

"You want to know how to destroy them," I said.

"You're smarter than you look," he said with the twist of his lips that passes for a wry smile with him. "Disable them, if we can't outright destroy them. And soon."

I didn't even hesitate. "I got a good look at them, because I was curious," I said, which was one hundred percent true. "You know their mages have to draw on those boards to work magic, right? Well, these things have a sort of plate with a, um, design or picture or something like the ones they draw on their boards. I think they paint over the lines to make the magic work and fire the projectiles." That was fifty percent guess, because those th'an might be to make it move, but they're different enough from the ones on the collennas I've seen that it was a guess I felt comfortable with.

"Interesting, but not totally helpful," Nessan said. "Didn't you see any weaknesses we can exploit?"

"That *is* the weakness," I said. "If we damage the plate, the picture won't be accurate anymore, and the thing won't work. Smash it, gum up the lines with rocks or something, tear the whole thing off. It's not easy, but it's simple."

Nessan had begun looking into the distance past my shoulder as I spoke. He was silent for a few seconds when I finished, then said, "Get the wallowers (this is what he affectionately calls our spies) and meet me at the southern picket line in ten minutes. Tell them to dress for speed, not warmth. No flapping coats, understand?"

"Since this is not my first time doing this, of course I do," I mock-snarled at him, and he returned the expression.

The spies were excited when I told them to get ready, and we reached the picket line two minutes early, about half an hour before sunset. Nessan was there exactly at the ten minute mark. He sneered at us, which is another way he shows approval, along with insults and sarcasm, though he's not as good at the latter as Cederic is. He was lugging a big canvas sack that clanked when he dropped it on the frozen ground in front of us. He didn't look winded, but his breath was coming more quickly, making little puffs of white when he exhaled. That should have warned me. I was stupid not to remember there are so many ways you can be detected that have nothing to do with sight.

But reproaches aren't going to change the past. Nessan dug into his bag and began handing things out: claw hammers, sacks of sticky mud that on inspection turned out to actually be wet clay, big metal tent spikes, and chisels. He explained what I'd told him about the th'an plates on the war wagons, then added, "We don't know what will work best to disable them, so you've got options. You'll work in pairs.

"Alessabeka and Rutika, you're going to circle around to the north, and Tobiak and Relania, to the south. Sesskia and I will drive up the middle. One of you distracts the operators—there's only two to a weapon, one to load, one to work the magic—and the other disables it. Get as many of them as you can, then pull out before they get their mages involved." He sighed, and a whole cloud of white mist blew from his lips. "This is what you trained for. Make me proud."

They all nodded or murmured assent, and we headed out through the camp and past the front lines, where we concealed ourselves and separated. I've never felt so anxious in my life. It was like when our warrior mages faced battle for the first time, except this was worse because stealth and cunning were the only weapons these mages had, and as good as they'd become, they had almost no experience. To distract myself, I said to Nessan, "You'd better not give me away with all your tramping around. You hardly look like a Cas—an enemy soldier."

"Don't worry about me," he said. "You want to distract, or sabotage?"

"I'd better distract, because you're stronger than me and I think smashing the plate is the best solution," I said.

"Weakling," he said.

"Oaf," I said. "Here, take the tools."

"Good idea," he said. "You clank when you walk."

"I'm surprised you can hear that, what with you going deaf in your old age," I said.

We kept up the insults for about half a minute more, then went silent as we neared the camp. We came wide around its flank, me following Nessan as he made a path among the tents. He's good at using shadows and those gaps between places no one uses because they're not on a direct route to anywhere. He's also good at looking like he belongs when he can't avoid being hidden. I know I couldn't have walked through the Castaviran camp without my stolen uniform, which by the way I was wearing, just in case.

The war wagons were still being maneuvered into place when we arrived at their position, which was a higher piece of land that curved through the camp from north to south. It began sloping downward about two-thirds of the way into the camp, and since the war wagons were lined up along the ridge, that meant Nessan and I, and Tobiak and Relania probably, were in the middle of the God-Empress's camp, and Nessan and I, going for the middle of that line, were heading even deeper into it.

We walked along the low ridge and observed. Each war wagon had a white-coated mage behind it, drawing th'an in the grooves of the shining brass plates fastened to the rear. The th'an propelled the war wagons very slowly across the matted dead grass, which made me wonder why the war wagons weren't collennas, to move by themselves. I hadn't noticed those plates when I'd explored the chamber of death, but I'd been rattled, so I don't blame myself too much. Each war wagon was accompanied by a wheeled bin filled with projectiles, pushed by a soldier. It was all happening so slowly I chafed at the delay, but there was nothing we could do about it except wait for them to get into position.

Nessan walked past the war wagons, and I followed him to a spot near some of the command tents and looked around. The God-Empress's standard was about fifty feet away, which made me wonder where she was. Directing their attack? Demanding some irrational service that would slow or hamper that attack? I wasn't sure what I'd do if I saw her. No, that's not true, I knew what I'd do, I'd stand there and let her walk past. Mattiak's right, killing her wouldn't solve anything. And it's not my duty.

Eventually the battle mages found positions they liked, but then they spent another handful of eternities making their war wagons' barrels tilt up and down, using th'an to make a glowing amber circle they kept consulting—I think it helped them aim at their target, and knowing that made me even more anxious about what would happen if we failed.

Nessan whispered, "Stay here. I have to move or I'll be conspicuous," and then he was gone, leaving me with nothing to do but watch and plan ways to distract or overcome the mages. The mage operating the war wagon nearest me took her seat, and Nessan wasn't back. The young man with the bin full of projectiles heaved one up and slid it into the funnel at the back of the war wagon. Nessan wasn't back.

I leaned forward on the balls of my feet. I couldn't do this alone, I didn't even have the tools. The fire pouvra wasn't hot enough to melt brass, damn it, and I couldn't think of anything else to do short of killing both of them, which would ruin the whole plan.

Then a panicked, horrified thought struck me. Only the green-eyed mages could work magic. And mages wouldn't need the grooves to scribe the correct th'an. Our plan was useless. I looked up and down the line and, of course, saw nothing out of the ordinary. I had no way of warning our mages they were about to risk their lives for nothing. We were just going to have to go through with it and hope we all survived.

Nessan still wasn't back. I had to watch, helpless, as the mage dipped her brush into the tankard fused to the barrel's side and brought it out dripping with gleaming silver. Then, to my surprise, she swept the brush through the grooves, a tangle of graceful movements, and the wintry evening was ripped open by the loudest noise

I'd ever heard, louder than the thunder that follows lightning striking just feet from where you stand. I thought the sound echoed, but it was just more of the explosions, farther away, and now I was fighting to control my panic. I had nearly resolved to attack the mage and to hell with the plan when suddenly Nessan was at my ear, saying, "Do it."

The battle mage had a brushful of silver again, and I used the mind-moving pouvra to snap the brush in half, just in case. Then I pulled myself up on the back of the war wagon, kicking the boy in the face as he was about to load his projectile, looked inside the mage's neck and found the same veins I'd used to subdue Norsselen. The mage toppled, and I heard a muted clang as Nessan wedged the chisel into one of the grooves and struck it hard with the hammer, making it peel up into an unrecognizable mess. "Move," he said, and I leapt down and raced after him to the next wagon southward.

The noise was incredible. It felt like being inside a giant drum that wouldn't stop beating. I didn't even try to tell Nessan what I'd figured out; he couldn't have heard me, and it wouldn't have changed anything. We repeated our technique again, and again, before anyone realized the drumbeat was lessening. I couldn't hear anything over the noise of the war wagons, but I saw soldiers running to find out why the war wagon mages were unconscious.

The fourth wagon was unoccupied, or rather the mage was off his seat and shouting something unintelligible over the noise. He was pacing, moving enough that I had to grab him to hold him still enough to knock him unconscious. His eyes went wide, and he took hold of me in a way that told me he saw past the concealment. "Who are you?" he said.

This time, I managed not to say "none of your business." I kept my head even though my heart was pounding with fear, and without a word sent him unconscious. He fell, nearly taking me with him, and it took far too long for me to extricate myself from his grip. Nessan had to pull me to my feet, shouting, "One more, then we run!"

"We need to warn the others!" I shouted back.

"They know what to do! Give them a little credit!" Nessan said, and dragged me—this was when I realized I'd dropped concealment, and I decided it didn't matter anymore. We disabled our fifth one and kept running.

We passed one of the other war wagons, and I saw an unconscious battle mage on the ground and another one perched on the seat, painting rapidly and swearing (I think; it was too loud to hear). The war wagon was silent. I stopped and circled around to where I could see what he was doing. The brass plate was a smeared mess of clay filling the grooves, and silver paint coated it above the engraved th'an. As I watched, the mage tried again to paint the activation th'an on the flat, gleaming surface; nothing happened.

"Have you lost your mind?" Nessan growled into my ear, grabbing my wrist and towing me along after him. After a few seconds, I regained my balance, and we began moving as if we were panicked soldiers and not ruthless spies. Even though we were still in the Castaviran camp and therefore still in danger, I don't think I've ever felt so relieved. I'd forgotten how difficult it is to scribe th'an without lots and lots of practice. Those mages might have the innate ability to scribe the magic that makes the war wagons work, but they still needed the pattern of the grooves to do it. Our raid wasn't a waste of time, after all. Thank the true God. I don't think I could have forgiven myself, otherwise.

We came out of the enemy camp on the southeast and circled around back to our camp. It was full dark at that point, and Nessan stumbled so often I eventually took his hand to lead him in the moonless, cloudy night. Neither of us said anything about it, me because I didn't want to make him feel awkward and him, probably, because he didn't like the route I'd chosen, not that it was a bad one —he just doesn't like having to follow anyone.

Tobiak and Relania were at the picket line, our agreed-on meeting place, when we returned. "We only got four of our five," Relania said. "There were more battle mages at the fifth, surrounding it, so we couldn't get through. And I think one of them spotted us."

"Fair enough," Nessan said. "And it might be good they saw you, if they know you were concealed before that. Give them something to worry about."

"Rutika and Alessabeka aren't back, though," Tobiak said. "Should we go after them?"

"Even if they aren't concealed, you'd never find them in the dark," Nessan said, "and as I told your fearless leader, you should give them credit for knowing what to do."

"And they have farther to go, if they retreated north rather than trying to cross the entire camp to come out where we did," I said, trying to make myself feel better. I don't know how convincing I was.

We waited for a long time. Once or twice someone tried to start a conversation, but it never went anywhere. We were all too nervous, especially since after a while the pounding started up again, and we worked out there were three war wagons still active. If Rutika and Alessabeka hadn't disabled two of theirs...

My stomach felt full of acid, and I realized none of us had eaten recently. Nobody suggested getting food—I think I'd have thrown up anything I tried to eat at that point. Eventually, the pounding stopped with one last defiant blast. Then it was still and cold and black, thanks to the thick cloud cover that probably didn't mean snow, which would have delayed the inevitable attack in the morning.

Then someone was approaching, and I had enough time to register it was only one person and think *Why is she still concealed?* when Alessabeka stumbled and caught herself on one of the picket ropes, and sobbed, "They killed her. They saw her breath, and she tried to get away but she tripped and hit her head and lost conceal-ment, and we ran away but it was right into a couple of soldiers—I'm sorry I ran, I left her behind, I'm sorry I'm sorry—"

Relania put her arms around the weeping woman and said, "It would have been stupid for you to stay and be killed as well. Rutika would be the first to tell you that. Shh, shh."

I was—I couldn't even think. It had never occurred to me Rutika might be the one to fall. She was so good at all of it, and—damn her, she relied too much on that damn pouvra and it got her killed. I'm so mad at her I can't even s

I'm not mad. I'm grieving. What a waste. And they didn't

I can't believe I was about to blame a dead woman for failing to complete her job. The truth is, I'm irrationally blaming myself for not going after them the way I wanted to, the way Nessan told me not to. Irrational, because he was right, but I do this every time, think about what might have happened if I'd chosen differently.

All right. Suppose I'd gone north instead of south. We might all have been killed. I could have been drawn into a fight and been overwhelmed. Or worse, they could have captured me and dragged me to the God-Empress to be tortured to death. There's no reason to believe a different choice might have been a better choice. So I'm not going to think like that anymore.

We made a difference. I wish we could have stopped them before they managed to fire any projectiles, because they did a lot of damage in the camp, just not as much as if they'd been allowed to attack unhindered. Mattiak finally looked at me the way he used to, as a friend and a respected colleague, and that helped. But mostly we're all in mourning now.

It's...I don't know what time it is. Late. Or early. Nobody feels like sleeping, which is stupid because we'll need to be fresh in the morning when the real battle begins. I wish I had Cederic's th'an that helped me sleep when I kept having those nightmares about everyone I love being killed by the God-Empress. We could all use it now.

CHAPTER TWENTY-ONE

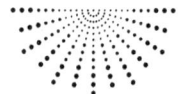

10 Seresstine, afternoon

We've been fighting for seven hours now and we're all exhausted. The battle mages were, as I predicted, prepared for our assault. They have defensive kathanas now, shimmering pale shields that protect them from missiles, and while they can't defend against fire, they can dismiss it before it does too much damage. The shields don't hold up against big missiles thrown really fast, but there are few of us who can do that. The only good thing about the shields is they make it easy for us to see our targets through the nightmare furor that is the battlefield—people milling around, clustering so we can't even tell our men from theirs.

Everyone is trying to come up with alternative forms of attack, even the pacifists, though their plans are more for how to sneak in and disable the remaining war wagons. I'm grateful for the following things:

1. The Castavirans don't have Cederic's shield. We'd have no chance against it.

2. The melee fighting hasn't reached us yet, not anywhere close.

3. The war wagons have stopped firing now they'll pulverize their own people as well as ours if they do.

4. The battle mages still have no idea who or where we are.

Number 4 can't last long. I've had our people move occasionally and spread out into little groups so we're not obvious, and of course I've forced them to abandon Norsselen's gesturing, but at some point someone's going to use logic, and then we'll be in trouble.

I'm going to nap, and maybe this will all look better later.

10 Seresstine, after dinner

A cease fire so the armies can collect the dead and wounded. I can't tell how things are going and I don't want to go to Mattiak for fear he'll think I'm weakening toward him. No casualties among the mages. Dinner tasted like sand, not the fault of our cook.

11 Seresstine, ~~maybe 9 a.m.~~ morning

I wonder if I should get a watch. I'm not usually in a position to care about the exact time, but if I'm going to make several entries a day, maybe I should be accurate.

That was a stupid thought. I don't care what time it is. I'm crossing that out. Fighting started again about an hour ago. This war is so stupid. We're all too tired to fight, so I sent everyone back to bed. Then I had a loud argument with Mattiak about it that ended with him shouting at me and me shouting at him, then me storming off to my tent. I know he's the commander, but he needs to *listen to me* when I tell him we've reached our limit.

11 Seresstine, a little later

Mattiak came to apologize. I apologized too. Then he tried to embrace me and I had to shove him away and shout again. Then I started crying. I hate this war. He had the good sense to leave without saying anything else.

11 Seresstine, evening

Back to work. Cianan and Kerkessa both killed, Cianan by a soldier who got past our guards, Kerkessa by a lightning bolt. I don't think it was on purpose, or rather I don't think the battle mage knew what Kerkessa was, or we'd have had several more bolts to deal with.

Saemon collapsed—I wasn't paying attention to how often he was using the mind-moving pouvra, maybe I didn't care because he's got the longest range of any of us and had the clever idea of targeting the mages themselves. So he was flinging one of the battle mages across the field and into the middle of the fighting, and then his eyes rolled up in his head and he folded up so fast no one even caught him. We took him back to his tent and Alessabeka's sitting with him. She still feels guilty about Rutika, though I think she knows it's inappropriate guilt, so whenever I can give her something to do that takes her away from the battlefield, I do.

We don't know how the battle's going, though Mattiak doesn't look grim, so I don't think we're losing. I hope. I'm writing this in between bites of bread and cheese, which is all we get for dinner because our "servants" are off fighting somewhere. Then I'm going back to try the fire-summoning pouvra again. There has to be a way to keep them from putting out the fires quickly. At least it keeps them from attacking our people, if not permanently.

11 Seresstine, late

Fighting's stopped for the night. They haven't used the war wagons against us again, don't know why. Had a talk with Mattiak about us changing tactics and attacking their officers. He approved. I told everyone the new plan. They are all so tired. I've never used so many pouvrin so often. It feels like the ground is pulling us down to meet it, the dead grass binding our feet so we can't move. I think we need to be more careful.

Saemon's still not totally recovered from his collapse and hasn't been able to work any pouvrin since then. I had to reassure him that magic isn't something that vanishes like water down a drain, but it's true I'm having more trouble bending my will to meet the pouvrin as the hours pass, so there might come a time when none of us can work magic. Trying not to dwell on that, as there's nothing we can do about it.

12 Seresstine, noon

It happened. The battle mages figured out where we were. The first I knew about it was when Aeddek, standing next to me, suddenly went still, and when I turned to look at him, he was clutching his throat like he couldn't breathe.

I shouted, "Get to hiding!" and grabbed him under the armpits and dragged him back to hide behind a wagon. I looked inside his throat and saw his windpipe being crushed as if some large hand had him by the throat. I reached inside him to open it up, but even as I did, the grip relaxed, and Aeddek took a huge choking breath and began coughing. I relaxed too, because I'd only been guessing that getting out of sight would keep the battle mages from being able to target us.

That was when the wagon went up in flames.

Aeddek and I stumbled away from it, and I instinctively worked the inverted fire pouvra on it, extinguishing it for only a minute before the distant battle mage lit it again. I'm still not sure I can do that when I'm not under pressure. I looked around and saw the rest of my warrior mages crouched behind whatever shelter they could find, wagons, tents, even a couple of horses (at the time we were near the picket line). "Fall back!" I shouted, and we moved away from the burning wagon, between the currently deserted tents.

"Now what?" Ryenn said. He's become my second in command, not because he's strong with the pouvrin—he's average—but he's logical and people listen to him. That might be because he's upper class, but I don't think so.

"I'm not sure. Any ideas?" I said.

Neomae said, "I think we need to observe them more closely. I noticed they don't all use the same magics. They're like us in that way —they specialize. We should target the ones who do the most damage."

"Good idea," I said. "Anything else?"

Relania began to speak, then subsided. "What?" I said.

She closed her eyes, then said, as if the words were being wrung out of her, "The shields are in front only, like actual shields. If you... take missiles from behind them, you can strike at their backs and avoid the shields."

I gaped at her. "Thank you, Relania," I said finally. "You shouldn't regret saying that."

"You know I think going to war is always the wrong decision," she said. "But we're here now, and I want to end this quickly, spare as many lives as possible."

"I agree," I said. "All right. We're going to move through the camp to the other side. Then we're going to spread out in groups of four, two mind-movers and two fire-summoners in each. Find the mages who, hmm…let's strike at those who've been sending fire our way. Pick your target, then fire-summoners, you keep them busy while the mind-movers find something to hit them with from behind. Take turns, don't overexert yourselves. Let's move."

The plan went perfectly. Battle mages began dropping like lead balls. We must have killed seven mages before anyone realized anything was wrong. Then they started attacking us again—I bet someone came up with a kathana that would identify and target our kind of magic—so we had to back off, but we were celebrating. We're all still tired, and I think about a third of us need full rest before they can work pouvrin again, but emotionally we're doing better.

12 Seresstine, very late

It's over. We won.

13 Seresstine, morning

Now that I've slept, and eaten something hot, I can write everything that happened. Unfortunately for future readers of this record, I didn't see much of it. After we had to retreat that last time, I decided we should take a rest—no, I forgot, I concealed myself and made my way around to where I could see the Castaviran mages.

I don't think I wrote that there really were only seven battle mage standards in the army, and Nessan's spies had counted far fewer than seventy mages—closer to forty, which is an incredible loss if those seven squads did have a full complement of battle mages before the convergence. I think we killed nineteen of them and injured most of the rest, though unfortunately not severely enough to remove them from the battle, and we'd only lost seven of our twenty-six, counting Paddrek and Rutika. So I was satisfied we'd done good work and could afford to rest. We ate, and I found a spot to curl up for a nap.

And the next thing I knew, Ryenn was shaking me awake and saying, "Something's happening, Sesskia."

We all went to where we could see, and to my shock, the enemy camp was overrun with our people, and the Castaviran standard, and the God-Empress's standard, were down. My nap had left me disoriented, and at first all I could think was *That was fast.* Then I realized I should find Mattiak, but one of his generals said he was gone to accept the enemy's surrender, and the warrior mages were to stay in the camp with his thanks.

I relayed this to my mages, and while they were celebrating, I went to where I could watch the end of the battle. Again, there wasn't much to see. I was so used to the tumult of the fighting, all those men and women clashing and withdrawing with a roar like storm waves striking a beach, that it felt strange to see nothing but the occasional soldier picking his way across the battlefield, looking for —I don't know. Anyone wounded but alive, maybe? I hope it wasn't looters.

I looked farther ahead, to where the enemy "camp" was—I don't know what they call it when they haven't pitched tents, theirs are farther back down the road, and we were backed into ours by the war wagons, even though they didn't succeed in making us flee. It, too, looked quiet, and for about half a second I was disoriented enough to imagine everyone was dead, and those of us who survived were going to have to rebuild civilization. Then that passed, and it was just a big, horrible battlefield.

I spent about an hour looking for survivors and found six people, four of them ours, two Castaviran. I called some of the other searchers to help me bring ours to the surgeon's tent, then pretended I was Castaviran to get help for the other two. The Castaviran soldiers who came to help eyed me skeptically, possibly because of my hair, but took them off my hands. Then I was feeling ill, so I came back here to write.

I'm glad we won. I wonder if the God-Empress did her little disappearing trick again, or if she had to surrender. I wish, now, I'd told Mattiak everything, and never mind the risk that he'd think me a traitor. He has no idea what she's like, and I don't think he can withstand her manipulation, given how persuasive she can be when she's in her right mind. And, of course, she's exceptionally beautiful, and some men are swayed by that.

Oh. It's only just occurred to me I'll need to stay out of her way unless I want all my secrets revealed. And Mattiak might want me to meet her. I should decide on a lie that will keep me away from her. Or I could ask him to send me back to Venetry to take word of our victory? No, he's probably already sent someone. Illness? That won't last long. Well, something, anyway. I wonder what the God-Empress will tell them, if anything. The rest of the Castaviran army is still out there somewhere.

Huh. If I'm not here, the God-Empress can't see me. No. I can't abandon my mages like that and strike out eastward. One more thing to figure out: how to attach myself to whatever force goes eastward to investigate what's happening in the heartland. Because I've done what I was asked to do, and once the warrior mages are back in Venetry, I am going to Colosse, one way or another.

13 Seresstine, later

I should have seen this coming. Not because there were any signs, just that this is *exactly* what was going to happen. The God-Empress isn't with the army. She hasn't been with the army for days. That first division we encountered, the one that routed our people and was defeated by us in turn? They were there to protect the God-Empress's flight northwestward. That was why the army looked so much smaller than when I saw it at Calassmir; it *was* smaller. She took several divisions and struck out toward Venetry nine days ago. She's probably there now.

We found this out—no, that happened later. They discovered the God-Empress was gone almost immediately, but her general wouldn't talk. Not that it mattered, because of course no one could understand him. *I* found out about it when I went to join the mages after I finished writing the last, and Nessan was there. "We're not sure what she thinks she's doing," he said, "because she can't have that many men with her. Possibly she's headed east again. Ran away to protect her own skin and left her men to die."

"How is Mattiak finding anything out?" I said.

"Gestures, mostly," Nessan said. "Their general isn't talking anyway. Makes it hard to deliver terms."

"It would," I said. "I'm going to talk to Mattiak now." I'd decided, somewhere in the middle of that conversation, I couldn't keep my language skills secret any longer, not if my being able to speak Castaviran could make a difference to our troops. And I was the only Balaenic who knew that if the God-Empress had gone missing, she was certainly going somewhere that would let her cripple Balaen. Besides, with her gone, there wasn't anyone who might give me away. Probably. I guess there was a chance another of those soldiers would recognize me, but nobody did. I was grateful for my good luck.

I ran across the battlefield where corpses still lay because the ground was too hard to easily dig graves, and went looking for Mattiak amid the mess. I found him in one of the Castaviran tents, staring down a Castaviran in a general's uniform, and saying to General Kalanik, "I can only mime so much. How the hell am I supposed to ask him if he'll give his parole?"

"*I* don't know," Kalanik said. "He won't even give his name."

"We need to know if they've got more forces on the way," Drussik said. "Where this leader of theirs went. Why they let a woman lead them, for that matter."

"He's acting like someone stalling for time," Mattiak said. There was a table between him and the general with a map of Balaen spread out on it. He gestured to include both of them, then stabbed at a point on the map. Then he pointed at the God-Empress's battle standard, propped against the tent wall. "Where?" he said, spreading his hand across the map. The general eyed the standard, sneered at Mattiak, and sat silent with his arms crossed over his chest.

"Mattiak," I said.

"Not the time, Sesskia," he said, not looking at me.

"I have a solution for you," I said. "But I'm not telling anyone but you."

He looked up at me warily. "Do you have magic that will let me talk to him?"

"Sort of," I said. "But in private."

He caught the eye of each of his generals in turn, and said, "Excuse us, gentlemen," and they all filed out, Kalanik looking annoyed, Drussik, as usual, looking suspiciously at me. When the tent was empty but for the three of us, Mattiak said, "Tell me."

"I speak their language," I said.

Mattiak sat back in surprise. "How?" he said.

"I can't explain everything," I said, "but I learned their language through magic, and I can translate for you."

Now he was frowning. "You could have told me this earlier," he said.

"There wasn't any point," I said, "and I didn't want you or anyone else pestering me with questions. Do you want my help or not?"

"You're not telling me everything," he said.

"No, I'm not," I said, "and maybe I'll tell you more later, but for now I think we need to talk to this man and find out what's happening." As I spoke, a plan occurred to me, and although I wasn't sure it was a good idea, it would solve a few problems.

I pulled up another stool and said, in Castaviran, "Hi. What's your name?"

He recoiled. "What is a Viravonian doing in this invaders' camp? Treachery!"

"He thinks I'm one of them," I told Mattiak, then said to the Castaviran, "Doesn't it occur to anyone there might be blond-haired people in both our worlds? I'm one of the, um, invaders, I happen to speak your language, and I'm here as a translator. This man is the leader of our army, and he wants to negotiate the terms of your surrender."

He sneered. "What terms? We are nothing. God is at the head of the army. You can't stop her."

"Maybe so," I said, "and I'll agree with you this is only a partial victory so long as the God-Empress is free. But we're not going to just let you go. Wait a minute, let me tell the General what you've said."

I turned to Mattiak and said, "So here's what he said. They worship their ruler as God—they call her the God-Empress. So this isn't only a military matter, it's religious. Which means he might not be willing to talk about her at all."

"We'll figure something out," Mattiak said. "See if you can at least figure out where she is, and what she's doing."

I turned back to the general. "Why are you so ashamed of God?" I said.

He looked first confused, then angry. "I am not ashamed of God! How dare you even speak of her, foreigner?"

"Because even a foreigner knows God's plans cannot be thwarted," I said. "If you don't want to tell us where she's gone, it must be because you think foreigners are capable of stopping her. It's lucky for you she's *not* here, because I can only imagine what she'd do to you if she knew you had such little faith."

"I am faithful to God!" he shouted, and now he looked afraid. "My loyalty has *never* been questioned."

"Until now," I said.

He lurched up from his stool and lunged at me. I leaned back as a couple of soldiers grabbed him and forced him to sit. "You are *nothing*," he said. "God's will cannot be thwarted."

"So tell us where she went," I said.

"Sesskia, is this safe?" Mattiak said.

"Sure," I told him, then to the Castaviran, "Show me how confident you are in God's will."

He glared at me, then leaned forward to trace a line with his finger. I gasped. The path curved northwesterly away from where the battle had taken place, all the way to a point marked with three stars. Venetry.

"She's gone to—" I said.

"I see it," Mattiak said. "How long ago?"

I asked the question. The general had picked up on my agitation and was looking smug. "Nine days," he said. "She took half our forces and has probably captured the city already. God will strike down your unholy cities and bring them under her protection."

I relayed this to Mattiak, who said, "She won't find it that easy, if her force was only the size of this one. Our troops have an excellent defensive position, and plenty of mages. I'm sure they can hold out until we can reinforce them. But we'll need to move quickly."

"What do you want to do with the Castavirans—that's what they call themselves," I added hurriedly, hoping he wouldn't remember the general hadn't said anything that sounded like that word.

"Just a minute," he said, and went to the tent door to call the rest of the officers back in for a discussion. I sat and looked at the general, who stared back at me. "I don't suppose you know what happened in Colosse after the convergence?" I said. "Oh, come on, what else do you have to do but talk to me?" I added when he gave me a mulish look. "I mean, didn't it matter to you at all that Perce Aselfos took control of the army there?"

"What?" he said, forgetting he didn't want to talk to me. "You lie."

"No," I said. "I don't know whether he was successful. I only know he tried to overthrow the God-Empress. I was wondering whether you knew anything, or if you'd just lost contact with Colosse the way everyone else did."

"You lie," he repeated, but I could tell he was thinking hard, reevaluating something in his head.

"Look—what's your name?" I said.

"Arnisen," he said, distractedly.

"I'm Thalessi," I said. "Arnisen, what would it mean if someone were capable of stealing some of the God-Empress's power? Doesn't that suggest to you that maybe she's not as omnipotent as she claims?"

"Do not blaspheme against God!" he shouted.

Mattiak turned quickly to see what was happening. "Sesskia, be careful," he said.

"I am," I assured him. I turned back to Arnisen, who was breathing heavily, his pupils dilated, and said, "Sorry. I don't know much about Castaviran culture and I don't want to criticize your religion. But I've seen her kill people whose only crime was saying the wrong thing at the wrong time. Not even the wrong thing— something she didn't like. I think your people deserve something better."

"Perce Aselfos should not dare to usurp God's place," he said in a low, harsh voice.

"Maybe not. I don't know if he's a better choice," I said. I looked at him more closely, and said, "You were relieved to be told to attack us, weren't you? Because you don't like what you have to do in Viravon."

He startled. "You know nothing of military matters."

"That is *entirely* true," I said. "But I think I know a little of what's wrong and what's right. And what's going on down there is wrong."

"Sesskia, what are you saying to him?" Mattiak said, startling me, because I'd been so rapt in my conversation with Arnisen I'd forgotten he was there.

"Just...talking about things," I said. "Trying to make him more inclined to give us information."

"Well, ask him if they understand parole in their country," he said. I relayed this to Arnisen, who looked mystified. "Well, what do you do with prisoners in Castavir?" I said.

"We haven't gone to war against anyone but Viravon in three generations," Arnisen said. "We execute Viravonian captives." Again that shadow flitted across his face.

"We haven't gone to war for seventy years," I said, "but even then we didn't execute prisoners. That seems barbaric."

"You know nothing of military matters," he repeated, but weakly.

"Well, General Tarallan isn't going to execute hundreds of enemy soldiers," I said. I felt confident about that even though I hadn't asked him. "And he's not going to just let you go. That's why he wants your word of honor you won't try to escape until you can be exchanged."

"It's my duty to fight to my death for the Castaviran Empire," he said.

I told this to Mattiak, whose face went grim. "I can't have them all executed," he said. "Convince him, Sesskia."

"What?" I exclaimed. "I can't do that!"

"Of course you can," Mattiak said. "I've heard you convince those mages of yours to work together, and they're the sort of people who'd argue about whether water was wet. And you're the only one who speaks his language. Please, Sesskia."

"I need some water," I said, because my mouth had just gone dry. I drank, then offered the flask to Arnisen. He took it with some hesitation, drank, then handed it back. I stared at it for a few moments. It had a leather case that slipped over its metal; the case felt smooth and rough at the same time. I set it aside. "Arnisen," I said, "how does your death serve the Castaviran Empire?"

He said, "It—" Then he shut his mouth.

"That's what I thought," I said. "It's your life that matters, isn't it? That's something I understand. Risking your life in the service of something important."

"Yes," he said. "Not allowing the enemy to defeat you. If I promise not to fight, I betray God."

"No, you betray the person you know yourself to be," I corrected him. "I understand that too. Am I right in saying you think offering your parole is the same as, for example, deserting your command?"

He nodded curtly. "I don't fully understand the concept myself," I said, "but I know it doesn't work like that. It's more like...being wounded. A wounded person can't fight, can he? Or do you execute your wounded for betraying their country in being wounded?"

"That's ridiculous," he said, but he looked uncertain.

"I know it is. You let a wounded person recover, then you send him back into the battle to serve again. That's what parole is. You're out of the battle for a while, then you're returned to your company to fight again. No shame. No dishonor. Just you serving your country in a different way."

"No," he said, quietly.

"Yes," I said. "Please. You may think I'm your enemy, but the truth is I'm on the side of those who want our two countries to find peace, not destruction. Please don't embrace death. Tell your soldiers not to fight. You'll rejoin the fight eventually, and have your chance to defeat us." I took a deep breath. "Or maybe you'll decide to take a different path. All I know is I don't want to see any more deaths. *Please.*"

Arnisen shook his head slowly, and my heart turned to lead. Then he said, "What is it we do, to offer our parole?"

I took another deep breath, and told Mattiak, "He accepts on behalf of himself and his soldiers."

Mattiak looked as relieved as I felt. He gave me a series of instructions I relayed to Arnisen, who eventually stood and offered his hand to Mattiak the Castaviran way. "Clasp his wrist," I told him, and they exchanged salutes. I was afraid to stand because I was fairly sure my knees wouldn't support me. That didn't matter, because they all left me sitting there while they went to arrange things. I looked at the map of Balaen, so familiar after all these years, then began mapping Castaviran landmarks onto it. The Arabel Mountains. Colosse. All those little ruins. I know so little of Castavir, but I don't want to see it destroyed any more than I want to see Balaen in flames. If only peace were as easy as convincing one Castaviran general not to embrace death.

Mattiak came back later to thank me. He also said, "You're a remarkable woman, Sesskia."

His voice had that intimate tone to it, and it made me weary. "That's what my *husband* thinks," I said, sharply.

"Then he's not a fool," Mattiak said. "I told you, Sesskia, I can wait."

"You're going to wait a long time, because *I* told *you* he's still alive," I said.

I wasn't looking at him—I didn't think I could keep from losing my composure if I did—so all I knew was he was silent for a bit. Then he said, "You know, I hope he is, true God help me," and left the tent. And I had to write or explode like one of those projectiles.

I'm starting to feel hungry, which is a relief, because I felt overwhelmed enough for a while I wasn't sure I could feel anything else. I'm not sure what happens next. How do they enforce parole, if the army has to pack up and get back to Venetry as quickly as possible? Mattiak doesn't seem too worried about the defenders in the capital, though he might just be putting a good face on it. But Venetry's walls are high and solid, and Arnisen said the God-Empress only took five war wagons so they wouldn't slow her down, though she compensated for it by taking twenty battle mages. That makes me suspicious, why she didn't take more

Lots of noise. It's coming from the east.

Ten minutes later, and I'm writing this quickly in case I don't have time later. The road to the east is *teeming* with movement. Soldiers. Lots of pennants. I think it's the Castaviran Army. It's *huge*. We're all dead.

CHAPTER TWENTY-TWO

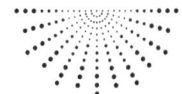

14 Seresstine

No fires tonight, which is awful because the mind-moving pouvra has exhausted all of us. I didn't get more than a nap last night. Not that anyone else has, either, since we saw the distant glinting of thousands of Castaviran soldiers coming down that highway. Between that and the unmarked snow on either side of the road, they were almost too bright to look at.

Mattiak stared at them for a full minute, then said, "Kalanik. Bronnok. Have everyone strike camp. Drussik, gather the captives on the north side of the road and make sure they're all bound securely. And no putting the boot in. They've given their parole and we'll treat them honorably."

"As if I'd treat a helpless man that way," Drussik growled, and he and the other generals left. Mattiak said, "Sesskia, I need you to translate again."

We went back to the tent where Arnisen still sat with his pair of guards. Mattiak said, "Tell him about the oncoming army. Remind him of his parole and tell him we're leaving our captives here. It's up to him whether his honor means anything."

"I don't think he'll see his parole as binding," I said, but I repeated everything to Arnisen. Surprisingly, he didn't taunt me with anything about how they were going to crush us now. He just said, "Who is leading those troops?"

"I don't know," I said. I was trying not to let myself become excited at the possibility those troops might be led by people opposed to the God-Empress. There was no way in hell Mattiak was going to sit there and take a chance on that, and as I think I've written before, there's no guarantee someone who hates the God-Empress is going to be our ally.

"And you expect us not to fight even though we will no longer be your captives?" he said.

"That's what parole means. I told you I don't understand it. It's up to you what you do. I think we can't afford to take you along, because you'll slow us down."

"You'll go to your capital?" he said.

I turned to Mattiak and said, "Should I tell him our plans? Or is that something we don't give away to our enemies?"

"We don't have any options," Mattiak said. "Go ahead and tell him we're leaving for Venetry to defeat the God-Empress before her army reinforces her."

"He says there's a chance they're not her allies," I lied, and briefly explained about the attempted coup. It was *so good* not to have to pretend not to know things.

"Interesting," Mattiak said when I finished, "but not something we can rely on. Tell him what we're doing and see if he gives up anything else."

I relayed this to Arnisen. "You're all dead," he said. "Even if you reach your city in time, you'll never be able to defeat the God-Empress before the rest of the army arrives. And they will crush you whether they ally with God or not."

"We don't have any options," I said, echoing Mattiak. "Unless you want to join forces with us."

Arnisen's lip curled in a sneer. "That truly would be faithless," he said. "You might as well kill me now."

"You know we're not going to do that," I said. I told Mattiak what he'd said, and Mattiak frowned at his captive.

"Bind him and put him with the others," he told the soldiers guarding Arnisen. "Leave their camp as it is," he said to his aides. "Let the enemy have to maneuver past it. We're leaving immediately."

The aides scattered, and I followed Mattiak out of the tent and back across the battlefield. We could see tents folding and collapsing like the drabbest butterflies you could imagine, folding their wings as they lighted on the ground. "Tell your mages to pack quickly, because we can't afford to lose any time," he told me. "Our only advantage now is speed."

"*Can* we outrun them?" I said.

"Let's hope not," he said cryptically, and before I could ask him to elaborate, we were at the mages' tents and he was gone.

Our tents were already being folded, and the mages had their gear and were sitting around the table in the dining pavilion, looking lost. I told them everything that had happened, and Saemon said, "Why wouldn't we outrun them?"

"I have no idea," I said. "It's probably some military code. Is everyone feeling rested? Because if we *can't* outrun them, and that turns out to be a bad thing, we'll need to fight."

It took a few hours—remarkably few—to break camp and form ranks for marching. Our wagon was at the rear of the procession, which made us all feel exposed and unhappy that we were slowing the army's pace. Everything nonessential had been abandoned, the supply wagons had gone on ahead long before the rest of us were ready to move, and even our wagon seemed to roll faster, as if the horses could feel how urgent this journey was.

After an hour or so, the rises and dips in the road put our former captives out of sight along with the oncoming juggernaut that was the Castaviran army. That didn't stop me looking back down the road, sometimes working the see-through pouvra in hopes of seeing how far the enemy had gotten. Unfortunately, I couldn't make it work past more than one rise, so I gave up and tried to join the mages' conversation, but I was too distracted.

I kept thinking *I could flit back and see who's in charge*, kept having to restrain myself. If they were enemies, which they almost certainly were, my learning that wouldn't change anything, and if they were friends, how was I going to convince Mattiak of that without looking like a traitor?

I'm pretty sure, after what I've done to serve Balaen, he'll give me the benefit of the doubt, but even if he doesn't think I'm a traitor when I tell him the truth about my experiences in Castavir, he's not going to risk most of the Balaenic Army just on my say-so.

So I practiced the binding pouvra (still nothing) and some of the other ones I haven't used recently, and that got the other mages practicing, and it kept me distracted enough I didn't notice where we were until the wagon stopped and the driver said, "Time to walk."

We'd stopped at the edge of the forest—I hadn't even realized we'd entered the forest, that's how preoccupied I'd been. The driver repeated his instruction, and we got down, clutching our bundles and looking around. Nessan came out from between the trees, scowled at us, and said, "Time for you to earn your pay again."

"What's going on?" I said.

The wagon jerked into motion and turned to go under the trees, where it barely fit. We were now the only people on the road. The army had vanished. "We're going to take a detour," Nessan said, "and we don't want those bastards knowing about it. The plan is to travel northward through the woods, keeping ourselves hidden, then wait for the enemy to get ahead of us and come up from behind to push them up against Venetry's wall."

"Is that why Mattiak wanted me to tell Arnisen where we were going? So he'd give false information to the Castaviran Army?" I said.

"And why we didn't bother taking any captives," Nessan said. "Let them think we're running scared."

"Isn't it a bad thing to let the troops we defeated join up with the God-Empress's forces?" Ryenn said. "To increase their numbers?"

"Worse for us if they catch us on the road," Nessan said, "and this way we harry them enough that the defenders of Venetry will have an advantage. Nothing worse for a besieging army than to be attacked from the rear."

"So what are we supposed to do? You know the concealment pouvra can't hide an entire army," I said.

Nessan waved his arm at the ground between the road and the trees. It was a mess of trodden snow and crushed branches. "You're going to clean this up so it doesn't look like an army came through," he said.

I whistled. "I had no idea you had such faith in us," I said.

"It's the General who does," Nessan said, scowling again. "I told him he was crazy."

"Well, we can try," I said, and turned to the mages. "Any ideas?"

"Well, the mind-moving pouvra, obviously," Elleria said. "We can bring in snow from all around to cover the tracks."

"Make new tracks in the road so they'll stay focused on following the 'army,'" Saemon said.

"That sounds good," I said. "Let's do it. And hurry."

We did such a good job even Nessan was impressed. Even I could move snow, and we finished by working together to move air to blow the snow crystals evenly across the ground. "We have to make sure we don't leave our own footprints," I said, and we backed into the trees, filling our prints as we went, until we were far enough in that the road was invisible. Then Nessan led us to where the army was camped between the trees, and we had something to eat before the spies had to go out again to make sure the camp couldn't be seen.

Mattiak wouldn't let us creep back to see if the army had believed our ruse, saying there was nothing we could learn that was worth the risk of revealing everything to the enemy. But I had trouble sleeping, and when we woke in the morning, we were told we were leaving the wagons behind because the forest northward was thick enough horses could barely navigate it. The wagons are heading west to get behind the Castaviran Army and pick us up again later.

So we walked all day, which we were completely unaccustomed to, and now I'm so tired if I didn't care so much about having a complete record of my journeys, I would just have written "Hid army, walked much, sleep now." And I'm so cold. I wonder how Jeddan and our mages are doing against the God-Empress. I wonder if they have to wear the King's stupid uniform, and if it's made them as much a target as I fear. I wonder if we'll be able to do any good against the Castaviran army, because we're maybe two-thirds their size and we've got a lot of wounded.

Hid army, walked much, sleep now.

15 Seresstine

More walking. We're deep in the forest now, though it's not the forest I remember. The pre-convergence forest that passes behind Hasskian ends about a hundred miles south of here, and this one is much thicker even than that one was. Fortunate for us. Not that we're anywhere near where the Castavirans are; Mattiak estimates they've reached that destroyed crossroads and are preparing to move north along the Royal Road. We're camping here for a few days to give them time to get ahead of us.

So—we're a couple days' march east of the Royal Road and two days' march north of where we were, which means we'll wait here for two days before striking out westward. (I didn't work that out myself, it's what Mattiak told me. I just thought I'd make myself look intelligent for once. That's a joke. I'm not stupid except about military affairs.)

Had dinner with Mattiak, who didn't do or say anything to discomfit me. I'm starting to feel as if I can forgive him, but our friendship can't go back to where it was before. I feel sad and guilty, which is stupid because *I* didn't do anything wrong. I guess it's because I still think Mattiak is a good man, and I wish he'd find someone who will love him the way he deserves.

I've been thinking maybe I should tell him the truth about why I speak Castaviran, and how I know all these things about their culture. He probably won't think I'm a traitor, and I'm growing increasingly worried that no one knows to be very, very suspicious of anything the God-Empress might do.

I'm too tired to think clearly about this. Tomorrow we won't be marching, and maybe I can make a decision then.

16 Seresstine

Telling Mattiak the truth was uncomfortable, but I'm convinced it was the right thing to do. We had dinner together again, and as we were finishing, I said, "I need to tell you something. I haven't been completely honest with you, and it's likely you're going to be upset, but I've never lied about being your friend, and I hope that friendship will let you listen to my whole story before you decide how you're going to react."

His eyebrows went up, and he leaned his elbows on the table. "You fill me with dread," he said. "You know I've already figured out you're a thief."

"It's not about that," I said. "I told you there were things I couldn't explain about why I speak Castaviran. I think you deserve to know what those are."

He stood and went to the tent flap to summon his servant, then stacked the dishes himself. "If it's that important," he said, "I think it would be better if we weren't interrupted."

Once the table was clear, he sat down again and spread his hands to indicate I should proceed. Naturally that made all my thoughts too jumbled for me to speak, so I took a moment to organize myself, then said, "A couple of months before the event, I was traveling near the Fensadderian border...."

I tried to sum up as much as possible. I didn't tell him any details about developing friendships or my relationship with Cederic; I wasn't trying to keep secrets, but it's a long story and I cut out as much irrelevant material as I could. I ended with the final kathana, the one that left me half-naked in the middle of a forest, then sat back and watched his face. He looked thoughtful, tapping his fingers rhythmically on the table top, his eyes fixed on a point somewhere between us. "Well," he finally said.

"I'm not a traitor," I said.

That startled him. "Is that what you thought I'd think?" he said.

"I'm married to a Castaviran mage," I said. "You can see how that, combined with everything else, might make it look like I would have reason to ally with Castavir against Balaen. But I don't. I'm not. Our worlds, our cultures, don't have any choice but to live side by side. I want that to happen peacefully, not Balaen conquering Castavir or the other way around. But I'll back any side that's in opposition to the God-Empress, because she's insane and she'll destroy either country, or both of them, if she's in control." He was still silent. "I've fought for Balaen all this time," I pointed out.

"I know," he said. His fingers resumed their drumming on the table top. "Why are you telling me this now?" he said. "There's no reason anyone would ever have to know."

"Because Balaen needs to know the God-Empress will try to destroy it," I said. "And because eventually I will find Cederic, or he will find me, and I'm not going to conceal my marriage just to keep myself from looking like a traitor."

"I understand," he said. He stood up and paced from one side of the tent to the other. I've seen him do this many times—it helps him work out serious problems. "I don't think anyone needs to know this," he said. "I'll give out that I learned about the God-Empress from interrogating that general. We already learned some of it from him, anyway."

"Actually, that was me feeding you information so I could pretend it didn't come from me," I said.

He laughed. "I don't know why you didn't tell me all of this then," he said. "I would have believed it all came from that Castaviran."

"I don't know either," I said. "Probably because you *wouldn't* have believed he was that forthcoming. Or that he'd be willing to admit his God was insane."

"True," he said. He came to a stop in front of me and put his hand on my shoulder, a friendly gesture, not a romantic one. "Thank you for trusting me with this, Sesskia," he said. "You're right, I might have thought you a traitor and had you executed."

I went briefly insubstantial so his hand fell through my shoulder to hang at his side. "Let me know when you figure out how to do that," I said with a grin.

"I am *so* glad you realized you're not an assassin," he said, returning my grin. "I'd never sleep again."

"We've agreed that I, of course, would never sneak into your tent at night," I said.

He laughed again. "Why *were* you there that night?" he said. "If it wasn't to make amorous advances."

"Nessan stole your watch and made me put it back," I admitted.

He rolled his eyes. "You *are* allowed to tell him to go to hell," he said. "I don't need two Nessans running around this place."

"I'll tell him you made me say it, and we'll see what happens," I said, and after a few more pleasantries, I came back here to write it all down. I still can't believe it was that easy. Not that I regret waiting this long, because I think Mattiak and I had to develop a real friendship so he'd be able to react so calmly.

It surprises me to discover I still consider him a friend, despite what's happened between us. If I'm being honest with myself, I can admit that as angry and heartsick as I was when Mattiak made that first advance, I appreciate that he was at least forthright enough to tell me the truth about how he felt—feels—about me instead of hiding it. Not that it's an excuse for him leading me on like that, but I think I've forgiven him.

Unless Mattiak is only pretending to be reasonable. I wish I hadn't thought that. I wish I weren't so paranoid. He didn't *sound* like he was pretending. Wonderful. And I taunted him about not being able to hold me against my will. If he puts Nessan to work on that problem, I'm doomed. *I* don't even know how to do it, but I know Nessan will figure something out. I'm never going to be able to sleep tonight.

17 Seresstine

More camping. Worked on pouvrin today, teaching everyone the see-in-dark pouvra. No real progress, but we're starting to get a feel for how to learn effectively. Nessan didn't come for me in the night.

18 Seresstine

We struck camp and began marching this morning. It took most of the day to emerge from the forest, where we found the supply train and our wagon waiting. Made some more progress before camping. Still no stealth attack by Nessan. I'd ask him myself if he has any secret orders about me, except I'm afraid it would give him ideas.

19 Seresstine

Practiced pouvrin on the road—not a road, we're cutting across country, which slows us and makes the wagon ride almost unbearably bumpy. Waiting for full dark so we can see if anyone mastered the see-in-dark pouvra, but after today's ride I don't have high hopes.

20 Seresstine

Reached the Royal Road early this morning. It's a wreck from the Castavirans passing through, but still paved smoothly and the wagon ride feels like a dream compared to the last two days. We made better time. Advance scouts report the army is a little more than a day's travel away, far enough ahead they can't see us trailing them. They are going to be *so* surprised when we come up behind them. What would be even better is if they don't attack Venetry at all, but the God-Empress's forces—let her batter them for a bit before we encounter them.

True God forgive me, I forgot my real loyalties just now. I don't want Balaen to slaughter the Castaviran army, I want them to find common ground. But that's not likely, is it? Even though I told Mattiak the truth, I don't think he agrees with me that compromise is possible. His loyalty is to Balaen, and the King's safety depends on his ensuring the "invaders" don't overcome Venetry. So we'll attack the Castavirans whether they join with the God-Empress or not, and we won't try to make peace with them even though Mattiak has a translator, and they're enough bigger than we are that even if we win, it will be at a huge cost. I'm so sick of war.

21 Seresstine

We're another two days south of Venetry, which means the Castaviran army will reach its walls either late tomorrow or early the day after. There's a big storm coming in, so it might take longer. These northern storms have been known to last for days. I hope I'm wrong about how the weather looks, but I've traveled rough long enough to know the difference between a light squall and a full-on tempest. I think the officers feel the same way, because they sent runners north to find a good location for us to camp. Oh, well, if we have to be stuck here, at least:

1. We will have plenty of time to learn and practice pouvrin;

2. The Castaviran army will be stuck too;

3. The odds are good the storm will reach as far north as Venetry, which will interfere with the God-Empress's attack; and

4. Storms are nice if you're in a cozy tent rather than stumbling around hoping to find shelter.

I've been trying not to think about what's happening at Venetry. I'm not worried about Jeddan; he knows what he's doing, and the mages listen to him. Mostly I'm worried I'm wrong, and the God-Empress has been able to overwhelm our defenders, and we'll arrive just in time to besiege our own city. And if she kills the King…it's better if I don't think about it at all, since I can't do anything about it. I'm going to sleep now, and hope I dream of Cederic again.

22 Seresstine, afternoon

The storm caught us about an hour ago—I say "caught us" but we actually saw it coming a long way off and had plenty of time to prepare. The wind is beating against the tent walls so loudly I feel as if my thoughts are shouting over it. The mages worked on pouvrin, and griped about not being able to practice the see-in-dark pouvra until someone suggested doing it outside in the storm, and it's a sign of how bored we all were that we were willing to try it. The experiment didn't last long, but it did amuse us, and a couple of the mages even succeeded!

But I've felt a little low today, like I'm coming down with a cold, so eventually I excused myself and came back here to re-read some of my records, all the nice ones like the rest day at the Darssan and the first night Cederic and I spent together. It was obvious, as I read that one again, that if I *had* been Castaviran, I would have been sending all sorts of signals that I wanted to marry him right then. In fact, it's surprising *he* wasn't offended by what to him must have looked like brash forwardness.

And it's no wonder he was so adamant I understand why he couldn't spend the night with me after letting me fall asleep in his arms; a Castaviran woman might have taken that as a breach of promise. I wonder how many other cultural misunderstandings we'll have, when we're finally together again to have them.

I can't think of anything else to write. I think I'll go find Nessan and see if he can think of any exercises you can do in a snowstorm.

I can't believe I'm that desperate for entertainment.

23 Seresstine, noon

The storm blew itself out in less than twenty-four hours, and we're getting ready to strike camp and move on. In fact, we're waiting for the runners to come back with the news that the Castavirans are on the move—wouldn't want to run into them too soon. I don't feel like practicing pouvrin now; I feel achy and tired and I'm definitely coming down with a cold. It had better be gone before we reach Venetry, because the way I feel, I'm not sure I could bend my will to anything more strenuous than drinking a cup of hot tea. Not that

Just had a messenger from Mattiak. People coming down the road from the NORTH, carrying red and black flags. Castavirans. I'm to go interpret. My heart is pounding so hard, but I had to write this in case the worst happens—hah. Like this record is going to matter if we're overrun by the army. But that doesn't sound like an attack. Could be anything. Going now.

CHAPTER TWENTY-THREE

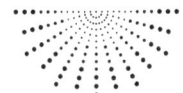

24 Seresstine, very early

It's been a long, busy day, and I still feel achy and stuffed-up, but I woke up about twenty minutes ago—some noise or other outside the tent—and couldn't fall back asleep. So I decided I might as well write, since I haven't had any time for that since I jotted down my last entry. I can't believe it was only about fifteen hours ago I put my book away and ran to the command tent (this was a guess, the messenger hadn't actually said where I was to go) which I reached in time to meet Mattiak approaching it. "Who are they?" I said, which of all the questions bubbling up inside me made the least sense.

"They stopped about half a mile from us and set up a tent," Mattiak said, answering the question I would have asked if my head hadn't been aching with my cold. "Battle mages. Five of them, carried by moving shells, or cups—our sentries were too shaken by their appearance to be very coherent—and a couple of what we think are ordinary soldiers. I don't suppose you know what a red diamond on a black background means?"

"I don't," I said, "but that sounds as if they want to talk. As if they want to seem non-threatening."

"That is what we are going to discuss," he said, and held the tent flap open for me. Generals Kalanik and Drussik were already there, and three or four majors, and all their aides, and in general it was so full of Balaenic military masculinity I felt stifled. I found a seat off to one side and watched Mattiak pace, bringing all the other quiet conversations to a halt. When the only sound in the tent was that of his boots striking the cold ground, he said, "Your thoughts, gentlemen?"

"They're trying to draw us out," Drussik said. "Those things they came in on are unnatural. Who knows what other magics they might be able to turn against us?"

"I want to know how they discovered us," said a major whose name I didn't remember.

"That was always a risk," Mattiak said. "All they needed was to send scouts in the right direction. I think if they had magic to locate us, they'd have come after us through the forest."

"I don't see that we have much choice now," Major Melekst said. "They won't let us pass. We'll have to make our attack here."

"And be overwhelmed by their superior numbers?" General Kalanik sounded angrier than I'd ever heard him before. "Think sense, man! We have to meet with them if only to give ourselves time to repulse their attack."

"But it has to be a trick," Drussik said. "Why wouldn't they approach and ask for a proper parley? It's all a ruse. They want to remove our leadership and weaken us. Trust me, Tarallan, if you go to this meeting, you'll be going to your death."

"They'd be going to a hell of a lot of trouble just to engineer one man's death," Melekst said. "And I mean no offense by this, Commander General, but as important as you are, the Army won't come to a shuddering halt if you're not here to direct it."

"I'm not offended, and you're right, Major," Mattiak said. "So if that's what they have in mind, throwing us into disarray by killing me, their leaders aren't very intelligent."

Something Drussik had said finally made it all the way to a part of my brain that could understand it. "If they don't speak our language, they *couldn't* ask for a parley, could they?" I exclaimed, cutting across Mattiak's next words.

"That's why it's a trick," Drussik said. "They're counting on us being curious enough to go out to meet them. And then they kill our envoys."

"They outnumber us," Kalanik said. "If they wanted us dead, they'd have just turned on us. No need for this elaborate game."

"What if, in their culture, this is how they parley?" I said. My heart was beating faster. If they were willing to talk to us instead of attacking, they couldn't be hell-bent on conquering Balaen, which meant whoever was in charge...actually, I couldn't think of a way to complete that thought. I couldn't assume someone I knew was in control of that army. "What if they haven't sent anyone because they think it's polite to allow us to decide the terms on which we meet them?"

"You sound as if you have some special knowledge, Sesskia," Mattiak said, eyeing me narrowly.

"I don't," I said. "It's just I can't help thinking—"

"Your thinking has no military basis," Drussik said, slapping his palm impatiently on his thigh. "You don't even have a true command."

"They carry flags we've never seen before," I forged on, starting to feel desperate. "They're well outside the range of their magic. And as General Kalanik said, they could have just marched on us—they discovered us before we knew *they* knew we were here, right?" (I was hoping, in writing this, to make it sound more coherent, but I'm still slightly ill. That's my excuse, anyway.)

"That's a nice fabric you've woven, but there's no proof of it," Drussik said. "I say we march on them and hope to take them by surprise. We have to prevent those battle mages from reporting back to their camp."

"No!" I exclaimed, coming off my seat to stand in front of Drussik. He's short and slender, with lots of white hair, and since he was standing already my movement put me eye to eye with him. "They're here in good faith and you want to betray that?"

"Don't try to involve me in your fantasy, girl, the rest of us have to live in the real world," Drussik said.

I glanced at Mattiak. He was looking at me impassively. I had no idea why he wasn't stepping in here, but that was just as well, because I didn't feel like I could stop myself, even for him. I looked back at Drussik, who was scowling at me. "Then let's talk about the real world," I said. "There aren't a lot of possibilities here. They clearly want us to come to them. Either they want us in a position where they can kill our leaders to throw us into confusion, or they want to talk, maybe to enter into an agreement, or maybe to present us with the terms of our surrender. Are you with me so far, General Drussik?"

Drussik's eyes were glazed with incomprehension, but then I *had* been talking rather quickly, partly because of my aching head, but mostly because I felt restless at how long this stupid discussion was going. "The thing is," I went on, "both those possibilities mean meeting the Castavirans is the best course of action."

"That's ridiculous," Drussik said, regaining his composure. "Why would we walk into their trap?"

"Because it's not a trap if you know about it," I said. "You go to meet them, prepared for betrayal, and you can defend against their attack and maybe even gain the upper hand if it turns out that's what they're after. If it isn't, then you can discuss whatever they *do* have in mind, and you both benefit. Even if they just want us to surrender, at least you've prevented unnecessary bloodshed. But *I* think they're here to deal honorably with us."

I turned to face Mattiak, and said, "I think I should come with you, though, in case I'm wrong and those battle mages turn on you. And to translate, of course."

"But—" Drussik sputtered.

"Sesskia's argument is compelling. We'll leave in fifteen minutes," Mattiak said. "Drussik, I leave the camp in your hands. Wyoth, Steless, you'll come with me. Sesskia, choose another mage—one capable of tearing a battle mage apart, if you don't mind? And meet us at the northern picket line."

He left the tent before anyone else could start an argument. I think that's why he's the commander of the Army—he knows when to leave a room. I hurried after him. "Why did you make me do all the talking?" I said. "It's your army. They're your generals. I'm just the mage auxiliary leader who doesn't even have a real title or uniform."

"I didn't expect you to do that," he said in a low voice. "I was giving you a chance to tell them your secret, if that's what you wanted to do. Now I'm wondering if I should put you in command of a division."

"That's not funny," I said, but the image of me waving a riding crop and leading men into battle was pretty funny.

"I'm only half joking," he said. We'd been walking all that time, and now we reached his tent and stopped. He didn't look joking at all. "You think you know who these people are."

I shook my head. "Maybe. But even if it is someone I know, he might not be an ally."

Mattiak sighed. "Bring one of your best mages," he said, and ducked into his tent.

I rounded up the mages and explained what was happening, then told Elleria to come with me before anyone could start arguing, and we put on our warmest gear—the sun might as well have been a yellow circle in a child's painting for all the heat it gave off, and there was a wind that felt like knives against exposed skin. The coat I bought in Venetry is ugly, but warm, and when I pull the hood up all the way it hides my face. Not that I did that on purpose, but I'm sure it made for a great dramatic element later.

We were first to the picket lines, and I shaded my eyes and looked out across the plains, but with all the loose snow kicked up by the frigid wind, I couldn't see our Castaviran friends. I was pondering the possibility of a see-far pouvra when the men arrived, and Mattiak said, "Neither of you know how to ride, do you?"

"You know we don't," I said.

He shrugged. "Wyoth, if you don't mind?" he said, and Kalanik stepped forward and offered his hand to Elleria, lifting her into the saddle before she could do more than let out a tiny yelp of surprise. Then Mattiak extended his hand to me.

"I don't—" I said, and then I was high above the ground, and Mattiak had mounted behind me. I had the same unnervingly unsafe feeling I'd had riding the God-Empress's collenna—just far enough off the ground that falling would hurt. I reminded myself of the many times I've scaled walls and dropped from windows and done other things that would terrify anyone else, and clung to the horse's mane even though I had a feeling that was the wrong thing to do. Sure enough, Mattiak's hand came around to pry my fingers free of the hairs that clung to my gloves and guided me to clutch the saddle horn.

"It's all right, I won't let you fall off," he said. He had a scarf wrapped around the lower half of his face, but I could tell he was grinning wickedly. He held the reins in one hand and put his other around my waist, but I was straddling the horse more securely now, and I no longer felt as if I were about to fall.

Even so, I didn't tell him to let go of my waist, though I felt uncomfortable at his nearness. He didn't make an issue of it, and I was eventually able to relax and enjoy—hah. I don't think I'll ever enjoy riding a horse. Maybe I'm wrong, and I'd like it if I were the one in control, but they're big and they smell funny and I'm sure they can tell when their riders don't appreciate them. If Mattiak hadn't been there I think ours would have knocked me off and then laughed at me.

It was too cold for conversation, and that's *another* reason not to like horses, you get so cold sitting up there exposed like that! But that's not important. We rode in silence, and I used the time to go over possibilities:

1. Aselfos, or his pet general, was there, and my presence would make them inclined to make peace with our army.

2. Aselfos was there, but didn't care that I was with the Balaenics and it would take forever for both our sides to learn to trust each other.

3. The army was controlled by someone I didn't know who was reasonable and wanted an alliance. I didn't know enough to even guess at what that might be.

4. They were there to demand our surrender.

What I couldn't figure out is why the negotiating party was all mages. Why not a military presence? Unless the mages had military rank as well...it's not as if I know anything about the Castaviran military. But Drussik's whining aside, our party had a huge advantage in the form of Elleria and myself, since I was certain we could neutralize their mages before any of them had the time to bring out their boards. I hoped it wasn't necessary.

The longer we rode, the more worries I came up with. I'd been acting on emotion when I argued this course of action, and if I had led Mattiak wrong...

By the time we reached the Castavirans' camp, I was ready to leap down and flit back the other way. Not that I would have done it, but it would have relieved my tension. And I would have regretted it so much.

The Castavirans had set up a single large tent that looked exactly like a Balaenic military tent. I guess there are only so many ways you can build a tent and still have it be useful. It was white canvas instead of drab brown, and I'm sure someone intended it to be attractive, but the white showed every splotch of mud, so it just looked in need of a wash.

Four thick poles were driven deep into the ground in front of the tent, and tethered to them were the strangest collennas I'd ever seen. Not that I've seen that many of them. They were small versions of the God-Empress's rose-colored collenna, maybe five feet around but lower to the ground, and shiny black like a beetle's carapace. In fact, they did look like headless beetles. Their tethers were stretched out taut as if they were straining to break free. Mattiak helped me down and I went to look more closely at them. "Don't do that," he said.

"They aren't dangerous," I said, though I didn't touch any of them, in case this kind of collenna responded to something other than th'an. No, there was the grooved faceplate, and the seat that looked like it could fit two people if they didn't mind being squeezed together, and the brushes and pots of silver ink. I wondered what all those unemployed collenna masters were going to do with their lives now.

Mattiak took my shoulder. "Everyone's here," he said. Kalanik was helping Elleria down. The other general was tethering the horses to a rail the Castavirans seemed to have put there for just that purpose. Two women in Castaviran military uniforms, or at least military trousers and boots (their jackets were concealed by their heavy coats) stood at attention near the tent door. Mattiak made a few gestures that made his men fall into a formation that looked intentionally lopsided. Elleria and I trailed along at the rear, not being privy to Balaenic military code, though as we weren't Balaenic military I guess that didn't matter. As we approached, the soldiers drew the tent doors open, and we all filed through.

It was blessedly warm inside. I'd forgotten until that moment how wonderfully practical Castaviran magic could be. Th'an glowed on all the tent poles near the roof, and tangles of those lights I remembered from the Darssan looped around all the horizontal poles and down the corner uprights. It looked warm, and felt warm, and the throbbing in my head eased.

Mattiak and the other two men were like a wall in front of me, blocking my view of the Castavirans. I was taking a few steps to the right to be able to see around them when I heard Mattiak say, "I am General Mattiak Tarallan, Commander General of the Balaenic Army —oh." He took my arm and drew me forward, saying, "You'll need to translate."

And I came around to where I could see everything in time to hear Cederic say, in unexpectedly drawling Balaenic, "My name is Cederic Aleynten, and I speak for the Castaviran Empire. Thank you for accepting our offer of parley."

My knees buckled from utter surprise, and I grabbed Mattiak's coat and clung to it to keep from falling over entirely. That made him lurch, and since everyone was looking at him, everyone transferred those looks to me, Cederic with a polite non-interest that was like a punch to the stomach until I remembered he couldn't possibly see past the fur of my hood.

Mattiak took hold of my elbow and helped me stand. "You speak our language," he said, and then his hand on my elbow gripped more tightly as the name registered.

"Cederic Aleynten," he said, rolling the words around on his tongue. "I think we have already found common ground." He transferred his hand from my elbow to the small of my back and gave me a push in Cederic's direction.

I turned to look over my shoulder at Mattiak, still feeling stunned. He had a strange look on his face I've only just now realized was regret. I think he really did believe Cederic was dead, or wasn't coming for me, and it was only a matter of time before I fell in love with him. That makes me so sad. I hope he finds the happiness he deserves.

I turned to look at Cederic, who'd already lost interest in me and was saying, "I do not believe we need fight with one another." He was wearing the red Kilios's robe, which confused me at first because he burned his robe with all our other clothes the day Vorantor was murdered by the God-Empress, but then I noticed this robe's color was faded and it was frayed at the collar and cuffs. His eyes were shadowed as if he hadn't been sleeping well, and when his hand came to rest on the back of the chair he was standing behind, I saw it tremble.

I saw all of that in the time it takes to draw breath and release it, and it made me so nervous I couldn't think straight, though some of that was probably my cold. It was as if he were a stranger, someone I'd been told was important to me, but not why. I'd had him with me only in memories for so long I was afraid those memories were wrong, that they didn't match the reality of him, and that he wouldn't even recognize me because to him I was just a woman from a dream, too.

That last thought, thank the true God, was absurd enough that I remembered the truth: I'd crossed half of Balaen hoping to be reunited with my husband, only to let ridiculous fears get in the way of that reunion. I pushed back the hood of my coat and said, "Cederic."

I think he didn't realize who I was at first. He stopped in mid-word when I interrupted him and turned politely in my direction, as if waiting to hear what I'd contribute to the discussion. Then his eyes met mine, and a look of complete, uncharacteristic astonishment crossed his features. Somewhere nearby I heard Terrael shout my name, but I couldn't stop staring at Cederic.

He didn't look as if he remembered how to move. He closed his eyes and shuddered once, the way he does when he's trying to contain a powerful emotion. Then he opened his eyes, and said, "Sesskia," and I was in his arms with no memory of how I'd crossed the intervening distance, laughing and sobbing at the same time, not caring how it must look to my Balaenic friends.

Cederic held me close and whispered, "I'm sorry, love, so sorry, please forgive my stupidity," and I said, "I meant to find you sooner, I truly did, I'm sorry," and then I started laughing harder, I'm still not sure why, except I was so emotional it was either that or bark at the noonday sun like a madwoman.

I'd forgotten about our audience, but Cederic hadn't, and after a few more whispered endearments, he released me—not far, I still had a grip on his hand—and said to Mattiak, "General Tarallan, I am not certain what question to ask next."

"I'm nearly as surprised as you," Mattiak said. "I assure you this wasn't a ploy to threaten or coerce you."

"I believe you," Cederic said. "But I think it changes the nature of these discussions."

"I hope it means we don't have to waste time deciding whether or not to trust each other," Mattiak said. "May we sit?"

"Please," Cederic said, and there was some shuffling as everyone found camp stools or folding chairs. I took a moment to hug Terrael, who for a miracle wasn't babbling. He looks different, and I don't know if that's because he's lost his magic or because he has so many more responsibilities now or just the haircut—but I learned all that later.

We ended up in two lines facing each other, Castaviran and Balaenic, with me sitting on the Balaenic side despite my extreme reluctance to let go of Cederic's hand. He didn't look happy about it either, but we both knew where I belonged for this meeting, though I could see by how impassive Cederic became he was struggling not to ask a million questions that had nothing to do with the issues at hand.

Mattiak gave me a look, when I sat at the end of our row, that was filled with a respect I'm not sure I deserved. I smiled back and him, and shrugged, and he nodded once, then turned to face Cederic.

I was opposite a mage I didn't know, with Terrael at the other end of the row, which was fortunate because I'm not sure I could have stayed focused on what was happening if I'd been looking at his familiar, eager face.

"We did not realize you had doubled back until yesterday morning," Cederic said, "and then we did not expect to find you trailing us so closely. We feel fortunate you did not seem inclined to attack us, because we were unprepared for that contingency."

"We were waiting for the right time," Mattiak said. "I'd like to know why you didn't attack *us* when you discovered where we were."

"We are not interested in attacking Balaen," Cederic said. "We are pursuing Castaviran troops who are under the command of a madwoman who *is* intent on conquering Balaen."

"Your God-Empress," Mattiak said. Cederic's gaze flicked to me and away again. I wanted so badly for this meeting to be over, because he hadn't even kissed me and I wanted that more than anything.

"She is no longer Empress," Cederic said. "She was ousted from power during the convergence. Castavir currently has no ruler."

"It's not you, then?" Mattiak said. "You said you spoke for the Empire."

I gave Cederic a horrified look. "Cederic, you're not *Emperor*, are you?" I blurted out, not caring that everyone turned their attention on me. I was caught in the grip of a vision of myself dressed in the God-Empress's cloth-of-gold robes, seated on a throne next to Cederic, and I felt faint.

He gave me a little smile. "I am not," he assured me. "General

Tarallan, the former Empress has no heir, and while there are many contenders for the throne, none has a claim sufficiently strong as to emerge the unchallenged victor. I speak for Castavir, for the moment, because my rank as chief of the priest-mages of the Empire gives me the power to anoint a successor. But before I can do so, the former Empress must be apprehended so she cannot challenge the new regime."

"And executed?" Mattiak said, arching one eyebrow. I swear I'm going to learn to do that someday.

Cederic turned his tiny smile on Mattiak. "If she cannot be convinced to retire peacefully." His smile said clearly what he thought of the likelihood of the God-Empress doing *anything* peacefully.

"And then you will declare a new Emperor. Or Empress," Mattiak said.

"Not exactly," Cederic said. "Bad enough that there is no obvious choice to hold the throne; the lure of power is great enough that many of the candidates passed over by me will not see my decision as binding on them, despite my right to make that decision. Civil war is coming to Castavir, and it will sweep Balaen along with it. Therefore, once we have defeated the God-Empress, I intend to offer the throne of Castavir to the King of Balaen."

I sucked in a horrified breath. The other Balaenics didn't look happy either. Mattiak looked as if he were struggling to find words that would not be treasonous. "The King...I don't think he...Balaen is a great responsibility in itself..."

"We are aware of the King's...limitations," Cederic said. He looked as impassive as ever, but I could tell he was no happier about this than the rest of us. "But he is the best solution to both our countries' problem. Many of those in Castavir who would revolt at one of their fellows being elevated above them would find no legitimate reason to prosecute their claim to the throne should a non-Castaviran hold it. None of them would be able to make common cause against Balaen because if they successfully defeated your country, they would simply be in the same position of being at one another's throats. And

Castavir's military forces are in the hands of people who agree with my—our—solution."

"But your citizens will never stand for it," Mattiak said. "To be ruled by a foreigner—"

"We have been laying the foundation for that in the past months," Cederic said. "We will, of course, insist on establishing the conditions under which the King of Balaen will take power. He will remove his court to Colosse, our capital city. There will be a council of advisors drawn equally from Balaenics and Castavirans. And we will expect him to marry a Castaviran woman. There are other conditions, but these are the ones on which we will not compromise."

"And if he refuses?" Mattiak said.

"Then there will be war," Cederic said, and his control slipped enough to show how the idea saddened and angered him. "That is not a threat; we are not interested, as I said, in attacking Balaen. I will select a ruler from among a pool of suboptimal choices, and Castavir will burn, and it will take Balaen with it."

Mattiak curled his hands, which were resting on his knees, into fists. "I am not the one you should tell this to," he said.

"I want the support of your army in defeating our former Empress," Cederic said. "I think it would have been hard to convince you of the necessity had I not shared this plan. And I would appreciate your advice as to how we might present our proposal to your King that would be effective. It is crucial he be induced to see our sincerity."

Mattiak let out a deep breath. "I can't ally with you," he said, and Cederic went even more impassive. "That's something King and Chamber have to approve. But I am free to pursue enemies of Balaen, and your former Empress falls solidly into the category. And, naturally, if we're attacking the same foe, it makes sense we should coordinate those attacks. We wouldn't want to step all over each other."

Cederic nodded. "And on the other matter?"

"I owe my loyalty to my King," Mattiak said, his face as impassive as Cederic's. "I should not share such information with a foreign diplomat, if that's what you are. But I am not the only one who's observed the King closely." He looked directly, blatantly at me, and I had to make myself sit up straight and look alert and helpful instead of shrinking from, again, the attention of everyone in the tent.

"I understand," Cederic said. "I respect your sense of honor. Is there anything you would ask of us? Of me? I feel myself very much in your debt." He *didn't* look at me, but I knew—and I'm sure everyone else did too—that as far as Cederic was concerned, he and I were the only ones in that tent.

"I'm curious as to how you speak our language," Mattiak said, "and why you sound like a Barrekellian."

This had made me curious as well—not the part about Cederic speaking my language, since I've given up being astonished at the things he's able to do, but the fact that he speaks it with a long, drawling accent like that of those living in the southeast, especially around the city of Barrekel. It's not that it's a bad thing, but they all sound bored, all the time, and the contrast to the precision of Cederic's Castaviran speech was pretty funny.

"We have a kathana—a kind of magic—that allows a mage to speak and understand, but not read, another language," Cederic said. "I was not aware it gave us any particular accent."

"I wouldn't mind being able to speak yours," Mattiak said. "It would be a tremendous advantage."

"I am afraid it would not work on you," Cederic said. "It only affects mages because their minds have the right flexibility from working magic. Unfortunate, I think, but we have also met Balaenics who are learning to speak Castaviran the traditional way, and they tell us it is not difficult. Your language is far more complex," he added, and he sounded impressed, which made me proud on behalf of my culture.

"Perhaps when this is all over, I'll make time," Mattiak said. "I think I should meet with your commander—you did say that was someone other than yourself?"

"General Gael Regates," Cederic said. "She was not convinced this meeting was a good idea, but I think she will be glad to learn we could make common cause. She has not yet mastered your language, but we will provide translators. Shall we arrange for the two of you to meet here at another time?"

"No need," Mattiak said, rising from his stool. "If it's all right with you, we'll go to your camp now. I understand the former Empress is besieging Venetry at the moment, and I don't think we should waste any time."

Cederic stood when he did, with the rest of us rising raggedly after him. "This has been an unexpected meeting in every way," he said. "I am grateful to find such a sensible man in command of the Balaenic Army. I had anticipated a much greater struggle to reach consensus."

"I've heard a great deal about your character in the past weeks," Mattiak said, "and I trust the source completely." I was so grateful no one understood that comment, because it made me blush to know how much he respected me even if I didn't return his affection.

"Though it makes sense," he said, extending his hand palm-out to Cederic, "that Sesskia's husband would turn out to be the spokesman for an Empire." That sent up a lot of murmuring on our side as my greeting of Cederic suddenly made sense to everyone, and I blushed harder and couldn't meet anyone's eyes.

Cederic placed his palm against Mattiak's with no hesitation. "Sesskia's husband is simply very grateful to be reunited with her," he said.

Mattiak nodded. "I take it those...things...outside are some form of transportation?" he said.

"Yes," said Cederic. "They are somewhat faster than horses, so we will outpace you, but I think we should arrive in advance of you anyway, to warn our sentries." Finally, *finally* he turned to me, and extended his hand. "Sesskia," he said, with such depth of emotion in his voice that I shivered, "ride with me. I think we have much to talk about."

"Yes," I said, my tongue tangling on other possible responses like *Damn right we do* and *I am* never *letting go of you again*. I let him help me into the collenna, which had a tendency to shift if you pushed on it the wrong way, and Cederic released its tether and it started rolling forward slowly. Then he traced a couple of linked th'an on the brass faceplate with his fat writing tool, and I shrieked and clutched at him when it jerked, then sped off faster than any horse, spraying up the snow that still covered the road into a fine white mist.

Cederic chuckled and put his arms around my waist to steady me. "That was an unexpected bonus," he said, and I pressed my lips to his and stifled whatever else he was going to say.

He had to pay attention to driving the collenna, or I don't think I would have stopped kissing him until we reached their camp. As it was, we managed a few kisses in between battering each other with questions. First, of course, was the pressing matter of why I'd been separated from him in the first place. It turned out Cederic Aleynten, Kilios and undisputed master of magic, had in his hurry to finish the convergence kathana left out a few simple but key th'an that would have returned me to the palace once the convergence was over. It took a *lot* of kissing to get him to stop apologizing for it.

Less amusing was the way he looked when he described how rewriting the locator kathanas kept being pushed aside in favor of more urgent problems, like bringing order to Colosse and inventing a translation kathana, though that last was Terrael's work. I seized on that and said, trying to distract him from his bleak memories, "So he didn't lose his magic, after all?"

Cederic frowned. "He did," he said, "and I think you have guessed the common factor between all who can still work magic."

"The eyes," I said. "Poor Terrael. But he seemed—I didn't have time to look at him, but he didn't seem incapacitated."

"There was a time when we thought we would lose him," Cederic said. "He fell into a deep depression from which even Master Engilles could not rouse him. It took him some time to realize he had not lost his genius, and that his knowledge of magic was still extraordinary even if th'an no longer activated when he drew them. He and Master Engilles have become a powerful pairing, more so, I think, than even marriage can account for. He devises kathanas which she performs and adapts, and he acts as my aide. I think you will find him changed, but for the better."

"I'm glad. I was so worried for him and for Sovrin," I said.

"Master Peressten's translation kathana works even on those mages who can no longer work magic, which has given them a new role in our endeavor," he said. "Master Ustanz supervises our corps of translators, who travel to Balaenic cities to explain what has happened and ask for their help in bringing our countries together. She is a remarkable leader and an effective diplomat."

"Are they with the army, then?" I asked.

"All of the mages who worked on the convergence kathana are with us," he said. "They will be overjoyed to know you are well. When the locator kathanas failed, all we could do was prove you were alive, and it was two weeks before we had the ability and time to do that." He clenched his hand tightly on mine. "Two weeks," he repeated, his eyes going unfocused, and I hugged him tight—tighter, because I hadn't let him go from the moment the collenna started moving.

I told him the short version of my adventures, from meeting Jeddan to fighting the God-Empress's army, and he listened in the intent way he does, then said, "Why do you think the convergence created so many mages?"

"I have no idea," I said. "All I can think is it must have been traumatic on some level we're not aware of. Or that something about the combined worlds allowed the magic to wake up on its own terms, like how only the green-eyed mages can work magic now. But they're able to learn magic the way Jeddan and I did, if faster—that might be part of the difference too."

"I look forward to meeting your friend," Cederic said. "I owe him a debt for not leaving you entirely alone, after I—"

I kissed him again. "I thought I told you no more talking like that," I chastised him.

Wry humor touched his eyes. "If you intend to kiss me every time I express my apologies for failing you," he said, "that will almost certainly accomplish the opposite of what you intend."

"I could stop kissing you entirely," I pointed out.

"I think," he said, pulling me close, "you are unlikely to follow through on that threat."

When we finally came up for air, I said, breathlessly, "I'm sure Jeddan wants to meet you too. I certainly talked about you enough."

"To General Tarallan, too, it seems," he said. "You must be friends, that he uses your praenoma."

"We are," I said.

Cederic linked his fingers with mine. "And he is in love with you," he said.

"I was hoping you couldn't tell," I said.

"Better for both of us that I could," he said. "I might have said or done any number of cruel things in my ignorance."

"I was afraid you might be..." I trailed off because I wasn't sure what I'd thought Cederic might be. Jealous? Angry?

"Is it too arrogant for me to say I am certain of your love for me?" Cederic said. "I understand perfectly why a powerful, honorable man might fall in love with you, Sesskia. And I could see by your behavior you feel nothing more for him than friendship. So no, I feel no jealousy other than what I feel toward everyone who was able to share your companionship these past weeks when I could not. Sadness, possibly—though not enough that I would be willing to stand aside and allow him to win your heart."

"Now I'm annoyed you think I need your permission to fall in love with someone," I said, teasing him.

"Not permission, certainly," he said, straight-faced again, "but I assure you if I thought there were someone you felt an attraction to, I would do everything in my power to remind you I am the superior choice."

"I already know that," I said, which set us to kissing again.

Now I'm feeling sleepy—I still don't have a watch, so I don't know what time it is, but I'll have to sum up the rest. We arrived at the Castaviran tent, and Cederic tethered his collenna—they don't stop moving until the magic runs out naturally, so the...paddock, maybe? The place where they keep them, anyway—it's full of these giant black beetles straining at their leashes, which is fun to watch for a few minutes, and then it's boring.

I watched them for more than a few minutes while Cederic gave orders concerning the Balaenics who were following, then he took my hand and we went to his command tent, where Sovrin stopped talking to a couple of men in an unfamiliar uniform, shrieked, and flung herself on me, hugging me until we both cried. Then it was Audryn, who looked so tired because SHE IS PREGNANT and I can't believe Cederic failed to tell me this!

We had a long talk, Sovrin and Audryn and I, while Cederic was off with his generals, and then with our people (I mean the Balaenics), and Audryn said she still felt embarrassed about becoming pregnant, because in Castavir the women are solely responsible for contraception if that's what they want, and it's a big semi-religious thing. And on their wedding night, Audryn was so happy about Terrael loving her and miserable over Cederic's humiliation she didn't take any precautions, and it only took the one time. ("Four or five times," she said later, grinning.)

So what with that and with Terrael being suicidally depressed, she had a rough couple of weeks. And she was bearing the burden of her pregnancy alone because—I didn't understand this very well, but I guess there's some stigma attached to becoming pregnant when you haven't said your legal vows in front of a priest, and she felt ashamed about telling anyone.

But eventually she broke down and started shouting at Terrael while he was curled up in that black despair, and the knowledge that he was going to be a father managed to wake him up, and now everything's fine, except they *still* haven't said their vows, and I guess that's not good. But Terrael—Cederic was right that he's changed; he's openly sharing a tent with Audryn, and while he's still eager and bright, he's not bouncing with excitement all the time anymore. And I like the change.

Audryn being pregnant woke *me* up a bit, because Cederic and I haven't taken any precautions either. I'm definitely not ready for a baby, not while everything is so uncertain, and I didn't think I could put the burden of responsibility on my husband the way we do in Balaen, so I flitted north up the Royal Road a few miles to a respectably-sized Balaenic city and found an apothecary who had what I needed. Because there was no way in hell I was *not* sleeping with Cederic that night.

And I did. And it was wonderful. Those camp beds are pretty narrow, but there's plenty of room for two people who love each other to sleep close together—and plenty of room for them to show that love to each other if they're creative. Which we were. More than once.

Cederic looks so relaxed now. He fell asleep before I did, and I didn't wake him getting out of bed, so I can imagine how exhausted he must have been. My heart aches to think of how he must have suffered, not knowing if I was alive, having to bring Colosse out of the flames of riot, fighting absolutely everyone to take control of the government, knowing he would have to hand that control over to a weak king—I don't know how he learned what kind of man Garran Clendessar is, but he knows well the odds of Balaen's King being a good ruler of two countries are small. I hope our being reunited makes Cederic's work easier. I know I feel better having his strength behind me.

I think I can sleep now. Tomorrow—hah, later today—we'll meet with the generals of both armies and plan a strategy. And then we move out. Two days, and we'll be at the gates of Venetry. I hope it's not too late.

CHAPTER TWENTY-FOUR

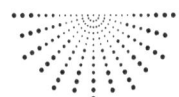

24 Seresstine, evening

I'm taking advantage of Cederic being in yet another meeting with his generals—with our, I mean the Balaenic, generals too, discussing what both armies are going to do when we arrive in Venetry tomorrow. It will probably be late tomorrow, too, and I gather that's part of the discussion, deciding whether to attack immediately or camp and look threatening. Cederic wants to send an envoy demanding they turn over the God-Empress to us, see if we can avoid fighting altogether, and I think that's probably the way they'll go.

No wonder Cederic was so tired; the Castaviran Army is composed of several divisions the way the Balaenic Army is, and their generals all argue like cats in a sack. Even he has trouble keeping them all focused on their goal. Having seen them, I can understand how having the King of Balaen ruling Castavir is the best of a lot of bad options.

I rode with the Balaenic mages all morning, telling them the whole story of my experiences in Castavir before the convergence, and about how Castaviran magic works, and answering all their questions. The first questions were almost entirely about my personal life; they met Cederic this morning, when he came back with me to our camp, and they were curious about him and the other Castaviran mages. A few of them wanted to know how Jeddan was going to feel about it, since it seems some of our people thought he and I were romantically involved. I wanted to laugh at that.

The rest of the questions were about Castaviran magic. They're all deeply interested in the possibilities inherent in th'an and pouvrin being related, and we talked about the binding pouvra (some of them may have learned it, but since it doesn't do anything, there's no way to tell) and the concealment pouvra, and one or two of them asked about doing it the other way—turning a pouvra into a th'an or kathana. I hadn't thought of that before, but of course it's just as possible (or impossible) as making a pouvra out of th'an. Something to work on after we capture the God-Empress.

After we stopped for lunch, I rode with Cederic, who was heart-breakingly glad to see me even though we'd only been separated for a few hours, and we talked about the King of Balaen. Cederic said what they knew of him was built out of conversations the translator mages had had with Balaenic citizens as they went through the country building good will.

(All that noise Mattiak made about the center of Balaen being conquered by Castavir was based on our not receiving messengers from those cities, but that was because most of them were busy trying to communicate with their new Castaviran neighbors. And he might have been exaggerating a bit in his attempt to win my heart.)

Cederic had inferred correctly that the King allowed the Chamber to make most of the policy decisions that affected the average Balaenic citizen, and that his presence was felt sporadically as he took up new enthusiasms and then let them fall, usually before he'd completed whatever project it was. The citizens the mages had spoken to were respectful of the King, but he was a very distant part of their lives.

I told Cederic what I'd observed of King and Chamber, how the King was motivated primarily by fear for the security of his reign, and how he'd wanted to keep the entire corps of mages in Venetry for his personal protection no matter how that affected the defense of the country. I also told him what I knew of the Chamber Lords, especially my suspicions that Crossar believes himself better qualified to hold the throne than Garran Clendessar. "You should watch out for him," I said. "He's the one most likely to object to your plan."

"From what you have said, it's likely he would do so obliquely," Cederic said. "If he can be persuaded he will wield greater power as a member of our new council, it might keep him contained. It also helps that he has no personal army. He is much like Perce Aselfos, personally ambitious but dependent on others for the resources he needs to pursue those ambitions."

"Where *is* Aselfos?" I said. "Still in Colosse? What happened to him?"

"He and General Regates were unable to maintain control of the army after the convergence," Cederic said. "The entire army, I should say; they controlled about two-thirds of it. He approached me about throwing my support behind him, after it became clear our mages had succeeded in pacifying much of the city where the army could not. I told him he would, in fact, throw *his* support behind *me*, and he has proved to be a capable ally who has learned leadership is not to his taste, after all."

"I wish I'd been able to hear that conversation," I said.

"As do I," Cederic said. "So how do you suggest I approach the King?"

I considered that for a bit. "Don't give any more of your attention to the Chamber Lords than you have to for politeness's sake," I said eventually. "Make it clear you think the decision should be made entirely by him. He responds well to that kind of flattery—I mean, if you tried to tell him how smart and wise he is, he'd know you were playing him, but displaying respect for him as the King...I don't think he gets that very often, because everyone knows how powerful the Chamber Lords are. And make sure he sees how confident you are, because that will make him feel better about himself, like he's good enough to command the respect of someone like you." I fingered the neck of his robe. "And find something nicer to wear. He won't know what a Kilios is, so you'll look like a poor supplicant to him."

"This robe belonged to the first Kilios," Cederic said, "but I take your meaning." He sketched another th'an on the faceplate, making the collenna shift its direction, and said, "Will you stand with me before him?"

"I don't know. Do you think I should?" I said.

He sighed. "I would like to say yes," he said, "but since your King knows who you are, it is likely he would see your presence at my side as a betrayal, and he would be even more fearful. But I think we should find a way for you to be present, and not only because it would give me strength. You and your mages represent a new power in Balaen, and I think if Garran Clendessar could be convinced you support him, he would feel as if he were treating with Castavir on a better than equal footing. I'm told your mages tore through ours like this collenna plows through snow."

"It was a lot harder than that," I said, "and most of it was luck and cleverness rather than power. Castaviran magic is still more flexible."

"The goal is to bring the two together," he said. "We have not had leisure to examine the possibilities, but now the worlds are united, we should be able to discover what magic was meant to be. Master Peressten believes the unified magic will be far more powerful than either Balaenic or Castaviran individually, but not what that unified magic is. We know only that it is not as simple as combining Balaenic and Castaviran magics, but, as with so many other things, the project has been pushed aside in favor of other things."

"I have the same problem," I said. "I could only justify learning the flitting pouvra—oh! I never showed you that."

"Showed me what?" he said.

I directed him to turn to one side, out of the path of the main army, then jumped out of the collenna—this was hard, it was still moving pretty fast—and before he could do more than shout, I flitted ahead a couple hundred feet and dodged out of his way as he once again sped past me. I did it a few more times until the magic on the collenna faded and it slowed enough that I could jump back on. Cederic looked as if he'd turned to stone. "Amazing, huh?" I said.

"Please give me time to overcome my urge to shout at you for leaping from a moving collenna," he said.

"It wasn't dangerous," I said. "Well, not *very* dangerous. And don't you think that pouvra is wonderful?"

"I do," he said. "It is a kind of magic we have lost; we know of its existence, but no mage has ever been able to replicate the kathana. Where did you learn it?"

"It's one of the ones our new mages spontaneously manifested after the convergence," I said. "Only Jerussa and I know it, though Jeddan might have learned it by now, if he had time during the siege."

"We will—" He closed his eyes and drew in a deep breath, then released it slowly. "It is one more thing we can investigate when the former Empress is defeated and our countries have become one," he said. "I look forward to resuming my academic pursuits."

"Will you be able to? It seems as though they all look to you for guidance," I said.

He took my hands in his and said, "Once the King of Balaen has been crowned Emperor of Castavir, I will direct the formation of his guiding council. It is perhaps not truly my responsibility, but I think I command enough respect that my decisions will be given great weight. And I think it is important this council be composed of individuals who can...balance the new Emperor's impulses. Then I will take up the mantle of most high priest—I cannot avoid that—and set about reorganizing the priesthood to have meaningful power rather than representing the whims of Renatha Torenz.

"But when that is done, and when I feel the priest-mages can manage themselves, I will be able to resume a semi-private life, conducting ritual on holy days but otherwise free to pursue my own interests." He sighed again. "I regret that I cannot continue as Wrelan of the Darssan, but there are other organizations in Colosse that would not mind admitting me to their number."

I laughed at that. "Yes, I'm sure it will be a struggle for them to decide whether to make Cederic Aleynten part of their group."

"My rank is sometimes intimidating," Cederic said, "and there are those whose pride would resist giving me a chance to outshine them.

But I will find something—or start my own institution, perhaps." He put his arm around me and squeezed gently. "And outside pressures will no longer dictate what *we* do."

I leaned into his embrace and said, "There are so many things I've had to put off as well. I'm reluctant to make plans until we know for sure what will happen. I'm used to adapting as circumstances change, but that was when my plans involved sneaking into some treasury after a forgotten book, and circumstances changing meant taking the roofs instead of the stairs. I don't want to get excited about the future only to have it change under my feet."

"I understand," Cederic said. "Although I would like to know if children are part of any of your futures."

I was glad I wasn't in a position to meet his gaze. "Maybe," I said. "Mam wasn't the best example of parenting. I'm not sure how good I'd be at it. But I'm willing to discuss it, after everything...however things fall out."

"Understood," he said, and if I hadn't known I loved him before, I would have discovered it then, because he didn't say anything like "you'll be a wonderful mother" or "you don't have to be like your parents," just held me and said nothing as we rode along. After a while, we started talking again, mostly about strategies my warrior mages might use if it did come to fighting against the God-Empress's troops, or tricks we might use against the battle mages. Occasionally one of us would say something that reminded the other of something that had happened while we were apart, so we'd tell that story.

About mid-afternoon we came to the place where the Castaviran Army was going to camp; they were stopping early to give the Balaenic Army time to catch up. Our army (I still think of Balaen as my country) broke camp before sunrise and were marching at their fastest speed, and they managed to come within four miles of the Castaviran camp by sundown. I went back to our camp to have dinner with the mages and talk about what Cederic and I had discussed, then flitted to the Castaviran camp, and that brings me to now.

I know I said I don't like making plans when there's no guarantee they'll work out properly, but it's hard not to imagine what will happen once we have the God-Empress in custody. I have no idea how the King will react to Cederic's proposal. He might even think it's a trick and reject it on those grounds. I pray the true God he believes Cederic and sees the virtue of ruling both countries.

It will still be hard. Cederic's assurances aside, I can't help thinking a lot of Castavirans will be unhappy about being ruled by a foreign monarch. The communication barrier is still a problem. There will be land disputes, which will mean disputes over who gets to arbitrate the land disputes. But this is how the world is now. People will eventually come around. Maybe Viravon will get its independence, even.

Damn. I started making plans. All right, the only plan I have is to spend the night with my husband, whenever he finally comes to bed. Sex might be involved, but what I want more than anything is to wake the way I did this morning: snuggled up against a warm body, with loving arms wrapped around me, and the most beloved voice in the world murmuring "Good morning" into my ear. It was almost better than sex.

Almost.

25 Seresstine, mid-morning

I'm writing this in the wagon, which is why my handwriting is so uneven. This would be an awful drive in the summer, with dust kicked up by the horses and the wagons and the thousands of marching feet. Right now it's bumpy despite the excellent condition of the road. Everyone's straining for a glimpse of Venetry, hoping not to see smoke rising from behind its walls. I considered riding with Cederic, out in front of both armies, but decided it was better I stay with the mages in case we come under attack and my direction is needed. Besides, I can be at the head of the Castaviran Army in less than a minute if I'm needed there instead.

Messenger from Mattiak approaching, waving at me. Let's see what he wants.

25 Seresstine, half an hour later

So this is strange. General Regates of the Castaviran Army sent a messenger by collenna to tell us their advance scouts have reached Venetry, and there's no movement. At all. The God-Empress's forces are there, but they're not attacking the city, even from a distance with war wagons. The main body of the Castaviran Army will reach Venetry in four hours, at which point they can send messengers demanding the God-Empress's surrender. We'll be there three hours later. Mattiak's sent messengers to our army, the defenders of Venetry, now, hoping to learn what's going on.

I asked if I could go on ahead, but he was concerned that a woman unexpectedly appearing in front of them might make them lethally surprised. He has a point. Still, it's killing me not knowing if Jeddan's all right. Anything might have happened. We still don't know how long the God-Empress has been here. About all the advance scouts could tell us, other than that the armies were at a standstill, was the walls of Venetry hadn't been breached. That's something, anyway.

25 Seresstine, seven hours later

We can finally see Venetry. Sure enough, it doesn't look like it's been overcome. I'm writing this as the wagon draws closer for lack of anything better to do—I'm not allowed to be part of the Castaviran negotiation with the God-Empress's forces, not being Castaviran, and Mattiak hasn't called for me, hopefully because there's no news. Or maybe I should say it's worrisome that there's no news; our messengers never came back. Granted they don't move *that* much faster than the army does, but they should have been back by now.

I can see the Balaenic defenders we left behind on the walls, inside the main gate with that stupid clock over it. Something, possibly a war wagon projectile, hit it hard, caving in the hands so they point almost directly away from the clock face. I wonder if they'll try to repair it.

I wish we could see the God-Empress's forces, but they're ahead and a little to the right of our direction of march, which puts most of the Balaenic Army between us (the mages) and them. If Cederic hadn't explicitly told me to stay behind, I'd flit over there to take a look. I might have disregarded his instructions if he hadn't had the look I see so rarely, the one that says he needs me to obey without question, and I figure if he can trust me when I tell him I have to do something, I can return the favor when it matters to him.

There. Finally, movement from the direction of Venetry. Someone on horseback, waving a flag and riding in our direction. I don't know what the flag means—the only one I know is the red-bordered white one that asks for truce of parley, and this is blue. Well, Mattiak never told me I had to stay here, so I'm going to find out what's going on.

CHAPTER TWENTY-FIVE

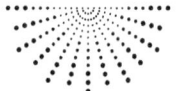

31 Seresstine

I don't know how long I'll be able to sit up, but I'm recovered enough that I feel restless at being confined to bed. So I'll see how much I can write before I need to sleep again.

It feels like much longer ago than six days I wrote about the messenger approaching (I found out somewhere the blue flag means "clear the way" literally, but it's symbolic of an urgent message that must be passed directly to the commander) and went looking for Mattiak. I tried the command tent first, but he wasn't there; he'd gone to meet the messenger himself. It took me a while to find out where that was, and when I finally found Mattiak, he had dismissed the messenger and was saying to General Drussik, "I don't like this."

"Neither do I," Drussik said. "It doesn't make any sense."

"What happened?" I asked, not caring that I was interrupting.

"Nothing to concern you, girl," Drussik said.

"We sent a message to the defenders of Venetry about half an hour ago," Mattiak said, "asking for information. General Shansselen just sent his reply. The fighting was heated until two days ago, when the former Empress's forces called for a cease fire for negotiations. A group of them were allowed inside the gates under guard."

"A few hours later, they returned to their camp, and the next day, another group went inside, this one led by a woman, presumably Renatha Torenz herself. Several hours after *that*, Shansselen received orders to cease hostilities, but to remain on alert. They haven't received any other orders since then. And the Castavirans—the former Empress's forces, I should say—haven't moved at all, though messengers have come through from the city to their camp twice."

"So what does it mean?" I said.

"Shansselen said the battle was going their way," Drussik said. "Don't know why the King didn't want the foreigners battered into submission. No doubt their God-Empress is a hostage against their good behavior."

"But then why hasn't he made any demands of her army?" Mattiak said. "It doesn't make sense."

"The King will almost certainly send orders soon," Kalanik said. "I don't suppose we've heard back from our Castaviran 'allies'?"

"Nothing yet," Mattiak said, "and I don't dare send a messenger, in case we're being observed and someone takes it the wrong way. All I know is they've been in communication with the other Castaviran forces."

"I can find out," I said. Mattiak frowned at me.

"Sesskia, I appreciate your willingness to turn your magic to our service, but I want to keep the mages out of this," he said. "Right now the King has likely forgotten you mages can do anything other than the martial pouvrin, and once the war is over, he'll assume there's no more you can give him. If anyone sees you, and he is reminded you can do other things as well, he'll want to put you in permanent service to him—not to Balaen, but to him. And true God forbid he learns about flitting. You'd end up his personal messenger. Stay put."

That made me uneasy. He was right in his assessment of the King's attitude toward magic, but I hadn't realized I might be in as much danger from him as I had been from the God-Empress, though in a completely different way. I prayed Jerussa and Jeddan hadn't revealed the flitting pouvra to him. Then I remembered I'd promised Cederic about not approaching the Castaviran camp, so I couldn't have gone on that errand anyway. So instead I stuck close to Mattiak, but in an unobtrusive, non-annoying way, and waited.

Nearly an hour later, a Castaviran mage I didn't know came to our camp the long way around to avoid being noticed by anyone, friend or foe, though at that point those words had ambiguous definitions. He told us the following:

1. When the Castavirans arrived and sent a demand to the God-Empress's camp for her to surrender to them, they were told she was already in the city and would General Regates please not attack them.

2. The God-Empress has been in the city for two days already, along with some of her high-ranking officers, and has been sending uninformative messages back to the camp that amounted to "stay where you are." Based on her messages, they think she's a captive, which makes sense to me, but as long as those messages keep coming, they don't want to attack the city again. That also makes sense to me. Disobeying the God-Empress's command is the same as stabbing yourself through the heart.

3. Cederic sent a messenger (Terrael) to the King explaining what they were after and asking for a meeting. That was two hours ago and they haven't heard anything since.

Mattiak told the messenger what we'd learned and sent him back to Cederic. "Now what?" I said.

"Nothing's changed, Sesskia," he said. "We wait for orders. You should get some rest. I promise I'll send for you if anything happens," he said, forestalling my objections. So I went and had something to eat, though I was too anxious to appreciate it. The mages and I talked about what might happen, and whether the war might actually be over without any more fighting. We were so ridiculously naïve.

It was around sunset that a runner came for me, and I arrived back at the command tent once again to find a messenger just leaving. "Who knows what they have in mind? We could be taking them to their deaths," Kalanik was saying as I entered, and his words sent a chill through me.

"That message wasn't informative enough to make us draw that conclusion," Mattiak said. "And I'm sure Aleynten knows the danger."

"What danger?" I said, alarmed.

Mattiak held out a sheet of paper to me. "We're to assemble an escort for a Castaviran delegation to the King," he said. "A royal summons. No more information than that."

I read the paper, which said exactly what he'd just told me. "Who's going?"

"Of our people, or theirs?" Mattiak said. "I don't know who they'll send. For us, they said ten soldiers and as many officers as I deem necessary. That will be me, Bronnok—don't argue with me, Wyoth, I need you here in case we end up fighting the Castavirans after all—Melekst, and Kyrran."

"And me," I said.

Mattiak looked as if he'd forgotten I was there. "You're not coming," he said.

"Yes, I am," I said.

"Sesskia, you aren't part of the military," Mattiak said. "You weren't summoned. If the King is at all in an irra—I mean, if the King decides to take offense at your presence, it could hurt the Castaviran negotiations. Aleynten would agree with me."

I concealed myself and enjoyed watching his eyes water as he tried to stay focused on me. "I think you misunderstand me," I said, strolling around the tent and observing the other men closely. They were clearly tracking me by the sound of my voice, and not doing a very good job. "My telling you I'm coming is a courtesy to you. Your approval has nothing to do with it. The God-Empress went into Venetry two days ago and hasn't been seen since. Anything might have happened. The one thing I'm sure of is that the King doesn't mean to treat honorably with the Castavirans, and that means they'll need whatever edge they can get. I am that edge, Mattiak, I have been from the beginning. Cederic understands that."

Mattiak managed to locate me after a few seconds and was following me with his eyes, turning as I circled around him. "Your concealment is not invisibility," he said. "And while the King might not be capable of seeing through it, I can assure you Caelan Crossar will."

"Only if he knows to look for me," I said. "And I intend to stand well away from the people he *will* be paying attention to."

Mattiak scowled. "It's not as if I can stop you," he said.

"I take it from the way you are addressing empty air Sesskia has made a decision neither of us will like," Cederic said, entering the tent at the head of a procession of people. Some of them were friends from the Darssan, including Sovrin; others were people in military uniforms, including General Regates, who'd turned out to be Aselfos's co-conspirator. She looked grim. All of them looked unhappy and concealed it more or less successfully.

"I'm going with you to meet the King," I said, still concealed.

Cederic focused on me with some effort. "If you are revealed, it will not go well with us," he said.

I dismissed the concealment pouvra and said, "I don't intend to be revealed."

"Of course you do not," Cederic said, "and I agree the likelihood of that is small."

"And you yourself said you thought I should be there," I said.

"That was when I believed you could be present in support of Garran Clendessar, but in this case, when you have not been summoned, the consequences should the King discover you could be severe," Cederic said. "Master Peressten sent a written message instructing us as to exactly who would be members of this delegation. He included within it a code that said 'all is not as it seems.' We must assume we are walking into danger.

"As I pointed out to Mattiak, you need every advantage you can get," I said. "Suppose the King intends treachery. I don't know why he would, but it's possible. If he attacks you unexpectedly, the mages won't have time to ready a defense, and your mind-moving pouvra can't work in all directions at once, unless you've developed powers you haven't told me about. And if the King has some of my mages in there, I'm better equipped to fight them than any of you. *And* if the King is plotting treachery, him discovering I'm there won't matter to how he treats you."

"Do you really think the King is plotting treachery?" Mattiak said, though what he was actually saying was *Do you think the King is capable of successfully plotting treachery?*

"Probably not," I said, "not on his own, anyway, but I've survived this long thanks to paranoia and the ability to stay out of sight, and to be honest, this isn't even close to the riskiest thing I've ever done."

Mattiak looked over at Cederic. "I don't suppose you've figured out a way to confine her?" he said. "Some magic to counter that walk-through-walls pouvra she's so fond of?"

"General Tarallan, I would never even try," Cederic said. He looked at me, and added, "Sesskia, please do not take unnecessary risks. Master Peressten's code indicated he was being observed when he wrote that message. I have no idea what we will find inside the city."

I embraced him, not caring that everyone in the tent was watching us. "I never take unnecessary risks," I said, "and suppose Terrael needs rescuing? Besides, Jeddan is in Venetry, and we haven't heard anything about the mages, and that worries me. I'd go if only for that."

He laid his forehead against mine and sighed. "You would not be who you are if you were not willing to risk yourself," he said. "Something I should always remember."

"Yes," I said, then let him go and turned to face Mattiak. "I'll follow behind you," I said, "unless you think I should go first?"

He shook his head. "Behind," he said, and then it became a discussion about how our escort would be arranged. Then there was a bit of an argument about how I would get there, as everyone would be riding, and Mattiak looked cheerful for about five seconds in which he thought I'd have to stay behind, then I reminded him about flitting and he scowled. That's how I ended up standing, concealed, next to the gate, trying not to shiver in my heavy coat because I'd left the hood down so it wouldn't impede my range of vision. I'd never flitted while concealed before and had made the surprising discovery that I could go farther in that state. I wonder

I started a list at the back of this book of all the things I want to investigate. Since it looks like it'll be a long time before I can get to any of them, I don't want to forget. I'm close to the end of this book, but I can spare a few pages.

I think that's a sign I should rest now. My back burns if I sit for too long, and my vision gets blurry. Not that I would ever tell Cederic that. He worries too much.

1 Hantar

A new year. We're sort of making a fresh start, but nobody's celebrating. I don't know what Castavirans do to celebrate the new year, anyway, though this confirms that our calendars are in sync at least to some degree.

I had to re-read my last entry to remember where I'd left off. The gate was heavily guarded, which made sense given that we were still at war, as far as I knew, and Cederic and Mattiak and everyone took so long to arrive I was tempted to run around the guards and taunt them. But that was too risky, even if I hadn't promised Cederic, so I leaned against the city wall and let my mind wander. I thought about Jeddan and the mages, and about pouvrin, and I practiced the binding pouvra some more, and made a mental list of pouvrin I wanted to learn, or invent, but it was so long I don't want to reproduce it here.

I don't know how long it took for the others to arrive, but I was thinking about climbing the city wall just to give myself something to do by the time I saw them. (I think it was really only twenty minutes. When I'm on edge I bore easily.)

Mattiak rode up to the gate and said, "The Castaviran delegation to see King Garran Clendessar." The guards hurried to open the gate —huh, I only just realized I'd never seen it closed until then. Everyone filed through, with me bringing up nearly the rear; if I were actually behind everyone, I'd risk being shut into the door, not that that would have much effect on me, but still.

It was well after sunset at this point, with a trace of pink tinting the clouds on the western horizon, and it was going to be another beautifully clear night. Mattiak was at the head of our procession with Cederic beside him, and I think they rode slowly so I'd be able to keep up. The few pedestrians stopped to stare at us, fourteen Balaenic soldiers surrounding twenty Castavirans in assorted robes and military uniforms.

Cederic had borrowed someone's golden ceremonial robe—I don't know why anyone had brought one, but I wonder if they wanted to be prepared to perform religious rites, and now I want to know why whoever the robe belonged to couldn't have witnessed Terrael and Audryn's vows. Not that it matters now.

Anyway, he looked elegant and handsome and exactly the kind of person you'd expect to see leading a delegation to a king. I can't believe I ever thought he looked arrogant and smug.

I was grateful to be trotting along behind the procession, because it kept me warm and forced me to stay alert and move quietly, good practice for the hard part, which was trying to remain undetected in Janeka Manor. I couldn't stay too close to the horses, because they were too stupid to be fooled by the concealment pouvra and fidgeted when I was near, so I trailed behind somewhat and observed the watching Venetrian citizens.

They were well bundled against the cold, so well bundled it was hard to tell which members of our group they were looking at. I don't know what they thought we were, but from my perspective the Castavirans looked like prisoners being escorted to the hangman, except Cederic was talking to Mattiak and their body language was not that of captive and captor. The pedestrians stood and watched us for far longer than I'd have expected, given how cold it was, not to mention the curfew was almost certainly still in effect, and while I didn't know when it started, I was pretty sure the city guard didn't want people hanging around in the streets after dark.

Slipping into Janeka Manor behind everyone else wasn't difficult, and the halls are broad enough everyone could spread out comfortably and I could find myself a place near the rear where no one would bump into me. Mattiak was greeted at the door by a functionary in full court dress who indicated we should follow him.

I guessed he was taking us to the larger of the two audience chambers, the room where the King hears legal cases that have been sent to him by the Lords Governor because they're too complex for their jurisdiction. It's supposed to be an honor, but everyone knows it isn't, because the King is indecisive and doesn't understand the law well, and his judgments aren't always fair. I should have realized it was an omen. Or maybe not. I've given up trying to decide what I should have anticipated in this whole mess.

The entrance to the audience chamber was flanked by two armed men in the uniform of the King's personal guard. They each took hold of one of the double doors and pushed it open so we could enter. Since I was at the back, I didn't see what brought the procession to a halt; to me it looked like a ripple of movement coming toward me, pushing everyone backward a few steps and forcing me to step even farther back or be run over. I heard some agitated murmuring, a few "what's happening" comments, and then the King said something I couldn't understand at all. And by that I mean it was in no language I recognized, and I think I've written before I know quite a few.

But I didn't become truly afraid until I heard Cederic say something in a loud voice—I'm sure he wanted me to hear clearly—and it was, again, in that same alien language, except for two words that sent ice water rushing through me: "Renatha Torenz."

I began prodding the people in front of me, whispering, "Keep going, damn it!" and eventually they all shuffled through the door and I could slip past them to stand at the front of the delegation, right behind Cederic and Mattiak. Now I could see the King and the God-Empress were sitting side by side on a dais that rose three steps above the rest of the room, and that made me feel both cold and sick, because none of the scenarios I'd entertained had the God-Empress as anything but a prisoner.

I should have anticipated the truth. I know well how the God-Empress can captivate someone, how compelling she is if you don't know she's mad, and I should have disregarded what the Castavirans said about her being a prisoner. Maybe if I'd been my usual paranoid self, things would have gone differently. But I guess I wanted to believe she was no longer a threat. So my being wounded is my own fault, and so is—no, I won't think that way. Most of what happened would have played out that way no matter how cautious we'd been. But I still can't help blaming myself.

The King was smiling and looked smug, as if he'd engineered some grand triumph he was about to reveal. The God-Empress was as beautiful as ever, though her roots were showing and her gown was an unadorned black silk. Soldiers stood behind them in a semi-circle against the walls (the room is a big oval), and some of the mages who'd remained in Venetry stood in two loose groups on either side of the dais. Jeddan wasn't there. Terrael wasn't there. The Chamber Lords were not present. The soldiers were blank-faced. The mages looked uncertain.

"—not represent the Castaviran government," Cederic was saying, and this time I understood him even though he was still speaking in that foreign language. The God-Empress's mages must have come up with a translation kathana. It didn't bother Cederic at all, because he went on to say, "She no longer holds the title of Empress."

"I am God's anointed and cannot be removed simply because an upstart palace functionary decides he would like to be Emperor," the God-Empress said. She looked neither mad nor dreamy nor cruel, but wore an uncomfortably acute expression that told me I shouldn't meet her eyes if I wanted to stay concealed. "You betray God when you misuse your priest's authority to support Perce Aselfos."

"It is you who have betrayed God, Renatha Torenz," Cederic said, "in abusing your position as ruler of the Castaviran Empire. Your ouster was just."

"The people can't be allowed to decide who rules them," the King said. "That way lies anarchy. Renatha's forebears stabilized the Castaviran Empire and brought it to glory, and you show disrespect to your ruler when you disregard that."

Dread replaced fear. The King using the God-Empress's praenoma was bad news. Cederic seemed to realize that. "Renatha

Torenz lacks the support of the citizens of Castavir," he said. "If she remains in power, the Empire will destabilize and civil war will result. As Balaen is inextricably tied to Castavir, it will be drawn into the conflict as well."

"Do not threaten Garran," the God-Empress said. Now I felt sick. The King using the God-Empress's praenoma might be excused by Castaviran customs being different, but he would only allow her to use his if he felt a personal connection. She laid her hand on the King's forearm and said to him, "You see how Cederic Aleynten seeks to increase his own power by challenging yours."

"I have no interest in political power," Cederic said, addressing the King and ignoring the God-Empress entirely. "My statement is not a threat, it is simple fact. Bringing two countries together requires a strong, unified government, not an Empress whose grip on the throne is insecure."

"I agree," the King said. "And I have a solution."

Cederic was caught in the middle of saying something else, and his head jerked up in surprise. "A solution, your Majesty?"

"Yes," the King said, and to my increasing horror took the God-Empress's hand in a caressing gesture. "Our two countries will be joined by marriage. Renatha and I will wed, and we will share the rule of Balaen and Castavir. I will bring stability to Castavir, and Renatha will lend her strength to Balaen."

The room went completely silent. For once, Cederic didn't know what to say. The God-Empress said, "Gael Regates, you may serve our united kingdoms if you renounce your association with the traitor Perce Aselfos now."

I turned to look at Regates, who seemed stoic, but whose eyes were wide and panicked. "You...I will not..." she said. The soldiers around her shifted, glancing at each other as if assessing their options.

"Perce cannot protect you," the God-Empress said. "But God is merciful. I choose to spare your life. Reject my gift, and I will have to destroy you. Your soldiers will not protect one whom God has turned away."

Regates was shaking now. She too glanced from side to side and, by her expression, didn't like what she saw there. "I...accept, God-Empress," she said, and I had to keep from sucking in a sharp, horrified breath.

"You will address me as Queen Renatha," the God-Empress said (I just can't stop thinking of her as that). "I choose to use the title bestowed on me by my future husband."

Regates bowed. "Yes, Queen Renatha," she said.

"Your Majesty," Cederic said to the King, his voice calm, but with an edge that revealed how much strain he was under. "Renatha Torenz is mad. She will give Balaen nothing but destruction. We are here to offer you the throne of Castavir—you need not ally yourself with her."

"Renatha told me you hated her, Aleynten," the King said, "but I didn't realize you were so far gone you would make such cruel accusations. I wanted to crush you and your followers, but she in her kindness chose to offer you the chance to put aside your bad feelings and accept her as your ruler again. I see you care nothing for peace."

"Castavir will not recognize her as its ruler," Cederic said. "We will fight to keep the throne from her."

"She has Balaen's support, and that of my army," the King said. "General Tarallan, take this man and his followers into custody."

Mattiak stepped forward. "Your Majesty knows I have been a loyal servant of Balaen for many years," he said. "But you are making a mistake. You are putting Balaen into the hands of someone who will turn on you when she has lulled you into believing you are in control. I will not be party to my country's destruction."

The King blinked as if he couldn't believe what he'd heard. "Commander General, I ordered you to take that man into custody."

"I will not," Mattiak said.

"General Regates," the God-Empress said, making a little gesture with her finger. Regates immediately drew her sword, followed swiftly by her soldiers. Cederic's mages went for their boards. Mattiak turned and gestured at his men, who also drew their swords—I can't believe they let everyone come into that room without disarming them, the King is an idiot—and moved to engage Regates' men. The soldiers along the wall came forward rapidly. The mages on either side of the dais exchanged glances, as if they weren't sure what to do. And Cederic roared, "STOP!"

I've written before that Cederic has a tremendous presence. Everyone actually stopped. Cederic turned in a slow circle to encompass the room in his gaze. To my eye, he looked as if he might snap if given the right provocation. "This is *ridiculous*," he said. "There are two countries lying inextricably entwined that must come together or go on clashing for a century or more. You, Garran Clendessar, have the opportunity to unite them. Castavir will throw its support behind you, but *only* if you do not ally yourself with this madwoman. Take what we are offering you. Embrace peace."

The King looked horribly conflicted. He glanced at the God-Empress, who gave him a look of such perfect wounded sorrow even I would have been fooled if I hadn't known she's madder than a bag of starving weasels. He looked back at Cederic. "I—" he began.

The God-Empress leaned forward and fixed Regates with her mad eyes. "Kill them all," she said.

Regates shouted a command, half her soldiers brought their swords up, and then it was carnage. The Castaviran mages, caught in the middle of the group, had no chance to use their boards. Mattiak's men dove in to protect them, but some of those swords found their marks, and two mages fell screaming.

I dodged out of the way of battling warriors, circling around to get nearer the King and my mages standing uncertainly beside him. Regates' soldiers were fighting each other as well as Mattiak's; it seemed not all of them were afraid of the God-Empress's threat. A few of Cederic's mages stood back to back and were scribbling madly, though they kept being interrupted by the jostling of the melee.

Then fire erupted and died as my mages attacked, only to realize they couldn't burn anyone without burning an ally, or maybe they weren't sure who their allies were. I shouted, "Attack the King's men! The soldiers!" That didn't do anything but confuse them, since I think only half of them recognized my voice, but I still didn't want to give up my concealment advantage even though I wasn't sure what I'd do with it. I kept shouting as I ran toward them, and to my delight one clever person both recognized my voice and understood what I said, because a couple of the King's soldiers flew backward into the wall ~~backward~~.

What a terrible place to stop telling the story, but I'm falling asleep and lost track of that sentence. I'll finish tomorrow.

3 Hantar

I spent yesterday with Audryn, who's having a really hard time and needed reassurance, and that left no time for writing. I think we managed to cheer each other up, at least as much as Audryn can be cheered with Terrael gone. That's far better than writing, any day.

So—Castavirans fighting Castavirans, Balaenics protecting the Castaviran mages, one of my mages knocking down some of the enemy soldiers. I turned reflexively to watch them fall and saw the God-Empress dragging the King by the hand—not literally, he was still on his feet, he was just dazed by the noise and furor—toward a small door at the rear of the room.

I darted after them, shouting something like "She's getting away!" and had to fling myself through the closed door because I got there just as she shut it in my face. It led to a narrow hallway I'd never been in before that I guessed let out in the King's living quarters, but we didn't get that far, because I shouted "God-Empress!" and dismissed the concealment. "Let go of the King." The translation kathana was still in effect, though I wasn't sure how much farther its range might reach.

The God-Empress turned around, still gripping the King's hand. "Sesskia!" she said, her voice filled with delight. "My dear sister! I so hoped you would come. I did tell you God would raise up more mages to serve her, didn't I? And you, as God's most high priest, did just that. I'm very pleased with my new priests. Thank you."

"You're her sister?" the King said, now thoroughly confused.

"She doesn't have any sisters, your Majesty," I said. "She had them all killed when she took the throne. She probably didn't tell you that, did she?"

"Don't listen to Sesskia, dearest, she's always been jealous of how the others take up all my time," the God-Empress purred. "Sesskia, I forgive you for everything you've done. I want us to be close again. Don't you want that?"

"I'd be afraid I'd get a knife in the back if I were close to you," I said. I lashed out with the fire rope. She moved fast as a snake and put the King between us, making him cry out in pain and forcing me to dismiss the pouvra. I couldn't get close enough to use the mind-moving pouvra, couldn't set her on fire without hurting the King, couldn't think of a single thing I could do to kill her. Because that was what it had come to—the two of us facing each other, and me the only hope Balaen and Castavir had of avoiding war. That feeling of rightness I'd had fighting Norsselen filled me again. I was pretty sure I'd feel sick later, but at the time, it seemed like the only solution that one woman's death would spare thousands of lives later. And I couldn't do a thing.

The God-Empress's expression turned into a snarl. "You spurn me," she said. "You spurn my gifts. I've never been anything but generous to you and this is how you repay me. I didn't even punish you for permitting Cederic Aleynten to disrespect me. I can't allow you to continue to live."

"I don't know how you plan to make that happen," I said. Her eyes focused on a point past my head, and I began to turn around, but I wasn't fast enough.

Sharp pain ripped through my back. I screamed and fell forward to get away from the soldier and the sword that slashed down at me again, barely missing me. It hurt so badly I forgot every pouvra I'd ever known, could think only of crawling away, but there was no away, there was only the swordsman and the God-Empress and the soft scratchiness of the rug that extended the length of the hall, red with my blood.

The God-Empress said, "Hold," and went to one knee in front of me. She grabbed my chin and forced me to look at her, making me cry out again. "I told you, Sesskia, God must not be mocked," she said. "You pretended to be my sister, but I knew all along you were false. Your death will not appease God, but it's a start." She let go of me, made a signal, and with my last ounce of concentration I worked the walk-through-walls pouvra and fell through the floor.

I didn't know where I was going, or if there were even a space for me to fall into; I just knew if I didn't get away, I'd be dead. Luckily, what was immediately below that hallway was an unused guest bedroom, and I went substantial before I landed on the bed. I lay there for a while, my head and ears buzzing from the gray mist surrounding me, then I got up, clenched my teeth on a scream, and set about finding something to bind my wound so I could make my way to safety without bleeding to death.

I dragged the sheets off the bed and tore one into pieces, a large piece to fold and press against my back, and a couple of long ones to bind the pad securely to me. Taking my coat off hurt like hell, and I had to sit down and rest a few times during this process, but eventually I felt capable of leaving the room. I was so tired. I remember trying to conceal myself, and flickering in and out of sight, so in the end I had to leave Janeka Manor the old-fashioned way, by sneaking out a side door and counting on darkness to conceal me until I could tumble behind a stone bench near the hedge bordering the property.

I made it out just ahead of several of the King's guard, who shouted and flailed about in the darkness, then I stumbled around to the front of the manor, where the clamor was even greater. I thought I heard Cederic's voice rise above the noise of shouting and screams as lightning snapped in short bursts across the broad, winter-dead lawn, but everything was echoing in my head, so I thought I must be mistaken. I know now it *was* Cederic, in a panic over not being able to find me, but that came later.

Once the guards were gone, I scrabbled around until I found a gap at the bottom of the hedge and forced my way through, biting back a scream as the branches dug into my wounded back. I found a hiding place in an alley of trees planted at irregular intervals and rested again, then realized I didn't know where to go. I would probably be safe at Fianna Manor with Jeddan and my mages, but that would leave me separated from Cederic again, and he would be truly frantic at not being able to find me.

I couldn't go to the God-Empress's army, obviously, and if Regates had survived the slaughter, the Castaviran Army might not be safe either, depending on how many of its officers and soldiers she was able to convince to follow her. That left the Balaenic Army, which had its own problems; I was pretty sure Mattiak wouldn't allow the King to retain control of it, but even if he managed to gather the troops that had been left to defend Venetry, the Castaviran Army still outnumbered him, especially with the God-Empress's troops rejoining it. So he would have to move.

Right. He'd have to leave. So I needed to move quickly before they left me behind.

I stepped out of hiding and began walking rapidly toward the main road. I'd chosen that hiding place because in winter the trees, in their unorthodox arrangement, cast strange shadows that obscured more ordinary ones. They also blocked vision enough to make flitting impossible. I was staggering when I came out into the open, and my back felt numb and cold from pain, but I turned in the direction of the front gate and did an experimental flit of about a hundred yards.

I nearly passed out, it hurt so badly. I wiped tears from my eyes, gritted my teeth, and did it again, and again. It took so many seconds to reorient between flits, and hurt so badly, that several times I thought about giving up and walking. Then, as I was bent over trying not to faint, I heard someone shout, "You! What are you doing out past curfew?" and I flitted again out of sheer panic, and kept going until I fetched up against the wall.

My coat is a dark gray—the blood didn't show in the darkness, not that anyone would have cared—and I was able to lean against the black stones of the wall and breathe deeply for a few seconds. I couldn't believe how nice the cold stone felt against my face, when only an hour before I'd been complaining about freezing.

The gate was about a hundred feet from where I stood, and the soldiers guarding it were alert but not active. Nobody there knew yet what had happened at Janeka Manor. Even so, they were unlikely to let me out no matter what I said. So I worked the walk-through-walls pouvra and went through the wall. Then I flitted once as far as I could go, not paying attention to my direction, just wanting to get away and out of sight.

I collapsed when I landed and lay on the snowy ground, unable to move my legs. I could see nothing but the snow and a sliver of dark sky, and I remember thinking there was some great significance to the two things being lined up together like that, but I realize now I was hallucinating.

Eventually I started to shiver, and I managed to push myself up and look around for the camp. I'd gone much too far, though at the time I was light-headed enough from blood loss I didn't even know which direction I was facing, much less whether the cluster of lights I was aiming at was the right one. I think I figured I was probably going to die if I didn't get help soon, and if I chose wrong, and they killed me, at least I'd made a decision. Then I flitted, and landed outside the eastern picket line of the Balaenic Army camp.

I staggered forward until I found a soldier, then I collapsed on him and didn't remember anything else until I woke up in the bed of a moving wagon, my back still aching but much less painful than it had been. The wagon's jolting sent little spikes of pain through my back, but it was the sort of pain that's easy to ignore because it reminds you you're still alive.

I lay there with my mind a white blur for a few seconds, then I tried to cry out for help, but succeeded only in making a faint croaking sound. I tried again and managed something louder that sounded like a cat's meow, and tried to get up, but failed utterly.

Moments later, the camp surgeon hopped into the wagon, followed closely, to my relief, by Cederic, who looked as if he hadn't slept for days. I'd never seen him so unkempt. He crouched beside me and took my hands in his, and he looked so distraught I said, "I'm not dead, you know."

"That is because your God-given reserves of luck have not yet been drained," he said. "You lost a great deal of blood, and you kept going insubstantial while the surgeon tried to stitch your wound. I am afraid you are going to have a very long, very crooked scar."

"I don't mind as long as I'm alive," I said.

"Let's check that wound," the surgeon said, and I had to submit to being prodded for a bit, and it hurt, but, again, not as much as being stabbed had. He changed the dressing, said, "You should probably lie on your side, if you can manage it," and left me alone with Cederic. He helped prop me up, and the pain diminished, though the little jolts kept on jabbing me. He made a seat for himself in the thick pile of bedding I rested on, and I held his hand while he stroked my hair with the other.

We sat like that for a while, not speaking. I was trying to decide whether I should tell my story first, or ask him to tell his. Then he said, "I am going to assume that was not an unnecessary risk."

"It wasn't," I said, and explained what had happened. "I feel so stupid about letting that soldier creep up behind me," I said. "I guess I was so intent on the God-Empress I wasn't paying enough attention. At least it wasn't a pouvra that betrayed me. I'm sorry I made you worry. It must have seemed to you as if I really had vanished."

"It did," he said. "We were halfway out of the manor when I realized you were not with us, concealed or otherwise. General Tarallan had to force me to stay with our people and not go running after you where I would certainly have been killed. He is extremely sensible."

"He is," I agreed. "Tell me what happened."

(I was going to write this all as a conversation, but the truth is I was still fuddled and I only remember bits of Cederic's exact words. Then I talked to Sovrin later and she told me more. So this next part is me combining the different stories so they make sense.)

Once the fighting started, everything was total confusion. There were at least four different sides ("our" group, most of General Regates' soldiers, the King's guards, and my mages) and even though my mages didn't do much, that was still a messy conflict. Eventually, the King's guard called for reinforcements, and our people had to retreat or be overrun. My mages stepped in at that point to help cover their retreat, though I think most of them still didn't understand what was going on.

I hope Jeddan's okay. I hope the King doesn't retaliate against them.

Our people fought their way free of the manor grounds, then had to run for it on foot because they didn't have time to spare to get the horses. Mattiak's furious about that, because he's had his horse for years and they're like old friends, which is the only bad thing I have to say about Mattiak's character, that and trying to part me from my husband, but he's given up on that.

They separated to return to their respective armies. Mattiak told Cederic he was stupid to go where he might be captured, but Cederic said he wasn't going to leave his mages to be hostages for the God-Empress, especially since she might decide to take out her wrath on the Darssan mages as proxies for Cederic.

So Mattiak gave the command for the army to break camp and move out, even though it was almost ten o'clock at night, and Cederic and his mages went to the Castaviran army, which hadn't yet gotten the word about Regates' change of heart, rounded up the rest of the mages, told them to pack what they could carry, and brought all of them to the Balaenic camp just as it was beginning to move. They had to leave a lot behind, including the collennas, which I think Cederic regrets, but better that than being dead.

I'd stumbled into camp twenty minutes before, but no one thought to inform Cederic of this because they were all busy saving my life, and at this point in the story I had to stop him and make him lift me so we could hold each other, because the look in his eyes as he described how it had felt to ride away from Venetry, thinking he'd left me behind, made me cry. But that was nearly the end of the story. The surgeon stitched me up, but I was restlessly unconscious for most of three days, waking long enough to drink some water now and then but otherwise looking as if I might not survive.

The army traveled eastward that whole time, getting as far from Venetry as it could, but with no other plan in mind. Now we're headed to Colosse, but not for long; it's not a terribly defensible city, no walls or anything, and we need more troops. So we're moving to Barrekel from there, where we hope to convince the Lord Governor of the rightness of our cause. From there...I don't know. There's going to be another meeting tonight when we camp, and I'm finally well enough I can attend. I can't believe I'm looking forward to a *meeting*, of all things, but I'm so glad to be out of this bed anything seems exciting.

CHAPTER TWENTY-SIX

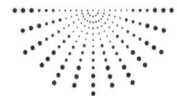

3 Hantar, late

I wish there were more pages left in this book. There's so much I want to write, so many things I need to work out that I can't talk to anyone about, not even Cederic. And I'm not well enough for love-making, which is awful because I think we could both use the comfort that comes with that kind of intimacy. In a few days, I hope things will look better, but right now the future is too difficult for me to contemplate.

Cederic carried me to the meeting despite my protests that I was well enough to walk. Finally, he shushed me—I wonder if that will ever not work on me—and said, "My love, I sat beside you for three days during which I did not know if you would ever wake again. Let me indulge my need to keep you close," and there wasn't anything I could say to that.

So he found me a chair someone padded with blankets, and sat next to me while we waited for Mattiak to arrive. There were a lot of people in the command tent, not only Mattiak's general staff but Cederic's trusted aides, including Sovrin and Audryn. Audryn's still not doing well because no one knows what happened to Terrael, but we all know there's a good chance the God-Empress had him killed.

He's close to Cederic, and even if he can't work magic anymore he's still a genius and might be able to thwart her plans. Not that anyone would say this out loud, and certainly not where Audryn could hear, but it's left all of the Castaviran mages (and me, of course) feeling very low.

Mattiak came in a few minutes after everyone was there. The tent was uncomfortably warm with all those people bundled together and me near the center, enough that the cold air that blew in with Mattiak felt good against my face.

Mattiak looked grim. He stood where everyone could see him and said, "About the only good thing I can tell you all is we moved quickly enough to put ourselves beyond the reach of the Castaviran Army. Our scouts report they have not moved from their position surrounding Venetry other than to combine their two camps. It seems those in the army in opposition to the former Empress were not able to overcome her supporters, if in fact they tried."

"Renatha Torenz is held in reverence by many people, even those who were part of our opposition forces," Cederic said. "They followed our banner primarily out of loyalty to their officers. If those officers chose to follow General Regates' example, their men and women would do the same. Even so, there are enough officers whose loyalty will not revert that I predict the Castaviran Army will be torn by factionalism and internal strife, which is no doubt the reason they have remained near Venetry. Their conflict can only benefit us." He didn't point out the obvious, which was that anyone who remained loyal to us would no doubt be killed.

Mattiak nodded agreement. "Our supply train has been cut off, so the first thing we need to do is find a place to wait the winter out, somewhere southerly. They won't field an army while the snow flies." He pointed to a map of Balaen that had had Castaviran cities added to it. "Lirilla is far south, and it's a port city with a strong economy. They should be able to support us for the winter. It's nearly four weeks away, so we'll need to stop somewhere to resupply, probably Barrekel—"

"I agree with your assessment, General Tarallan," Cederic said.

"But we have more urgent matters than supporting the army, which is still, for the moment, well supplied."

"What matters are those, Aleynten?" Mattiak said. He didn't look upset about being contradicted. In fact, he wasn't displaying any emotion at all, and that surprised me, because Mattiak's a very open person.

Cederic stood and went to the map, and flicked his finger at Colosse, lying nearly at the center of the map. "Colosse is not a defensible city," he said, "and occupying it would be disastrous for us. But it is the heart of the Castaviran Empire and carries much symbolic weight. We must go there first so I can anoint a new Emperor, or Empress, in whose name we can raise the country. The Castaviran people have suffered under Renatha Torenz's reign and will be, for the most part, happy to see it ended. But they are more likely to oppose her if they have a new ruler to give their allegiance to."

"How does that affect Balaen?" Kalanik said. "Are we going to ask Balacnics to support a foreign ruler over their own King? Granted that nobody really respects him, but if you ask them to accept a new ruler, they'd want it to be a Balaenic."

"I haven't lost sight of that, Wyoth, but Aleynten has a point. Who will you choose as Emperor?" Mattiak said.

Cederic sighed. "Dugan Lerongis is currently King of Helviran, which gives him as good a claim to the throne as anyone," he said. "Helviran has been part of the Castaviran Empire for centuries, which would make him acceptable to everyone. But Lelaena Osther of Endellavir is a stronger personality and would, I think, make a better Empress if it were not for her nationality. Endellavir has maintained its cultural traditions to the point that many feel it is not sufficiently Castaviran.

"Sai Veneta Amaleten has been head of the Firtha thanest for decades; she would have been most high priestess had Renatha Torenz not warped the priesthood to her own ends. Her ecclesiastical rank makes her a natural candidate to transition the Empire from the rule of a woman who claimed a divine mandate, but Sai Amaleten has a tendency to privilege the needs of mages over those of the secular community.

"And Moerton Taissatus, as consul of Colosse, has shown great leadership skills in serving as chief consul of the Castaviran Empire. My concern, however, is that he is perhaps not ruthless enough to provide the leadership we will need in the coming years, and I fear he would not be even-handed in his treatment of Balaenic citizens. But we have several days still until we reach Colosse, time enough for me to consider the candidates and make a decision."

"That sounds like a good solution," Mattiak said. "But I have a better one."

Cederic raised his eyebrow at Mattiak. "You do?" he said. "I was not aware you knew anything of Castaviran politics."

Mattiak ignored the humorous jab. "I don't," he said. "But I think we have a better candidate much closer to hand."

Cederic's brow furrowed. Then his impassivity cracked. "That's impossible," he said, sounding appalled.

"As I said, I don't know much about Castaviran politics," Mattiak said. He was as expressionless as Cederic was not. "But I know there's no precedent for choosing an Emperor outside the Torenz line. Nothing says he has to be of noble rank. What he *does* have to be is someone the Castavirans respect utterly. Someone who has demonstrated the ability to lead. Someone who has committed himself entirely to defending the Empire."

He flicked a glance at me. "And, if he wants to rule both countries, someone fair-minded enough to treat Balaenic and Castaviran citizens equally before the law...and someone who has a Balaenic wife."

That was when I realized what Mattiak was getting at. "*What?*" I shouted, incautiously standing up from my chair and then having to drop rapidly back into it as pain stabbed through my side. "Mattiak, are you out of your mind?"

"I don't think so," he said. "I say Cederic Aleynten is the best choice to rule a unified Balaen and Castavir."

The tent erupted into noise, men and women talking loudly over each other, some of them addressing Cederic, others shouting at

Mattiak. I grabbed Cederic's hand and made him sit down and look at me, bringing him out of the stunned reverie Mattiak's words had sent him into. "It's impossible," I said, echoing his earlier words. "You can't be Emperor. I can't be Empress, or whatever it is you call the Emperor's wife. I'm a thief! You're a scholar! The whole point of this was to turn power over to someone else!"

He looked impassive again, but his eyes were wide and still stunned. "He's right," he said. "There isn't anyone else. God help me, there isn't anyone else."

"You just listed four other people who could rule!" I said.

"None of whom will ever be entirely acceptable to the other three," he said. "I—" His grip on my hand tightened. "I never even considered this possibility. I saw myself as bringing order to two countries and never thought what it implied that I had the will and the ability to do so."

"You don't have to do this," I said.

"I think it is possible I do," he told me. He laid his hand gently along my cheek. "I have spent my life in the service of Castaviir," he said. "And I think—God help me, Sesskia—I think that life has been leading me here all along. Am I too arrogant, to think myself the best choice to rule both our countries?"

He sounded calm now, but his hand was trembling, and I put my other hand over our joined ones. "Not arrogant," I said. "Never that. But it isn't what either of us wanted."

"I know," he said. "You married an academic, not an Emperor, and I...will understand if it changes how you feel about being my wife. I should...offer to release you from your wedding promise."

That made me feel sick as well as horrified. "I would want to be your wife if you were nothing but an out-of-work collenna master," I said. "How fickle do you think I am?"

He squeezed his eyes shut and put his arms around me; reflexively I hugged him back, ignoring the pain. "I cannot bear this alone," he said. "If you tell me this is impossible for you, I will decline the honor, and we will find another way."

"Don't you dare put this burden on me," I whispered into his ear.

"I'm not making that decision for you. If this is what you think will save both our countries, then we'll face it together. I am your foundation, and you are mine. Don't you forget that."

He nodded, and released me, smiling sadly. Then he stood, and took a few steps to stand at the front of the crowd, which went silent immediately. "This is not the future I planned for myself," he said, "but it is the only future that makes sense. With your consent, I will accept the throne of a combined Balaen and Castavir, and we will bring our two countries to a peaceful union."

The shouting began again, but it was cheering, and approval, and a lot of unregal saluting. I'm still not sure whether everyone is supposed to address Cederic as Emperor when he hasn't been crowned, or even if they have to do it at all—it seems like

Oh, true God help me, I'm an Empress. Empress-Consort. Something like that.

It's just now hitting me, the magnitude of what we've taken on. The title is all we have—no capital city (should we capture Colosse if we can't afford to hold it?), no allegiance of the Kings and consuls of the Castaviran Empire or of the Balaenic Lords Governor, no income to support ourselves, let alone build the kingdom. We have nothing but two-thirds of an army, a double handful of mages, and determination, and determination can only win a war if it's backed up by military force. I don't even know what we have to do first to make this a reality. But Cederic does, and like the rest of us, I follow where he leads.

We talked again briefly before he went off to discuss logistics with Mattiak and his generals and the quartermasters. "Your policy of not making plans for the future when the present is uncertain is proving sensible," he said. "I, on the other hand, will have to suffer the disappointment of giving up the thanest I dreamed of founding."

"And I suppose we will have to have children," I said, with a grin so he wouldn't think I was resentful, because I wasn't. "Which I think is something else you were planning on."

He smiled. "It was," he admitted, "despite what you said. Not that I would have forced you into a decision to suit me."

"I know," I said. "But it will have to wait until you are seated firmly on the throne at Colosse. I still think the proposal you were going to make to the King was a good one. Move the capital to Colosse, set up a council drawn from both countries."

"Marry a Balaenic woman," he said, pushing back my hair from my face.

"You're so foresighted. It's as if, deep down, you knew it was going to come to this," I teased him.

He shook his head and sighed. "I have just remembered what you looked like the day you arrived at the Darssan," he said. "I could not have guessed then what you would mean to me, let alone that you would be my Empress-Consort one day."

"Is that what it's called?" I said. "How did I look that day?"

"Fierce," he said, smiling, and kissed me. "Fierce and beautiful, with those extraordinary eyes daring us to capture you."

"And you did," I said, which made him kiss me again.

He still hasn't come to bed. I foresee a lot of late nights in his future. Strange, I feel better now than I thought I would, writing about all of that. I was afraid it would make me feel more agitated, but instead I feel almost peaceful. There's still a lot to worry about— Terrael, and Jeddan and the mages, and finding a place we can wait out the winter so we don't run out of supplies, and learning what the God-Empress has planned—and I'm almost out of pages except the ones I'm keeping my pouvra notes in, but I feel now as if we can handle it, whatever "it" turns out to be.

Empress-Consort. True God help me.

THINGS TO STUDY

1. Why can I flit farther when I'm concealed than otherwise? Also, what happens if I'm concealed AND insubstantial and then flit? I'm a little afraid to try.

2. Still haven't given up on the enhanced hearing pouvra.

3. Or the memory pouvra.

Later—Cederic made a memory kathana. Might be a good starting point.

4. A locator pouvra. ~~Something not dependent on the landscape.~~ I don't even know what that means, so it might not matter to the pouvra.

5. Norsselen was obnoxious, but he did manage to learn two more pouvrin spontaneously. So how did he manage that? And is it something only "new" mages can do? Wish I had more "old" mages for comparison.

6. This binding pouvra has to be good for something. Or maybe not. Terrael said once there are a lot of th'an combinations that don't do anything. But I'm not giving up on it either.

7. Cederic's shield kathana as a pouvra.

8. Turning kathanas into pouvrin, just in general.

9. Turning pouvrin into kathanas. There are some pouvrin the Castaviran mages can't do. Focus on flitting?

10. I wonder if there's a way to counter the walk-through-walls pouvra. Maybe I *should* get Nessan working on it.

GLOSSARY AND PRONUNCIATION GUIDE

General note: in Sesskia's language (Balaenic), long A and long O are usually written "ae" and "oe," and she writes Castaviran words as they would be spelled in Balaenic (i.e. Coell (Coll) River)

Balaen (bah-LAIN) – Sesskia's home country

Barrekel (BEAR-uh-kell) – city in southeastern Balaen; inhabitants have a distinctive accent

Calassmir (cah-LAHS-meer) – southwesternmost city in Balaen

Castavir (CAS-tah-veer) – Empire formerly ruled by the God-Empress Renatha Torenz; also the central country of that empire

collenna (coh-LEN-nah) – engine, either self-propelling or attached to a loenerel

Colosse (col-LOSS) – capital of the Castaviran Empire

Endellavir (en-DELL-uh-veer) – country annexed a century ago by the Castaviran Empire

Hasskian (HASS-kee-ann) – Balaenic city on the Royal Road, south of Venetry

Helviran (HEL-veer-an) – country in the Castaviran Empire

kathana (ka-THAWN-ah) – ritual or spell composed of th'an

Kilios (KEY-lee-ohs) – "highest master"; a mage who has mastered all known th'an and all kathanas that can be performed by a single person

Lirilla (lih-RILL-ah) – southern port city in Balaen

loenerel (LOH-neh-rel) – a train-like vehicle that runs on any surface, not on rails

pouvra, plural pouvrin (POW-vrah, pow-VRIN) – a form of magic requiring no words, gestures, or th'an, that is instead manifested through the mage's will

praenoma, (plural) praenomi (pray-NO-ma, pray-NO-mee)— Balaenic first name; reserved for the use of close friends and family

Sai (sigh) – "great master"; a mage with advanced knowledge of magic

th'an (TH-AWN, with a glottal stop at the apostrophe) – magical pictogram or rune; may refer to a single rune or a simple combination of three or four

thanest (THAWN-est) – in Castavir, a place where magic is available to the public, usually for a price but sometimes for free

Venetry (VEN-eh-tree) – capital of Balaen

Viravon (VEER-ah-von) – country in the Castaviran Empire, annexed over a century ago, in rebellion against the God-Empress's rule

THE BALAENIC CALENDAR

Winter:
Hantar (30 days)
Jennitar (31 days)
Teretar (30 days)
Spring:
Shelet (30 days)
Dorinet (31 days)
Auret (30 days)
Summer:
Evray (30 days)
Senessay (31 days)
Lennitay (30/31 days)

Autumn:

Coloine (30 days)

Nevrine (31 days)

Seresstine (31 days)

THE BALAENICS:

(NOTE: the surnames of the noble houses all end in –ssar; these are the people who are allowed to serve as Chamber Lords and as Lords Governor of the major cities of Balaen)

Sesskia (SESS-key-ah) – mage of ten years' standing, married to Cederic Aleynten

Jeddan (JED-un) – "old" mage, Sesskia's friend and traveling companion

Baltan, Gismara, and Nanissa – "new" mages in a village in southern Balaen

Falak Endolessar (FAH-luk en-DOH-les-ar) – Lord Governor of Hasskian; "new" mage

Messkala (mes-KAH-luh) – Endolessar's major-domo

Garran Clendessar (GAR-un CLEN-des-ar) – King of Balaen

Caelan Crossar (CAY-lun CROSS-ar) – Chamber Lord of Defense

Merdel Lenssar (MUR-del LEN-sar) – Chamber Lord of Commerce

Jarlak Batekessar (JAR-lack BAH-teh-keh-sar) – Chamber Lord of Agriculture

Debarra Jakssar (deh-BAR-uh JACK-sar) – Chamber Lord of Transportation

Mattiak Tarallan (MAT-tee-ack tar-ALL-un) – Commander General of the Balaenic Army

Nessan (NESS-un) – leader of an elite special military force and trainer of Sesskia's spies

Hesskel Drussik (HES-kul DREW-sick) – Balaenic general, cranky and conservative

Wyoth Kalanik (WYE-oth KAL-uh-nick) – Balaenic general, Mattiak's friend

Taelon Bronnok (TAY-lon BRON-ock) – Balaenic general

Melekst and Kyrran (muh-LEKst, KEE-ran) – majors in the Balaenic army

General Shansselen (SHAN-sel-un) – leader of the Balaenic defenders of Venetry

THE BALAENIC MAGES (57 in all):

Corrmek Norsselen (COR-mick NOR-sel-un) – leader of the "new" mages

Relania Phellek (rel-AY-nee-ah FEL-eck) – "old" mage, familiar with Sesskia's research, a pacifist

Daerdra (DAYR-dra), Davik (DAV-ick), Paddrek (PAD-reck), Neomae (nee-OH-may) – primarily capable of the fire pouvra

Saemon (SAY-mun), Hasseka (HAS-uh-kuh), Aeddek (AY-deck) – primarily capable of the mind-moving pouvra

Rutika (RUE-tee-kah), Alessabeka (ah-less-ah-BECK-ah), Tobiak (toh-BYE-ack) – primarily capable of the walk-through-walls pouvra; pacifists

THE CASTAVIRANS:

Cederic Aleynten (SED-er-ic ah-LEN-ten) – Kilios and former head of the Darssan, Sesskia's husband

Terrael Peressten (ter-RAIL per-ESS-ten) – mage who can no longer work magic, married to Audryn; Cederic's aide and inventor of kathanas

Audryn Engilles (AW-drin en-GIL-is) – mage and friend of Sesskia; married to Terrael and his partner in invention

Sovrin Ustanz (SAW-vrin uss-TANCE) – mage who can no longer work magic; head of the translator corps and Sesskia's friend

Renatha Torenz (ren-AH-tha tor-ENCE) – deposed God-Empress of the Castaviran Empire

Wilfron Kasselen (WILL-fron KASS-uh-len) – Elder of Castaviran village in Viravon

Carlen Lisskestis (CAR-len lis-KESS-tis) – leader of captured Castaviran village near Hasskian; studied with Cederic

General Arnisen (AR-nih-sen) – commander of the Castaviran Army stationed in Viravon

Gael Regates (GAIL reh-GAH-tis) – commanding general of the main Castaviran Army; Aselfos's co-conspirator in ousting the God-Empress

Perce Aselfos (PERSS ah-SEL-fus) – former spymaster to the God-Empress and would-be Emperor

Dugan Lerongis (DOO-gan leh-RON-gis) – King of Helviran in the Castaviran Empire and candidate for Emperor

Lelaena Osther (leh-LAY-nuh OSS-ther) – Queen of Endellavir in the Castaviran Empire and candidate for Empress

Moerton Taissatus (MOR-ton TIE-sah-tus) – Consul of Colosse; chief of the consuls of the Castaviran Empire and candidate for Emperor

Veneta Amaleten (ven-EE-tah ah-MAH-leh-tun) – chief Sai of the Firtha thanest in Colosse; Cederic's former teacher and most high priestess, candidate for Empress

BONUS SCENES

CEDERIC'S DIARY

When I started writing *The Wandering Mage*, one of my original ideas was to write it as Cederic's diary, as a balance to Sesskia's diary in *The Summoned Mage*, and then maybe to write the third book alternating between the two. So what follows is the original beginning. I got as far as these entries before realizing that Cederic's story was a lot of boring administrative detail, and Sesskia was more interesting. So some of the details are different from the final version.

(15 Coloine)

Sesskia is missing. And it is entirely my fault.

I should never have taken so many shortcuts. Yes, the palace was coming down around us, and time was running out, but to have omitted such a crucial part of the kathana—how could I have been so stupid? I wish I could blame it on the mages who scribed the foundations of the kathana, but they did so under my instruction. And now she is gone.

I should not indulge in self-pity when there is so much still to do.

The palace lies in ruins before us; it is a miracle we all escaped alive, though our fallen dead remain within, buried under the rubble. Denril is there, somewhere, and I find it difficult to mourn him, though we were friends for more than ten years, became Sais together, shared joy and sorrow—but now I wonder how much resentment he hid beneath the façade of friendship. That he could attempt to have me executed for treason...I still don't understand it, but it does not matter now.

We have found a refuge in the coliseum that lies across Eddon's Road from the palace. It survived the merging more or less intact, and people have been gathering all morning. The palace was not the only edifice leveled by the destruction. Colosse is in turmoil, looting and violence are rampant, and the God-Empress's army, which should enforce some level of order on the confusion, is engaged in fighting itself. It seems Aselfos's coup was not aborted by the merging.

We have thrown up defensive shields around the coliseum and organized the refugees into groups, but soon we will need to feed everyone, and although what little food was brought here has been put into a common pool, it is not enough. We will have to expand our territory—though I think from what the refugees say, we could not help but do that, not and still call ourselves human. We mages represent one of the few forces of order with any power in this beleaguered city, even though the destruction has overwhelmed many of us to the point that they are unable to participate in the shield kathana. We all need time to regain our composure, and time is something we do not have.

I understand now why Sesskia found such comfort in her book. It gives me a measure of peace to lay everything out on paper, even as it tears at my heart to be reminded of her in this small way. There has been no time to establish whether she is even alive, though I refuse to believe otherwise. In pain from the kathana, yes (how I wish I could have spared her that!), but she definitely succeeded at her task, and there is no reason to believe it killed her. Oh, my love, forgive my mistake!

We will attempt to push our shield out further. Soon all our mages will recover, and we will begin to reclaim Colosse.

(16 Coloine)

I knew the world would change when its parts were reunited. I simply did not anticipate this change, and I once again berate myself for my stupidity. In this case, though, my stupidity did not cause the problem, simply prevented me from anticipating it.

I thought that it was overwork and emotional distress that prevented some of us from being able to work the shield kathana. I was wrong. The mages who worked the original kathana intended to create a world in which anyone, with time and perseverance, might learn to do magic. And they succeeded—for as long as the worlds stayed apart. Now that they are joined again, the original conditions surrounding magic have been restored, to all our sorrow, for it seems most of our mages are no longer able to work magic.

We have always known that those with the peculiar green-gray eyes are drawn to magic. It seems that in this restored world, they are the only ones capable of working magic. It is a tremendous blow. We have lost some two-thirds of our mages, including, to everyone's dismay, Master Peresten. To say that he is devastated would be a cruel understatement. I am grateful to Master Engilles, whose presence has been as much a comfort to him as is possible under these circumstances, but I worry that her continued ability to work magic may be a strain on their marriage in the future.

For now, I am faced with the challenge of protecting the men and women within our shields with a much diminished cohort of mages. Despite their loss, all of them are facing this new challenge with determination and resolve. I have never been prouder of my fellow mages than I am this day. They look to me as their leader, and I refuse to let them down.

Brave words. I cannot show any of my uncertainty, for fear it will demoralize them just as they need to feel most strong. They do not know how inadequate I feel to this task. People have been pouring into our sanctum, which now extends three streets north and two west of the coliseum, and the flood shows no signs of abating. These refugees bring tales of horror, of uncontrolled troops looting and raping their way through Colosse, and I wish we could bring the entire city under our protection even as my soul quails from the terrible challenge that would be.

I need Sesskia so badly now, but I cannot indulge in thinking of what might or should be; I have a task ahead of me, and no time for idle fantasy. The one good thing about all of this turmoil and horror is that it leaves me little time to worry about my wife and what she might be facing now.

In half an hour we will push further north, which will allow us to encompass the Firtha th'an*est*, and with luck we will find more mages to bolster our numbers. I pray they have not already been over-whelmed.

(16 Coloine, later)

The Firtha th'an*est* was well-defended, and we nearly had a bloody conflict before we were able to convince them we were not the God-Empress's battle mages. It seems they had to fight off a troop of soldiers several hours ago, but it sounds as if the army's losses with regard to their mages is at least as great as ours has been, for that troop had only two mages where they ought to have had seven. I believe the army's numbers may even be more reduced than ours, since the green-eyed mages have historically been drawn toward academia and the priesthood rather than the military. If I am right, this could be an unlooked-for boon; the fewer battle mages we are forced to fight, the better.

Seventeen of the sixty mages in the Firtha th'an*est* retain their ability to work magic. The chief Sai is not among them, but she is a talented administrator and I have been grateful to turn the logistics of running what is fast becoming a refugee camp over to her. She has organized them by neighborhoods and established leaders to take responsibility for each group, leaders who then report to one of the mages, who report to her. Even so, I find I spend an increasing amount of time handling small crises, and while I try to direct most of those petitioners elsewhere, it is clear that many of them simply want the reassurance only the Kilios can provide. Turning them away might prove demoralizing, and if my status can do anything to alleviate the strain those under our protection are suffering, then I am happy to turn it to that purpose.

It is growing too dark to see these pages. We will be posting watches throughout the night, those capable of the shield kathana taking their turn at it—I believe I can improve the kathana to expand the size of the shield, but that will not be possible before morning, and we will all be exhausted by then. Our...I have no idea what to call them, those mages whose magic is lost. They are *not* former mages, I refuse to think of them as such, not when they have all of them labored for so many years to gain that knowledge. Our mages who cannot work magic will set a traditional watch, joined by men and women of the refugee camp.

I think we will survive this night, which is more than I can say for the rest of Colosse. It breaks my heart to hear the shouting, and the screams, that come from beyond our walls. Wayn and Cybel want to lead an attack, to push our shields even farther, but in this darkness we would accomplish nothing, and I refuse to risk the lives of those already under our protection.

Sesskia would think nothing of the darkness. She would likely already be gone, searching for those who need protection, bringing them back to us. I barely understand this magic that has...she called it "waking up," but to me it feels like a beast breaking free of a cage that will overwhelm me if I do not leash it. I cannot even imagine the pouvra that would let me see in the dark. I will put this away until the morning, and I will try to sleep before I take my turn with the shield kathana.

I do not know if I should wish to dream of Sesskia, or fear it.

(17 Coloine)

We have all survived the night, though the need for food is once again becoming urgent. It is time for us to send out a scavenging group. I wish I could go, to sweep the street ahead of us with this pouvra, but I am needed here, to keep everyone else's spirits up. I never thought my primary purpose in life would be to be a mascot—

no, that is too cynical, I am for good or ill their leader, and they look to me.

Master Peresten is very ill, though it is an illness of the spirit and not of the body. He responds to no one but Master Engilles, and only rarely to her. I wish I had time to spare for him, but we are about to move our shield eastward, skirting what is left of the palace and moving toward the storehouses. It is likely they have already been looted, but we must take the chance.

(17 Coloine, later)

The storehouses were guarded by troops—Aselfos's troops, as it turned out, with five battle mages. The soldiers looked reluctant to engage with us, almost afraid, but the battle mages had no qualms about turning their magic on us, and seven of our people (three of them refugees, one of them a child) were killed before we could kill them. The loss of their battle mages made the soldiers even more reluctant to attack, and a few sweeps with the mind-moving pouvra convinced them to throw down their arms and flee.

We took possession of the storehouses, all of them intact, and waited for our scavenging group to return. They brought back more than a hundred more refugees, but very little in the way of supplies, so it is fortunate Aselfos thought to guard the storehouses from the depredations of people like us.

Unfortunately, we have reached the limit of what territory we can keep shielded. People continue to seek shelter here, but we will soon be at capacity, and I have no idea what to do next. We have what I think can be called a council, Sais and mages and citizens, and we will meet to discuss our options. Then I will try to speak with Master Peresten. Master Engilles tells me he has not eaten for nearly twenty-four hours. Mage or no, he has the finest mind in Castavir, and I will not see him lost to his despair.

(18 Coloine)

We have decided to seek out Aselfos and attempt to treat with him. His coup attempt failed—at least, I call it failure because he has been unable to maintain order in the city, and it is clear no one rules in Colosse—but he is not insane, and we may be able to work together to restore civil order. A group led by Lineta Arnisen will seek him out. Mrs. Arnisen has a strong presence and has kept the peace within our sanctum, and I was surprised to learn that she is no community leader, but a householder and mother of three children, only two of whom survived to find refuge here. Strange how, in times of crisis, leadership arises from the least likely places.

Those of us who remain behind are working to bury our dead and make better arrangements for supplying our groups. There have been more disagreements as our numbers grow, and I am called on more frequently to mediate disputes and, in some cases, stop fights. I used to hate the Kilios's robe, but now I wish I had it, because it commands respect in ways I more fully appreciate now.

I overheard a conversation in which one of the Firtha mages asked one of ours how I can remain unmoved by tragedy, whether I am as heartless as I seem, and I felt like taking the man by the throat and shaking him while I howled out my grief and anguish. The city is in ruins, people are dying, there is no one to set it right, and I must stumble along and turn a blank, unfeeling face to the world because if I once give in to the emotions that threaten to overwhelm me, my authority would vanish, and I would be useless.

If only Sesskia were here—oh, my love, I am so selfish that I think only of how much I need you and not of what you might be enduring. But every time I begin to be afraid for you, I think of how much you have already survived, and it heartens me to know that you are not defenseless. I swear I will find you, and soon.

Now that we have achieved some small measure of stability, it is time to put the mages to work. I may possibly be motivated by selfish desires—how many of these people have also lost loved ones?—but as wretched as Colosse's situation is now, how much worse will it be when we encounter the people of Balaen? We will need someone who can communicate with them, and as Master Peresten continues unresponsive, Sesskia is crucial to our efforts. Tomorrow, then, we will begin our search.

(19 Coloine)

Utter failure. Did I once consider myself a talented mage? Why, then, did it not occur to me that our search kathanas are all calibrated to a Castavir that no longer exists? The coming together of the worlds has altered the landscape in a way we do not know how to correct for. The only positive thing that came from this debacle is proof that Sesskia is, in fact, alive. Alive, but nowhere that we can find her.

My momentary elation has now given way to the stomach-clenching dread that is my constant companion. I cannot see clearly —I sleep poorly these days, between the demands of my position and the knowledge that if not for my stupidity, I would not be sleeping alone. I need another mind to see this problem anew, and that mind is in danger of being lost to us forever.

(19 Coloine, later)

I don't know whether Sesskia tried to record conversations, or how she managed to remember the details. For most of the discussions I have had over the last three days, it has been sufficient for me to summarize the outcomes. But now I wonder if I should have been making more of an effort to record the specifics. So I devised a kathana to improve memory over short periods of time, and used it when I spoke with Master Peresten. The effect is very odd. Words take on a metallic echo, and even now that the kathana has faded, I find that I can recall the words of our conversation perfectly, not just the words but the tone of voice and the gestures each of us made. I am not sure if I will use it again, but it may yet prove useful.

Our territory contains a number of houses as well as some larger buildings, and Master Peresten and Master Engilles have a bedroom in one of these houses. Master Engilles looks worn out, and I think she has not slept more than four hours at a time since the merging. "He's worse," she told me when I arrived. "I still can't get him to eat."

"Will he let me speak to him?" I said.

"He probably won't know you're there, Sai Aleynten," she said, but let me into the bedroom. It had been a young woman's room, once, with brightly colored blankets on the bed and matching curtains pulled back from the windows to let in the light. A vase under one of those windows contained a handful of dying flowers, pink and gold, that felt uncomfortably like an omen, as if Master

Peresten's health were tied to these wilting blooms. Master Peresten lay curled up on his side under the colorful blanket with his fists pressed against his chin, his blue eyes wide open and staring at nothing. I pushed his legs gently to the side so I could sit next to him. "I would like to be alone with him, if you don't mind, Master Engilles," I said, and she nodded and left the room, shutting the door behind her.

I sat and looked at the young man's face for a while. I cannot begin to imagine what he must have felt, to scribe that th'an and see no effect. He would have been Kilios in less than two years, at the rate he was going, but the rank was only the result of what truly mattered to him, which was magic. I have never seen anyone with such a thirst for knowledge, never known anyone with such a brilliant mind. What might he have become, in a world that had never been divided? A linguist? An historian? It all seemed like so much waste that it infuriated me.

I whipped the blanket off him and grabbed the collar of his shirt, and hauled him up so his head was close to mine. That got a reaction; he flailed a little for balance, and his round eyes focused on me, though he still seemed confused and a little dull. "Terrayel Peresten, you will listen to me," I said, trying hard not to let him hear the full fury that surged through me at the thought of losing that brilliant mind to whatever dark depression had its claws sunk into him.

"You have had a loss no one but I can possibly begin to comprehend. Your life has changed forever. You knew what your future held and now that future is gone. I am sorry for that. But it is past time you got out of that bed and found out what your new future holds. No, *look at me*," I said, grabbing his chin and forcing his head up from where it had begun to droop. "I need you, Terrayel. You may not be able to work magic anymore, but there is no one more capable of understanding it than you. Sesskia is missing. Our search kathanas will not work. I cannot find her without your help."

His eyes focused on me again. "The magic won't work," he said in a hoarse voice. "It's all gone. Broken and drained away."

"Then I will perform the kathana, and you will tell me which th'an to use," I said. "Don't you dare look away from me, Terrayel. Or did your brains drain away with the magic? Have you forgotten all of the fifteen languages you speak? The history of the Castaviran Empire and all its rulers? The laws of mathematics? You are still a genius, with or without magic, and you have never once disappointed me in all the times I have asked you for something. Don't disappoint me now. *Please*. Help me find my wife."

I think it was the last word that woke something in him. He struggled away from my hand and leaned back, supporting himself against the headboard of the bed. "Sai Aleynten," he said, "what can I do? What can I ever do again?" He began sobbing, and that, strangely, reassured me; if he could finally mourn his loss, maybe he would not sink into that black emptiness again. I laid my hand on his head, briefly, then went to the door, where Master Engilles had clearly been listening. She rushed past me to put her arms around Master Peresten, pausing only briefly to give me a look of thanks. It seems we both had the same idea.

Now I will wait for Master Peresten to come to me. I feel more optimistic than I have since this whole fiasco occurred. We will find Aselfos and treat with him, we will bring order to this city, and we will bring Sesskia home.

The Meeting (24-25 Seresstine)

Cederic reached up and traced over a th'an whose glowing outlines had begun to fade. The negotiation tent was as warm as they could make it, but the bitter cold outside meant the magic drained more rapidly than usual. It was warm enough that he could do without his coat, displaying the Kilios's robe clearly. It still awed him, when he thought about it, that he was wearing a piece of Castaviran history. Haelen Quelten, first Kilios, had donated her robe to the Royal Museum in Colosse before her death, and Cederic's mages had liberated it so Cederic would have an outward symbol of his rank to command respect, having burned his own robe after Denril's murder by the former God-Empress. He stopped himself picking at a frayed spot on the sleeve. He had never had that kind of nervous habit before, not since—

He stopped himself before he could be drawn into a reverie tinged with guilt and sorrow. His fault, that Sesskia was lost somewhere in this new world. He had never erred in a kathana in his entire life, and the one time he made a mistake...his failure could only have been worse if he had killed her with his flawed kathana, and it was cold comfort that he had only failed to return her to his side. No more thinking of her. He needed all his wits focused on the meeting at hand.

"They haven't responded, Sai Aleynten," Master Peressten said, entering the tent and bringing a flash of bright sunlight with him. "Are you sure this is a good idea?"

"I am not sure of anything," he said, "save that we should not approach them first. The stealth of their approach tells me that they were prepared for an attack, and I think we should not do anything that might be construed as provocative. We will wait, and if they choose not to approach...then we will plan again."

Master Peressten nodded and ducked back out of the tent. How strange, that losing his magic had made him more confident rather than less. Or perhaps it was the discovery that what made him the man he was had nothing to do with magic. In either case, he was an exceptional aide, and Cederic was grateful for him. Grateful for all of them, the survivors of the convergence kathana, bound together now by that experience. It broke his heart that necessity was turning them into battle mages, though they didn't seem upset by it; if anything, they were enthusiastic about the promise of being able to serve Castavir, or whatever country might arise from the post-convergence world, in any way they could.

He had taught them all the shield kathana he'd invented to divert Renatha Torenz's wrath, hoping it would be enough to protect them. He hadn't exactly lost his confidence in his magic, but he felt less certain these days, without—he was doing it again. He sat in one of the camp chairs and put his face in his hands. Tomorrow he would return to the locator kathanas, and he would not allow other business to get in his way. He would simply tell anyone who needed his advice or magic or judgment that he was unavailable. He needed to stop lying to himself.

"Cederic, they're coming," Wayn said, hurrying into the tent. "Three horses, but at least one of them is carrying two riders."

"Get everyone inside, please," Cederic told the short, compact Sai, who nodded and called something out the door of the tent. Now was where they learned whether the Balaenics would listen to his proposal. They were at least a little reasonable, that they'd sent only a few people to this meeting rather than a column of armed soldiers, and brave, to come out to meet a handful of battle mages with no protection.

Cederic stood and paced, going over his words for what seemed the thousandth time. Perhaps it was the wrong decision, telling them so much about Castaviran politics, revealing their weaknesses, but if he had any chance of convincing them to aid him, they needed to know everything.

The mages came into the tent, Master Peressten bringing up the rear. "Definitely five people," he said. "Five of us, five of them. They've come to negotiate."

"I wonder what they think we're here for," Wayn said. "Our army by far outnumbers theirs—they might think we want surrender."

"So long as they are reasonable, and disinclined to panic," Cederic said, "they can think anything they like about our intentions."

They stood, and waited. Cederic felt his hand tremble, and gripped the back of the camp chair to still it. This was not the time to be mastered by emotions. He closed his eyes and took a few calming breaths. This would work. And if it did not, well, they would simply have to proceed without the Balaenic Army's aid. Capturing Renatha Torenz was still possible. He hoped.

Hooves beat a steady rhythm on the packed snow, drawing closer. Cederic forced himself to remain calm, listening to the cadence and trying to pick it apart into the sound of three horses slowing to a stop outside the tent. The jingling of harness. Boots landing on snow. The rustle of fabric against fabric as people walked toward the tent. Cederic straightened and faced the door, flanked on each side by two mages. It would work. His hand was still trembling.

The soldiers outside parted the door flaps, and three men entered, followed by two smaller figures. One of the men and both the smaller figures—women?—were hooded against the cold so no part of their faces showed. Cederic wished his own coat were so all-enveloping; the fur trim looked warm. The man in the center was tall and broad, with pale blond hair and gray eyes that met Cederic's in a direct, penetrating gaze. Cederic returned his gaze with equal confidence, concealing a moment's unease. This man had power, and knew it, but power did not always translate into reasonableness, and if his confident gaze indicated mulishness rather than understanding, Cederic's task would be nearly impossible.

The blond man said, "I am General Mattiak Tarallan, Commander General of the Balaenic Army—oh," he said, turning and extending a hand to one of the women. "You'll need to translate," he told her, drawing her forward.

"I am Cederic Aleynten," Cederic said, "and I speak for the Castaviran Empire. Thank you for accepting our offer of parley."

The woman stumbled and clutched at General Tarallan's coat; his hand more firmly supported her elbow. Cederic glanced once at her, then back at the general, who said, "You speak our language," somewhat surprised. Then he said, "Cederic Aleynten," wonderingly, as if the words were the key to some mystery, and continued, "I think we have already found common ground." He helped the hooded woman stand and gave her a little push in Cederic's direction.

"I do not believe we need fight with one another," Cederic said, feeling a little irritated at this disruption of their meeting. General Tarallan's expression had gone from wondering to—could that be regret? Cederic closed his hand on the camp chair and tried to focus. Then the woman put back her hood and said, "Cederic."

He looked in her direction, wondering what new interruption she'd come up with, and thought, *How strange, she looks so much like*

Sesskia. He blinked, focused again, took in the round face, the mass of dark blonde hair imperfectly contained by brass hair clips, the green-gray eyes fringed by thick black lashes, and felt as if he'd been flung headlong from one of those collenna*s* into the frozen ground, because he could not remember how to breathe.

He closed his eyes, opened them again, fearing that his first glance had been correct and this was merely some Balaenic woman who resembled his wife. Her eyes were still fixed on him, and she stood poised on the balls of her feet, waiting. Waiting for him to react. *"Sesskia,"* he said, and she flung herself at him, sobbing and laughing at the same time, something only she could manage. He put his arms around her and clung to her, words pouring out of him that even he couldn't understand, though "sorry" and "my fault" seemed to be most of them.

"I wanted to find you sooner, truly I did, things just kept happening, I'm sorry," Sesskia babbled, then lifted her head from his shoulder to look at him, and her laughter increased, making him smile as joy filled his chest, buoying him up as much as her strong presence did.

"How are you here?" he murmured to her.

"I—it's too long a story," she said. "What about you?"

"Also too long for right now," he said. He released her and turned to face General Tarallan again, only dimly aware of the man's presence because all his attention was focused on the gloved hand tucked into his. "General Tarallan, I am not sure what question to ask next," he said.

"I'm nearly as surprised as you," the general said. "I assure you this wasn't a ploy to threaten or coerce you." He looked at Sesskia as he said this, and surprise, then uncharacteristic rage, threatened to overwhelm Cederic, because the look he bestowed on Sesskia was not that of a friend. Cederic glanced at his wife. She was looking at Cederic with such love in her eyes that it dispelled his anger entirely. Foolish of him to hate the general simply because he had the good sense to realize how wonderful Sesskia was.

He nodded at the general. "I believe you," he said. "But I think it changes the nature of these discussions."

"I hope it means we don't have to waste time deciding whether or not to trust each other," General Tarallan said. "May we sit?"

"Please do," Cederic said, and there was a general commotion as everyone found a seat, forming two lines facing one another, Balaenic and Castaviran. Sesskia withdrew her hand from his, smiling sadly, and went to take a seat on the Balaenic side. Cederic's hand felt colder than the air could account for, and he closed it into a fist. Now he regretted the necessity for these negotiations. What he *wanted* was to take Sesskia somewhere that they could be alone and learn where she had been all this time, what she had done, to wrap her in his arms and kiss her until they both forgot their own names. What he was going to do was talk to this man and convince him of the rightness of Cederic's cause.

This man who has the effrontery to fall in love with my wife, he thought, then dismissed the ignoble thought. He rested his hands palm-down on his thighs and examined his counterpart. General Tarallan had a rugged face that at the moment wore an amused, rueful expression, and Cederic found himself filled with compassion for the man. *How did I feel, all those weeks when my love for Sesskia was not returned? And he has no hope at all.*

When everyone was settled, Cederic said, "We did not realize you had doubled back until yesterday morning, and then we did not expect to find you trailing us so closely. We feel fortunate that you did not seem inclined to attack us, because we were unprepared for that contingency."

"We were waiting for the right time," the general said. "I'd like to know why you didn't attack *us* when you discovered where we were."

"We are not interested in attacking Balaen," Cederic said. "We are pursuing Castaviran troops who are under the command of a madwoman who *is* intent on conquering Balaen."

"Your God-Empress," the general said. Cederic flicked a glance at Sesskia, who looked as if she were as eager to have this conversation over with as he was. What had she told them about Castavir, or the convergence? Would they think she was a traitor for having such close associations with a Castaviran mage?

"She is no longer Empress," he said. "She was ousted from power during the convergence. Castavir currently has no ruler."

"It's not you, then?" General Tarallan said. "You said you spoke for the Empire."

"Cederic, you're not *Emperor*, are you?" Sesskia blurted out. She looked utterly horrified.

Cederic gave her a reassuring smile. "I am not," he said. "General Tarallan, the former Empress has no heir, and while there are many contenders for the throne, none has a claim sufficiently strong as to emerge the unchallenged victor. I speak for Castavir, for the moment, because my rank as chief of the priest-mages of the Empire gives me the power to anoint a successor. But before I can do so, the former Empress must be apprehended so she cannot challenge the new regime."

"And executed?"

"If she cannot be convinced to retire peacefully, yes."

"And then you will declare a new Emperor. Or Empress."

"Not exactly," Cederic said. This was where it became tricky. "Bad enough that there is no obvious choice to hold the throne; the lure of power is great enough that many of the candidates passed over by me will not see my decision as binding on them, despite my right to make that decision. Civil war is coming to Castavir, and it will sweep Balaen along with it. Therefore, once we have defeated the God-Empress, I intend to offer the throne of Castavir to the King of Balaen."

The Balaenics, including Sesskia, reacted with varying degrees of shock. General Tarallan looked as if he'd eaten something foul. "The King...I don't think he...Balaen is a great responsibility in itself...." he said, as if he were searching for words that would not be treasonous.

"We are aware of the King's...limitations," Cederic said, hoping his own turmoil didn't show past the impassive façade he'd spent so many years perfecting. "But he is the best solution to both our countries' problem. Many of those in Castavir who would revolt at one of their fellows being elevated above them would find no legitimate reason to prosecute their claim to the throne should a non-Castaviran hold it. None of them would be able to make common cause against Balaen because if they successfully defeated your country, they would simply be in the same position of being at one another's throats. And Castavir's military forces are in the hands of people who agree with my—our—solution."

"But your citizens will never stand for it," the general said. "To be ruled by a foreigner—"

"We have been laying the foundation for that in the past months," Cederic said. "We will, of course, insist on establishing the conditions under which the King of Balaen will take power. He will remove his court to Colosse, our capital city. There will be a council of advisors drawn equally from Balaenics and Castavirans. And we will expect him to marry a Castaviran woman. There are other conditions, but these are the ones on which we will not compromise."

"And if he refuses?"

"Then there will be war," Cederic said, feeling the now-familiar sickness that threatened to overwhelm him when he thought of the consequences of failure. "That is not a threat; we are not interested, as I said, in attacking Balaen. I will select a ruler from among a pool of suboptimal choices, and Castavir will burn, and it will take Balaen with it."

General Tarallan curled his hands, which were resting on his knees, into fists. "I am not the one you should tell this to," he said.

"I want the support of your army in defeating our former Empress," Cederic said. "I think it would have been hard to convince you of the necessity had I not shared this plan with you. And I would appreciate your advice as to how we might present our proposal to your King that would be effective. It is crucial that he be induced to see our sincerity."

The general let out a deep breath. "I can't ally with you," he said, and Cederic's face tightened into greater impassivity. "That's something King and Chamber have to approve. But I am free to pursue enemies of Balaen, and your former Empress falls solidly into the category. And, naturally, if we're attacking the same foe, it makes sense that we should coordinate those attacks. We wouldn't want to step all over each other."

Cederic nodded. It was more than he'd dared hope for. "And on the other matter?"

The general's face was as impassive as Cederic's surely was. "I owe my loyalty to my King," he said. "I should not share such information with a foreign diplomat, if that's what you are. But I am not the only one who's observed the King closely." He turned his head to look directly, blatantly at Sesskia, who cringed a little when everyone's eyes followed his gaze, then sat up straight and glared defiantly back.

"I understand," Cederic said. "I respect your sense of honor." He looked away from Sesskia to once again meet General Tarallan's eyes. "Is there anything you would ask of us? Of me? I feel myself very much in your debt." *Thank you for bringing her here. Thank you for sheltering her. Thank you for restoring my heart to me.*

The general smiled as if he could read Cederic's thoughts. "I'm curious as to how you speak our language," he said, "and why you sound like a Barrekellian."

"We have a kathana—a kind of magic—that allows a mage to speak and understand, but not read, another language," Cederic said. "I was not aware it gave us any particular accent." He risked another glance at Sesskia—if he kept looking at her, he might lose control entirely—and wondered why she seemed so amused. Something to ask her later. Soon. Immediately.

"I wouldn't mind being able to speak yours," the general said. "It would be a tremendous advantage."

"I am afraid it would not work on you," Cederic said. "It only affects mages because their minds have the right kind of flexibility from working magic. Unfortunate, I think, but we have also met Balaenics who are learning to speak Castaviran the traditional way, and they tell us it is not very difficult. Your language is far more complex."

"Perhaps when this is all over, I'll make time," he said. "I think I should meet with your commander—you did say that was someone other than yourself?"

"General Gael Regates," Cederic said. "She was not convinced this meeting was a good idea, but I think she will be glad to learn that we could make common cause. Shall we arrange for the two of you to meet here at another time?"

"No need," General Tarallan said, rising from his stool. "If it's all right with you, we'll go to your camp now. I understand the former Empress is besieging Venetry at the moment, and I don't think we should waste any time."

Cederic stood when he did, with everyone else rising raggedly after him. "This has been an unexpected meeting in every way," he said. "I am grateful to find such a sensible man in command of the Balaenic Army. I had anticipated a much greater struggle to reach consensus."

"I've heard a great deal about your character in the past weeks," the general said, "and I trust the source completely." He smiled wryly, and this time Cederic could feel nothing but compassion for him, compassion and a sense of comradeship in their shared affection.

He extended his hand to Cederic, palm-out the Balaenic way, and added, "Though it makes sense that Sesskia's husband would turn out to be the spokesman for an Empire." That sent up a lot of murmuring on the Balaenic side. Apparently Sesskia had been at least a little circumspect in what she told her fellow countrymen.

Cederic placed his palm against the general's with no hesitation. "Sesskia's husband is simply very grateful to be reunited with her," he said.

The general nodded. "I take it those...things...outside are some form of transportation?" he said.

"Yes," said Cederic, "and they are somewhat faster than horses, but I think we should arrive in advance of you anyway, to warn our sentries." He saluted the others, then, finally, his heart pounding with joy, said, "Sesskia, ride with me." He extended his hand, and she took his and gripped it hard. "I think we have much to talk about."

She gave him a look that clearly said she thought that was the most profound understatement anyone had ever uttered. "Of course," she said, and let him help her into his collenna, which shifted under her weight because the previous th'an's magic had not yet run out. He climbed in after her, released the tether, and reflected that he had never fully appreciated how narrow its seat was; she fitted snugly in next to him, her hand still linked with his.

He leaned forward a little to draw the th'an on the brass face plate, bracing himself against the familiar jolt as the magic propelled the collenna forward. Sesskia, unprepared, squeaked and clutched at the front of his coat to steady herself. He laughed, and put his arms around her. "That was an unexpected bonus," he said, "I—"

She transferred her grip from his coat to his neck and kissed him, cutting off whatever he'd been about to say. He let the writing tool fall into his lap and pulled her closer to him, feeling like a starving man offered a ten-course meal as he returned her kisses. The reality of her presence was so much better than memory.

He had to break away from her to make sure the collenna was not veering off course, then drew her into his arms again and sighed with profound contentment. "I cannot express how I feel to have you with me," he said. "I am so sorry I failed you, my love."

"How did you fail me?" she said. She put her own arms around his waist and snuggled close with that brief shimmy of motion that always drove him mad with desire for her. Now he wished the collenna were larger. And enclosed.

"The kathana should have returned you to Colosse," he said. "I... was in a hurry, and...I omitted a few th'an. I never imagined I might make such a mistake."

She laughed, a low, rich sound. How long had they been separated, that he'd forgotten the sound of her laugh? "Cederic Aleynten, Kilios and undisputed master of magic, performs a flawed kathana— am I right that it's the first time you've ever done that?"

"You are," he said. "Sesskia, I am so sorry—"

She reached up to kiss him, firmly, then again when he tried to say something else. "No more apologies," she said. "I forgive you for making a mistake, and you should forgive yourself, considering that it probably made that whole negotiation possible. I wouldn't have been with the Balaenic Army, and you and Mattiak wouldn't have had such an instant rapport."

"You must be friends, to use his praenoma," Cederic said, trying to sound casual. Hearing her speak the man's name so off-handedly roused his irrational jealousy again.

"We are," Sesskia said, and now *she* sounded a little too casual. "He's a good man."

He tightened his grip on her, fractionally. "And he is in love with you."

Sesskia went tense. "I was hoping you hadn't noticed," she said.

The way she said it made the jealousy vanish, leaving him feeling guilty for ever having entertained it. "Better for both of us that I did," he said. "I might have said any number of cruel things in my ignorance."

"I was afraid you might be..." Sesskia's words trailed off. She brought her hand around to run her fingers along his hairline at the base of his neck. He wasn't sure how he would complete that sentence either.

"Is it arrogant for me to say that I am certain of your love for me?" he asked. "I love you, Sesskia, and because of that I can understand perfectly well how a powerful, honorable man might fall in love with you. And I can see that you feel nothing more for him than friendship. So no, I am not jealous of him except in the sense that I am jealous of everyone who was able to share your company these past months when I could not. Sadness, possibly, when I think of how *I* would feel if you did not return my love—though not enough that I would stand aside and let him win your affections."

"I'm a little annoyed that you think I need your permission to fall in love with someone," Sesskia teased.

"Permission? No," Cederic said, straight-faced, "but I assure you if I thought you were attracted to someone else, I would do everything in my power to convince you that I am the superior choice."

"I already know that," she said, and they kissed until the

collenna's th'an nearly ran out, making them lag far behind the others.

"Tell me what happened while I was gone," Sesskia said when he had refreshed the th'an. "I already know the locator kathanas stopped working, and I am *certain*—" she poked him in the side—"that you were so busy with other things that you couldn't spare the time to fix them and find me."

"Sesskia, I am sorry—"

She kissed him soundly again. "No more of that," she said.

He smiled wryly at her. "If you intend to kiss me every time I try to apologize for failing you so utterly," he said, "you will almost certainly achieve results opposite to what you intend."

"I could stop kissing you entirely."

"I think you are unlikely to carry out that threat." He kissed her forehead, then her lips, and the way she responded proved him right.

"Colosse was in flames, literally and figuratively," he said after a few minutes. "And we had so many mages who could no longer work magic. It took several days for us to marshal our resources, and more days to bring the city under control."

"Is Terrael...he lost his magic, didn't he?"

"He did. And I take it you realized the common factor among those who can still work magic."

"The eyes, yes. But I thought Terrael would be devastated. He seems...better than well, actually."

"There was a time when we thought we might lose Master Peressten," Cedric said, frowning at the memory. "He fell into a black despair that even Master Engilles could not rouse him from. It took him many days to realize that his life was not over, that he still understands magic in ways no one else ever has, even if th'an no longer activate when he scribes them. He is the one who devised the translator kathana, he and Master Engilles—he does the research, she performs the kathana. They work well together, better even than their marriage would account for. I think you will find them both changed, for the better."

"I hope so. Is Audryn with the army, then? And Sovrin, and the other Darssan mages?"

"All the mages who survived the convergence kathana are with us. Master Ustanz has also lost her magic, but as head of the translation corps she has proven her worth as an administrator and diplomat. They will all be relieved to see you. It was two weeks before we could even prove you were still alive." The memory of those two weeks, the horror of bringing Colosse out of chaos, the necessity of being strong for everyone else's sake when his strength had been torn from him, filled him again with pain. "Two weeks," he said again, faintly, and felt Sesskia's hand grip his.

"I had to believe you were still alive," she said. "I must have tried to go to Colosse to find you half a dozen times, but every time something more urgent came up. I discovered the God-Empress's army at Calassmir and Jeddan and I—Jeddan's a mage like me, the first one I ever met!—anyway, we had to go to Venetry to warn the King and Chamber so they'd send out the army. And then it turned out there were more mages, and they were being bossed around by some idiot, so I couldn't abandon them. Then I ended up as Mattiak's liaison to the army, and *then* the army marched out—you see how the story goes?

"I really did intend to find you. But now that we're reunited, I'm having trouble regretting all of those detours. I did so much good, Cederic. I can't wait for you to meet Jeddan. He's—you know I love you, and Audryn and Sovrin and Terrael are some of my best friends, but I never realized what it was like to be friends with someone who understands magic the way I do."

"I look forward to meeting him as well," Cederic said. "If only to express my gratitude to him for being company for you on the road."

"I did wish you'd been with me," Sesskia said. "There were so many—" She cut off in mid-phrase. "I'll tell you everything, but later," she said. "When we aren't rattling along in this collenna, freezing our noses off."

"I have other plans for later," he said with a tiny smile.

She looked at him uncomprehendingly. "What plans?"

He blinked at her, feeling suddenly awkward. "Well," he began, and she grinned at him and threw her arms around his neck.

"I can't believe you fell for that," she said.

"Neither can I," he said, feeling both relieved and embarrassed. "Though I must warn you that my bed is rather narrow and has a very thin mattress."

"Then it's a good thing that I don't mind being *very* close to you," she said.

He tethered the collenna in the yard when they returned to the camp and left Sesskia watching the things shift about and butt against each other as if they were living creatures while he went to make arrangements for General Regates and her staff to meet with the Balaenic party. Then he took her back to the mages' part of the camp and watched with pleasure as Sesskia's friends leaped on her and dragged her away to trade stories.

Then he was pulled away himself to be consulted on some matter of army business.

Then some of the mages needed his attention.

Then he was called on to perform some kathana that was just complex enough to require either four mages working together or one Kilios working alone.

Dinnertime passed, and he hadn't seen Sesskia for hours. He became irritable, and concealed it under an increasingly impassive demeanor that he knew was making everyone around him uncomfortable. Why did everyone come to him with their minor problems that anyone might have resolved?

Finally, feeling as if he might erupt if one more person asked him a question, he told those around him that it was late (it was barely after nine o'clock) and he was tired (emotionally, if not physically) and he would be available in the morning (though he did not specify at what time) and went back to the mages' camp as swiftly as possible.

The common area, with its open-sided pavilion and enormous cookfire, was empty. Most of the tents were dark, but lights burned in a few of them, including his own. He pushed the flap aside and entered. It wasn't a very big tent, but it held a table where he made notes on kathanas and tactics to share with General Regates, and a small trunk where he kept his things, and a narrow camp bed—that was currently occupied.

Sesskia, buried under a pile of blankets and the fur rug he usually left bundled on his trunk, rolled over to face him, then propped herself on her elbow. Her hair fell loose over her bare shoulders. "I hope you don't mind," she said, "but I didn't bring anything to sleep in, and your tent is cold. I don't suppose you can think of a way to warm me up?"

Cederic began unfastening his robe, astonished at how fumble-fingered he'd become. "There are th'an that generate heat," he said, pulling his robe off over his head and tackling his trousers.

"Is that the best solution?" she asked, sitting up further and letting the rug slip off her shoulders. He groaned and yanked at his boots, which were in the way of his trousers.

"The best solution," he said, flinging first one boot, then the other, across the tent, "is skin to skin contact."

"Really? I'm not sure I believe that's better than magic," she said.

Naked, he crossed to the bed and slid in next to her. It wasn't as narrow as he'd thought. "It has a magic of its own," he said, and laid her down beneath him.

He slept as he hadn't in months, deep and untroubled by dreams, surfacing occasionally to reassure himself that she was still there, then falling back into the depths. Sunrise finally woke him, but gently; he was first aware of a warm body nestled against his, then of the smell of her hair tangled across her face, then of her quiet breathing, and he lightly traced the line of her shoulder and felt her wake at his touch. "Good morning," he murmured into her ear, and she rolled over to face him, smiling with such happiness that he thought his heart might break from pure joy.

"That's the best way to wake up anyone ever thought of," she said, reaching out to push his hair behind his ear.

"I think we can do better," he said, and bent to kiss her.

Later, tangled together and breathing heavily, Sesskia said, "I'm surprised no one's tried to rouse you yet. I thought, with how everyone wanted your attention yesterday, that they'd be lined up outside the door."

"Everyone in this camp knows I spent the night with my wife," he said. "I daresay they are afraid of what they might interrupt."

Sesskia began laughing. "How circumspect of them," she said. "I'm grateful for it. And hungry. Can we get something to eat? And..." Her mirth died away. "I should return to the Balaenic camp soon."

"No," he began, seeing once again that bleak emptiness, then shook his head to dispel it. "You are correct," he said. "Much as I would prefer to keep you with me, your country needs you."

"The mages will want to know where I was all night," she said. "By now everyone probably knows that my missing husband is a Castaviran mage, but that will only increase the number of questions they'll have. I don't know if it's something about mages in general, or just Balaenic mages in specific, but friendly argument seems to be their default state."

"I would like to return with you this morning, to meet them. I wish we had time for me to observe their pouvrin."

"So do I. I'll have to show you the new ones I've learned, later. It's been a huge boon to have other mages like me to share experiences with." Sesskia climbed out of bed and began hunting for her clothes. "Though it also made me eager to rejoin you so I could explore some of the possibilities I've discovered."

"I might have known your desire for me was not your only motivation for returning. You would no doubt have been content to wander indefinitely so long as you were capable of learning something."

"You taught me a few new things last night," Sesskia said with a grin. She tossed his robe at him, and he caught it in midair. "Oh, Cederic, I missed you so much. I want all this to be over so we can go back to just being ourselves, owing no duty to anyone."

"With the aid of the Balaenic Army, we have great chances of success," Cederic said. He pulled on his trousers and bent to put on his boots. "Two more days, and we will know better what those chances are. Renatha Torenz has only a fraction of our combined forces, and there are those among her officers who may choose to throw their fortunes in with us."

Sesskia nodded, but her smile was gone. "Cederic," she said, "there's something I should tell you."

"Come here," he said, and put his arms around her. "You have the look of someone who needs reassurance."

"Yes," she said. "I killed a man. With magic."

His grip on her tightened. "When was this?"

"About two months ago. We were on the road—Jeddan and I—and we were attacked by bandits. Their leader would have...Jeddan had taught me the see-inside pouvra, and I looked inside his chest and used the mind-moving pouvra to crush his heart. It...was so easy, it frightened me."

She looked up at him, her beautiful eyes shadowed with memory. "I don't regret his death any more than I do that of the man who tried to rape me. And Mattiak and I talked about it, and I know it doesn't mean I have to use those pouvrin that way just because I can. But I can't help wondering, after you said the God-Empress might need to be executed, if it might not be better for everyone if I just sneaked into her camp—"

"No," Cederic said, appalled at the image. "We are not that desperate. Take her life if she threatens yours, certainly, but you are no killer, my love, and I would prefer that you not become one."

"I know," she said, relaxing just a little. "But I thought I should ask."

"You should consider getting medical training," he said. "We have kathanas that do what you describe, but they require at least three people. If you can perform the same magic alone, what an advantage that would be."

"I hadn't thought of that." She sounded more cheerful, and it relieved his heart. Sesskia as assassin. It was too awful to contemplate.

He changed his grip on her to hold her at arm's length. "I find I am extremely hungry," he said, "so let us join the others for a meal, and then I will, with extreme reluctance, restore you to your people."

"I'll ride with you this afternoon. I still have a lot to tell you." Her eyes went wide. "And speaking of telling people things, how could you not tell me that Audryn is pregnant? I was so surprised!"

"So was she, as I understand it," Cederic said. "I think her condition played a large part in returning Master Peressten to us."

"The way she told it, she broke down completely after two weeks of his silence and had a hysterical fit, screaming things about how she wasn't going to raise their child alone, and that finally got through to him. *He* said you also took him by the collar and told him his brains hadn't gone the way of his magic. He's different now. Less restless, more centered. I like the change."

"So do I," Cederic said. "I am resigned to the fact that he will never be Kilios, which I had anticipated with great pleasure. I think none of us knows exactly what he will become now, except that it will be something remarkable."

They were late in rising, and people were breaking camp all around them, but they shared their meal with Master Engilles, who was also a late riser these days. He was accustomed to eating with all the mages now and not just the Sais; the artificial barrier of status that had formerly separated them was gone, cleared away by the shock of the convergence and the grueling weeks that had followed it. They still treated him with respect, and he knew the formality of his demeanor kept them at a distance, but it was not so great a distance as before. He'd never realized he was lonely until Sesskia came along, and never realized how much he needed human companionship until she was gone.

They rode in the collenna back to the Balaenic camp, which had begun traveling before sunrise in their effort to narrow the gap between their companies. Sesskia's mages were refreshingly informal with him—they had no idea what his rank meant, were impressed with him mainly because he was Sesskia's mysterious husband and a foreign mage. He had time only for a few moment's conversation before he had to return to his duties in his own camp, but he was struck by how much their enthusiasm and curiosity about magic matched Sesskia's.

Are we so inherently different, then? he wondered as he rode back alone. *Or is it the nature of how they became mages that drives them to increase their knowledge? They are inventing, or reinventing, an entire school of magic where Castaviran mages can rely on learning what has already been discovered. What will we be able to teach each other, when there is finally time?*

He had to work at not being irritable and distracted that morning. *I am Kilios, and their leader,* he reminded himself, *and they deserve my full attention.* But he was still heartened when, as they stopped for a noon meal, he saw Sesskia coming toward him, munching on a piece of bread folded around a thick slab of cheese. "I was too eager to wait for anything more complicated," she said. "That collenna of yours seems as eager to be off as I am."

He hadn't realized how much he still had to tell her until they were riding along, trading stories. Most important was learning what she had to tell him about the King of Balaen, none of which made him less anxious about the course they'd chosen. "He's weak," Sesskia said bluntly. "And he's afraid for his own safety. He almost didn't let any of my mages come with the army, even though that's what we'd been training to do, because he wanted them for his personal protection. Sheer chance that it turned out to be a good thing that half of them stayed behind, if the God-Empress is besieging Venetry."

"So his councilors are the stronger personalities," Cederic said.

She shrugged. "Some of them. Caelen Crossar certainly believes he'd make a better king than Garran Clendessar. He might even be right. I don't understand enough about politics to know why he hasn't tried to overthrow the King, but I know he's going to be the one whose opposition to your plan you need to worry about. Jakssar is strong in her own way, but I think she's overly conscious of having a lesser role because she's a woman. I hate to criticize her when I, again, don't really know how it works, but I think she'd be stronger if she weren't so worried about whether or not they respect her.

Batekessar is an old reactionary and hates change, but he's ineffectual, and Lenssar is as much a coward as the King, plus he's terrified of magic."

"But will the King accept my proposal?"

"I think, if you can make him feel that you chose him because you respect him, that he'll go along with it. My feeling is that flattery won't work because deep down, he knows he doesn't deserve it. Put it in terms of him doing something noble to save two countries, and he might believe that."

"You've observed him closely, to know all of that."

Sesskia shrugged again. "He's not a very complicated person. Cederic, are you *sure* this is the only way?"

"You met the rest of our generals yesterday," he said. "The king of Helviran and the queen of Endellavir are both possible candidates, and their representatives here are as unyielding and fractious as they are. The other two candidates are just as absorbed in their own importance. Elevate one above the others, and there will be war. It took all my persuasiveness to convince them that they will have greater power on the new Emperor's council than they would if they tried to defend their throne against their rivals." He sighed. "Something I will no doubt have to convince the Chamber of as well. At least we will have balance, if we can put all of them on the new council. Four Balaenics, four Castavirans. And a handful of others with more good sense to steer them in the right direction. I intend to discuss the problem with General Tarallan and see if he has any recommendations."

"Well, when you meet with the King, try not to pay any more attention to the Chamber Lords than you have to for politeness's sake," Sesskia said. "Show respect, but not flattery. And be confident. He'll feel better about himself if he believes he's good enough to command the respect of someone like you. Also—" She picked at the neck of his Kilios's robe where it frayed a little. "Wear something nicer. He won't know what a Kilios is and you'll just look like a shabby supplicant to him."

"Understood," he said. "I would like you to be present, if we can manage it."

"I can't stand with you, of course."

"No, but your mages represent a new power in Balaen, and I think if that power stands with your King, he will feel himself more on equal footing with us." He put his arm around her shoulders and enjoyed how she fitted herself to his body. "I'm told your mages tore through ours like this collenna plows through snow."

"Most of that was being unexpected, and some of it was luck," she said. "It was actually very hard. Castaviran magic is still more flexible."

"We ought to be putting our efforts toward finding commonalities between the two," he said, frustrated. "We have not had leisure to examine the possibilities, but now that the worlds are united, we should be able to discover what magic was meant to be. We know only that it is not as simple as combining Balaenic and Castaviran magics, but, as with so many other things, the project has been pushed aside in favor of other things."

"I know. I could only justify developing the flitting pouvra—oh!" She sat up. "I never did show you that."

"A new pouvra?"

"It's how I returned from the Balaenic camp this afternoon—didn't you wonder about that?"

He hadn't wondered, being so happy to see her that he didn't care about anything else. "What does it do?"

"I'll show you," she said. She stood up, glanced behind herself, and tumbled out of the collenna.

"*Sesskia!*" he shouted, nearly falling out himself. They were going at such a speed that she was a tiny figure in his wake before he could do more than that. Then she vanished. He looked around wildly, saw a figure in the distance ahead, and had just enough time to see her wave at him before he left her behind again. Astounded, he watched her vanish and reappear half a dozen more times before the collenna's magic drained enough to slow down so she could climb back in.

"Amazing, yes?" she said, a little breathlessly.

"Please give me time to restrain my urge to shout at you for leaping from a moving collenna," he said.

"Oh, it wasn't dangerous. Not very dangerous, anyway," Sesskia scoffed. "It's range of vision, more or less—I can flit up to three miles if I have an unobstructed line of sight, and it takes a total of five seconds to go that far."

"Remarkable," Cederic said. He could be amazed now that his terror over Sesskia's stunt was fading. "We cannot do anything like that. We know the knowledge once existed, but no one has been able to reconstruct the kathana. If ever there were a pouvra I would want to see turned into a kathana, that would be the one."

"Do you think it's possible? Pouvrin into kathanas, I mean?"

"If you can create a pouvra from a kathana, I see no reason why the opposite could not happen."

She snuggled back under his arm. "Damn the God-Empress anyway. She keeps interfering in our lives."

He held her tight. "In a few days, it will all be over." *One way or another.*

ABOUT THE AUTHOR

In addition to Convergence, Melissa McShane is the author of The Extraordinaries series, beginning with BURNING BRIGHT, the Crown of Tremontane series, beginning with SERVANT OF THE CROWN, as well as COMPANY OF STRANGERS and many others.

After a childhood spent roaming the United States, she settled in Utah with her husband, four children and a niece, four very needy cats, and a library that continues to grow out of control. She wrote reviews and critical essays for many years before turning to fiction, which is much more fun than anyone ought to be allowed to have.

You can visit her at her website **www. melissamcshanewrites.com** for more information on other books.

For news, new release announcements, and other fun stuff, sign up for Melissa's newsletter **here.**

If you enjoyed this book, please consider leaving a review at your favorite online retailer or on Goodreads.

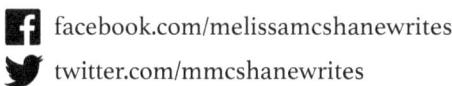

facebook.com/melissamcshanewrites

twitter.com/mmcshanewrites

ALSO BY MELISSA MCSHANE

THE DRAGONS OF MOTHER STONE

Spark the Fire

Faith in Flames

Ember in Shadow

Skies Will Burn (forthcoming)

THE CROWN OF TREMONTANE

Servant of the Crown

Exile of the Crown

Rider of the Crown

Agent of the Crown

Voyager of the Crown

Tales of the Crown

THE SAGA OF WILLOW NORTH

Pretender to the Crown

Guardian of the Crown

Champion of the Crown

THE HEIRS OF WILLOW NORTH

Ally of the Crown

Stranger to the Crown

Scholar of the Crown

THE EXTRAORDINARIES

Burning Bright

Wondering Sight

Abounding Might

Whispering Twilight

Liberating Fight

Beguiling Birthright (forthcoming)

THE LAST ORACLE

The Book of Secrets

The Book of Peril

The Book of Mayhem

The Book of Lies

The Book of Betrayal

The Book of Havoc

The Book of Harmony

The Book of War

The Book of Destiny

COMPANY OF STRANGERS

Company of Strangers

Stone of Inheritance

Mortal Rites

Shifting Loyalties

Sands of Memory

Call of Wizardry

THE CONVERGENCE TRILOGY

The Summoned Mage

The Wandering Mage

The Unconquered Mage

THE BOOKS OF DALANINE

The Smoke-Scented Girl

The God-Touched Man

Emissary

Warts and All: A Fairy Tale Collection

The View from Castle Always

www.ingramcontent.com/pod-product-compliance
Lightning Source LLC
Chambersburg PA
CBHW060153260626
47160CB00001B/254